PRAISE FOR *HOUR OF* ...

"A powerful, well-crafted, and fascinating look into the Ge... ...r Denmark during World War II, and the resulting bravery of those w... would aid and ultimately help evacuate the Danish Jews. A beautifully illustrated story you don't want to miss, *Hour of Need* is a fantastic tool to help understand a key piece of WWII history."
        —Andrew Aydin, #1 *New York Times* bestselling coauthor of *March* and *Run*

"A winning blend of inspiring history, page-turning action, and awesome comics!"
        —Steve Sheinkin, *New York Times* bestselling author of *Bomb*, *Fallout*, and *Undefeated*

"Absolutely amazing! A brilliant, beautifully written tale of hope and heroism that must be read. To never forget means to tell stories afresh which remind all future generations of the power of courage, kindness, and resolute determination—*especially* in the face of evil. *Hour of Need* is an outright triumph!"
        —Brad Thor, #1 *New York Times* bestselling author of *Rising Tiger*

"By saving almost the entire Jewish community under Nazi occupation, Denmark serves as an example of how to protect our humanity. This book shows that 'never again' is more than a deep-felt wish, it is a matter of choice."
        —Ronald Leopold, Executive Director of the Anne Frank House

"Eighty years have passed since the action against the Jews in Denmark, and we are now at a crossroads where it is becoming even more important to hear and preserve the testimonies and remember what happened. Ralph Shayne has turned his mother's experiences into a well told graphic novel (aided by the beautiful artwork of Tatiana Goldberg) that opens the story up for a younger audience and helps us all to remember, in a nuanced way. *Hour of Need* is recommended reading."
        —The Danish Jewish Museum in Copenhagen

"The citizens of Denmark provided a bright spot for humanity by coming to the aid of their Jewish neighbors in October 1943. Ralph Shayne's use of the graphic novel format to bring his family's personal Holocaust story to light in *Hour of Need* makes the story engaging and accessible to young readers. He highlights the simple decisions we can all make to stand with others being persecuted. This book is a great way for educators to bring the discussion of history we never want to see repeated into the classroom and spark lively discussions on the social pact we have with each other to be there for each other in our own hour of need."
        —Arne Duncan, US Secretary of Education under President Barack Obama

"I'm so grateful for *Hour of Need*. As a descendant of a German Jew who narrowly escaped Berlin during the war, I feel a deep connection to this moving story and these beautiful images. When we know personal stories, we have a deeper understanding of each other, and that empathy is vitally important at this moment in history. This graphic novel is a perfect way to engage, educate, and inspire younger generations to connect to the past and protect the future."

—Amy Landecker, American actress and activist

"We are approaching the day when the world will have lost its last Holocaust survivor. There is no better time for a book like *Hour of Need*. Ralph Shayne's profoundly personal story will move young people of all backgrounds and inspire them to show more compassion to those who suffer from senseless hate. *Hour of Need* is gripping, inspiring, educational, and deeply human.

—Joshua Malina, American actor

"A completely gripping story of escape and survival. I was holding my breath on one page and crying on the next. If you ever feel too pessimistic about human nature, read this graphic novel."

—Joe Weisberg, Emmy Award-winning television writer, producer, novelist, schoolteacher, cocreator of *The Americans*

"*Hour of Need* opens a new window on an aspect of history, and through its words and pictures, describes how history happens from new and unexpected angles. With wonderful art, an energetic pace, and human characters we can relate to, and at the same time, due to their Danish perspective, who are also fresh and unfamiliar, the book raises some difficult questions about the nature of collaboration, heroism, and how and when to act—as well as shining a light on how people cope and carry on. In the end, it seems to me, *Hour of Need* is about the joy of living, and living together, and why it's so important."

—Ken Krimstein, *New Yorker* cartoonist and author of the graphic narratives *The Three Escapes of Hannah Arendt: A Tyranny of Truth*, *When I Grow Up: The Lost Autobiographies of Six Yiddish Teenagers*, and *Einstein in Kafkaland*.

"With the last Holocaust survivors leaving us every day, it is essential to reach younger generations who will never have the chance to meet them and hear their stories, especially the inspiring ones. This is where graphic novels come in. Ralph Shayne's is an excellent contribution to this genre. His well-crafted story of his nine-year-old mother on the run from the Nazis and her family's protection by Danish Christians will have wide appeal."

—Jonathan Alter, author of *His Very Best: Jimmy Carter, A Life*

HOUR OF NEED

The Daring Escape of the Danish Jews during World War II

To the brave people of Denmark who came in my
family's hour of need, and to all who have not let the
memories of those lost in the Holocaust die

—RS

For my beautiful Aunt Gitte—though you're
not with us anymore, this book would not
have been the same without you

—TG

A Note from Illinois Holocaust Museum

Hour of Need provides the opportunity to learn and be inspired by the brave Danes, from
the King to ordinary people, who stood up for what was right and helped neighbors, friends,
and strangers alike survive the Holocaust. Illinois Holocaust Museum uses exhibitions,
programs, and innovative approaches to storytelling to preserve and promote the stories of
Holocaust survivors, eyewitnesses, and those who, against daunting obstacles, chose to be
upstanders rather than bystanders. We are proud to share the harrowing and inspiring story
of Mette Shayne, Svend Otto "John" Nielsen, Holger Danske, and the Danish people during
the dark days of World War II.

YELLOW JACKET
an imprint of Little Bee Books

yellowjacketreads.com

ISBN 978-1-4998-1357-9 (pb) 10 9 8 7 6 5 4 3 2 1 | ISBN 978-1-4998-1358-6 (hc) 10 9 8 7 6 5 4 3 2 1 | ISBN 978-1-4998-1359-3 (eb)

New York, NY | Text copyright © 2023 by Ralph Shayne | Illustrations copyright © 2023 by Tatiana Goldberg | Lettering by Martin Flink
All rights reserved, including the right of reproduction in whole or in part in any form. | Yellow Jacket and associated colophon
are trademarks of Little Bee Books. | Library of Congress Cataloging-in-Publication Data is available upon request.
First Edition | Manufactured in China RRD 0623

While the events described in *Hour of Need* occurred, in some instances space and time have been rearranged for storytelling purposes. Some dialogue
has been recreated or imagined from recorded history, and out of respect for non-historical figures, some names and characteristics have been altered.

For information about special discounts on bulk purchases, please contact Little Bee Books at sales@littlebeebooks.com.

HOUR OF NEED

The Daring Escape of the Danish Jews during World War II

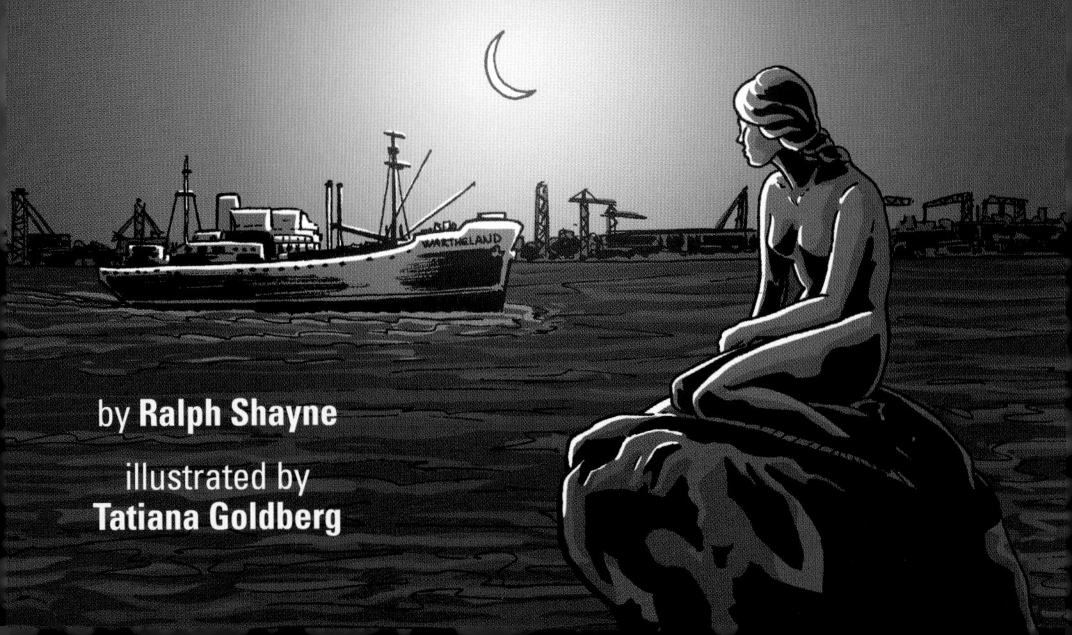
WARTHELAND

by **Ralph Shayne**

illustrated by
Tatiana Goldberg

"Should danger ever come, then Holger Danske will raise himself . . . 'Ah yes, remember me, you Danish people, keep me in your memory. I will come in your hour of need.'"
—*Holger Danske* by Hans Christian Andersen, 1845

"We are one people, one family, the human family, and what affects one of us affects us all."
—John Lewis

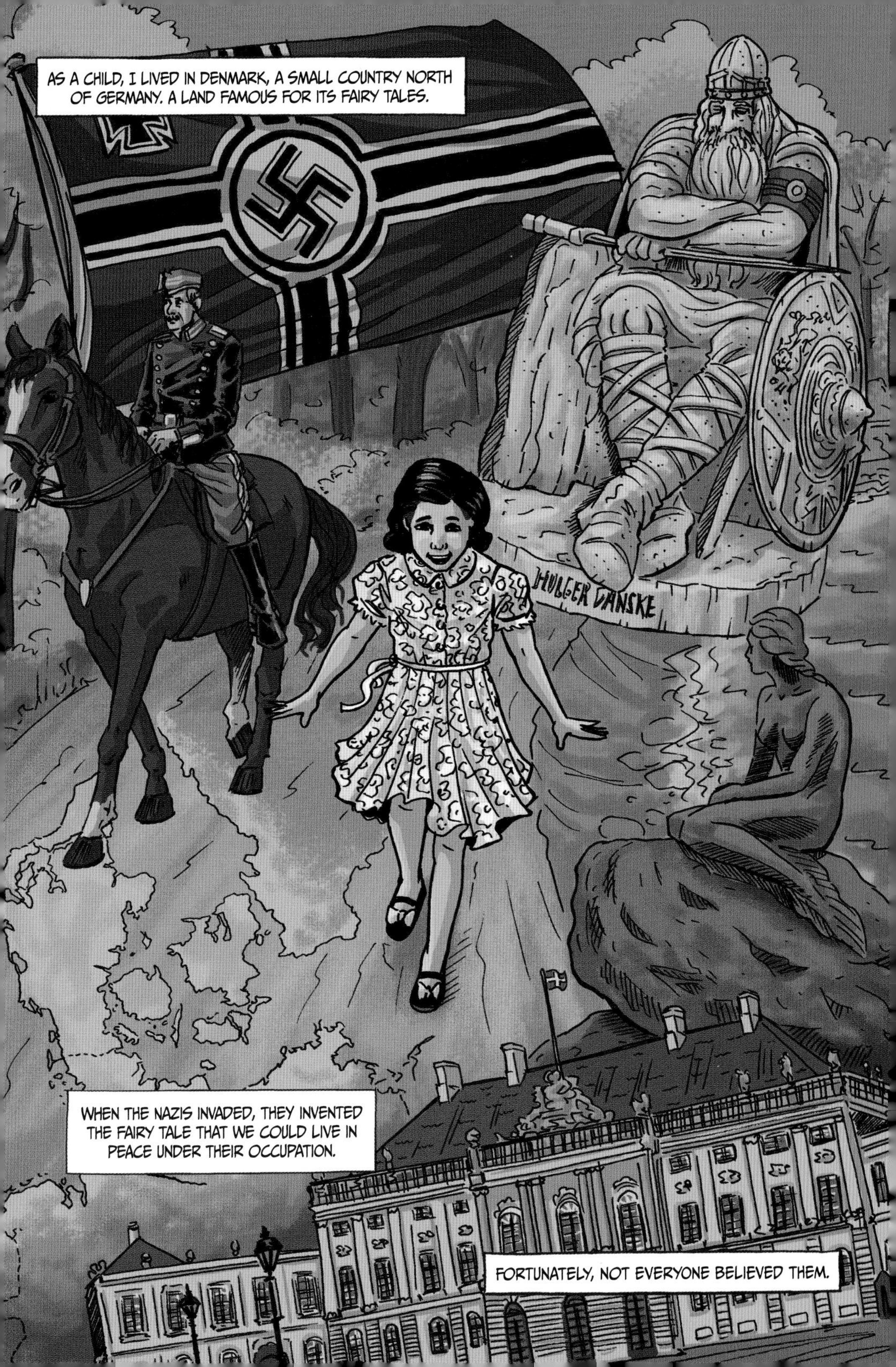
AS A CHILD, I LIVED IN DENMARK, A SMALL COUNTRY NORTH OF GERMANY. A LAND FAMOUS FOR ITS FAIRY TALES.
HOLGER DANSKE
WHEN THE NAZIS INVADED, THEY INVENTED THE FAIRY TALE THAT WE COULD LIVE IN PEACE UNDER THEIR OCCUPATION.
FORTUNATELY, NOT EVERYONE BELIEVED THEM.

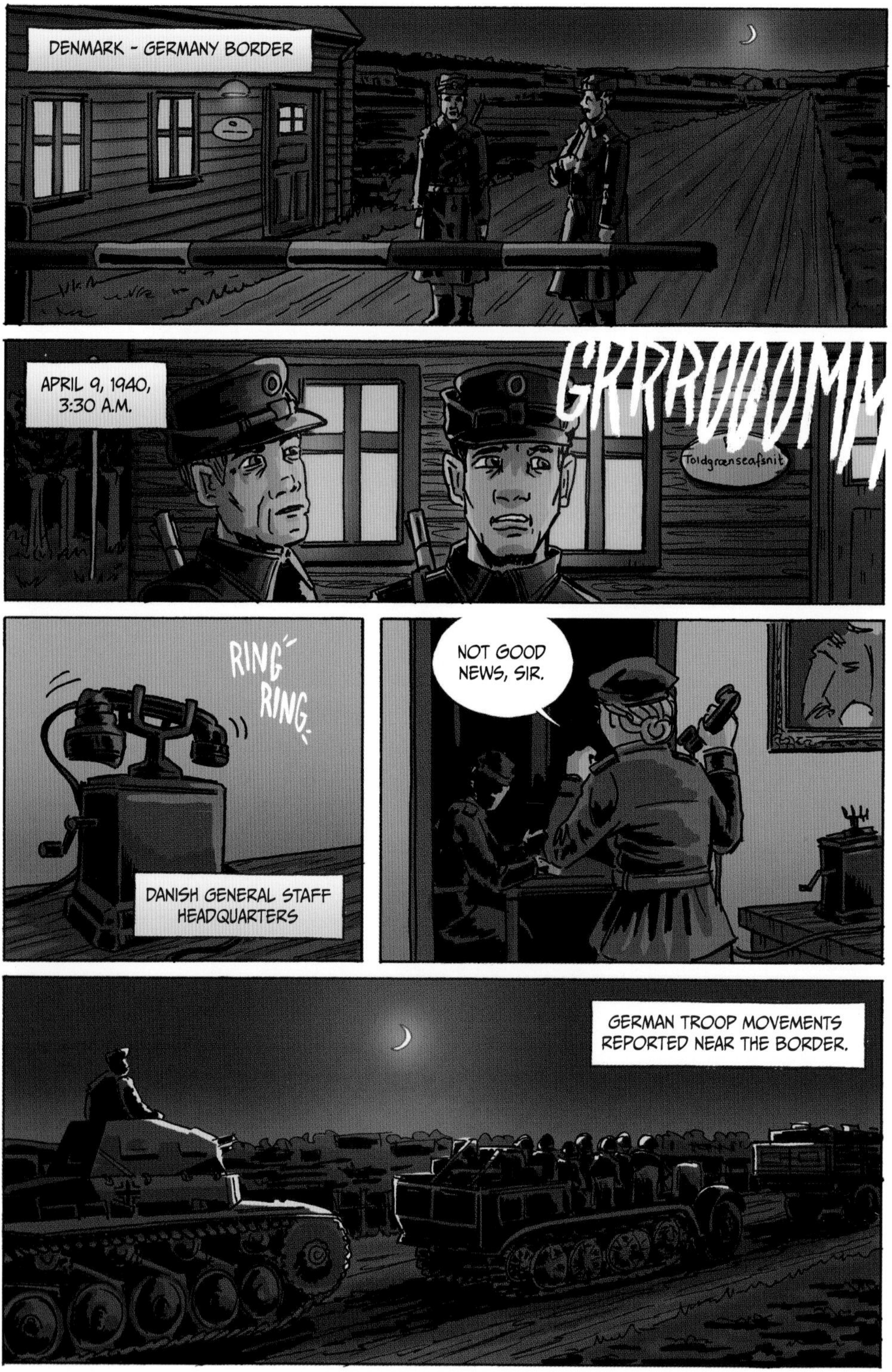
DENMARK - GERMANY BORDER
APRIL 9, 1940, 3:30 A.M.
GRRROOOMM
Toldgrænseafsnit
RING RING
DANISH GENERAL STAFF HEADQUARTERS
NOT GOOD NEWS, SIR.
GERMAN TROOP MOVEMENTS REPORTED NEAR THE BORDER.

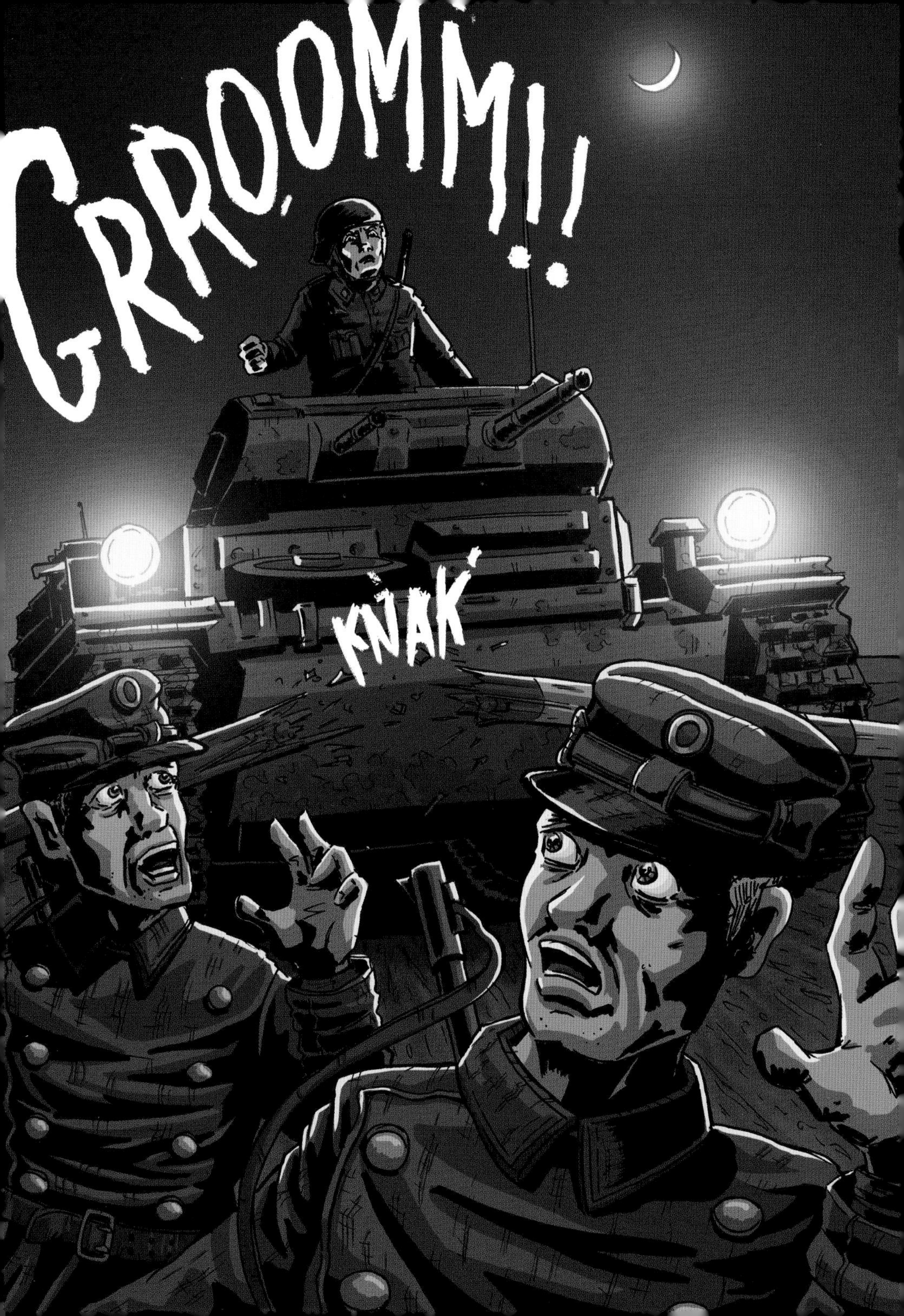
GRROOMM!!!
KNAK

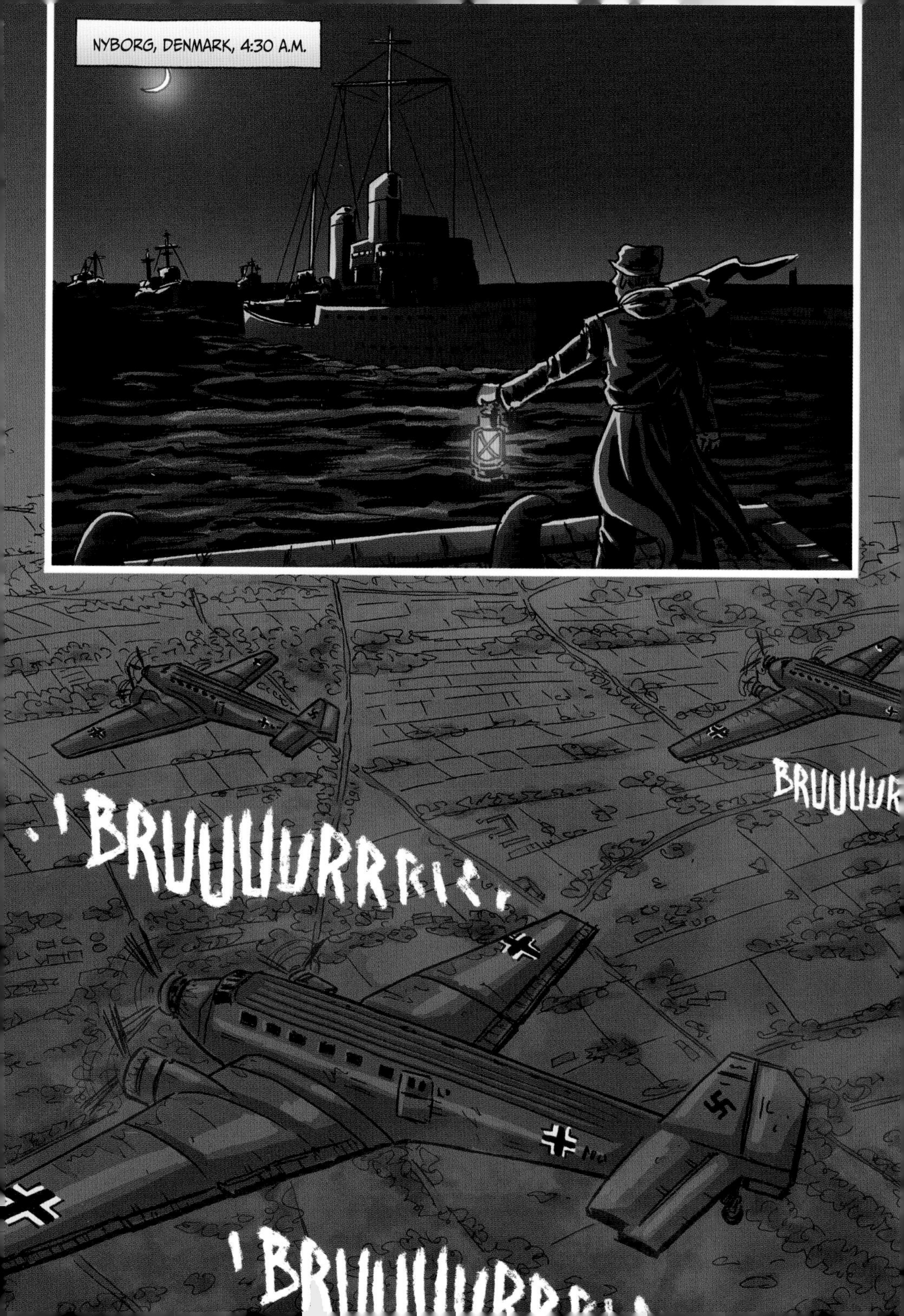
NYBORG, DENMARK, 4:30 A.M.
BRUUUUR
BRUUUURRR

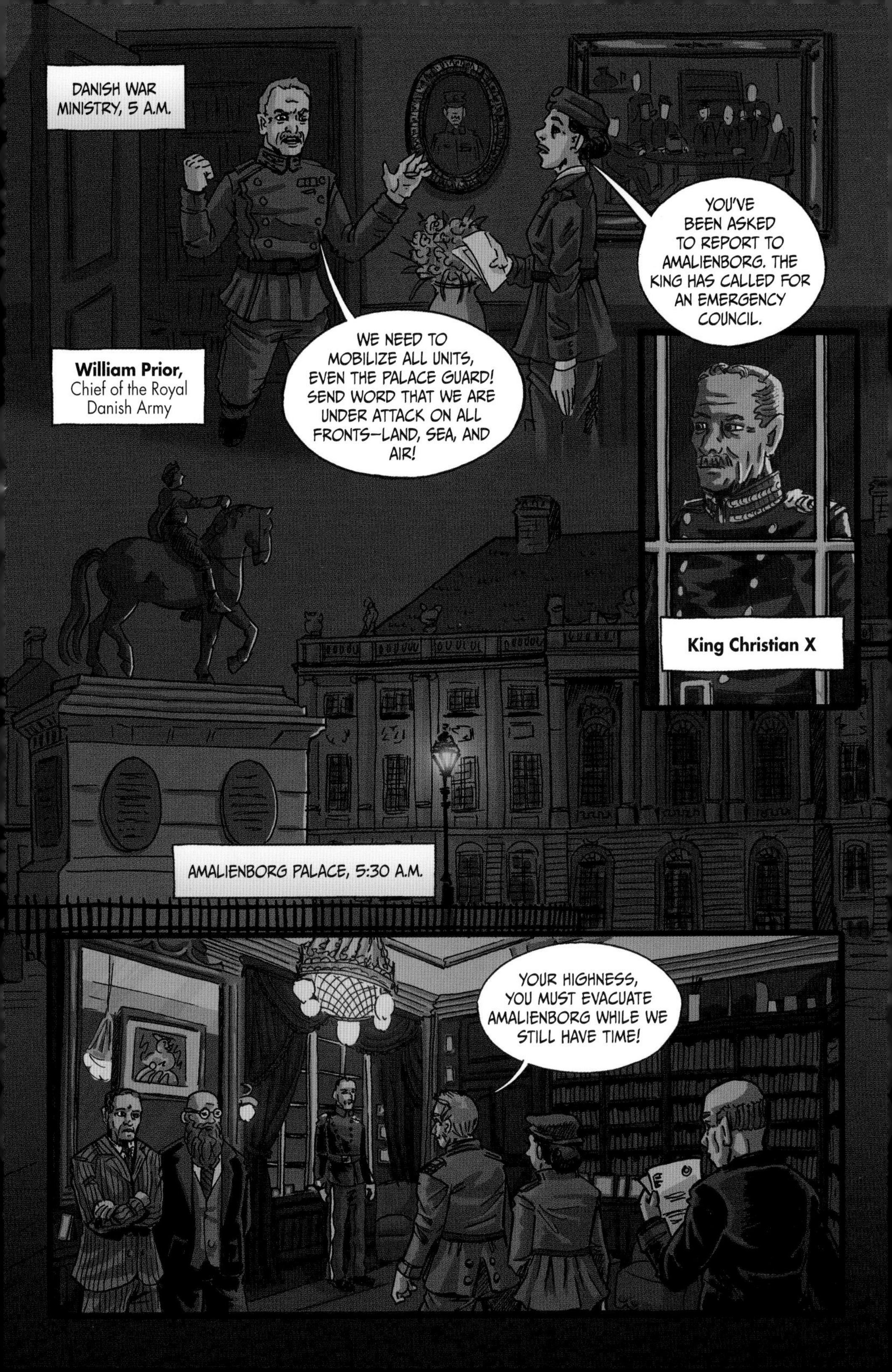
DANISH WAR MINISTRY, 5 A.M.
William Prior, Chief of the Royal Danish Army
WE NEED TO MOBILIZE ALL UNITS, EVEN THE PALACE GUARD! SEND WORD THAT WE ARE UNDER ATTACK ON ALL FRONTS—LAND, SEA, AND AIR!
YOU'VE BEEN ASKED TO REPORT TO AMALIENBORG. THE KING HAS CALLED FOR AN EMERGENCY COUNCIL.
King Christian X
AMALIENBORG PALACE, 5:30 A.M.
YOUR HIGHNESS, YOU MUST EVACUATE AMALIENBORG WHILE WE STILL HAVE TIME!

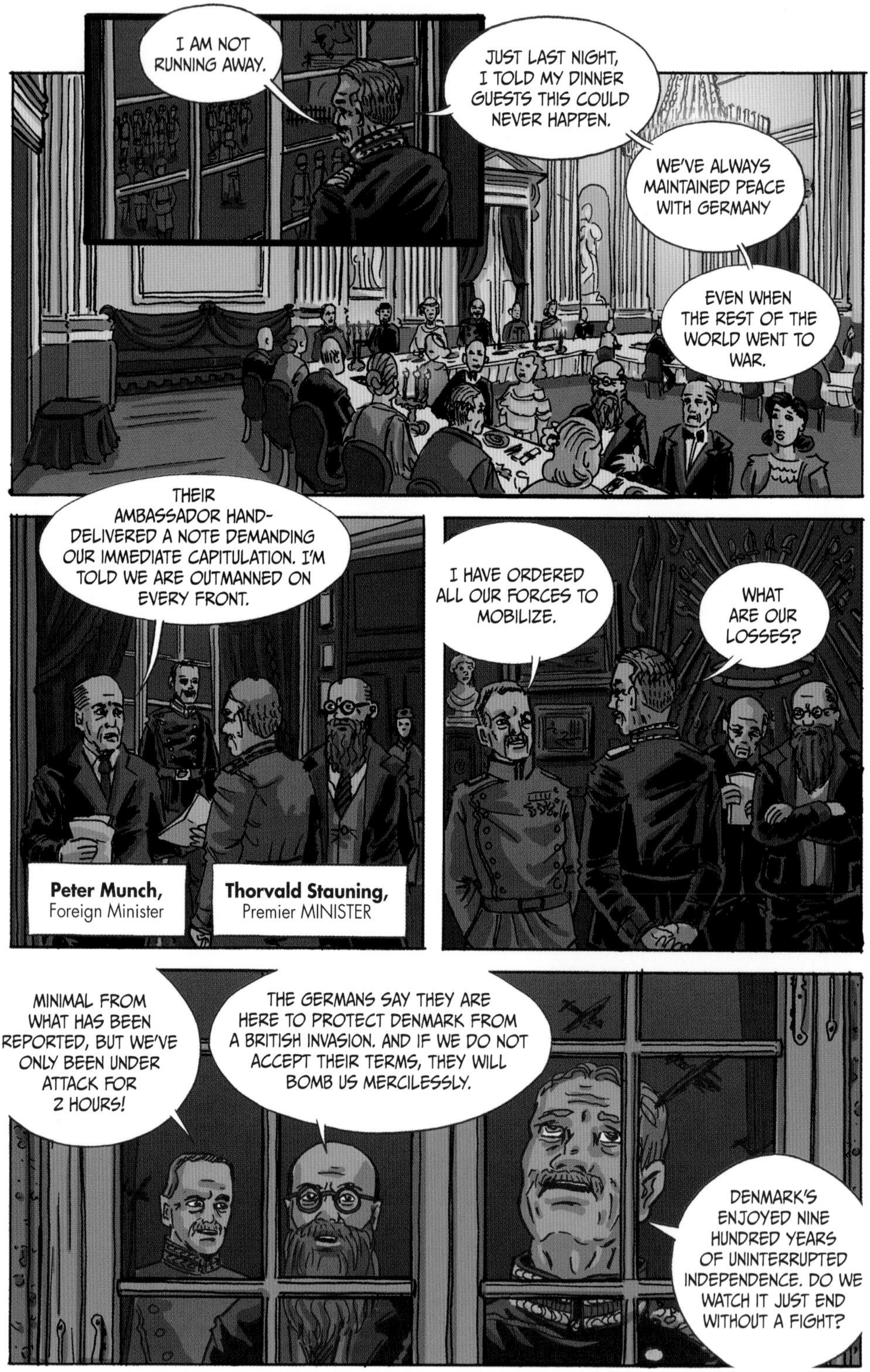
I AM NOT RUNNING AWAY.
JUST LAST NIGHT, I TOLD MY DINNER GUESTS THIS COULD NEVER HAPPEN.
WE'VE ALWAYS MAINTAINED PEACE WITH GERMANY
EVEN WHEN THE REST OF THE WORLD WENT TO WAR.
THEIR AMBASSADOR HAND-DELIVERED A NOTE DEMANDING OUR IMMEDIATE CAPITULATION. I'M TOLD WE ARE OUTMANNED ON EVERY FRONT.
Peter Munch, Foreign Minister
Thorvald Stauning, Premier MINISTER
I HAVE ORDERED ALL OUR FORCES TO MOBILIZE.
WHAT ARE OUR LOSSES?
MINIMAL FROM WHAT HAS BEEN REPORTED, BUT WE'VE ONLY BEEN UNDER ATTACK FOR 2 HOURS!
THE GERMANS SAY THEY ARE HERE TO PROTECT DENMARK FROM A BRITISH INVASION. AND IF WE DO NOT ACCEPT THEIR TERMS, THEY WILL BOMB US MERCILESSLY.
DENMARK'S ENJOYED NINE HUNDRED YEARS OF UNINTERRUPTED INDEPENDENCE. DO WE WATCH IT JUST END WITHOUT A FIGHT?

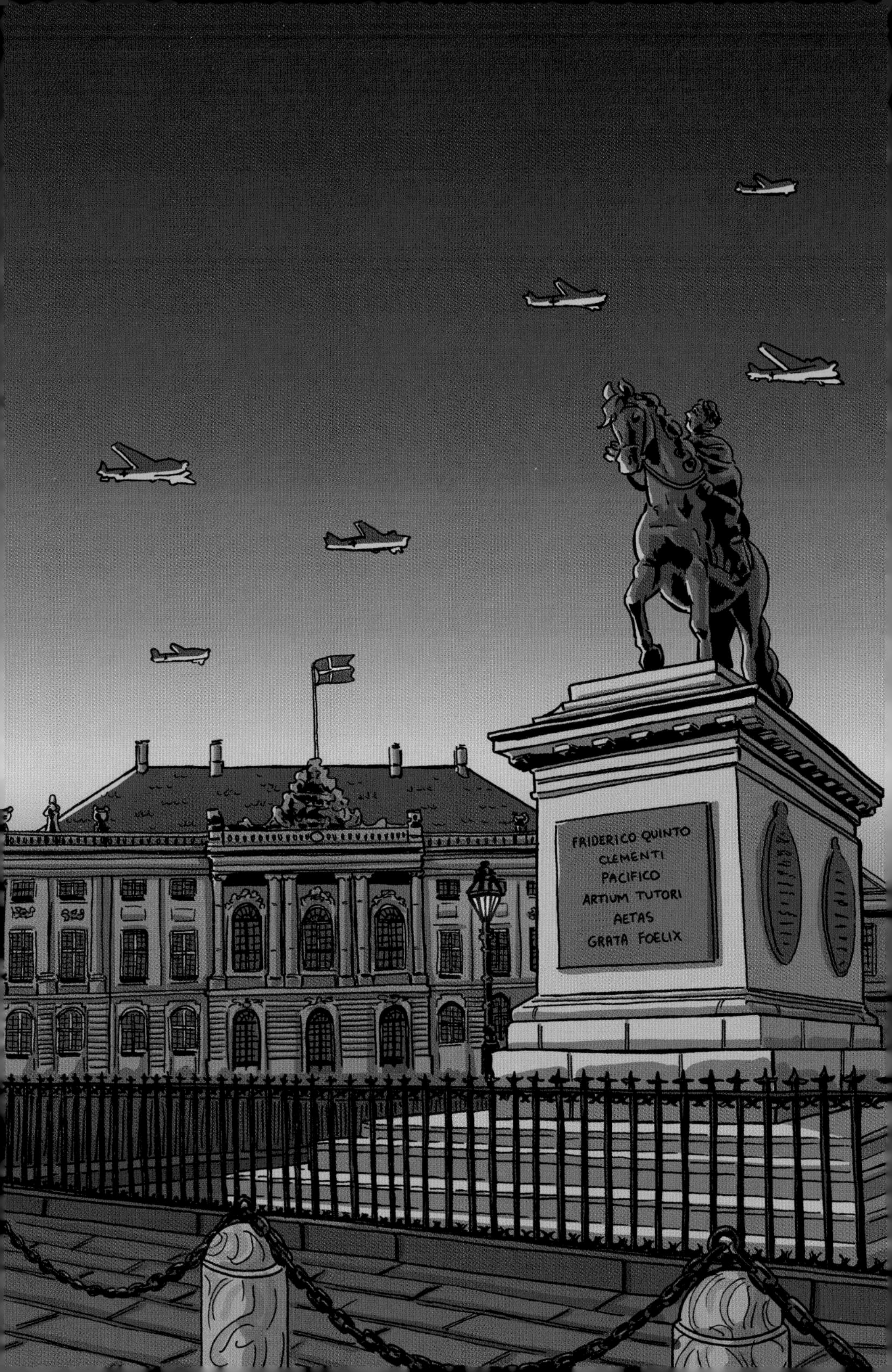
FRIDERICO QUINTO
CLEMENTI
PACIFICO
ARTIUM TUTORI
AETAS
GRATA FOELIX

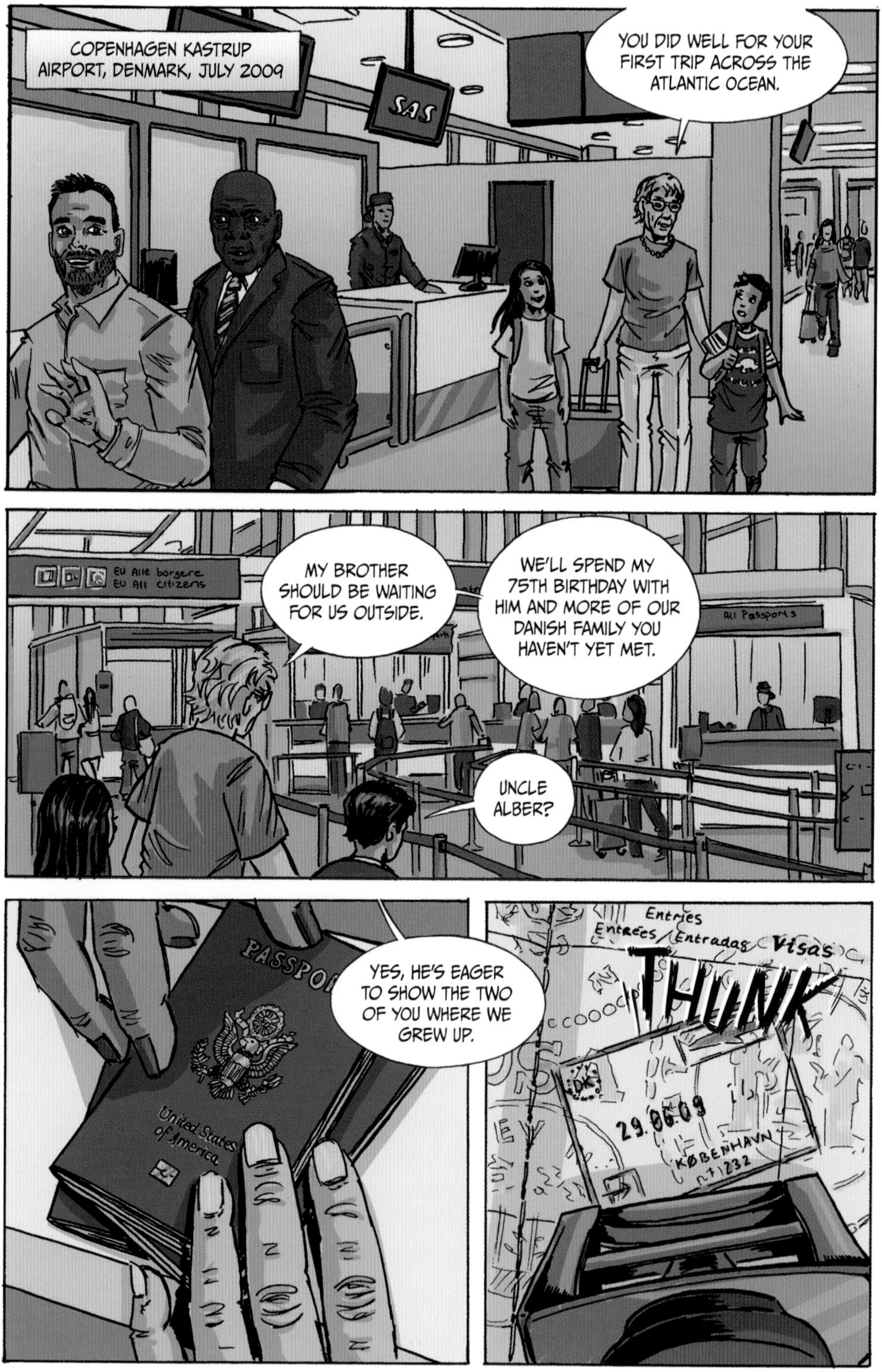
COPENHAGEN KASTRUP AIRPORT, DENMARK, JULY 2009
SAS
YOU DID WELL FOR YOUR FIRST TRIP ACROSS THE ATLANTIC OCEAN.
EU Alle borgere
EU All citizens
All Passports
MY BROTHER SHOULD BE WAITING FOR US OUTSIDE.
WE'LL SPEND MY 75TH BIRTHDAY WITH HIM AND MORE OF OUR DANISH FAMILY YOU HAVEN'T YET MET.
UNCLE ALBER?
PASSPORT
United States of America
YES, HE'S EAGER TO SHOW THE TWO OF YOU WHERE WE GREW UP.
Entries
Entrees/Entradas Visas
THUNK
DK
29.06.09
KØBENHAVN
232

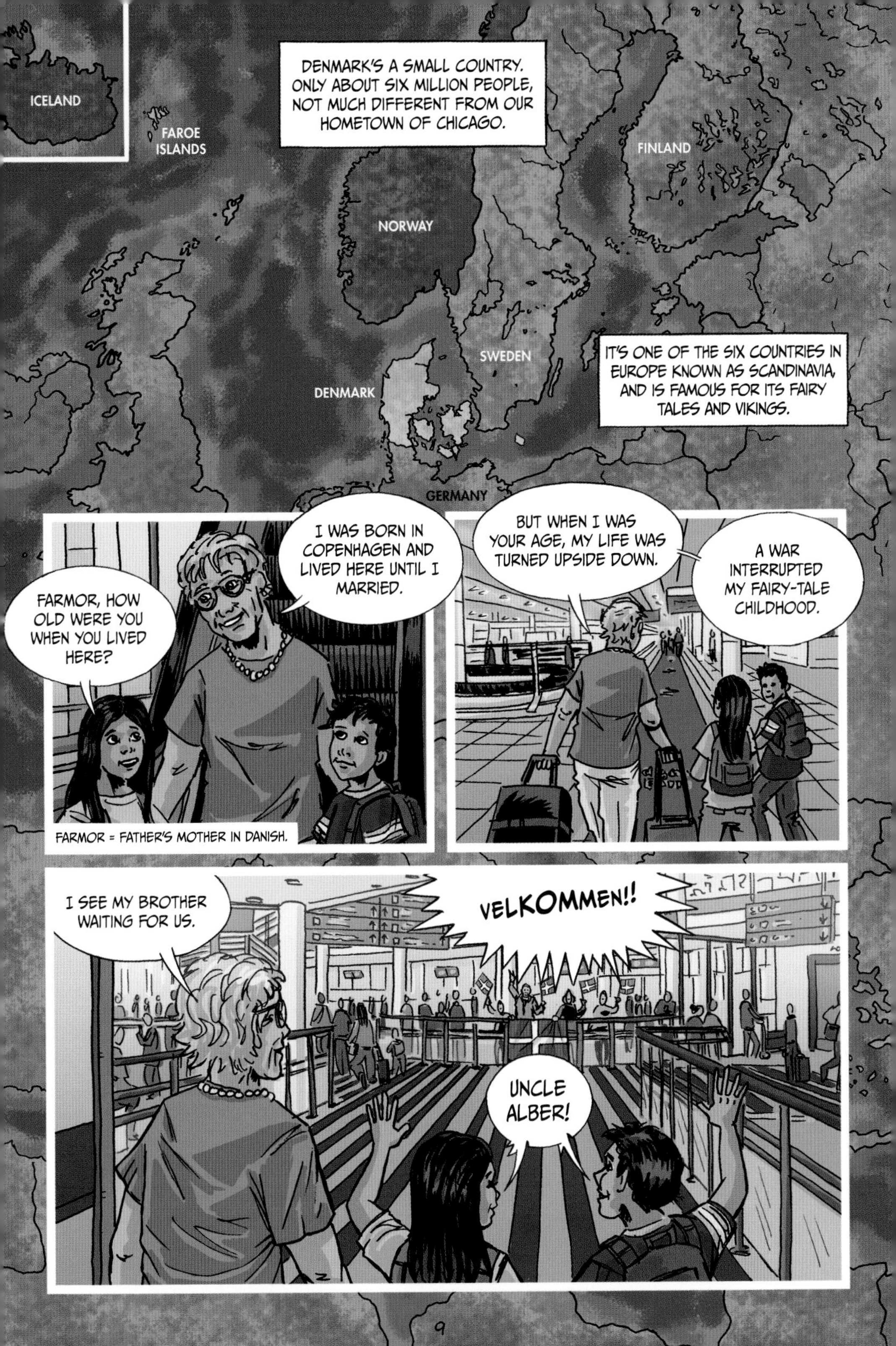
ICELAND
FAROE ISLANDS
DENMARK'S A SMALL COUNTRY. ONLY ABOUT SIX MILLION PEOPLE, NOT MUCH DIFFERENT FROM OUR HOMETOWN OF CHICAGO.
FINLAND
NORWAY
SWEDEN
DENMARK
IT'S ONE OF THE SIX COUNTRIES IN EUROPE KNOWN AS SCANDINAVIA, AND IS FAMOUS FOR ITS FAIRY TALES AND VIKINGS.
GERMANY
FARMOR, HOW OLD WERE YOU WHEN YOU LIVED HERE?
I WAS BORN IN COPENHAGEN AND LIVED HERE UNTIL I MARRIED.
FARMOR = FATHER'S MOTHER IN DANISH.
BUT WHEN I WAS YOUR AGE, MY LIFE WAS TURNED UPSIDE DOWN.
A WAR INTERRUPTED MY FAIRY-TALE CHILDHOOD.
I SEE MY BROTHER WAITING FOR US.
VELKOMMEN!!
UNCLE ALBER!

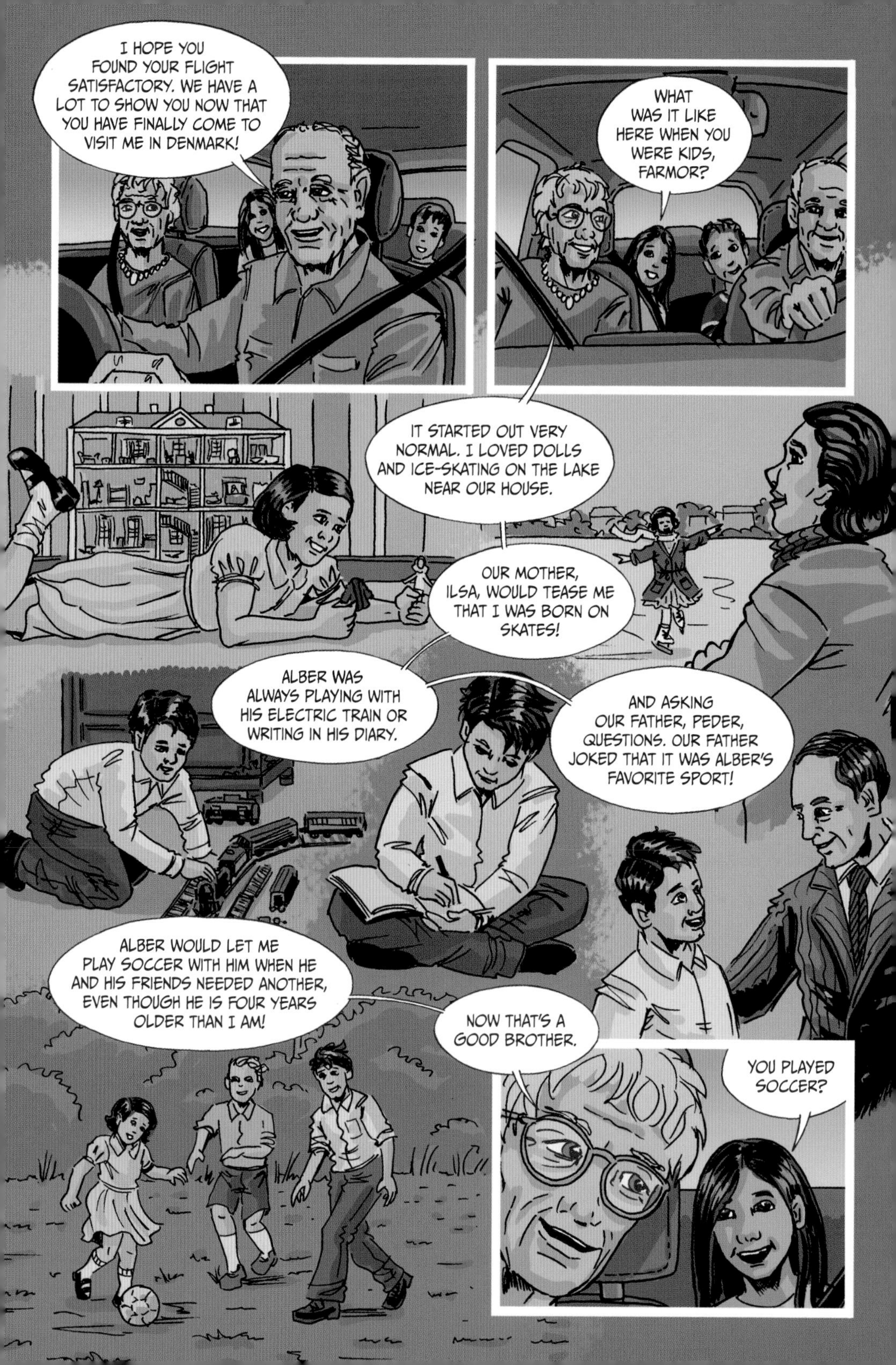
I HOPE YOU FOUND YOUR FLIGHT SATISFACTORY. WE HAVE A LOT TO SHOW YOU NOW THAT YOU HAVE FINALLY COME TO VISIT ME IN DENMARK!
WHAT WAS IT LIKE HERE WHEN YOU WERE KIDS, FARMOR?
IT STARTED OUT VERY NORMAL. I LOVED DOLLS AND ICE-SKATING ON THE LAKE NEAR OUR HOUSE.
OUR MOTHER, ILSA, WOULD TEASE ME THAT I WAS BORN ON SKATES!
ALBER WAS ALWAYS PLAYING WITH HIS ELECTRIC TRAIN OR WRITING IN HIS DIARY.
AND ASKING OUR FATHER, PEDER, QUESTIONS. OUR FATHER JOKED THAT IT WAS ALBER'S FAVORITE SPORT!
ALBER WOULD LET ME PLAY SOCCER WITH HIM WHEN HE AND HIS FRIENDS NEEDED ANOTHER, EVEN THOUGH HE IS FOUR YEARS OLDER THAN I AM!
NOW THAT'S A GOOD BROTHER.
YOU PLAYED SOCCER?

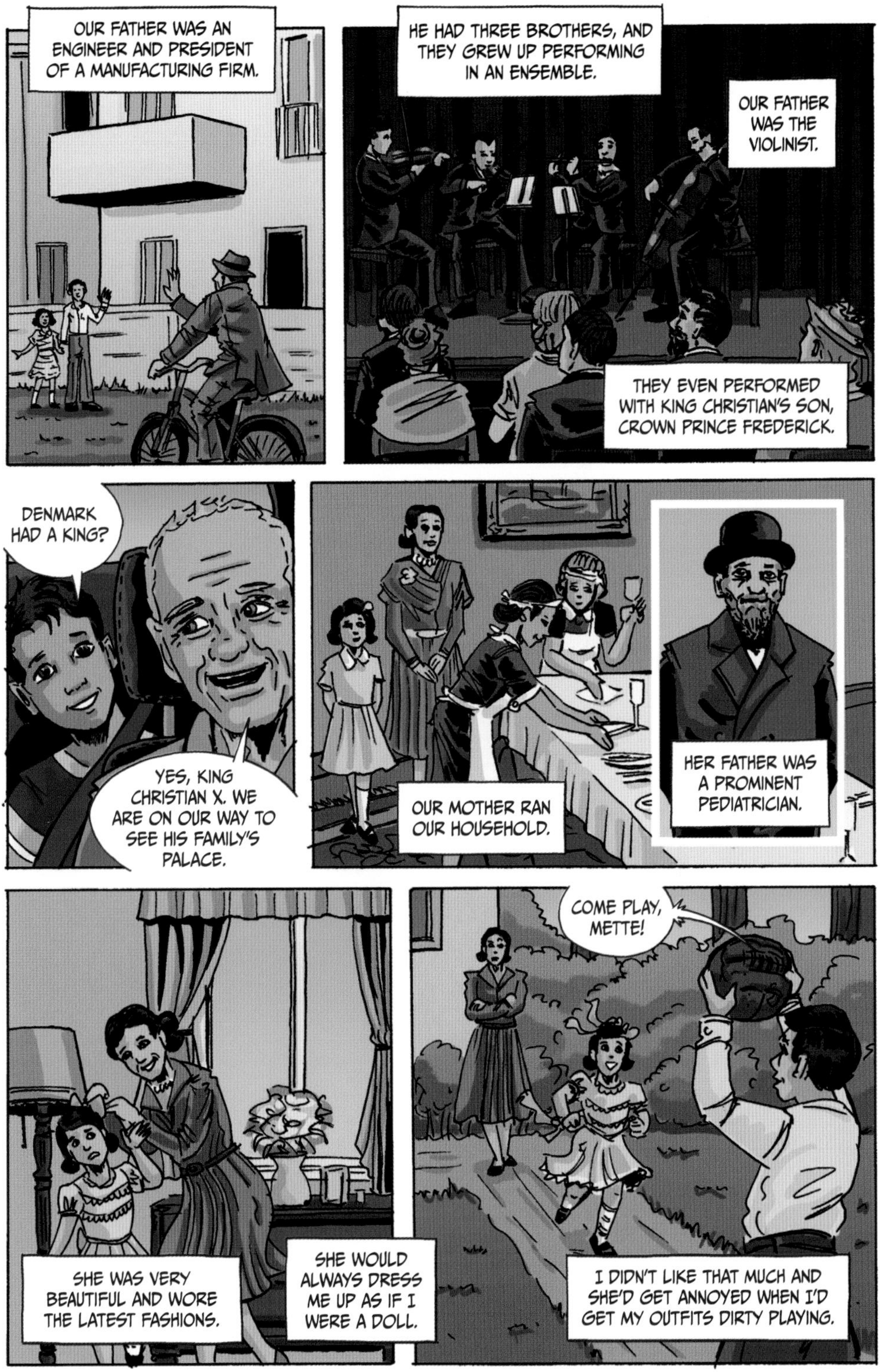
OUR FATHER WAS AN ENGINEER AND PRESIDENT OF A MANUFACTURING FIRM.
HE HAD THREE BROTHERS, AND THEY GREW UP PERFORMING IN AN ENSEMBLE.
OUR FATHER WAS THE VIOLINIST.
THEY EVEN PERFORMED WITH KING CHRISTIAN'S SON, CROWN PRINCE FREDERICK.
DENMARK HAD A KING?
YES, KING CHRISTIAN X. WE ARE ON OUR WAY TO SEE HIS FAMILY'S PALACE.
OUR MOTHER RAN OUR HOUSEHOLD.
HER FATHER WAS A PROMINENT PEDIATRICIAN.
SHE WAS VERY BEAUTIFUL AND WORE THE LATEST FASHIONS.
SHE WOULD ALWAYS DRESS ME UP AS IF I WERE A DOLL.
COME PLAY, METTE!
I DIDN'T LIKE THAT MUCH AND SHE'D GET ANNOYED WHEN I'D GET MY OUTFITS DIRTY PLAYING.

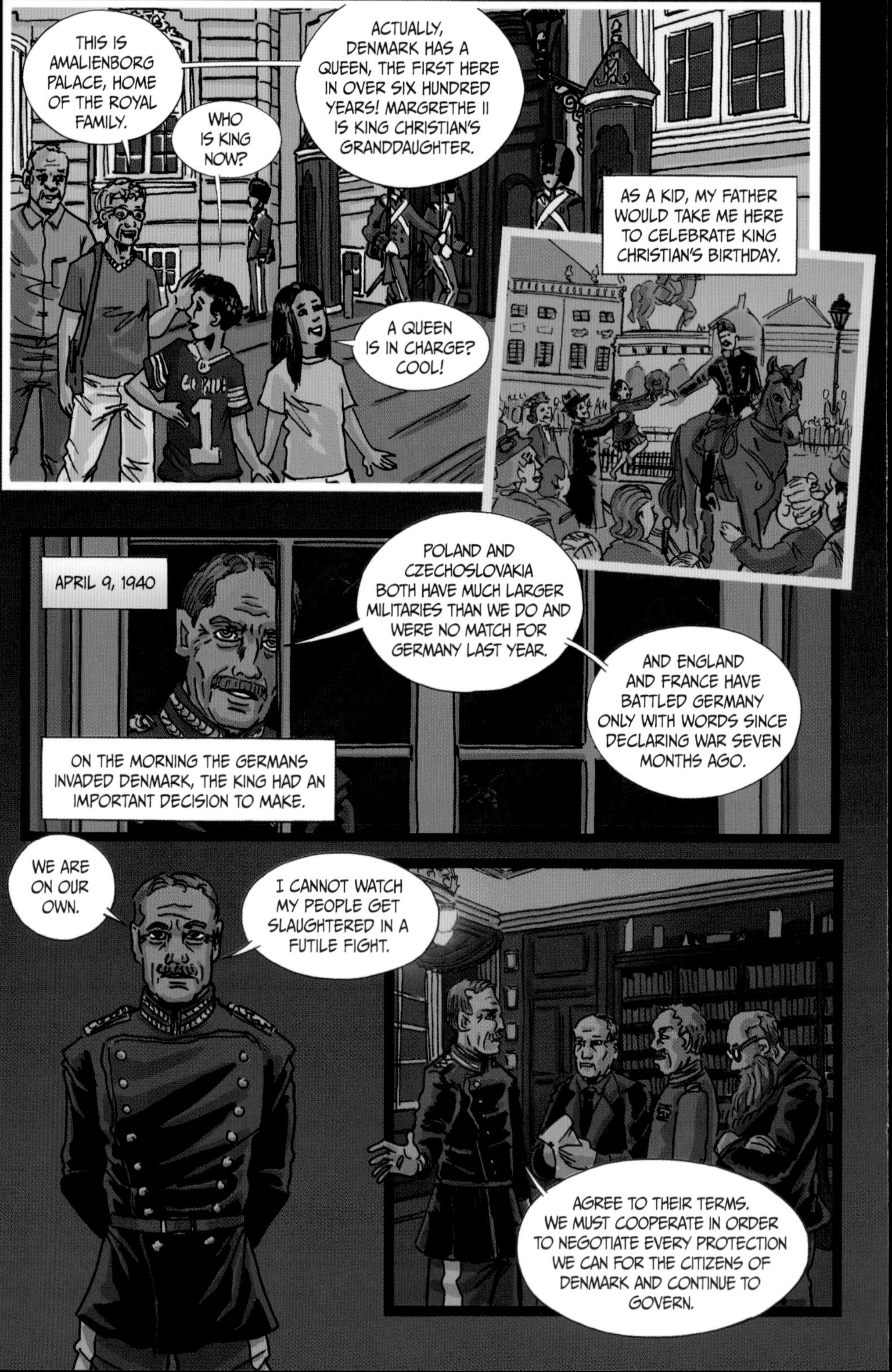
THIS IS AMALIENBORG PALACE, HOME OF THE ROYAL FAMILY.
WHO IS KING NOW?
ACTUALLY, DENMARK HAS A QUEEN, THE FIRST HERE IN OVER SIX HUNDRED YEARS! MARGRETHE II IS KING CHRISTIAN'S GRANDDAUGHTER.
A QUEEN IS IN CHARGE? COOL!
AS A KID, MY FATHER WOULD TAKE ME HERE TO CELEBRATE KING CHRISTIAN'S BIRTHDAY.
APRIL 9, 1940
POLAND AND CZECHOSLOVAKIA BOTH HAVE MUCH LARGER MILITARIES THAN WE DO AND WERE NO MATCH FOR GERMANY LAST YEAR.
AND ENGLAND AND FRANCE HAVE BATTLED GERMANY ONLY WITH WORDS SINCE DECLARING WAR SEVEN MONTHS AGO.
ON THE MORNING THE GERMANS INVADED DENMARK, THE KING HAD AN IMPORTANT DECISION TO MAKE.
WE ARE ON OUR OWN.
I CANNOT WATCH MY PEOPLE GET SLAUGHTERED IN A FUTILE FIGHT.
AGREE TO THEIR TERMS. WE MUST COOPERATE IN ORDER TO NEGOTIATE EVERY PROTECTION WE CAN FOR THE CITIZENS OF DENMARK AND CONTINUE TO GOVERN.

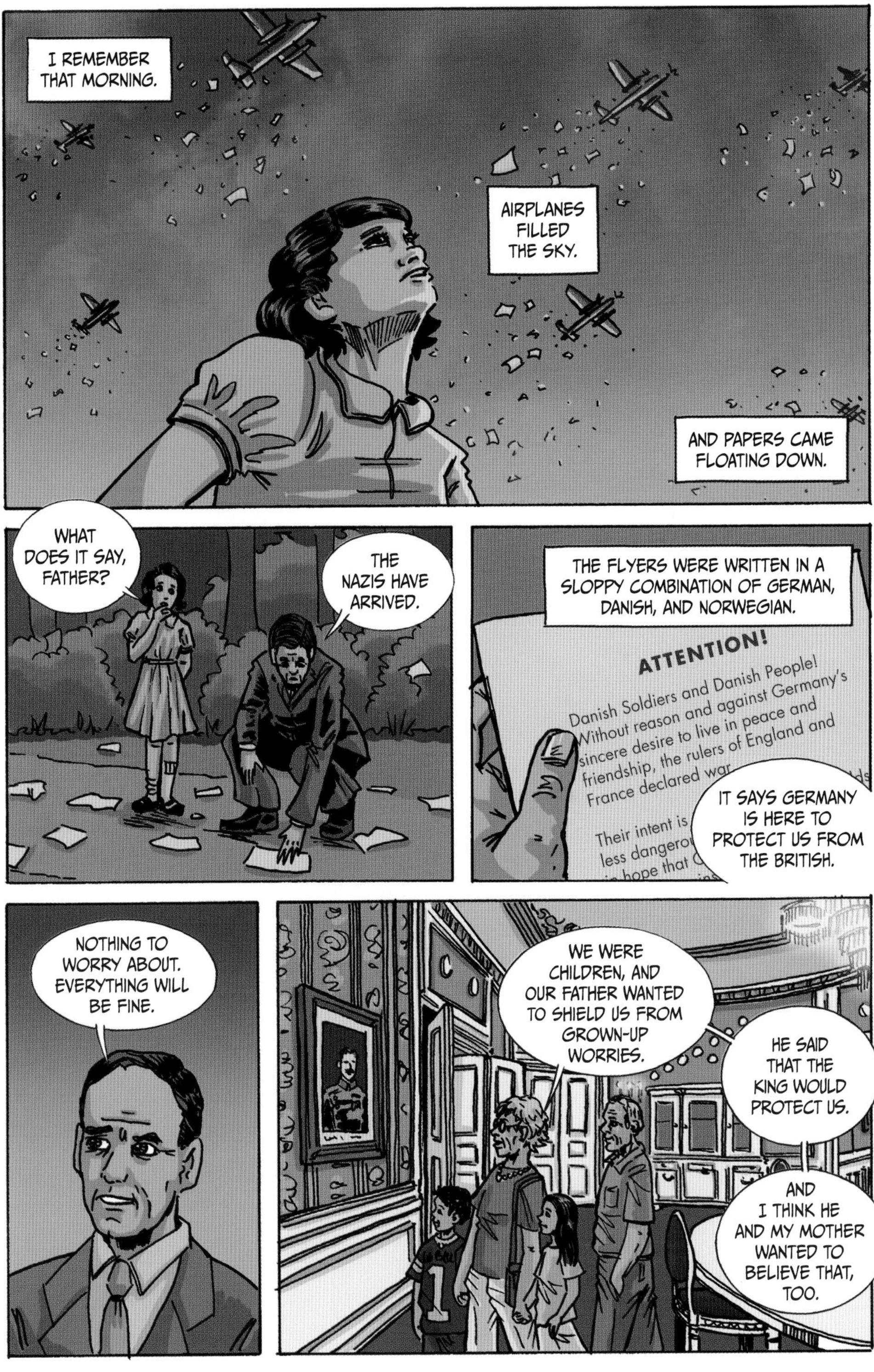

I REMEMBER THAT MORNING.
AIRPLANES FILLED THE SKY.
AND PAPERS CAME FLOATING DOWN.
WHAT DOES IT SAY, FATHER?
THE NAZIS HAVE ARRIVED.
THE FLYERS WERE WRITTEN IN A SLOPPY COMBINATION OF GERMAN, DANISH, AND NORWEGIAN.
ATTENTION!
Danish Soldiers and Danish People!
Without reason and against Germany's
sincere desire to live in peace and
friendship, the rulers of England and
France declared war
Their intent is
IT SAYS GERMANY IS HERE TO PROTECT US FROM THE BRITISH.
NOTHING TO WORRY ABOUT. EVERYTHING WILL BE FINE.
WE WERE CHILDREN, AND OUR FATHER WANTED TO SHIELD US FROM GROWN-UP WORRIES.
HE SAID THAT THE KING WOULD PROTECT US.
AND I THINK HE AND MY MOTHER WANTED TO BELIEVE THAT, TOO.

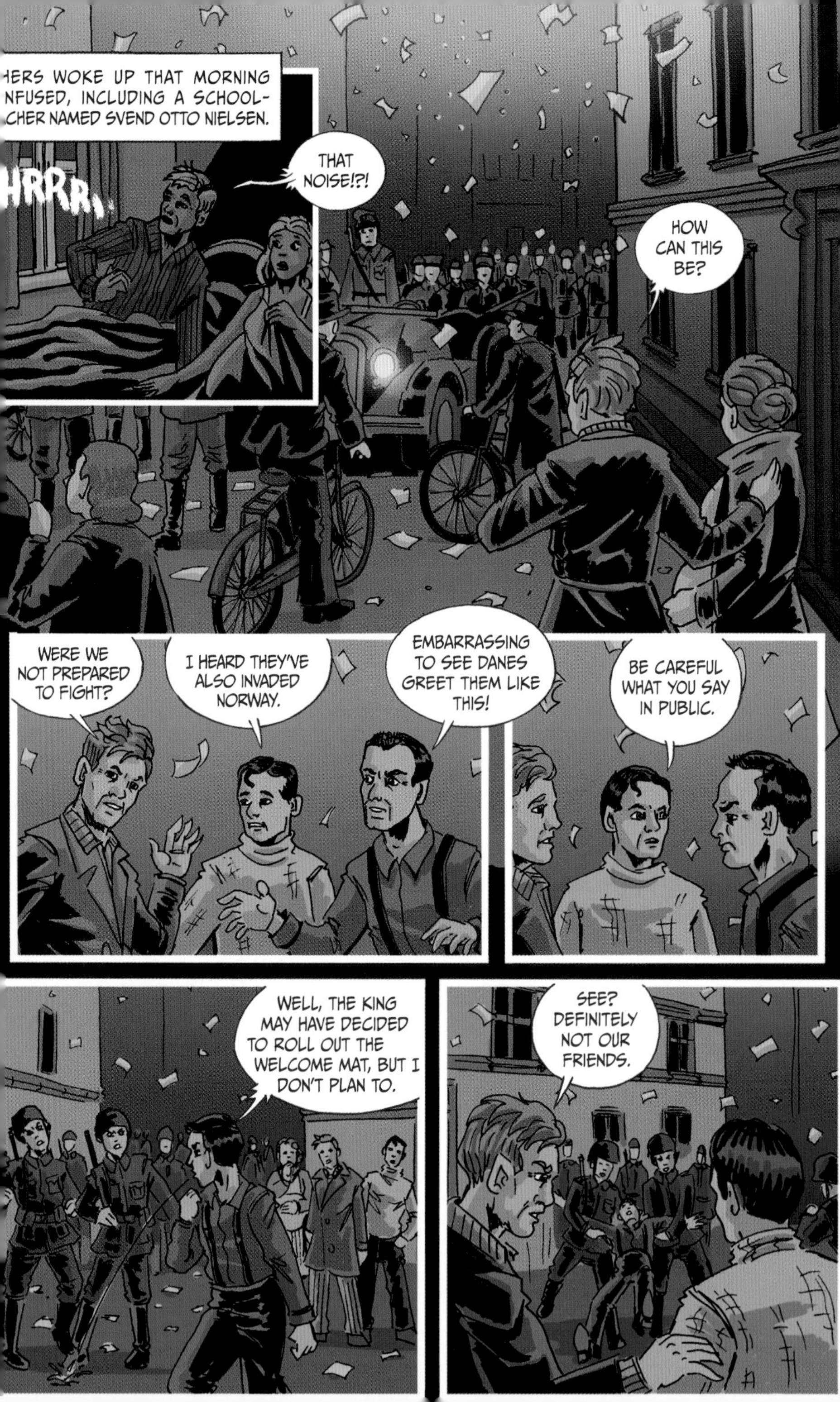

HERS WOKE UP THAT MORNING
NFUSED, INCLUDING A SCHOOL-
CHER NAMED SVEND OTTO NIELSEN.
HRRR
THAT NOISE!?!
HOW CAN THIS BE?
WERE WE NOT PREPARED TO FIGHT?
I HEARD THEY'VE ALSO INVADED NORWAY.
EMBARRASSING TO SEE DANES GREET THEM LIKE THIS!
BE CAREFUL WHAT YOU SAY IN PUBLIC.
WELL, THE KING MAY HAVE DECIDED TO ROLL OUT THE WELCOME MAT, BUT I DON'T PLAN TO.
SEE? DEFINITELY NOT OUR FRIENDS.

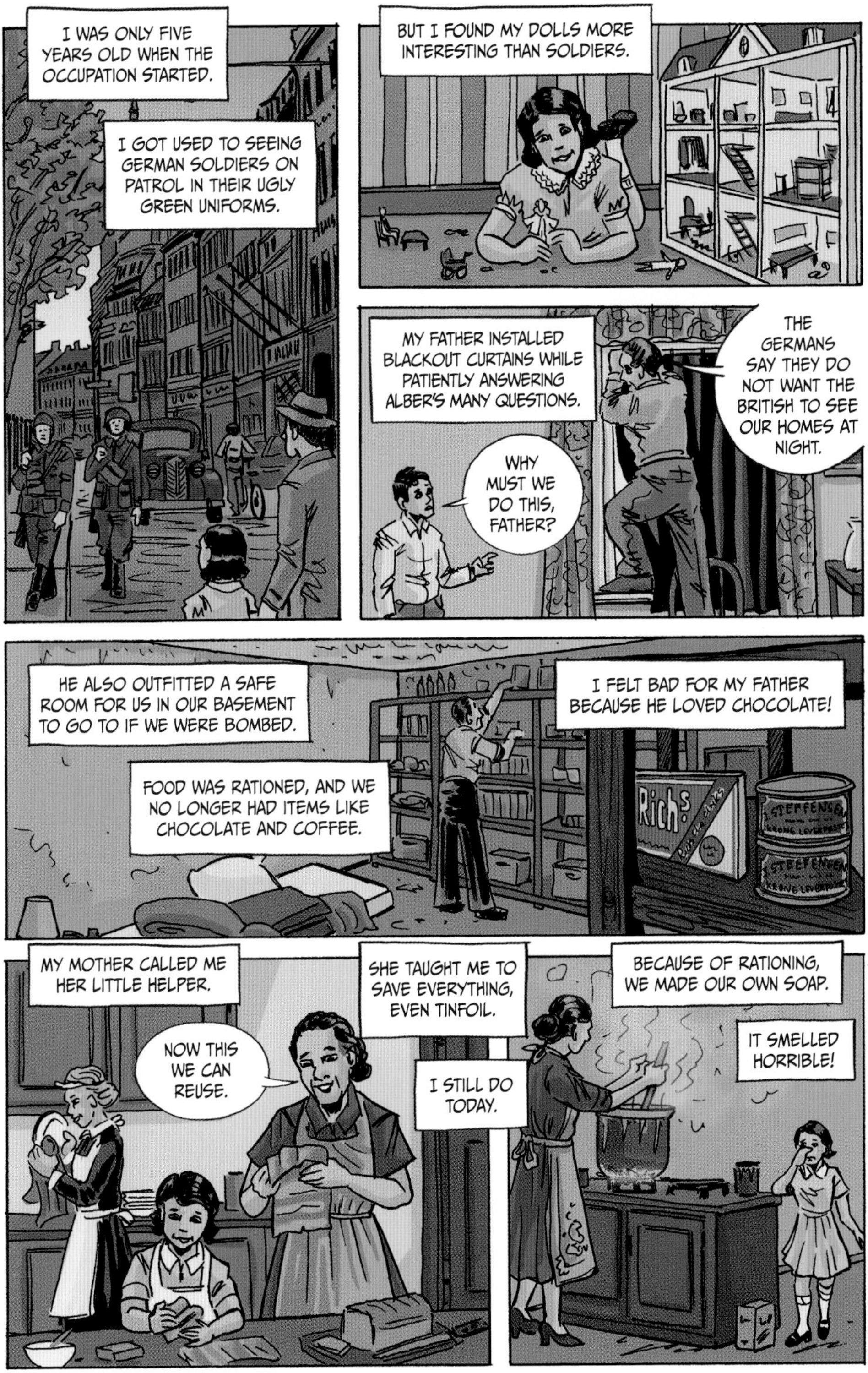

I WAS ONLY FIVE YEARS OLD WHEN THE OCCUPATION STARTED.
I GOT USED TO SEEING GERMAN SOLDIERS ON PATROL IN THEIR UGLY GREEN UNIFORMS.
BUT I FOUND MY DOLLS MORE INTERESTING THAN SOLDIERS.
MY FATHER INSTALLED BLACKOUT CURTAINS WHILE PATIENTLY ANSWERING ALBER'S MANY QUESTIONS.
WHY MUST WE DO THIS, FATHER?
THE GERMANS SAY THEY DO NOT WANT THE BRITISH TO SEE OUR HOMES AT NIGHT.
HE ALSO OUTFITTED A SAFE ROOM FOR US IN OUR BASEMENT TO GO TO IF WE WERE BOMBED.
FOOD WAS RATIONED, AND WE NO LONGER HAD ITEMS LIKE CHOCOLATE AND COFFEE.
I FELT BAD FOR MY FATHER BECAUSE HE LOVED CHOCOLATE!
MY MOTHER CALLED ME HER LITTLE HELPER.
NOW THIS WE CAN REUSE.
SHE TAUGHT ME TO SAVE EVERYTHING, EVEN TINFOIL.
I STILL DO TODAY.
BECAUSE OF RATIONING, WE MADE OUR OWN SOAP.
IT SMELLED HORRIBLE!

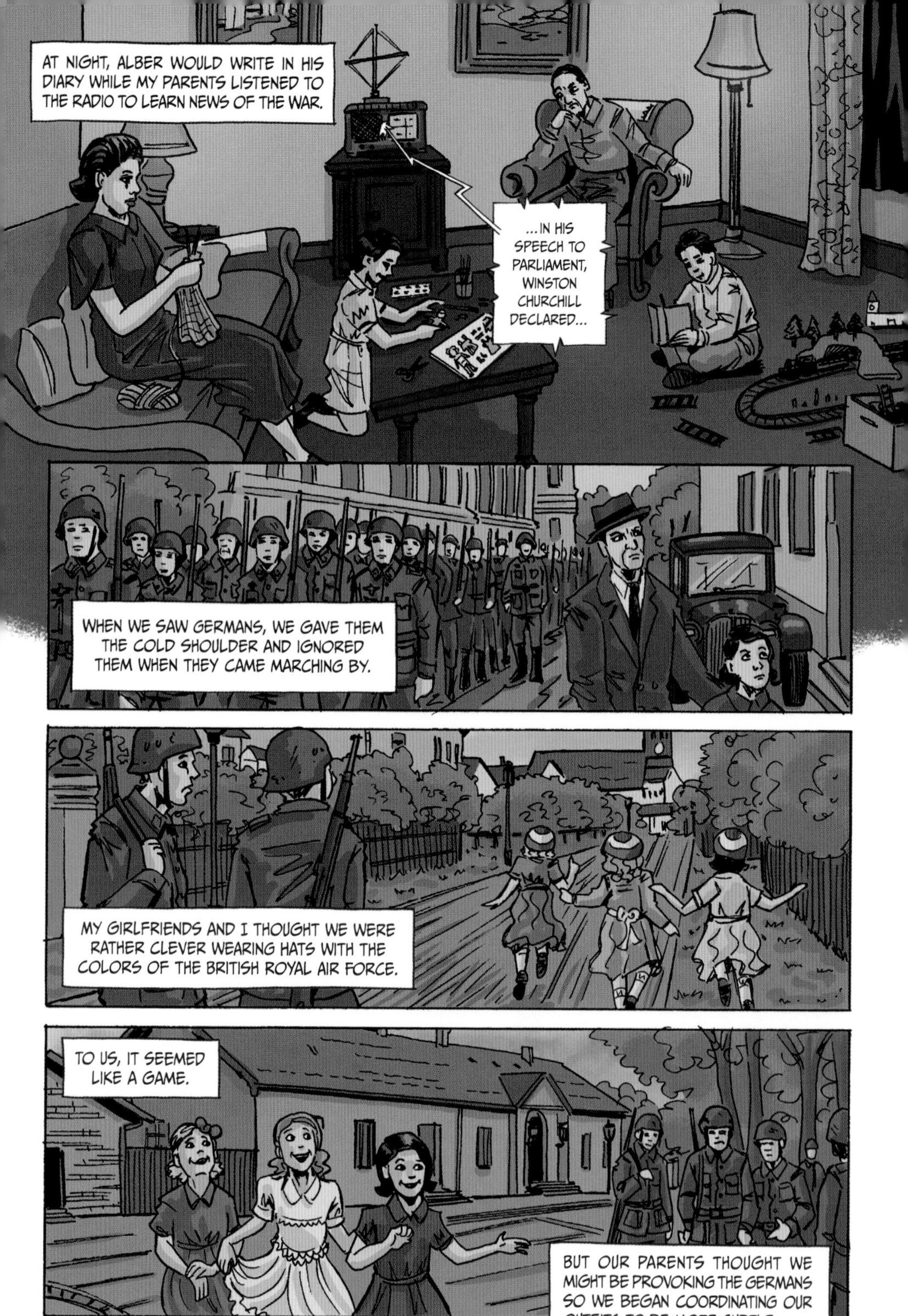
AT NIGHT, ALBER WOULD WRITE IN HIS DIARY WHILE MY PARENTS LISTENED TO THE RADIO TO LEARN NEWS OF THE WAR.
...IN HIS SPEECH TO PARLIAMENT, WINSTON CHURCHILL DECLARED...
WHEN WE SAW GERMANS, WE GAVE THEM THE COLD SHOULDER AND IGNORED THEM WHEN THEY CAME MARCHING BY.
MY GIRLFRIENDS AND I THOUGHT WE WERE RATHER CLEVER WEARING HATS WITH THE COLORS OF THE BRITISH ROYAL AIR FORCE.
TO US, IT SEEMED LIKE A GAME.
BUT OUR PARENTS THOUGHT WE MIGHT BE PROVOKING THE GERMANS SO WE BEGAN COORDINATING OUR OUTFITS TO BE MORE SUBTLE.

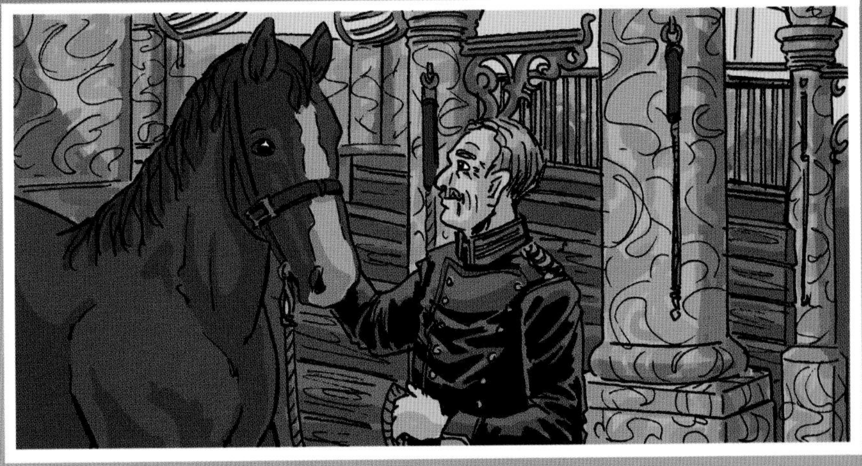

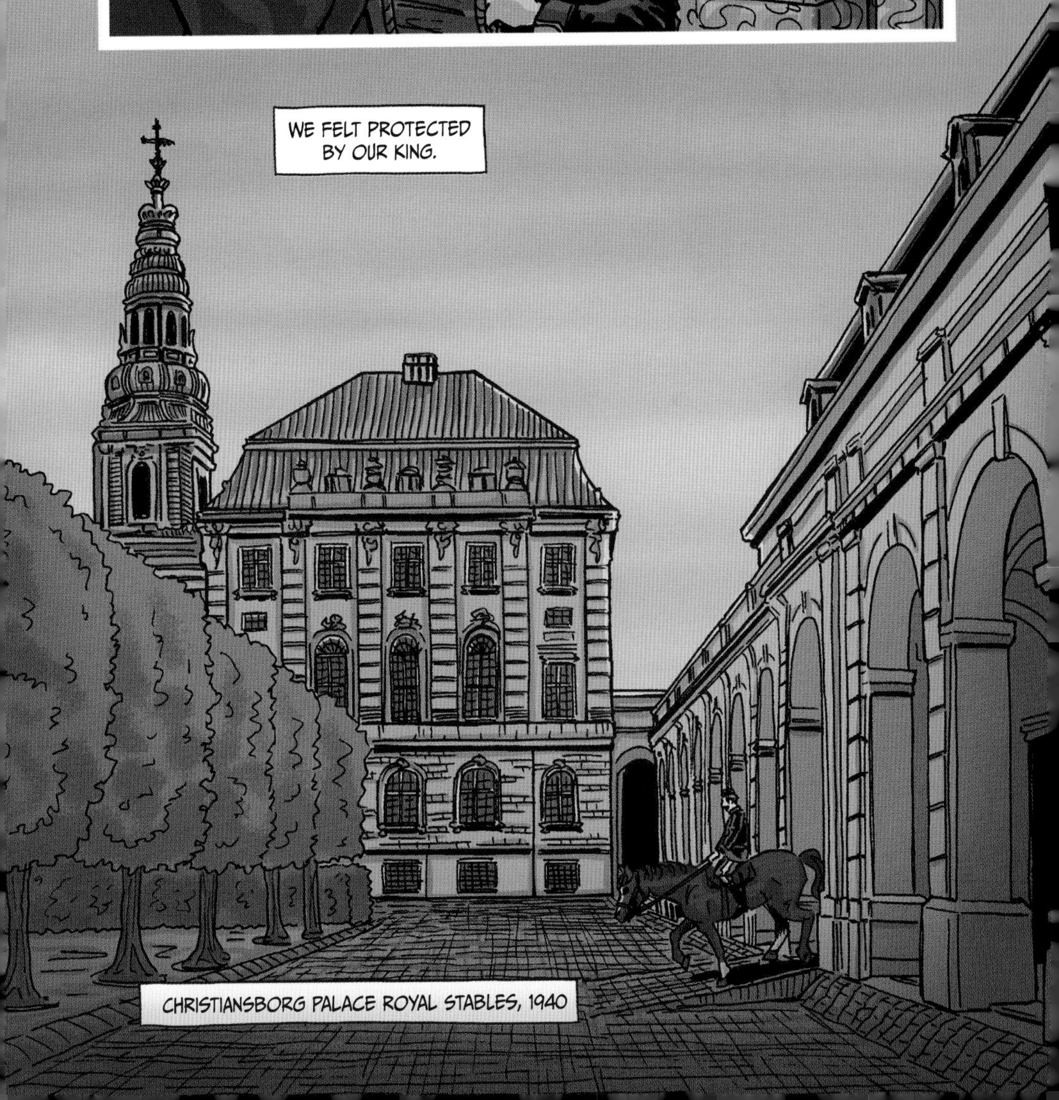
WE FELT PROTECTED
BY OUR KING.
CHRISTIANSBORG PALACE ROYAL STABLES, 1940

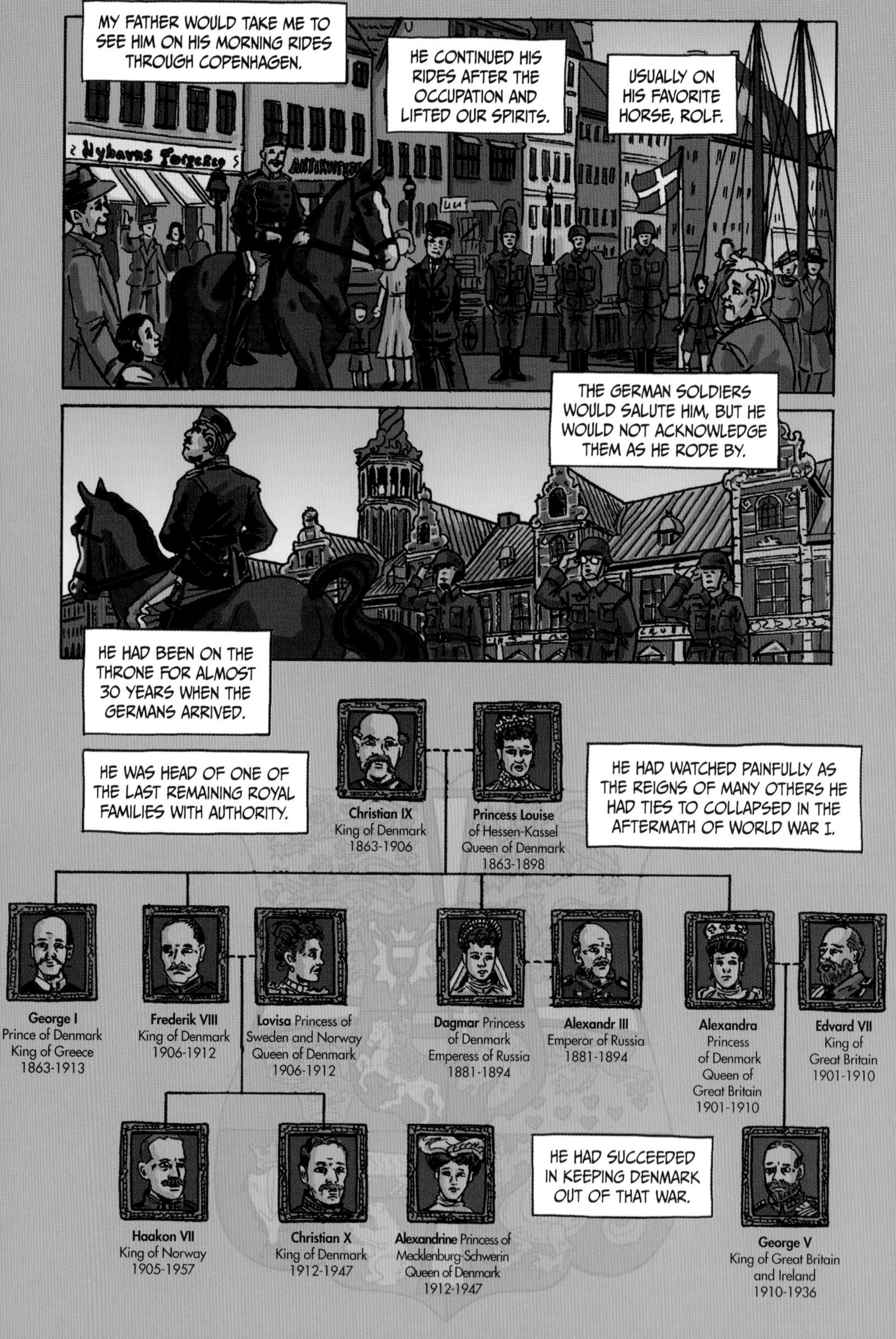
MY FATHER WOULD TAKE ME TO SEE HIM ON HIS MORNING RIDES THROUGH COPENHAGEN.
HE CONTINUED HIS RIDES AFTER THE OCCUPATION AND LIFTED OUR SPIRITS.
USUALLY ON HIS FAVORITE HORSE, ROLF.
THE GERMAN SOLDIERS WOULD SALUTE HIM, BUT HE WOULD NOT ACKNOWLEDGE THEM AS HE RODE BY.
HE HAD BEEN ON THE THRONE FOR ALMOST 30 YEARS WHEN THE GERMANS ARRIVED.
HE WAS HEAD OF ONE OF THE LAST REMAINING ROYAL FAMILIES WITH AUTHORITY.
Christian IX King of Denmark 1863-1906
Princess Louise of Hessen-Kassel Queen of Denmark 1863-1898
HE HAD WATCHED PAINFULLY AS THE REIGNS OF MANY OTHERS HE HAD TIES TO COLLAPSED IN THE AFTERMATH OF WORLD WAR I.
George I Prince of Denmark King of Greece 1863-1913
Frederik VIII King of Denmark 1906-1912
Lovisa Princess of Sweden and Norway Queen of Denmark 1906-1912
Dagmar Princess of Denmark Empress of Russia 1881-1894
Alexandr III Emperor of Russia 1881-1894
Alexandra Princess of Denmark Queen of Great Britain 1901-1910
Edvard VII King of Great Britain 1901-1910
Haakon VII King of Norway 1905-1957
Christian X King of Denmark 1912-1947
Alexandrine Princess of Mecklenburg-Schwerin Queen of Denmark 1912-1947
HE HAD SUCCEEDED IN KEEPING DENMARK OUT OF THAT WAR.
George V King of Great Britain and Ireland 1910-1936

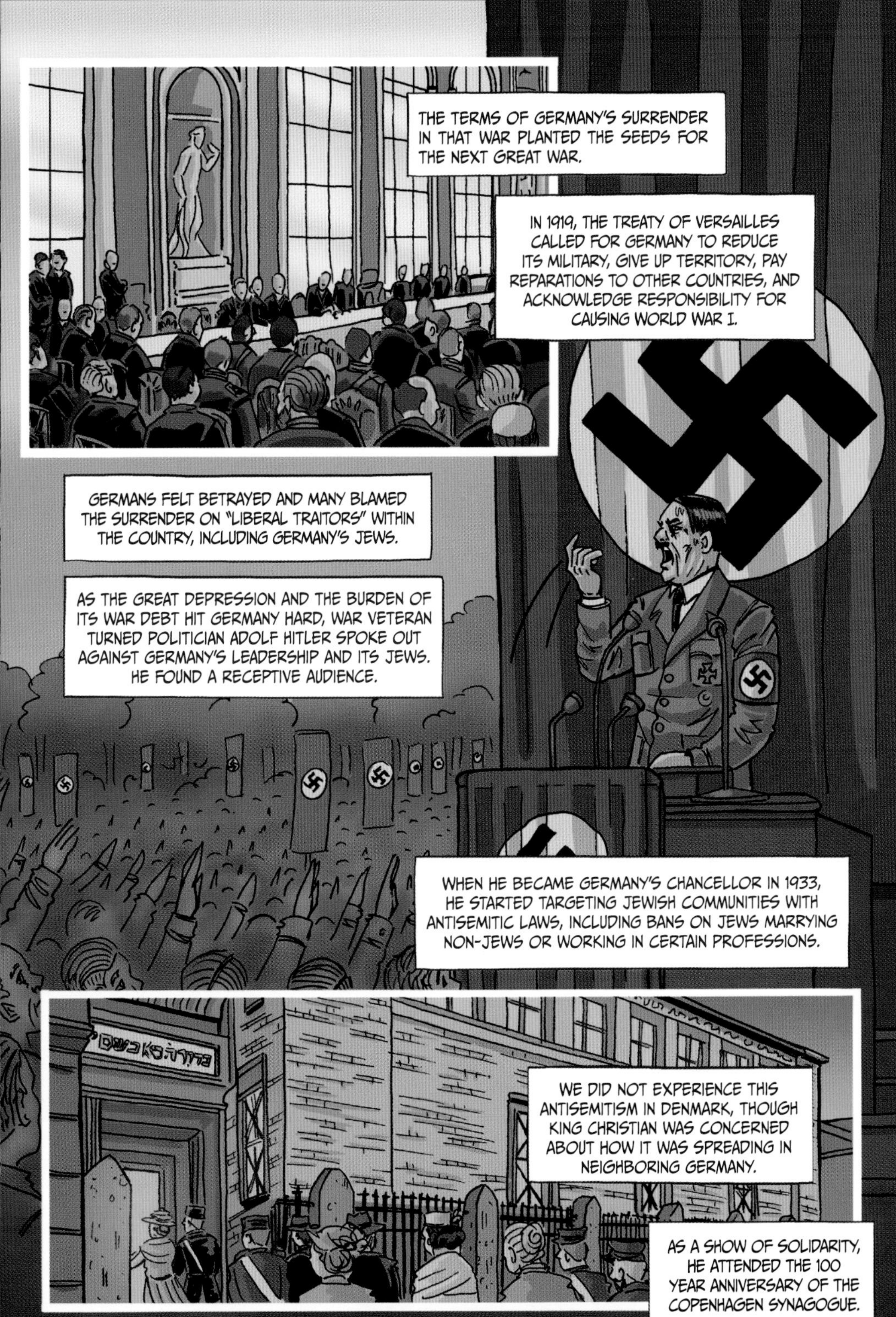
THE TERMS OF GERMANY'S SURRENDER IN THAT WAR PLANTED THE SEEDS FOR THE NEXT GREAT WAR.
IN 1919, THE TREATY OF VERSAILLES CALLED FOR GERMANY TO REDUCE ITS MILITARY, GIVE UP TERRITORY, PAY REPARATIONS TO OTHER COUNTRIES, AND ACKNOWLEDGE RESPONSIBILITY FOR CAUSING WORLD WAR I.
GERMANS FELT BETRAYED AND MANY BLAMED THE SURRENDER ON "LIBERAL TRAITORS" WITHIN THE COUNTRY, INCLUDING GERMANY'S JEWS.
AS THE GREAT DEPRESSION AND THE BURDEN OF ITS WAR DEBT HIT GERMANY HARD, WAR VETERAN TURNED POLITICIAN ADOLF HITLER SPOKE OUT AGAINST GERMANY'S LEADERSHIP AND ITS JEWS. HE FOUND A RECEPTIVE AUDIENCE.
WHEN HE BECAME GERMANY'S CHANCELLOR IN 1933, HE STARTED TARGETING JEWISH COMMUNITIES WITH ANTISEMITIC LAWS, INCLUDING BANS ON JEWS MARRYING NON-JEWS OR WORKING IN CERTAIN PROFESSIONS.
WE DID NOT EXPERIENCE THIS ANTISEMITISM IN DENMARK, THOUGH KING CHRISTIAN WAS CONCERNED ABOUT HOW IT WAS SPREADING IN NEIGHBORING GERMANY.
AS A SHOW OF SOLIDARITY, HE ATTENDED THE 100 YEAR ANNIVERSARY OF THE COPENHAGEN SYNAGOGUE.

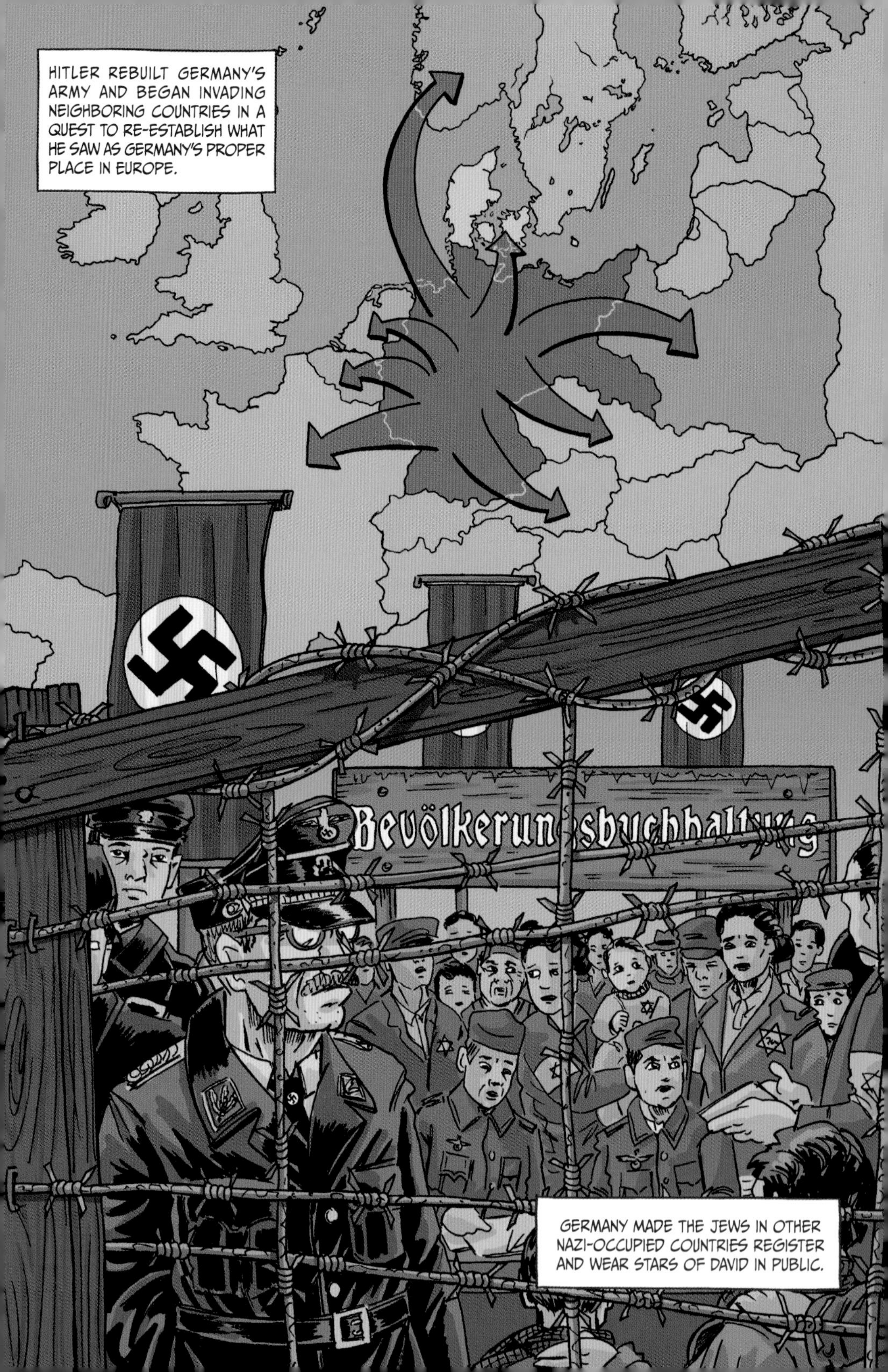
HITLER REBUILT GERMANY'S ARMY AND BEGAN INVADING NEIGHBORING COUNTRIES IN A QUEST TO RE-ESTABLISH WHAT HE SAW AS GERMANY'S PROPER PLACE IN EUROPE.
GERMANY MADE THE JEWS IN OTHER NAZI-OCCUPIED COUNTRIES REGISTER AND WEAR STARS OF DAVID IN PUBLIC.

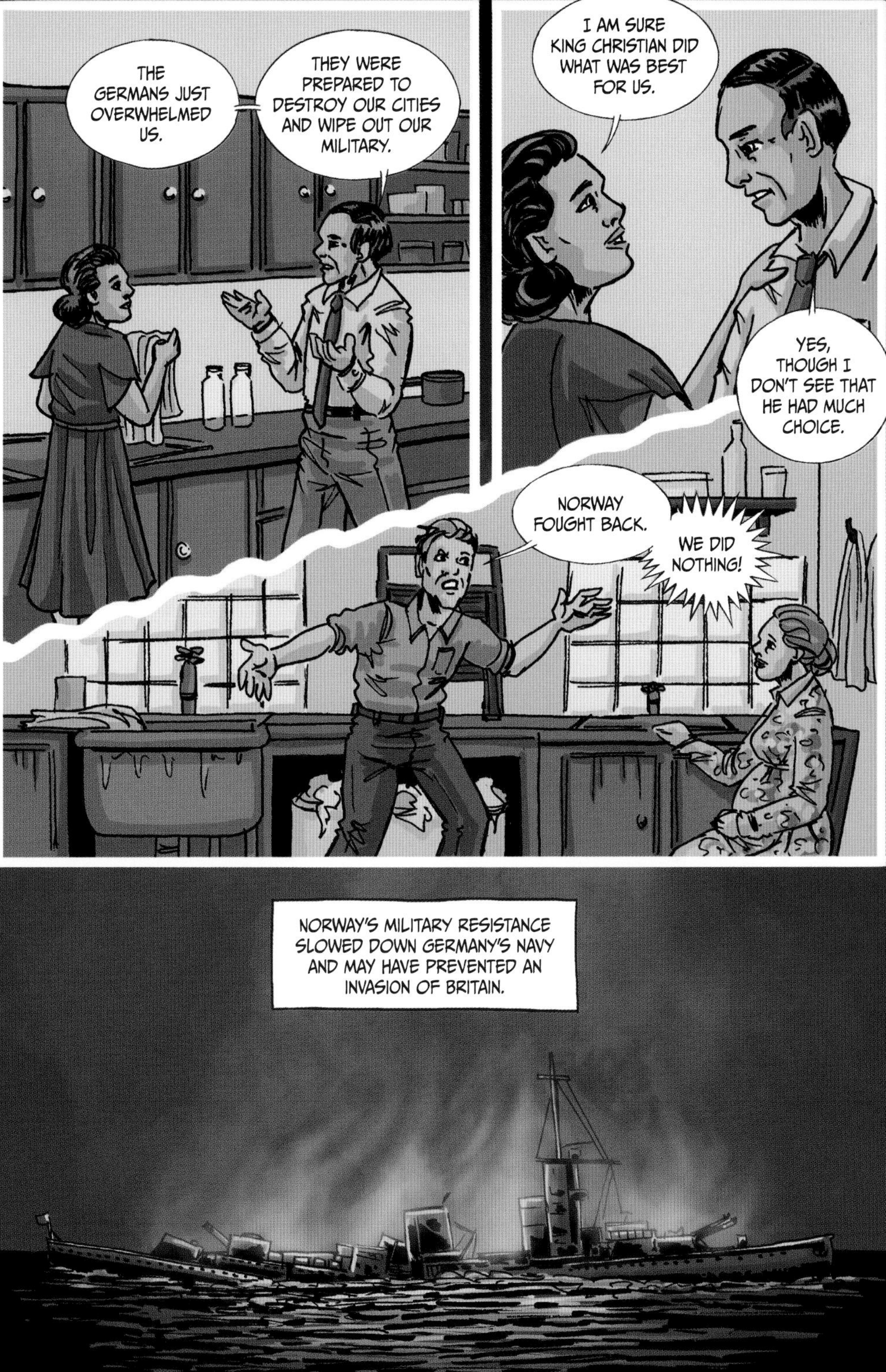
THE GERMANS JUST OVERWHELMED US.
THEY WERE PREPARED TO DESTROY OUR CITIES AND WIPE OUT OUR MILITARY.
I AM SURE KING CHRISTIAN DID WHAT WAS BEST FOR US.
YES, THOUGH I DON'T SEE THAT HE HAD MUCH CHOICE.
NORWAY FOUGHT BACK.
WE DID NOTHING!
NORWAY'S MILITARY RESISTANCE SLOWED DOWN GERMANY'S NAVY AND MAY HAVE PREVENTED AN INVASION OF BRITAIN.

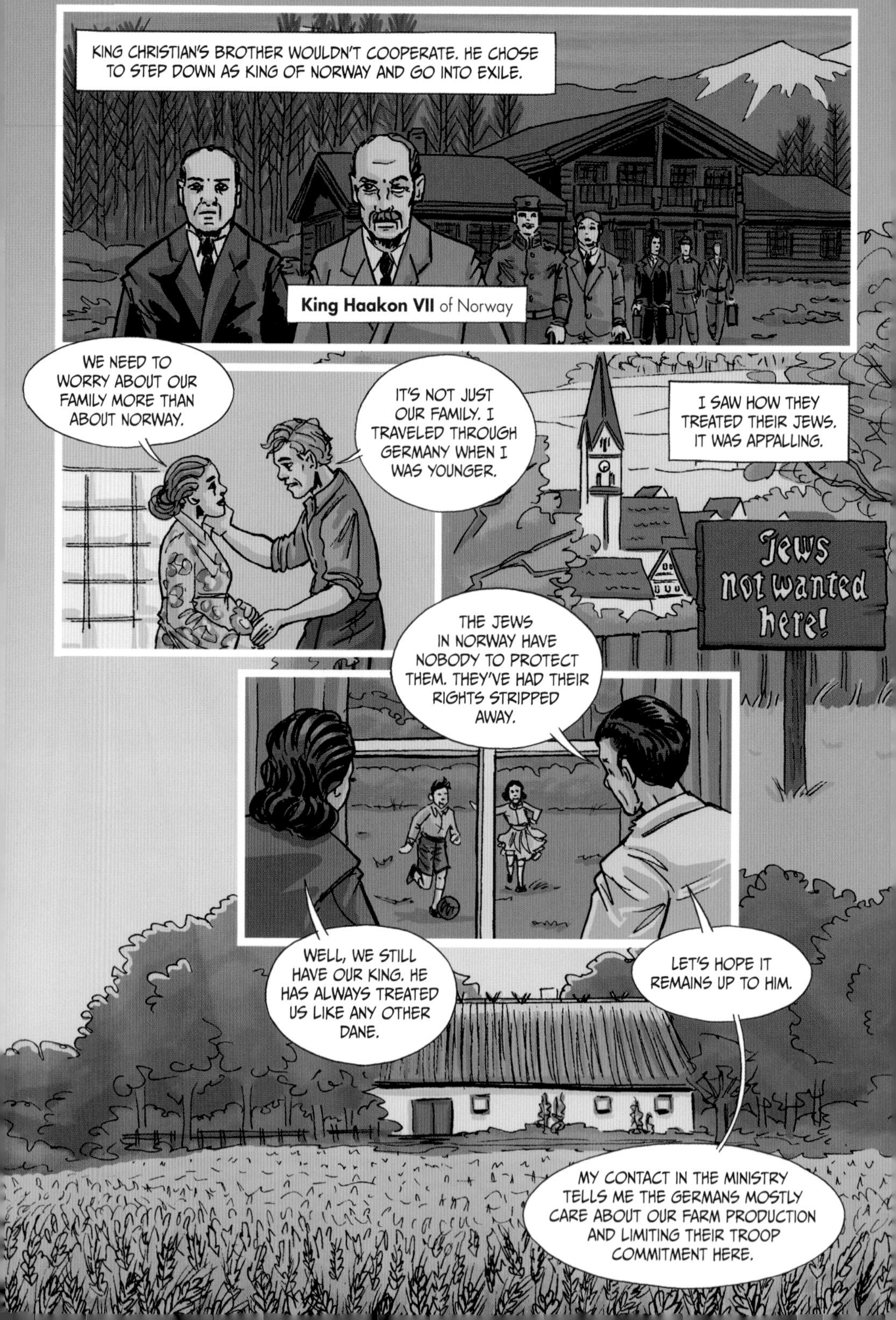

KING CHRISTIAN'S BROTHER WOULDN'T COOPERATE. HE CHOSE TO STEP DOWN AS KING OF NORWAY AND GO INTO EXILE.
King Haakon VII of Norway
WE NEED TO WORRY ABOUT OUR FAMILY MORE THAN ABOUT NORWAY.
IT'S NOT JUST OUR FAMILY. I TRAVELED THROUGH GERMANY WHEN I WAS YOUNGER.
I SAW HOW THEY TREATED THEIR JEWS. IT WAS APPALLING.
Jews not wanted here!
THE JEWS IN NORWAY HAVE NOBODY TO PROTECT THEM. THEY'VE HAD THEIR RIGHTS STRIPPED AWAY.
WELL, WE STILL HAVE OUR KING. HE HAS ALWAYS TREATED US LIKE ANY OTHER DANE.
LET'S HOPE IT REMAINS UP TO HIM.
MY CONTACT IN THE MINISTRY TELLS ME THE GERMANS MOSTLY CARE ABOUT OUR FARM PRODUCTION AND LIMITING THEIR TROOP COMMITMENT HERE.

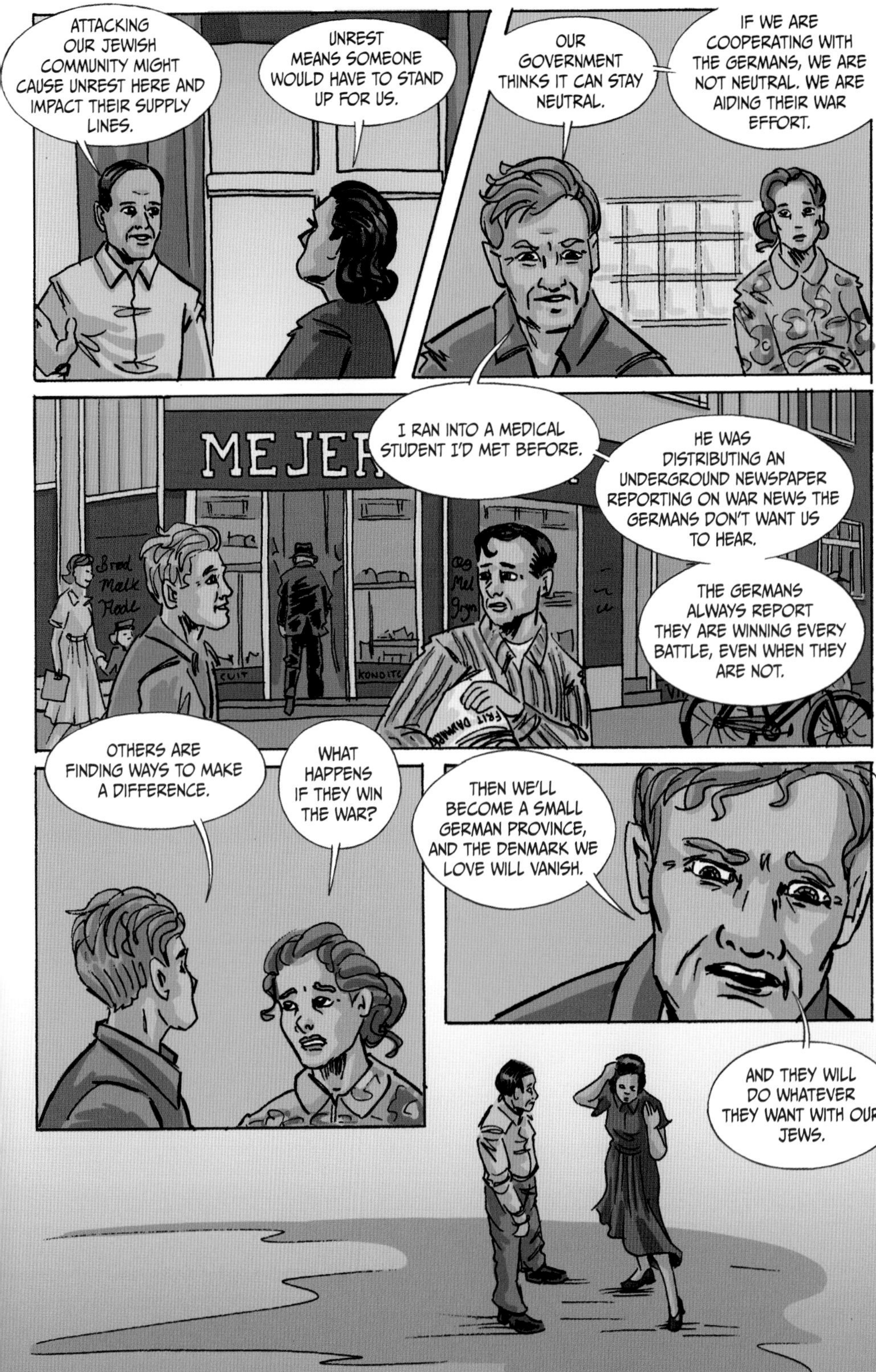
ATTACKING OUR JEWISH COMMUNITY MIGHT CAUSE UNREST HERE AND IMPACT THEIR SUPPLY LINES.
UNREST MEANS SOMEONE WOULD HAVE TO STAND UP FOR US.
OUR GOVERNMENT THINKS IT CAN STAY NEUTRAL.
IF WE ARE COOPERATING WITH THE GERMANS, WE ARE NOT NEUTRAL. WE ARE AIDING THEIR WAR EFFORT.
MEJER
I RAN INTO A MEDICAL STUDENT I'D MET BEFORE.
HE WAS DISTRIBUTING AN UNDERGROUND NEWSPAPER REPORTING ON WAR NEWS THE GERMANS DON'T WANT US TO HEAR.
THE GERMANS ALWAYS REPORT THEY ARE WINNING EVERY BATTLE, EVEN WHEN THEY ARE NOT.
OTHERS ARE FINDING WAYS TO MAKE A DIFFERENCE.
WHAT HAPPENS IF THEY WIN THE WAR?
THEN WE'LL BECOME A SMALL GERMAN PROVINCE, AND THE DENMARK WE LOVE WILL VANISH.
AND THEY WILL DO WHATEVER THEY WANT WITH OUR JEWS.

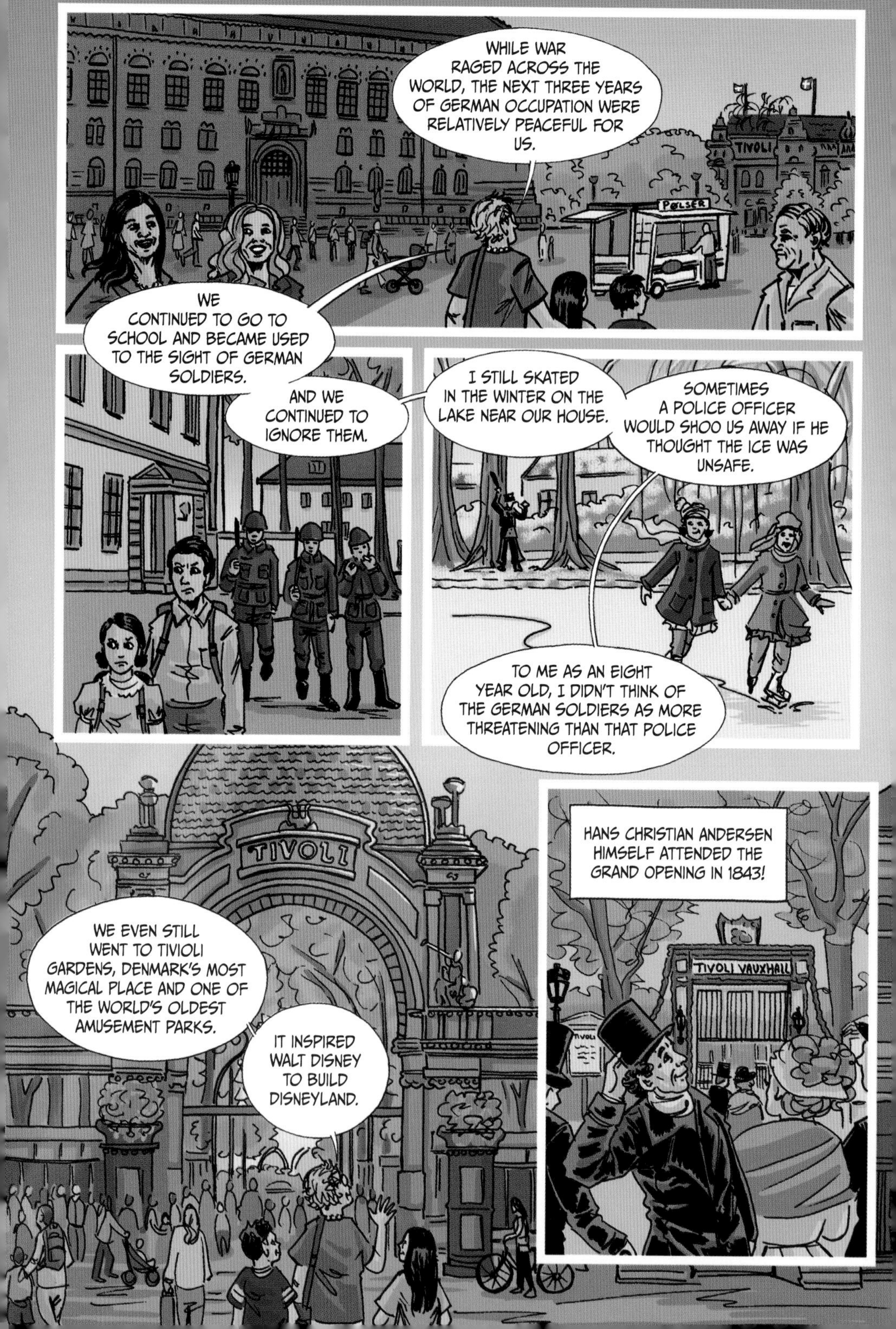
WHILE WAR RAGED ACROSS THE WORLD, THE NEXT THREE YEARS OF GERMAN OCCUPATION WERE RELATIVELY PEACEFUL FOR US.
TIVOLI
PØLSER
WE CONTINUED TO GO TO SCHOOL AND BECAME USED TO THE SIGHT OF GERMAN SOLDIERS.
AND WE CONTINUED TO IGNORE THEM.
I STILL SKATED IN THE WINTER ON THE LAKE NEAR OUR HOUSE.
SOMETIMES A POLICE OFFICER WOULD SHOO US AWAY IF HE THOUGHT THE ICE WAS UNSAFE.
TO ME AS AN EIGHT YEAR OLD, I DIDN'T THINK OF THE GERMAN SOLDIERS AS MORE THREATENING THAN THAT POLICE OFFICER.
TIVOLI
WE EVEN STILL WENT TO TIVIOLI GARDENS, DENMARK'S MOST MAGICAL PLACE AND ONE OF THE WORLD'S OLDEST AMUSEMENT PARKS.
IT INSPIRED WALT DISNEY TO BUILD DISNEYLAND.
HANS CHRISTIAN ANDERSEN HIMSELF ATTENDED THE GRAND OPENING IN 1843!
TIVOLI VAUXHALL
TIVOLI

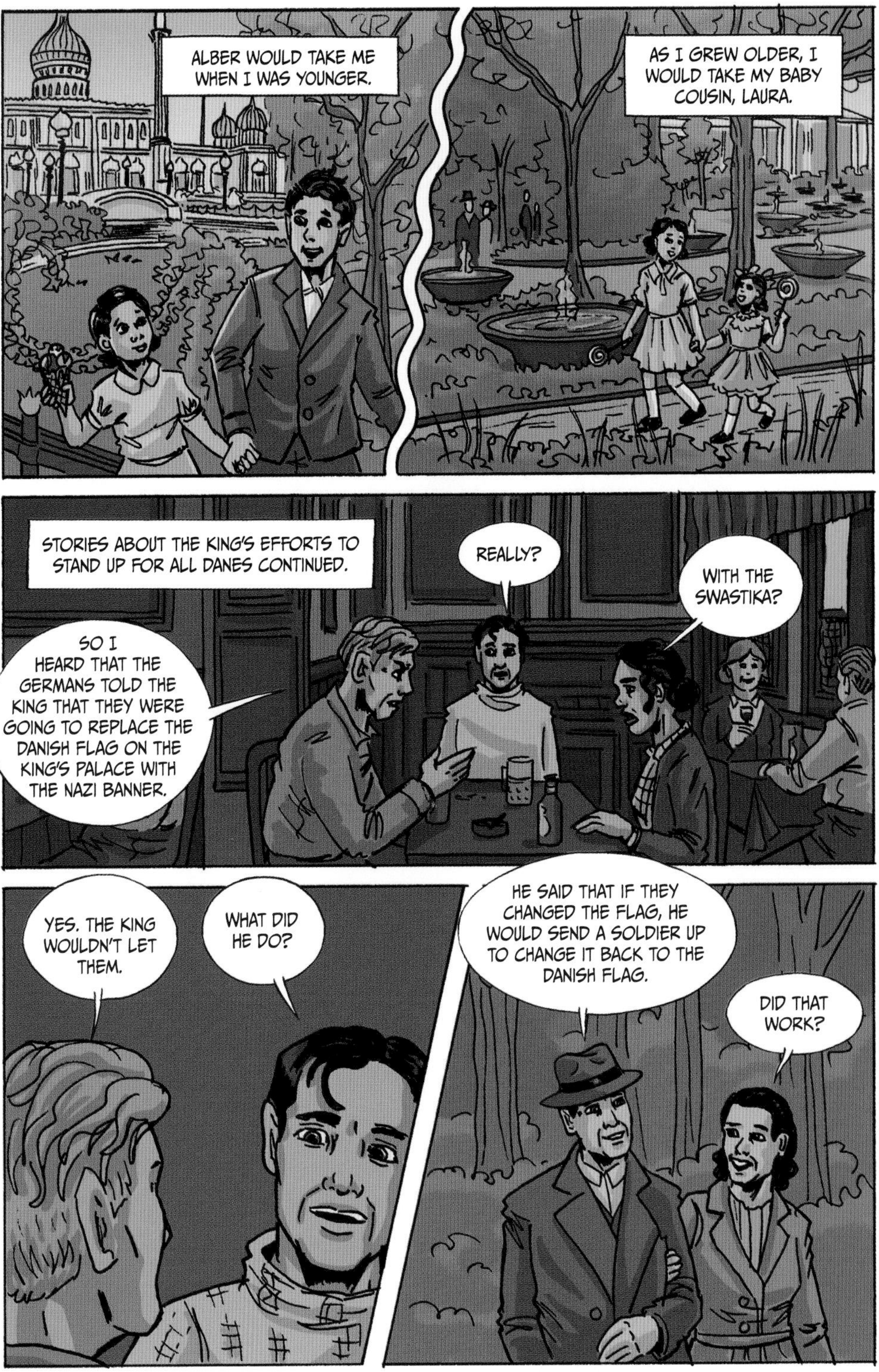
ALBER WOULD TAKE ME WHEN I WAS YOUNGER.
AS I GREW OLDER, I WOULD TAKE MY BABY COUSIN, LAURA.
STORIES ABOUT THE KING'S EFFORTS TO STAND UP FOR ALL DANES CONTINUED.
SO I HEARD THAT THE GERMANS TOLD THE KING THAT THEY WERE GOING TO REPLACE THE DANISH FLAG ON THE KING'S PALACE WITH THE NAZI BANNER.
REALLY?
WITH THE SWASTIKA?
YES. THE KING WOULDN'T LET THEM.
WHAT DID HE DO?
HE SAID THAT IF THEY CHANGED THE FLAG, HE WOULD SEND A SOLDIER UP TO CHANGE IT BACK TO THE DANISH FLAG.
DID THAT WORK?

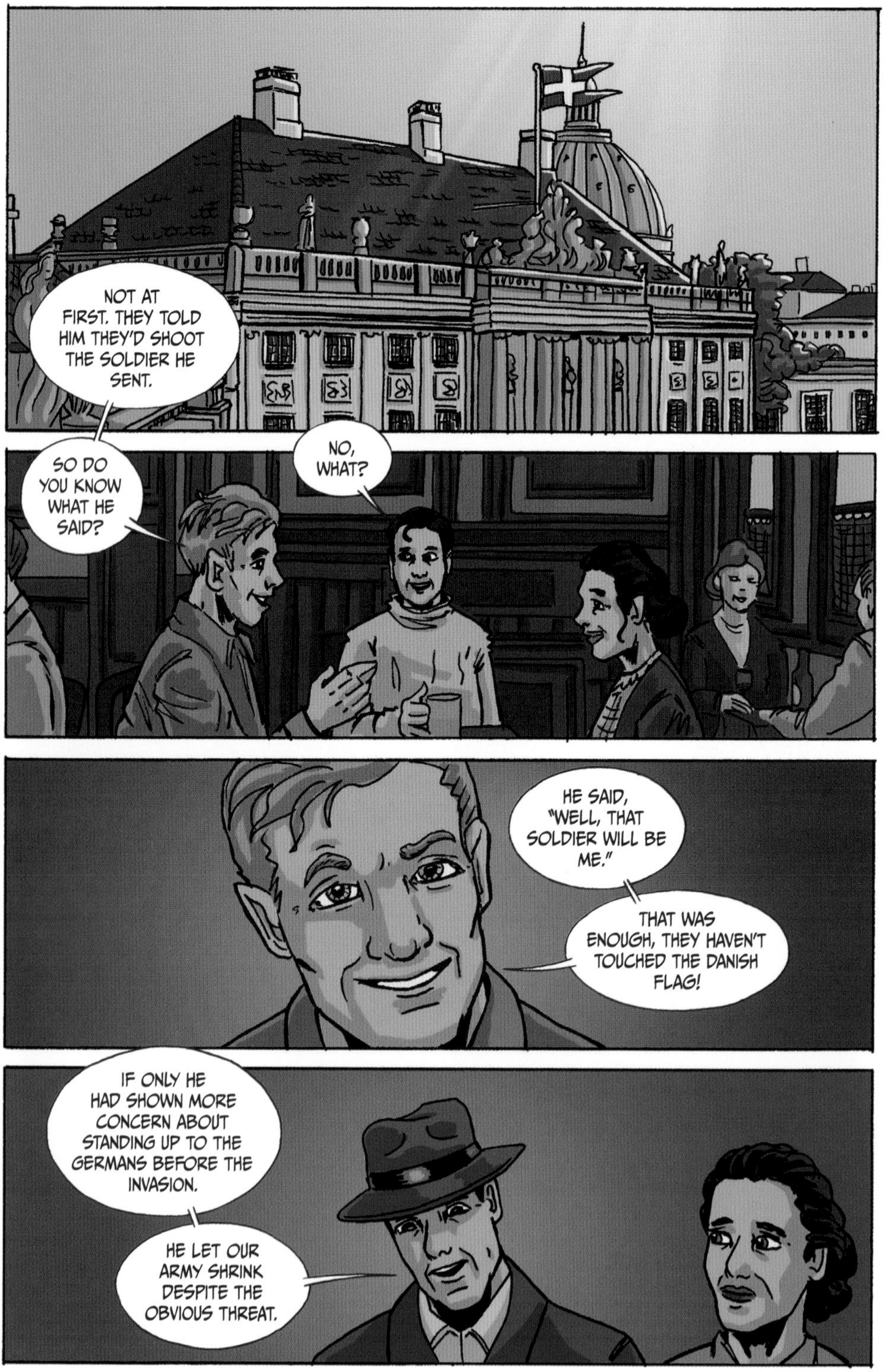
NOT AT FIRST. THEY TOLD HIM THEY'D SHOOT THE SOLDIER HE SENT.
SO DO YOU KNOW WHAT HE SAID?
NO, WHAT?
HE SAID, "WELL, THAT SOLDIER WILL BE ME."
THAT WAS ENOUGH, THEY HAVEN'T TOUCHED THE DANISH FLAG!
IF ONLY HE HAD SHOWN MORE CONCERN ABOUT STANDING UP TO THE GERMANS BEFORE THE INVASION.
HE LET OUR ARMY SHRINK DESPITE THE OBVIOUS THREAT.

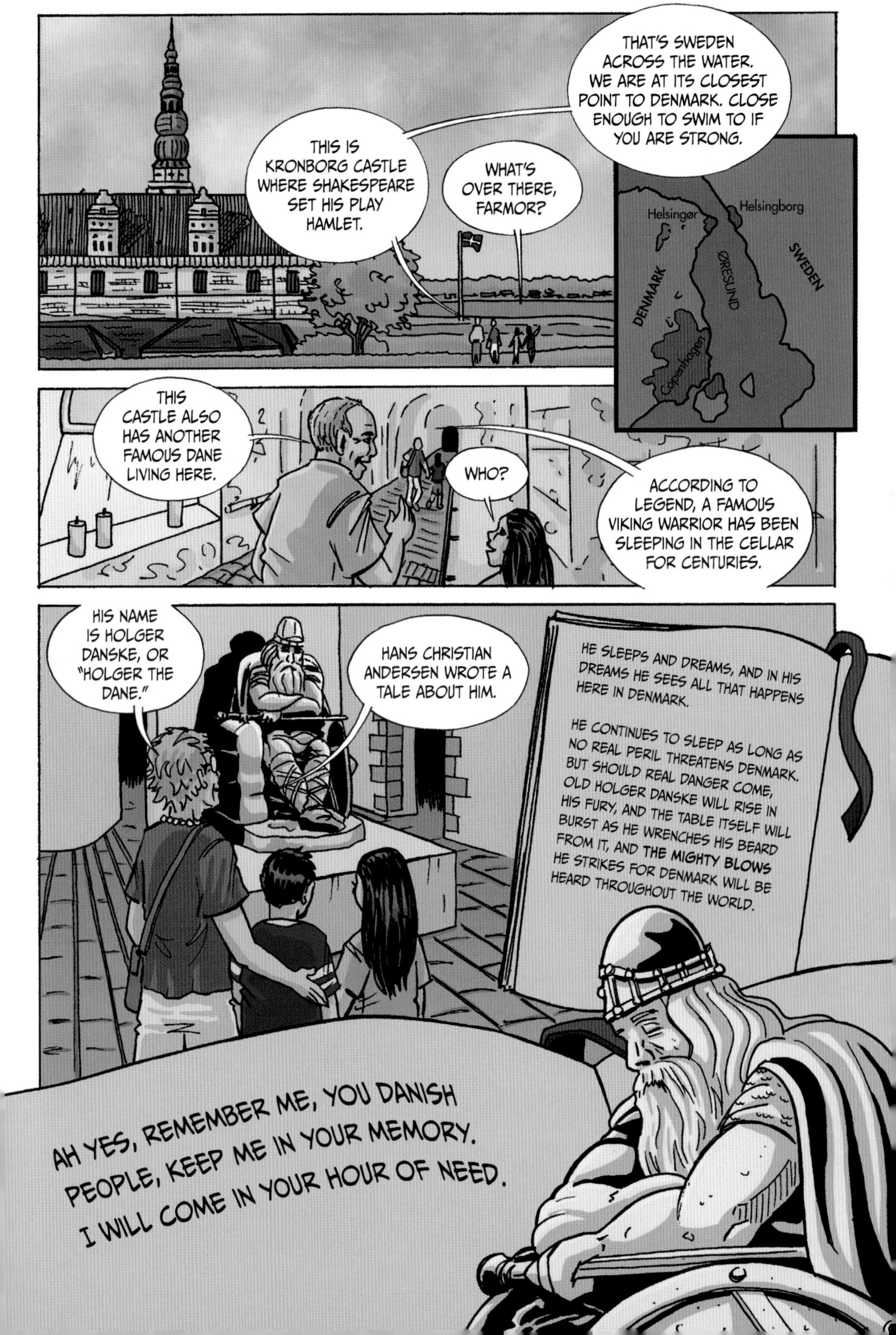
THIS IS KRONBORG CASTLE WHERE SHAKESPEARE SET HIS PLAY HAMLET.
WHAT'S OVER THERE, FARMOR?
THAT'S SWEDEN ACROSS THE WATER. WE ARE AT ITS CLOSEST POINT TO DENMARK. CLOSE ENOUGH TO SWIM TO IF YOU ARE STRONG.
Helsingør
Helsingborg
SWEDEN
ØRESUND
DENMARK
Copenhagen
THIS CASTLE ALSO HAS ANOTHER FAMOUS DANE LIVING HERE.
WHO?
ACCORDING TO LEGEND, A FAMOUS VIKING WARRIOR HAS BEEN SLEEPING IN THE CELLAR FOR CENTURIES.
HIS NAME IS HOLGER DANSKE, OR "HOLGER THE DANE."
HANS CHRISTIAN ANDERSEN WROTE A TALE ABOUT HIM.
HE SLEEPS AND DREAMS, AND IN HIS DREAMS HE SEES ALL THAT HAPPENS HERE IN DENMARK.
HE CONTINUES TO SLEEP AS LONG AS NO REAL PERIL THREATENS DENMARK. BUT SHOULD REAL DANGER COME, OLD HOLGER DANSKE WILL RISE IN HIS FURY, AND THE TABLE ITSELF WILL BURST AS HE WRENCHES HIS BEARD FROM IT, AND THE MIGHTY BLOWS HE STRIKES FOR DENMARK WILL BE HEARD THROUGHOUT THE WORLD.
AH YES, REMEMBER ME, YOU DANISH PEOPLE, KEEP ME IN YOUR MEMORY. I WILL COME IN YOUR HOUR OF NEED.

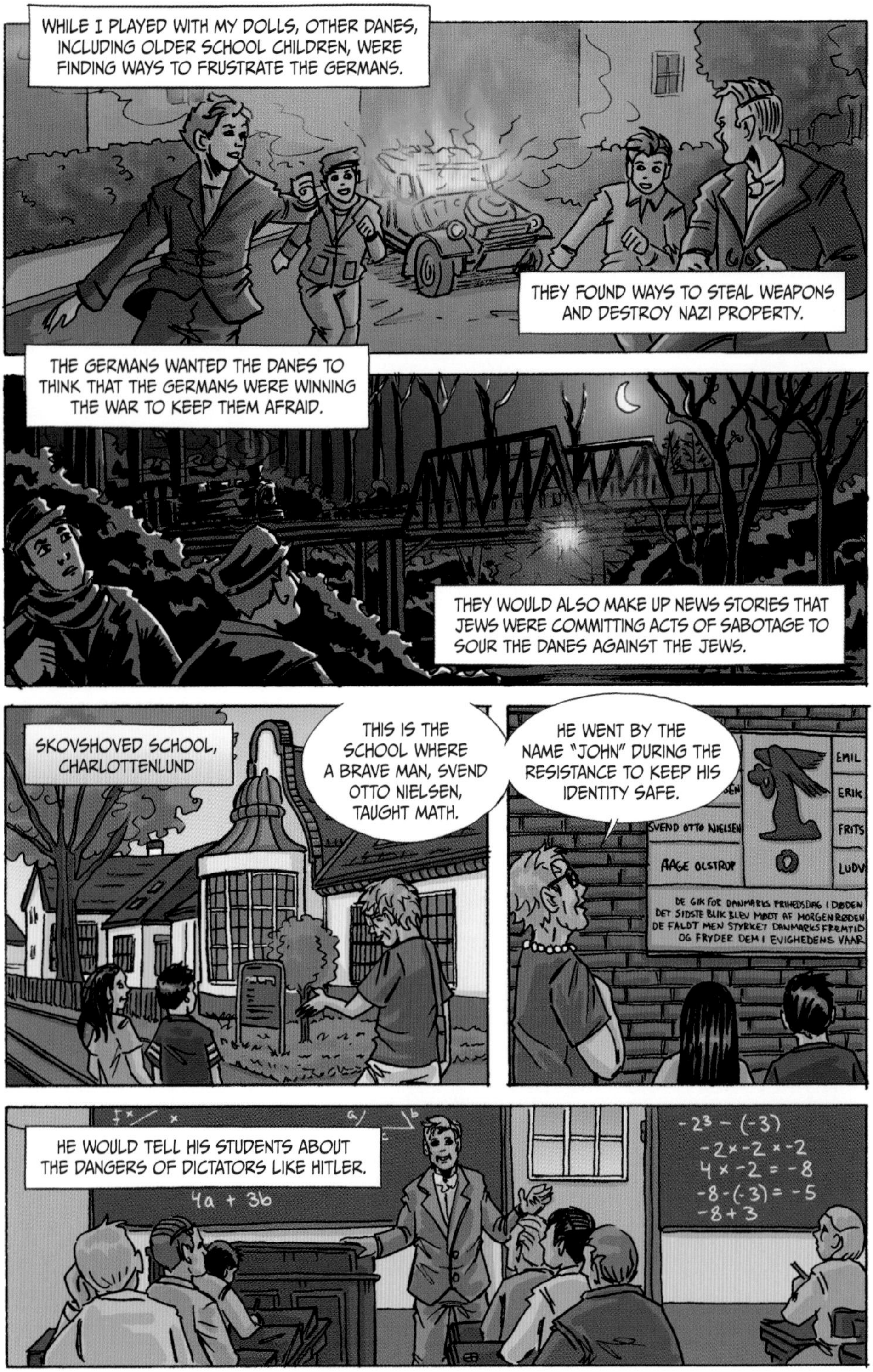
WHILE I PLAYED WITH MY DOLLS, OTHER DANES, INCLUDING OLDER SCHOOL CHILDREN, WERE FINDING WAYS TO FRUSTRATE THE GERMANS.
THEY FOUND WAYS TO STEAL WEAPONS AND DESTROY NAZI PROPERTY.
THE GERMANS WANTED THE DANES TO THINK THAT THE GERMANS WERE WINNING THE WAR TO KEEP THEM AFRAID.
THEY WOULD ALSO MAKE UP NEWS STORIES THAT JEWS WERE COMMITTING ACTS OF SABOTAGE TO SOUR THE DANES AGAINST THE JEWS.
SKOVSHOVED SCHOOL, CHARLOTTENLUND
THIS IS THE SCHOOL WHERE A BRAVE MAN, SVEND OTTO NIELSEN, TAUGHT MATH.
HE WENT BY THE NAME "JOHN" DURING THE RESISTANCE TO KEEP HIS IDENTITY SAFE.
SVEND OTTO NIELSEN
AAGE OLSTRUP
EMIL
ERIK
FRITS
DE GIK FOR DANMARKS FRIHEDSDAG I DØDEN
DET SIDSTE BLIK BLEV MØDT AF MORGENRØDEN
DE FALDT MEN STYRKET DANMARKS FREMTID
OG FRYDER DEM I EVIGHEDENS VAAR
HE WOULD TELL HIS STUDENTS ABOUT THE DANGERS OF DICTATORS LIKE HITLER.
4a + 3b
-2³ - (-3)
-2×-2×-2
4×-2 = -8
-8-(-3) = -5
-8+3

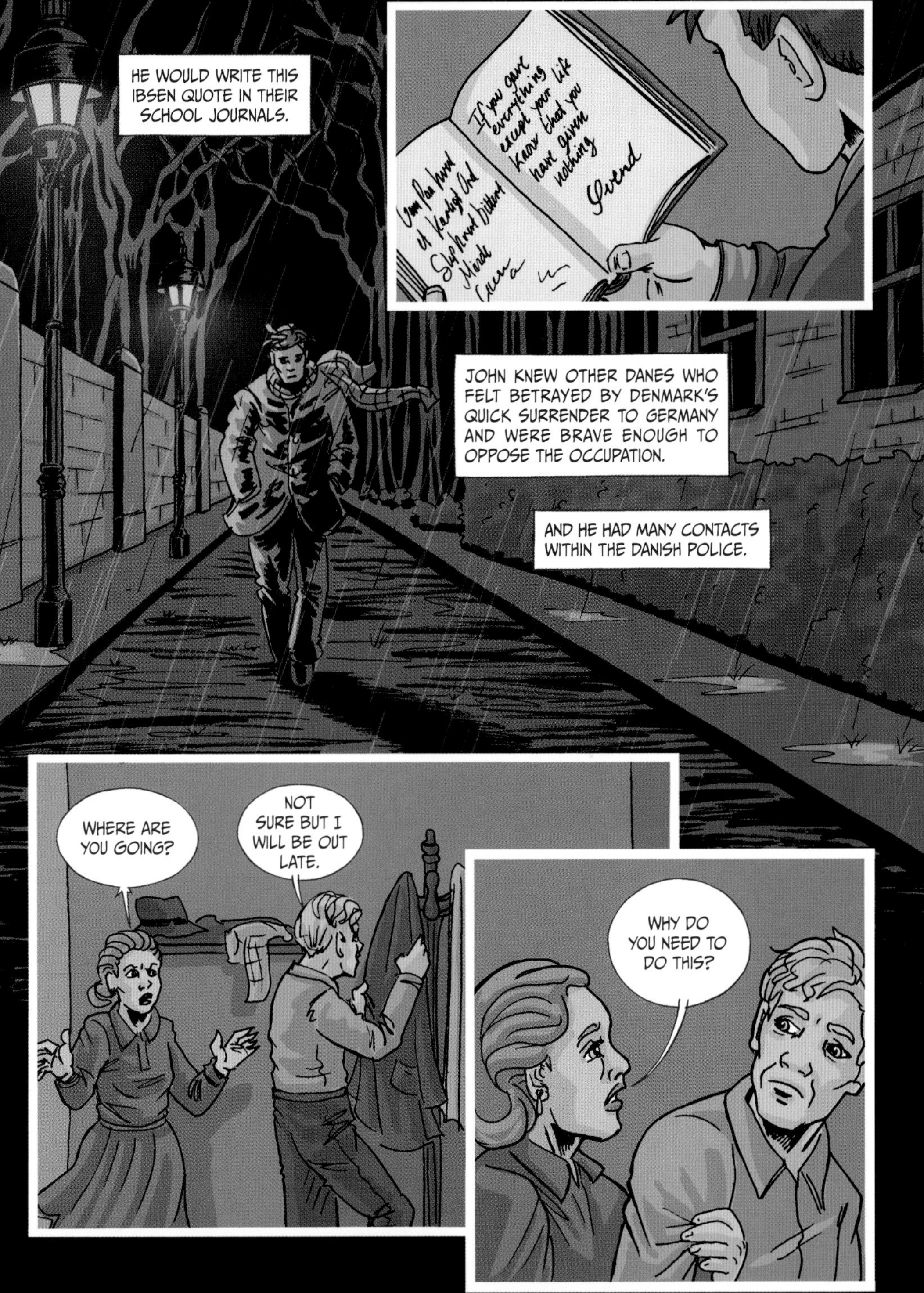
HE WOULD WRITE THIS IBSEN QUOTE IN THEIR SCHOOL JOURNALS.
If you gave everything except your life know that you have given nothing
Svend
JOHN KNEW OTHER DANES WHO FELT BETRAYED BY DENMARK'S QUICK SURRENDER TO GERMANY AND WERE BRAVE ENOUGH TO OPPOSE THE OCCUPATION.
AND HE HAD MANY CONTACTS WITHIN THE DANISH POLICE.
WHERE ARE YOU GOING?
NOT SURE BUT I WILL BE OUT LATE.
WHY DO YOU NEED TO DO THIS?

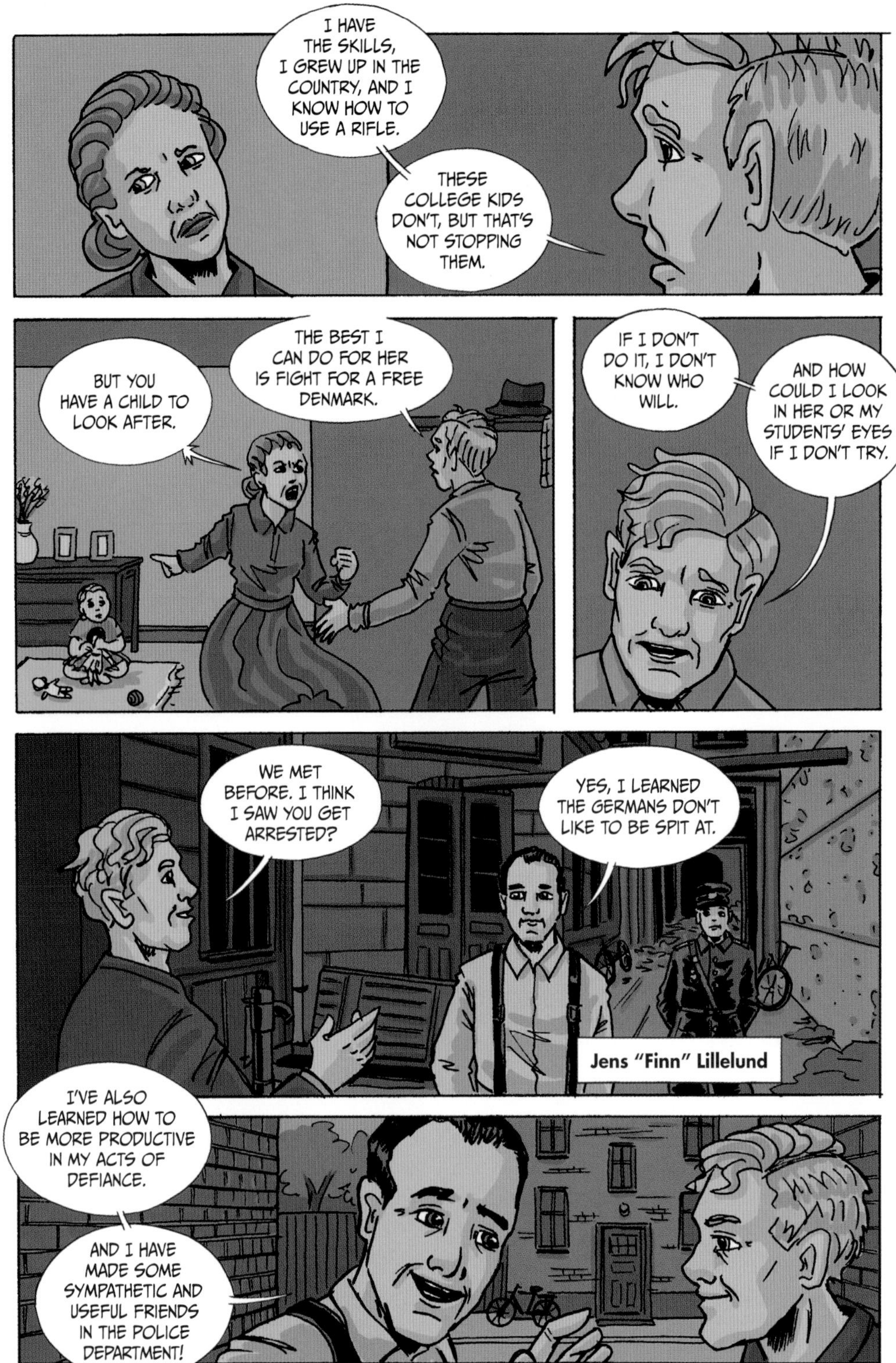
I HAVE THE SKILLS, I GREW UP IN THE COUNTRY, AND I KNOW HOW TO USE A RIFLE.
THESE COLLEGE KIDS DON'T, BUT THAT'S NOT STOPPING THEM.
BUT YOU HAVE A CHILD TO LOOK AFTER.
THE BEST I CAN DO FOR HER IS FIGHT FOR A FREE DENMARK.
IF I DON'T DO IT, I DON'T KNOW WHO WILL.
AND HOW COULD I LOOK IN HER OR MY STUDENTS' EYES IF I DON'T TRY.
WE MET BEFORE. I THINK I SAW YOU GET ARRESTED?
YES, I LEARNED THE GERMANS DON'T LIKE TO BE SPIT AT.
Jens "Finn" Lillelund
I'VE ALSO LEARNED HOW TO BE MORE PRODUCTIVE IN MY ACTS OF DEFIANCE.
AND I HAVE MADE SOME SYMPATHETIC AND USEFUL FRIENDS IN THE POLICE DEPARTMENT!

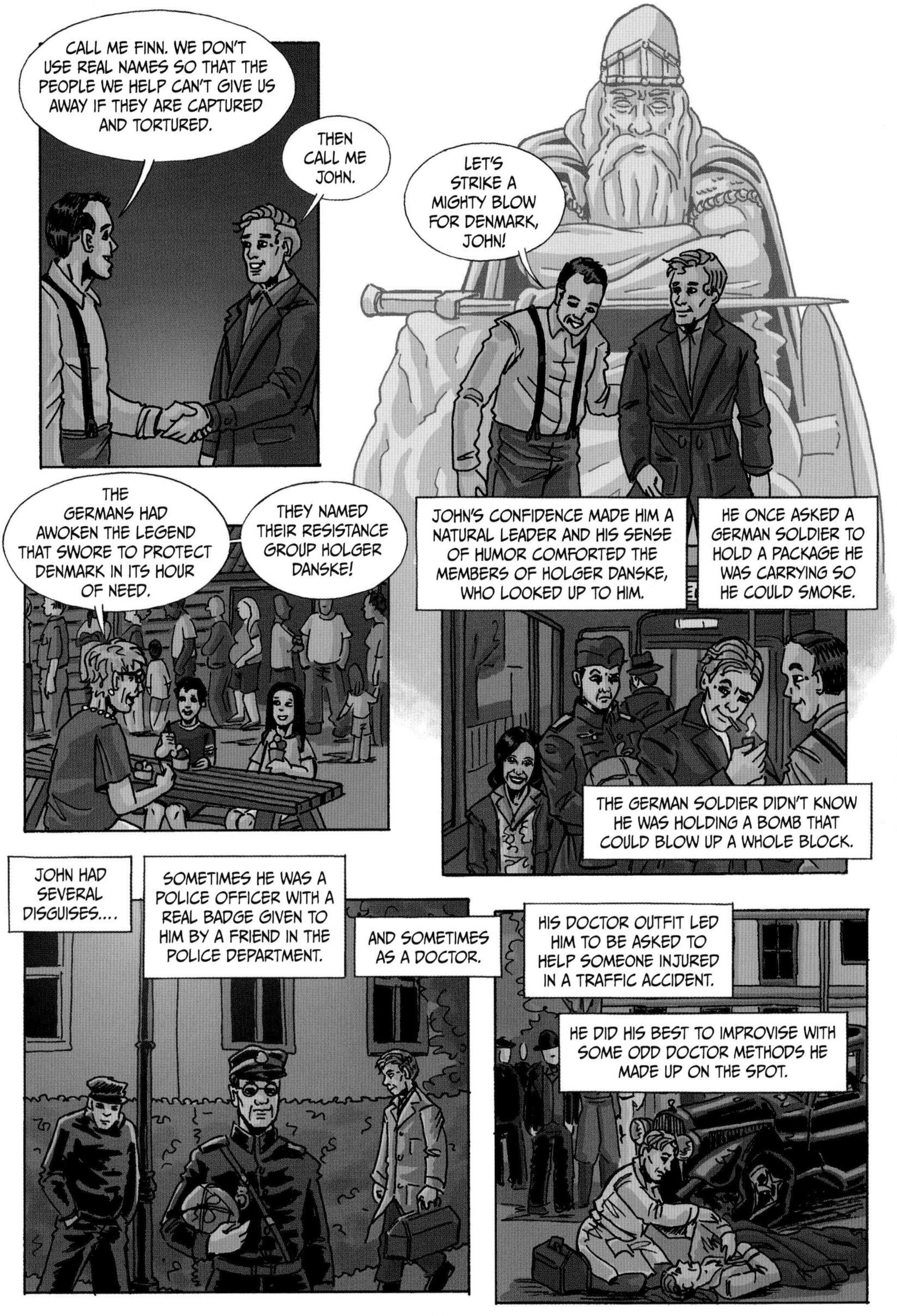
CALL ME FINN. WE DON'T USE REAL NAMES SO THAT THE PEOPLE WE HELP CAN'T GIVE US AWAY IF THEY ARE CAPTURED AND TORTURED.
THEN CALL ME JOHN.
LET'S STRIKE A MIGHTY BLOW FOR DENMARK, JOHN!
THE GERMANS HAD AWOKEN THE LEGEND THAT SWORE TO PROTECT DENMARK IN ITS HOUR OF NEED.
THEY NAMED THEIR RESISTANCE GROUP HOLGER DANSKE!
JOHN'S CONFIDENCE MADE HIM A NATURAL LEADER AND HIS SENSE OF HUMOR COMFORTED THE MEMBERS OF HOLGER DANSKE, WHO LOOKED UP TO HIM.
HE ONCE ASKED A GERMAN SOLDIER TO HOLD A PACKAGE HE WAS CARRYING SO HE COULD SMOKE.
THE GERMAN SOLDIER DIDN'T KNOW HE WAS HOLDING A BOMB THAT COULD BLOW UP A WHOLE BLOCK.
JOHN HAD SEVERAL DISGUISES....
SOMETIMES HE WAS A POLICE OFFICER WITH A REAL BADGE GIVEN TO HIM BY A FRIEND IN THE POLICE DEPARTMENT.
AND SOMETIMES AS A DOCTOR.
HIS DOCTOR OUTFIT LED HIM TO BE ASKED TO HELP SOMEONE INJURED IN A TRAFFIC ACCIDENT.
HE DID HIS BEST TO IMPROVISE WITH SOME ODD DOCTOR METHODS HE MADE UP ON THE SPOT.

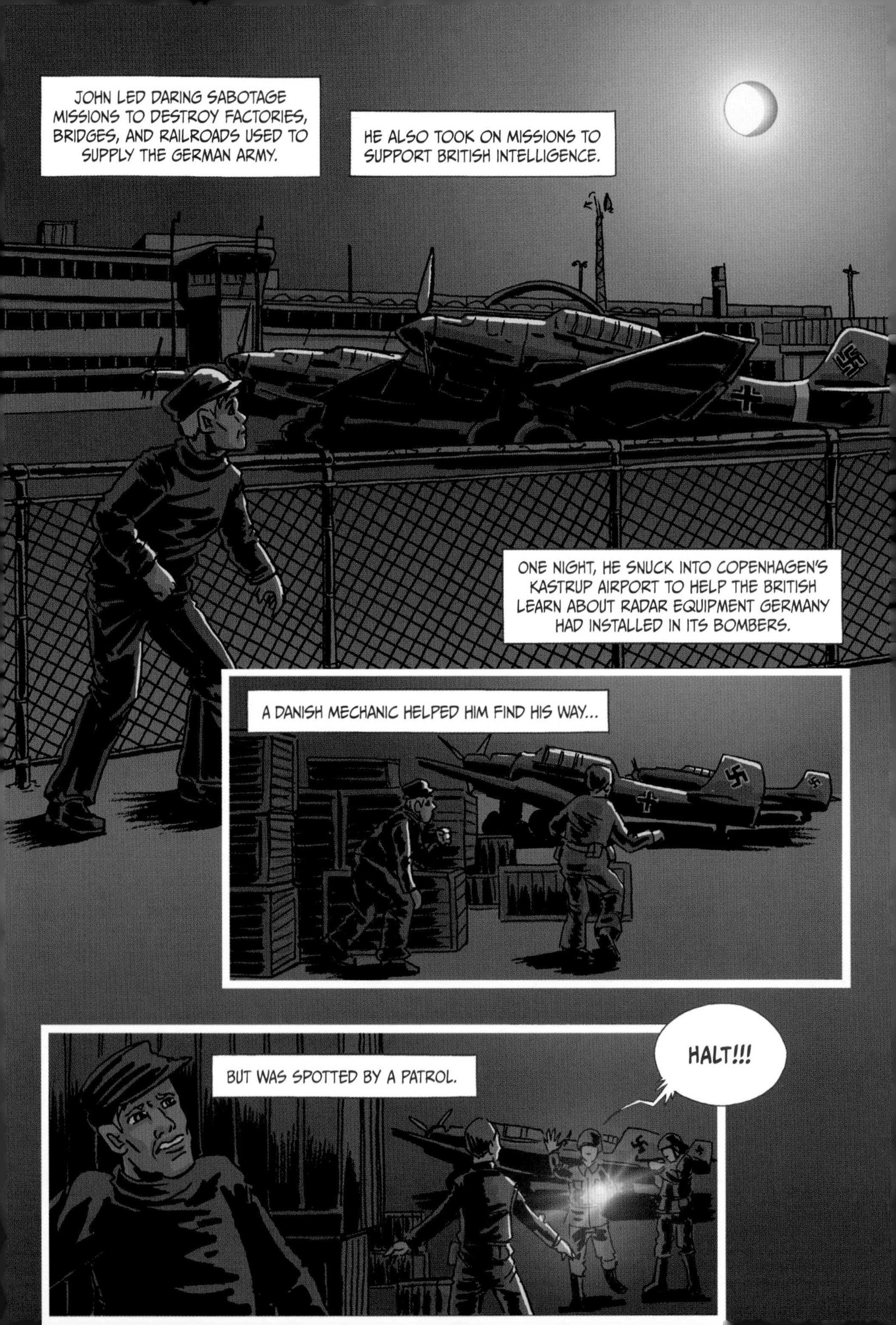
JOHN LED DARING SABOTAGE MISSIONS TO DESTROY FACTORIES, BRIDGES, AND RAILROADS USED TO SUPPLY THE GERMAN ARMY.
HE ALSO TOOK ON MISSIONS TO SUPPORT BRITISH INTELLIGENCE.
ONE NIGHT, HE SNUCK INTO COPENHAGEN'S KASTRUP AIRPORT TO HELP THE BRITISH LEARN ABOUT RADAR EQUIPMENT GERMANY HAD INSTALLED IN ITS BOMBERS.
A DANISH MECHANIC HELPED HIM FIND HIS WAY...
BUT WAS SPOTTED BY A PATROL.
HALT!!!

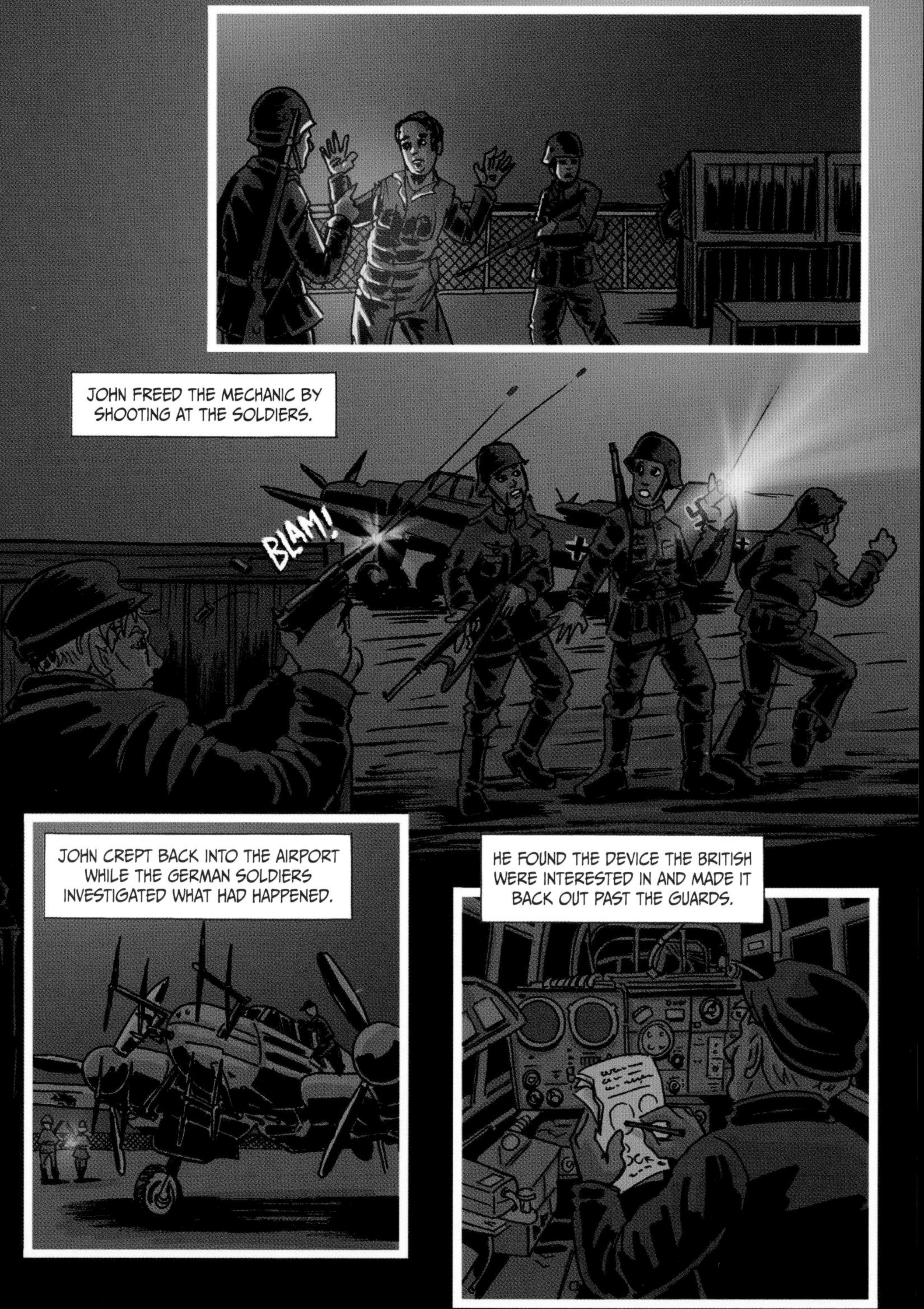

JOHN FREED THE MECHANIC BY SHOOTING AT THE SOLDIERS.
BLAM!
JOHN CREPT BACK INTO THE AIRPORT WHILE THE GERMAN SOLDIERS INVESTIGATED WHAT HAD HAPPENED.
HE FOUND THE DEVICE THE BRITISH WERE INTERESTED IN AND MADE IT BACK OUT PAST THE GUARDS.

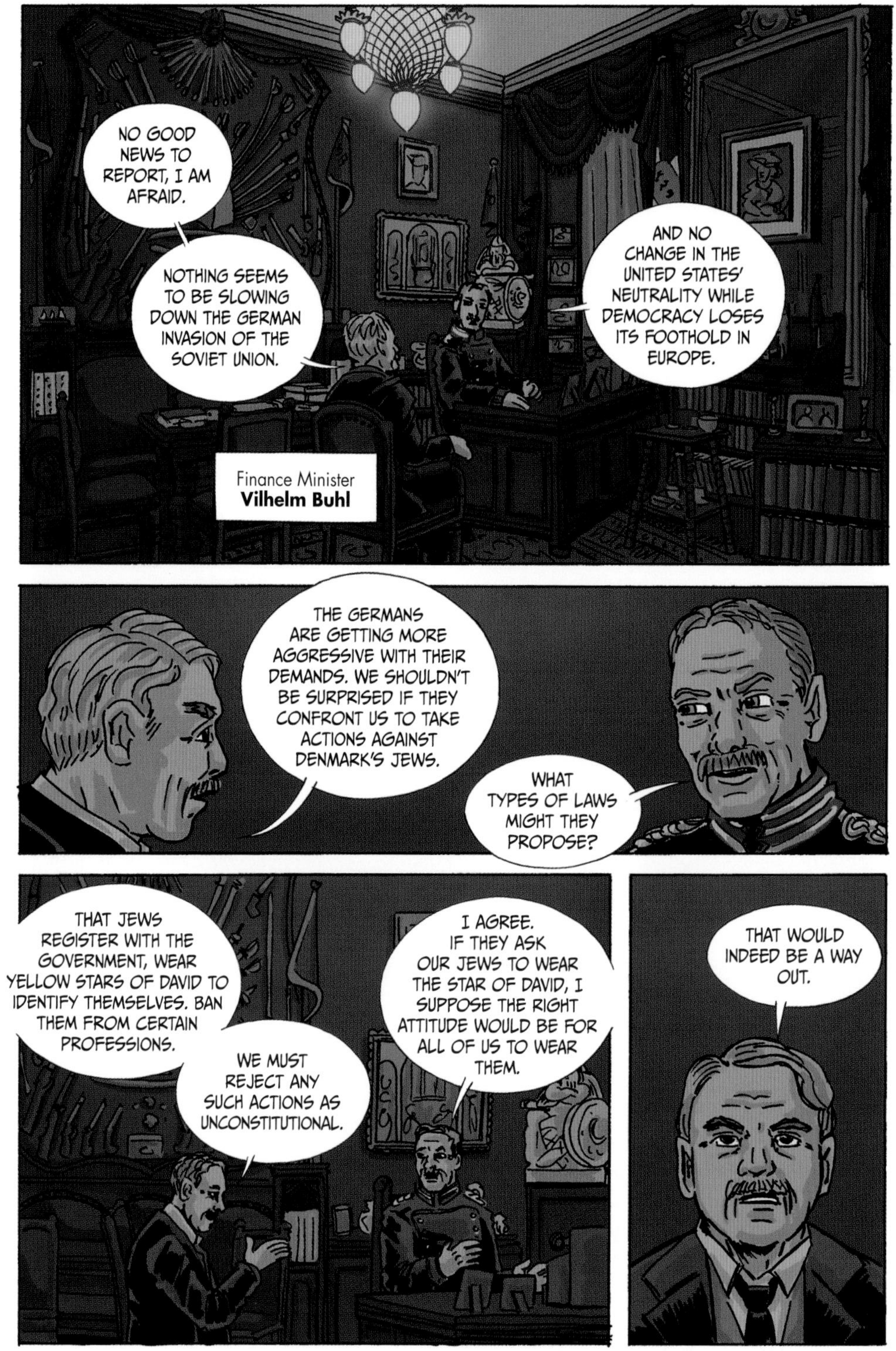
NO GOOD NEWS TO REPORT, I AM AFRAID.
NOTHING SEEMS TO BE SLOWING DOWN THE GERMAN INVASION OF THE SOVIET UNION.
AND NO CHANGE IN THE UNITED STATES' NEUTRALITY WHILE DEMOCRACY LOSES ITS FOOTHOLD IN EUROPE.
Finance Minister **Vilhelm Buhl**
THE GERMANS ARE GETTING MORE AGGRESSIVE WITH THEIR DEMANDS. WE SHOULDN'T BE SURPRISED IF THEY CONFRONT US TO TAKE ACTIONS AGAINST DENMARK'S JEWS.
WHAT TYPES OF LAWS MIGHT THEY PROPOSE?
THAT JEWS REGISTER WITH THE GOVERNMENT, WEAR YELLOW STARS OF DAVID TO IDENTIFY THEMSELVES. BAN THEM FROM CERTAIN PROFESSIONS.
WE MUST REJECT ANY SUCH ACTIONS AS UNCONSTITUTIONAL.
I AGREE. IF THEY ASK OUR JEWS TO WEAR THE STAR OF DAVID, I SUPPOSE THE RIGHT ATTITUDE WOULD BE FOR ALL OF US TO WEAR THEM.
THAT WOULD INDEED BE A WAY OUT.

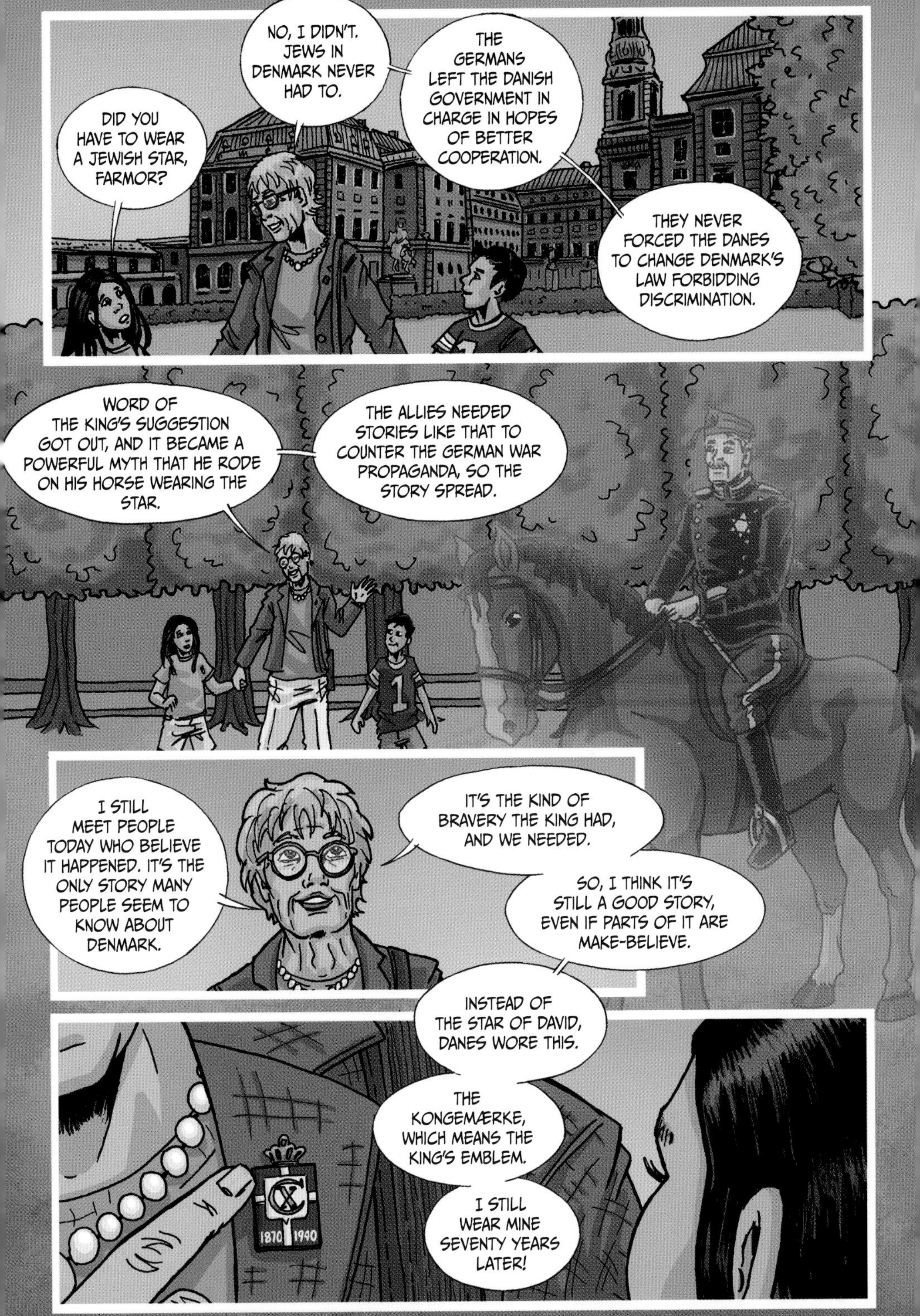
DID YOU HAVE TO WEAR A JEWISH STAR, FARMOR?
NO, I DIDN'T. JEWS IN DENMARK NEVER HAD TO.
THE GERMANS LEFT THE DANISH GOVERNMENT IN CHARGE IN HOPES OF BETTER COOPERATION.
THEY NEVER FORCED THE DANES TO CHANGE DENMARK'S LAW FORBIDDING DISCRIMINATION.
WORD OF THE KING'S SUGGESTION GOT OUT, AND IT BECAME A POWERFUL MYTH THAT HE RODE ON HIS HORSE WEARING THE STAR.
THE ALLIES NEEDED STORIES LIKE THAT TO COUNTER THE GERMAN WAR PROPAGANDA, SO THE STORY SPREAD.
I STILL MEET PEOPLE TODAY WHO BELIEVE IT HAPPENED. IT'S THE ONLY STORY MANY PEOPLE SEEM TO KNOW ABOUT DENMARK.
IT'S THE KIND OF BRAVERY THE KING HAD, AND WE NEEDED.
SO, I THINK IT'S STILL A GOOD STORY, EVEN IF PARTS OF IT ARE MAKE-BELIEVE.
INSTEAD OF THE STAR OF DAVID, DANES WORE THIS.
THE KONGEMÆRKE, WHICH MEANS THE KING'S EMBLEM.
1870 1940
I STILL WEAR MINE SEVENTY YEARS LATER!

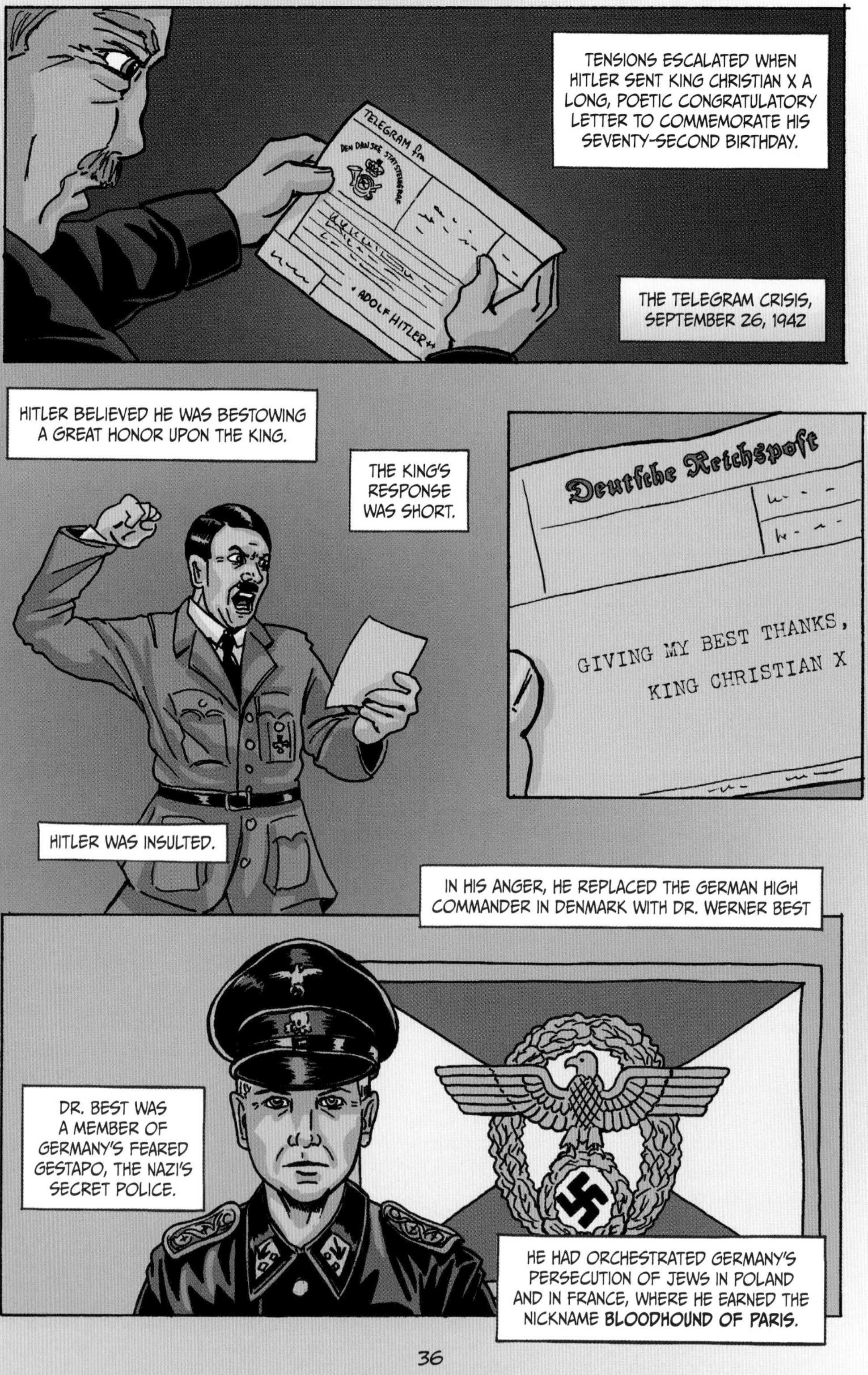
TENSIONS ESCALATED WHEN HITLER SENT KING CHRISTIAN X A LONG, POETIC CONGRATULATORY LETTER TO COMMEMORATE HIS SEVENTY-SECOND BIRTHDAY.
TELEGRAM fra
ADOLF HITLER
THE TELEGRAM CRISIS, SEPTEMBER 26, 1942
HITLER BELIEVED HE WAS BESTOWING A GREAT HONOR UPON THE KING.
THE KING'S RESPONSE WAS SHORT.
Deutsche Reichspost
GIVING MY BEST THANKS,
KING CHRISTIAN X
HITLER WAS INSULTED.
IN HIS ANGER, HE REPLACED THE GERMAN HIGH COMMANDER IN DENMARK WITH DR. WERNER BEST
DR. BEST WAS A MEMBER OF GERMANY'S FEARED GESTAPO, THE NAZI'S SECRET POLICE.
HE HAD ORCHESTRATED GERMANY'S PERSECUTION OF JEWS IN POLAND AND IN FRANCE, WHERE HE EARNED THE NICKNAME **BLOODHOUND OF PARIS**.

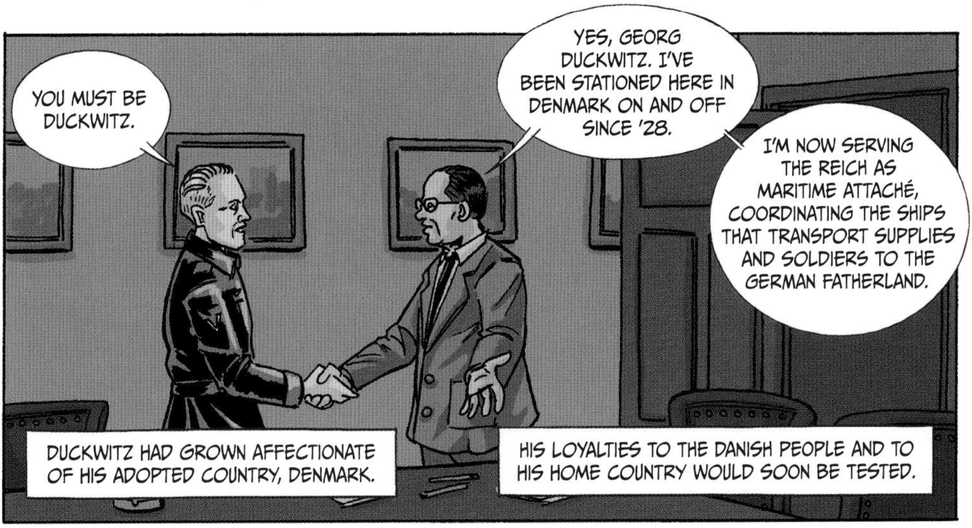
YOU MUST BE DUCKWITZ.
YES, GEORG DUCKWITZ. I'VE BEEN STATIONED HERE IN DENMARK ON AND OFF SINCE '28.
I'M NOW SERVING THE REICH AS MARITIME ATTACHÉ, COORDINATING THE SHIPS THAT TRANSPORT SUPPLIES AND SOLDIERS TO THE GERMAN FATHERLAND.
DUCKWITZ HAD GROWN AFFECTIONATE OF HIS ADOPTED COUNTRY, DENMARK.
HIS LOYALTIES TO THE DANISH PEOPLE AND TO HIS HOME COUNTRY WOULD SOON BE TESTED.

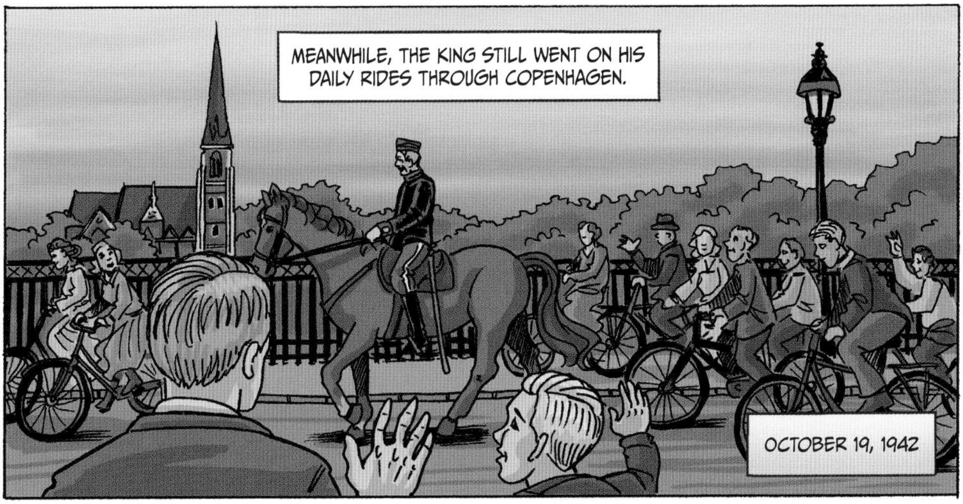
MEANWHILE, THE KING STILL WENT ON HIS DAILY RIDES THROUGH COPENHAGEN.
OCTOBER 19, 1942

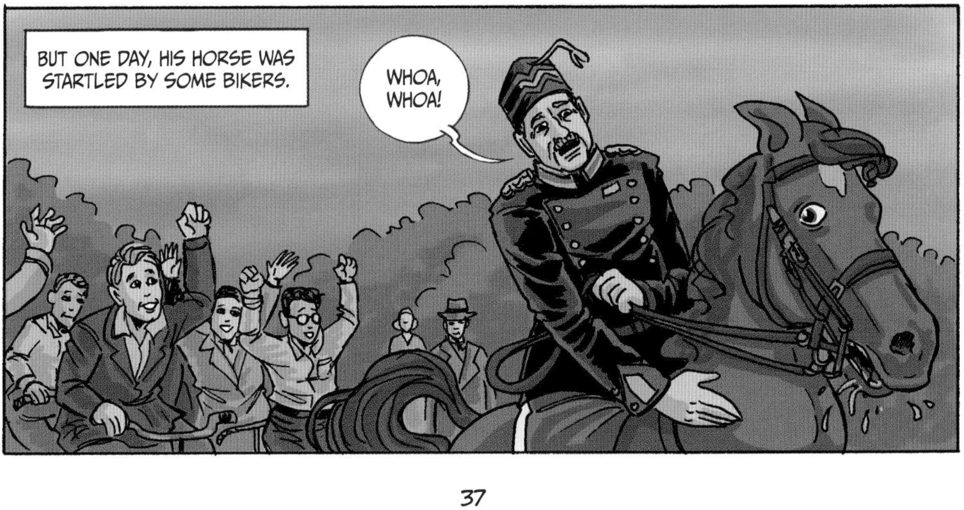
BUT ONE DAY, HIS HORSE WAS STARTLED BY SOME BIKERS.
WHOA, WHOA!

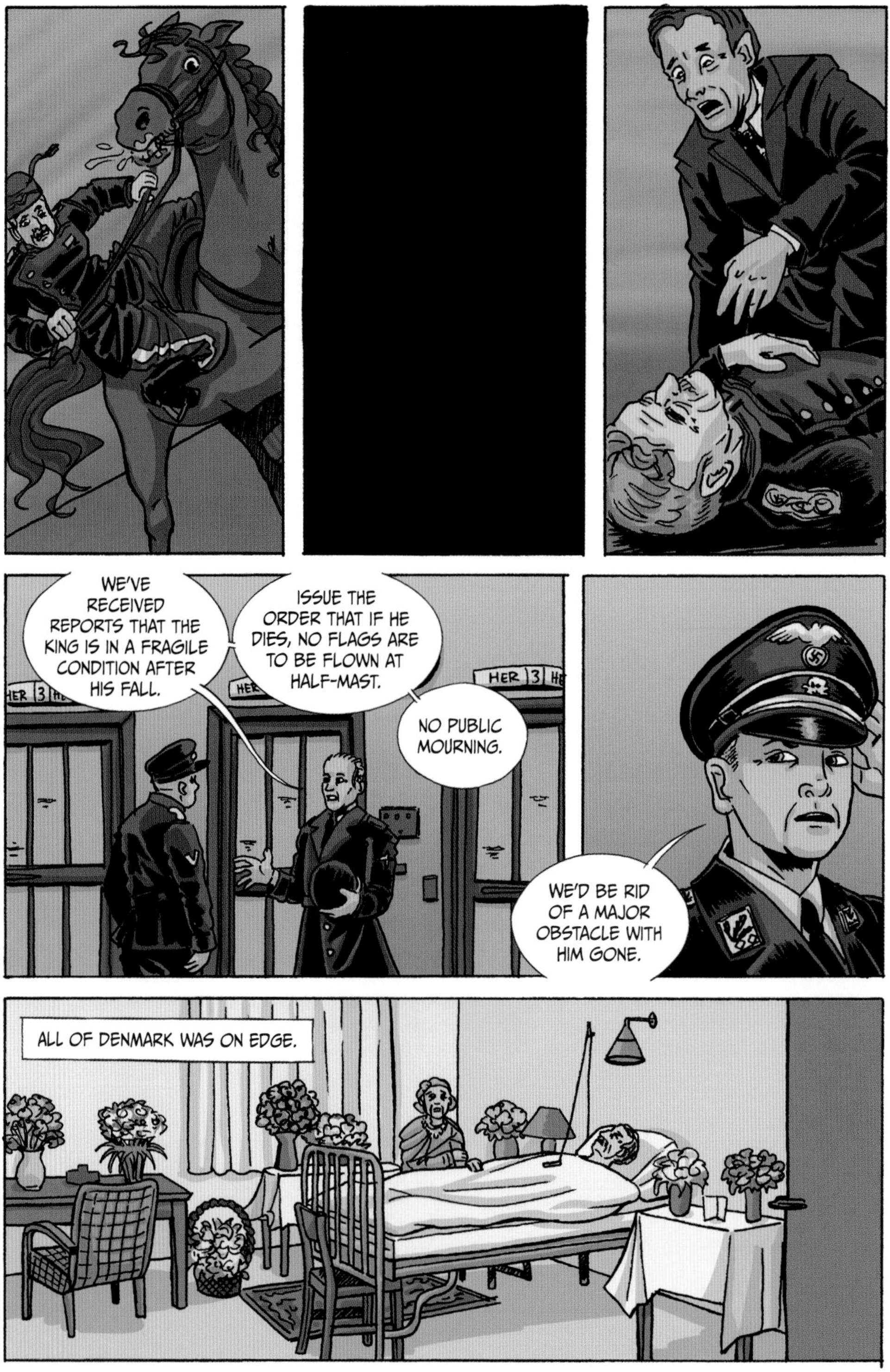
WE'VE RECEIVED REPORTS THAT THE KING IS IN A FRAGILE CONDITION AFTER HIS FALL.
ISSUE THE ORDER THAT IF HE DIES, NO FLAGS ARE TO BE FLOWN AT HALF-MAST.
NO PUBLIC MOURNING.
WE'D BE RID OF A MAJOR OBSTACLE WITH HIM GONE.
ALL OF DENMARK WAS ON EDGE.

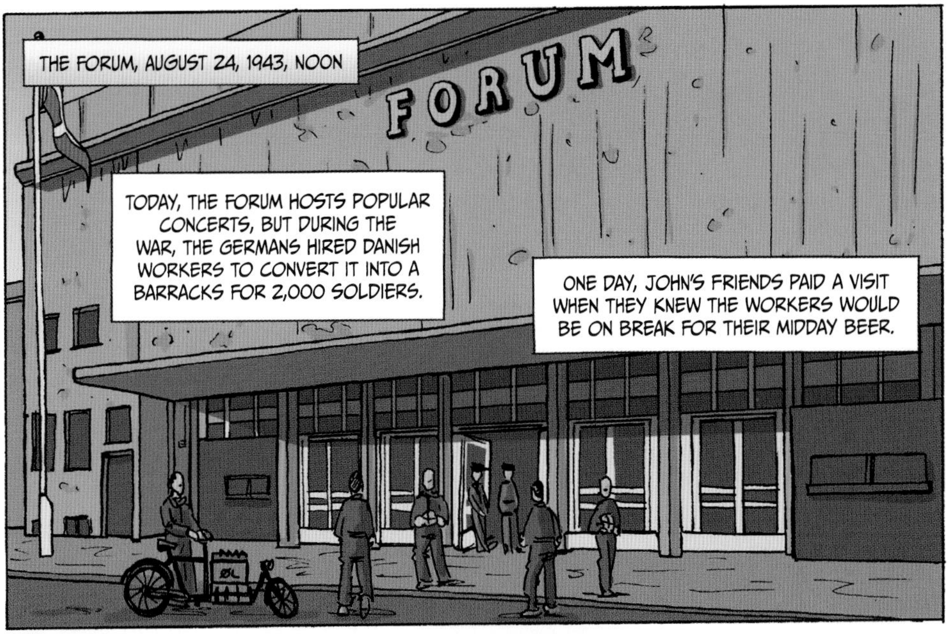
THE FORUM, AUGUST 24, 1943, NOON
FORUM
TODAY, THE FORUM HOSTS POPULAR CONCERTS, BUT DURING THE WAR, THE GERMANS HIRED DANISH WORKERS TO CONVERT IT INTO A BARRACKS FOR 2,000 SOLDIERS.
ONE DAY, JOHN'S FRIENDS PAID A VISIT WHEN THEY KNEW THE WORKERS WOULD BE ON BREAK FOR THEIR MIDDAY BEER.
ØL

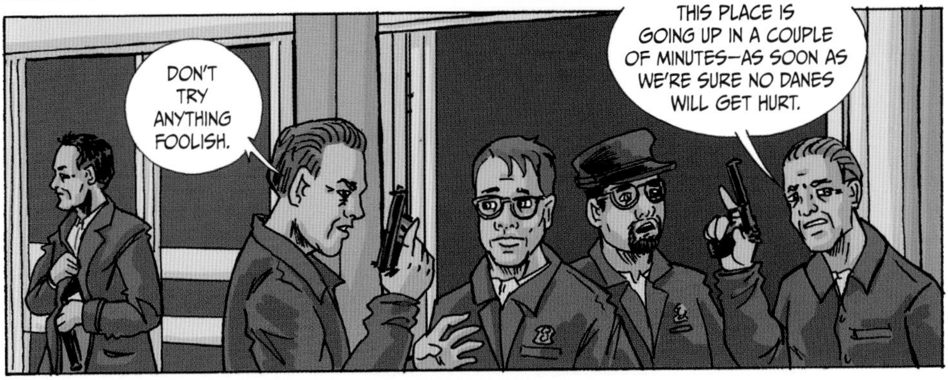
DON'T TRY ANYTHING FOOLISH.
THIS PLACE IS GOING UP IN A COUPLE OF MINUTES—AS SOON AS WE'RE SURE NO DANES WILL GET HURT.

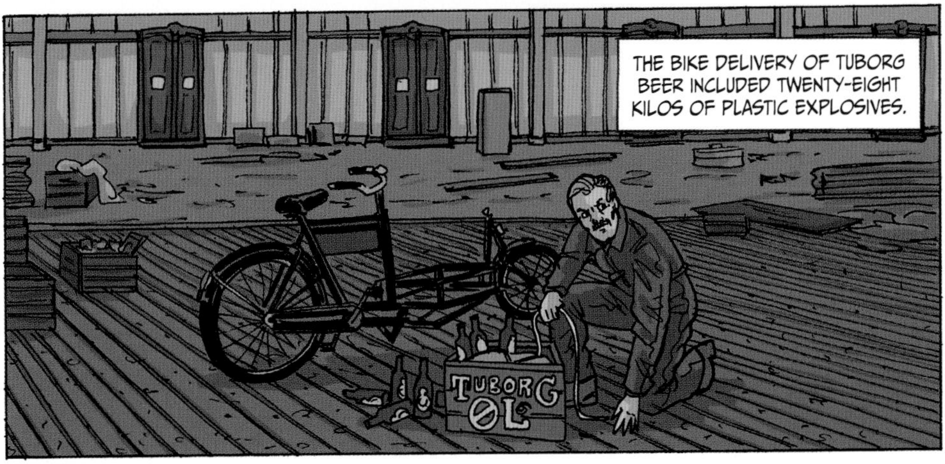
THE BIKE DELIVERY OF TUBORG BEER INCLUDED TWENTY-EIGHT KILOS OF PLASTIC EXPLOSIVES.
TUBORG
ØL

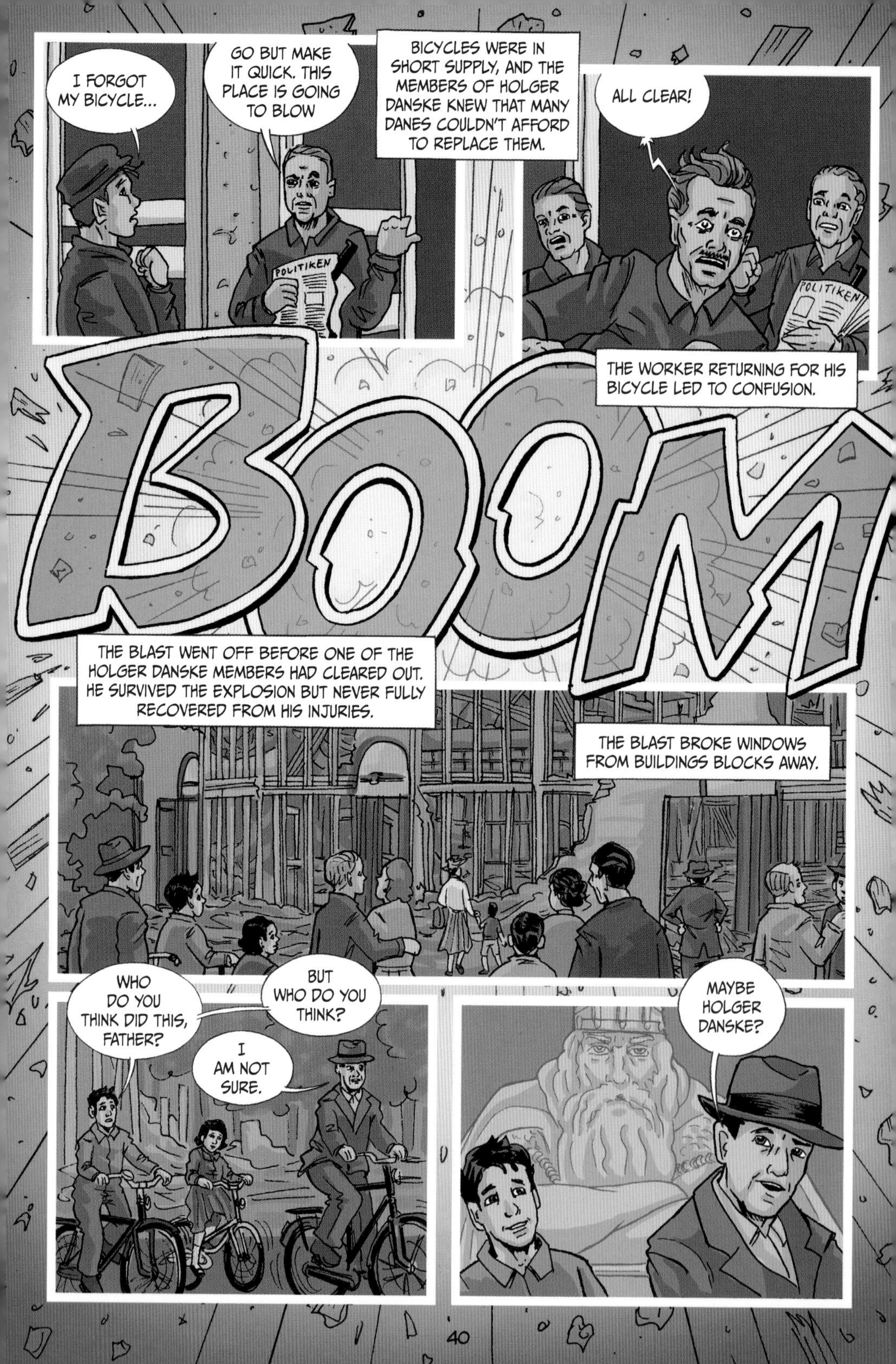
I FORGOT MY BICYCLE...
GO BUT MAKE IT QUICK. THIS PLACE IS GOING TO BLOW
POLITIKEN
BICYCLES WERE IN SHORT SUPPLY, AND THE MEMBERS OF HOLGER DANSKE KNEW THAT MANY DANES COULDN'T AFFORD TO REPLACE THEM.
ALL CLEAR!
POLITIKEN
THE WORKER RETURNING FOR HIS BICYCLE LED TO CONFUSION.
BOOM
THE BLAST WENT OFF BEFORE ONE OF THE HOLGER DANSKE MEMBERS HAD CLEARED OUT. HE SURVIVED THE EXPLOSION BUT NEVER FULLY RECOVERED FROM HIS INJURIES.
THE BLAST BROKE WINDOWS FROM BUILDINGS BLOCKS AWAY.
WHO DO YOU THINK DID THIS, FATHER?
BUT WHO DO YOU THINK?
I AM NOT SURE.
MAYBE HOLGER DANSKE?

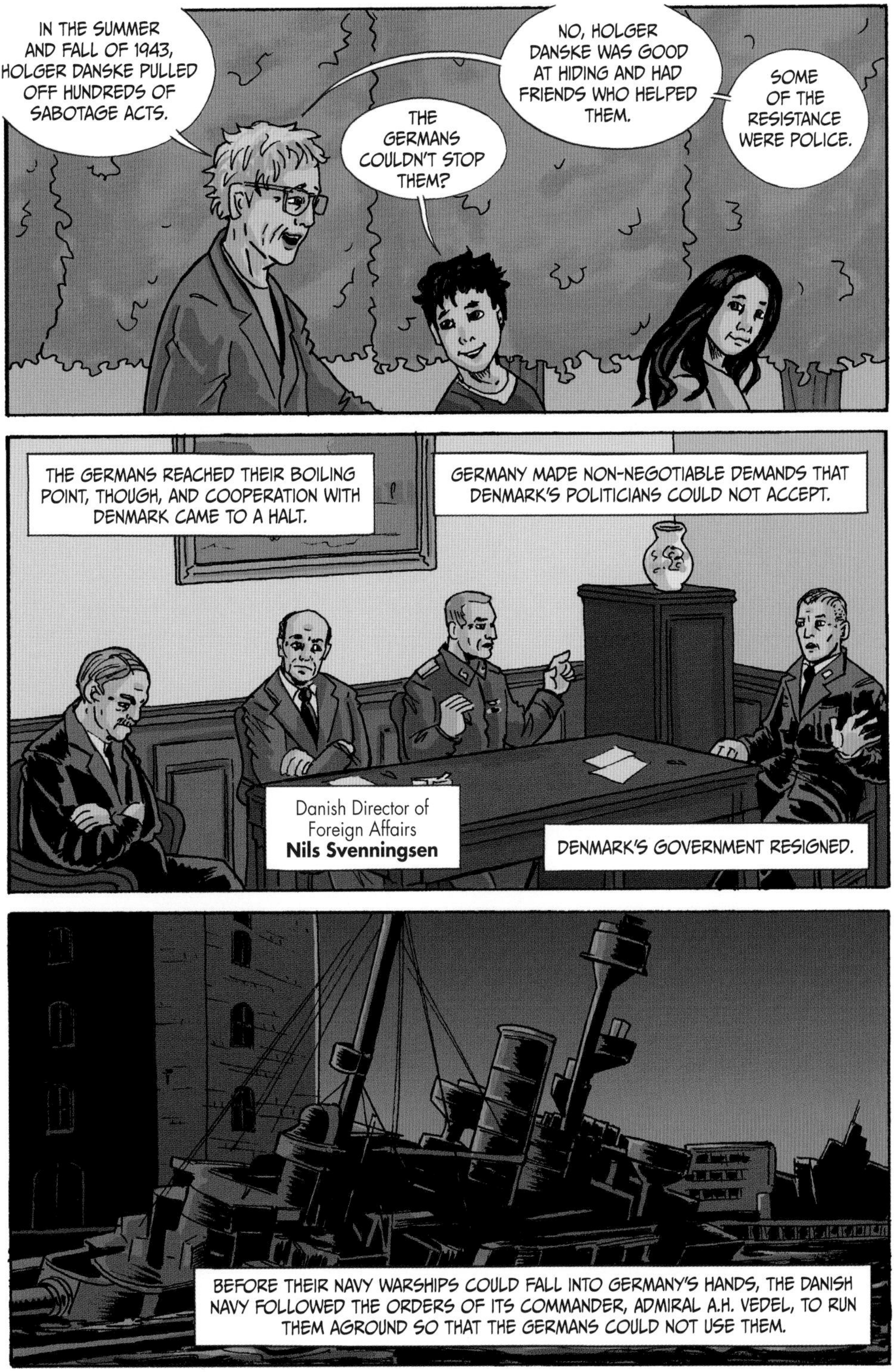
IN THE SUMMER AND FALL OF 1943, HOLGER DANSKE PULLED OFF HUNDREDS OF SABOTAGE ACTS.
THE GERMANS COULDN'T STOP THEM?
NO, HOLGER DANSKE WAS GOOD AT HIDING AND HAD FRIENDS WHO HELPED THEM.
SOME OF THE RESISTANCE WERE POLICE.
THE GERMANS REACHED THEIR BOILING POINT, THOUGH, AND COOPERATION WITH DENMARK CAME TO A HALT.
GERMANY MADE NON-NEGOTIABLE DEMANDS THAT DENMARK'S POLITICIANS COULD NOT ACCEPT.
Danish Director of Foreign Affairs **Nils Svenningsen**
DENMARK'S GOVERNMENT RESIGNED.
BEFORE THEIR NAVY WARSHIPS COULD FALL INTO GERMANY'S HANDS, THE DANISH NAVY FOLLOWED THE ORDERS OF ITS COMMANDER, ADMIRAL A.H. VEDEL, TO RUN THEM AGROUND SO THAT THE GERMANS COULD NOT USE THEM.

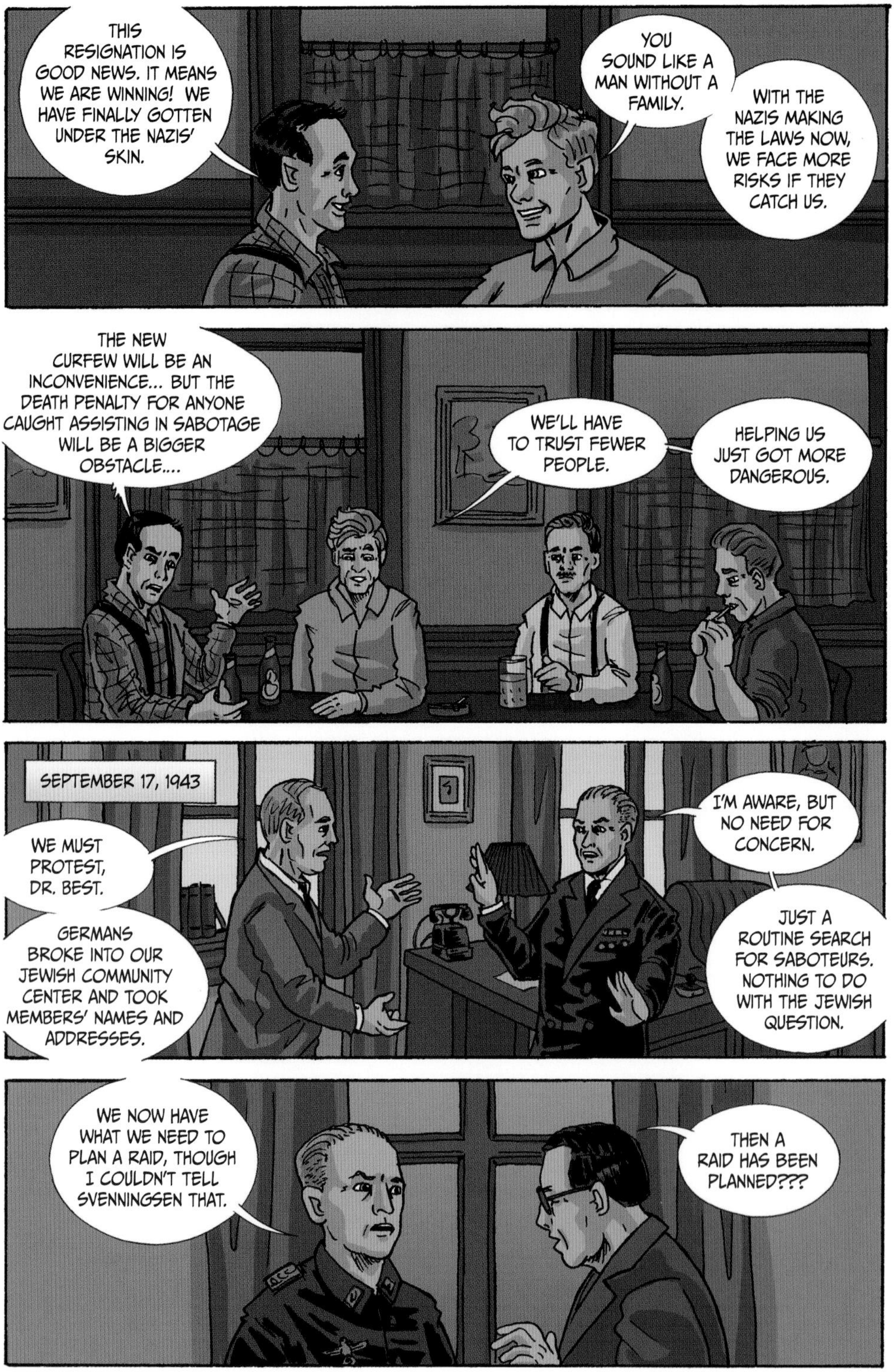
THIS RESIGNATION IS GOOD NEWS. IT MEANS WE ARE WINNING! WE HAVE FINALLY GOTTEN UNDER THE NAZIS' SKIN.
YOU SOUND LIKE A MAN WITHOUT A FAMILY.
WITH THE NAZIS MAKING THE LAWS NOW, WE FACE MORE RISKS IF THEY CATCH US.
THE NEW CURFEW WILL BE AN INCONVENIENCE... BUT THE DEATH PENALTY FOR ANYONE CAUGHT ASSISTING IN SABOTAGE WILL BE A BIGGER OBSTACLE....
WE'LL HAVE TO TRUST FEWER PEOPLE.
HELPING US JUST GOT MORE DANGEROUS.
SEPTEMBER 17, 1943
WE MUST PROTEST, DR. BEST.
GERMANS BROKE INTO OUR JEWISH COMMUNITY CENTER AND TOOK MEMBERS' NAMES AND ADDRESSES.
I'M AWARE, BUT NO NEED FOR CONCERN.
JUST A ROUTINE SEARCH FOR SABOTEURS. NOTHING TO DO WITH THE JEWISH QUESTION.
WE NOW HAVE WHAT WE NEED TO PLAN A RAID, THOUGH I COULDN'T TELL SVENNINGSEN THAT.
THEN A RAID HAS BEEN PLANNED???

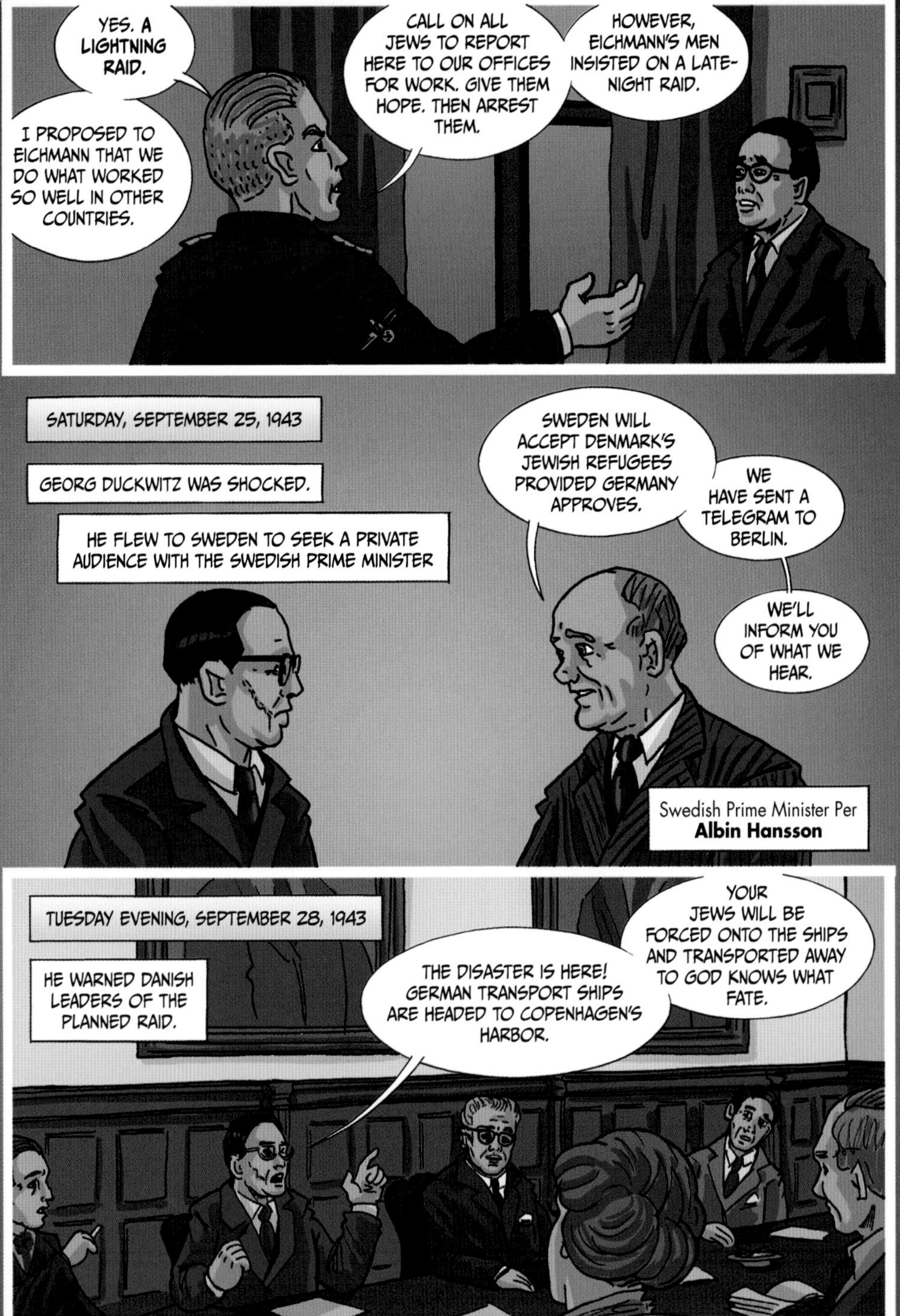
I PROPOSED TO EICHMANN THAT WE DO WHAT WORKED SO WELL IN OTHER COUNTRIES.
YES. A LIGHTNING RAID.
CALL ON ALL JEWS TO REPORT HERE TO OUR OFFICES FOR WORK. GIVE THEM HOPE. THEN ARREST THEM.
HOWEVER, EICHMANN'S MEN INSISTED ON A LATE-NIGHT RAID.
SATURDAY, SEPTEMBER 25, 1943
GEORG DUCKWITZ WAS SHOCKED.
HE FLEW TO SWEDEN TO SEEK A PRIVATE AUDIENCE WITH THE SWEDISH PRIME MINISTER
SWEDEN WILL ACCEPT DENMARK'S JEWISH REFUGEES PROVIDED GERMANY APPROVES.
WE HAVE SENT A TELEGRAM TO BERLIN.
WE'LL INFORM YOU OF WHAT WE HEAR.
Swedish Prime Minister Per **Albin Hansson**
TUESDAY EVENING, SEPTEMBER 28, 1943
HE WARNED DANISH LEADERS OF THE PLANNED RAID.
THE DISASTER IS HERE! GERMAN TRANSPORT SHIPS ARE HEADED TO COPENHAGEN'S HARBOR.
YOUR JEWS WILL BE FORCED ONTO THE SHIPS AND TRANSPORTED AWAY TO GOD KNOWS WHAT FATE.
HANS HEDTOFT, HEAD OF THE DANISH SOCIAL DEMOCRAT PARTY, BARELY HAD TIME TO SAY, "THANK YOU," BEFORE DUCKWITZ DISAPPEARED.

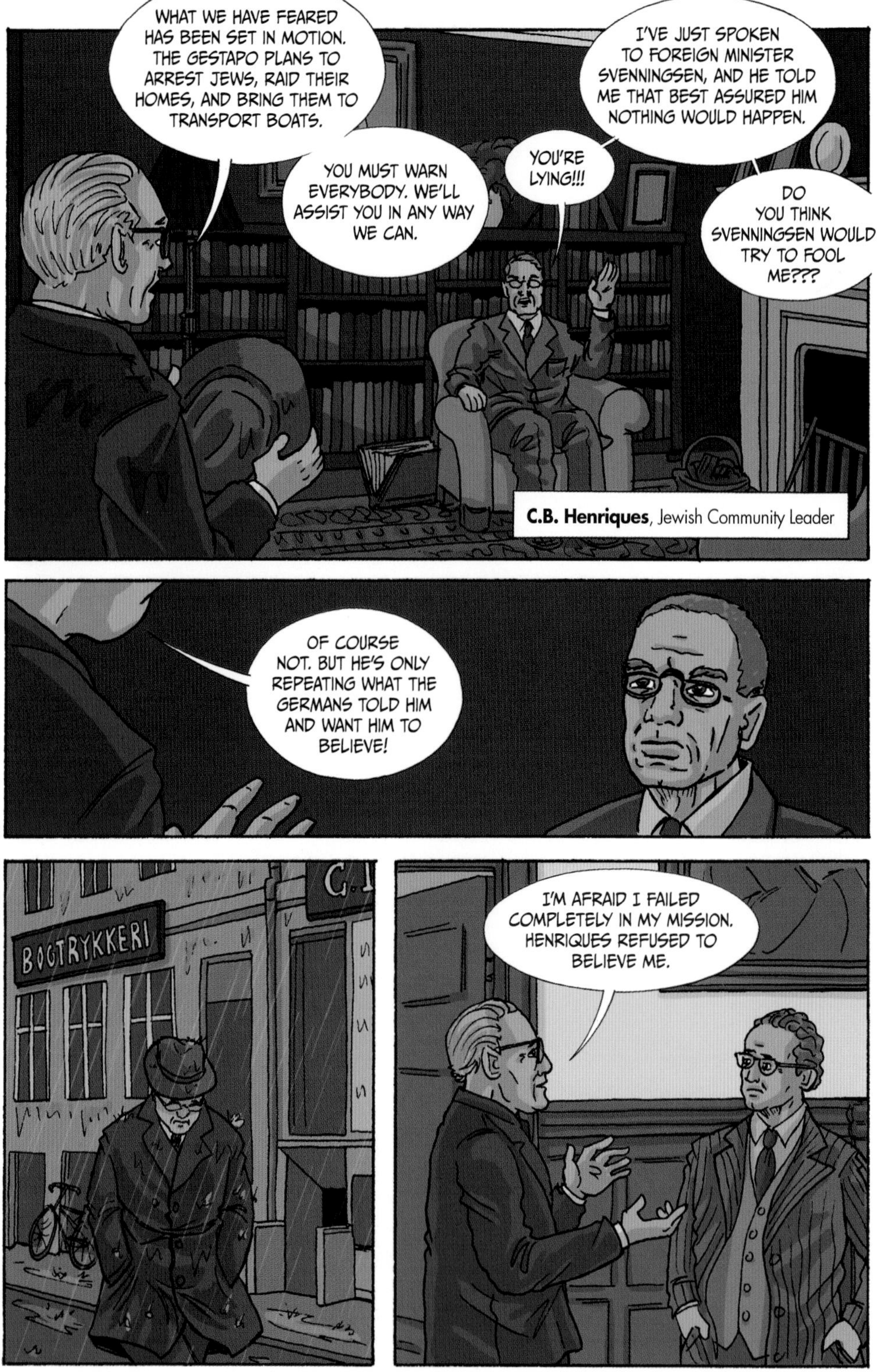
WHAT WE HAVE FEARED HAS BEEN SET IN MOTION. THE GESTAPO PLANS TO ARREST JEWS, RAID THEIR HOMES, AND BRING THEM TO TRANSPORT BOATS.
YOU MUST WARN EVERYBODY. WE'LL ASSIST YOU IN ANY WAY WE CAN.
YOU'RE LYING!!!
I'VE JUST SPOKEN TO FOREIGN MINISTER SVENNINGSEN, AND HE TOLD ME THAT BEST ASSURED HIM NOTHING WOULD HAPPEN.
DO YOU THINK SVENNINGSEN WOULD TRY TO FOOL ME???
C.B. Henriques, Jewish Community Leader
OF COURSE NOT. BUT HE'S ONLY REPEATING WHAT THE GERMANS TOLD HIM AND WANT HIM TO BELIEVE!
BOGTRYKKERI
I'M AFRAID I FAILED COMPLETELY IN MY MISSION. HENRIQUES REFUSED TO BELIEVE ME.

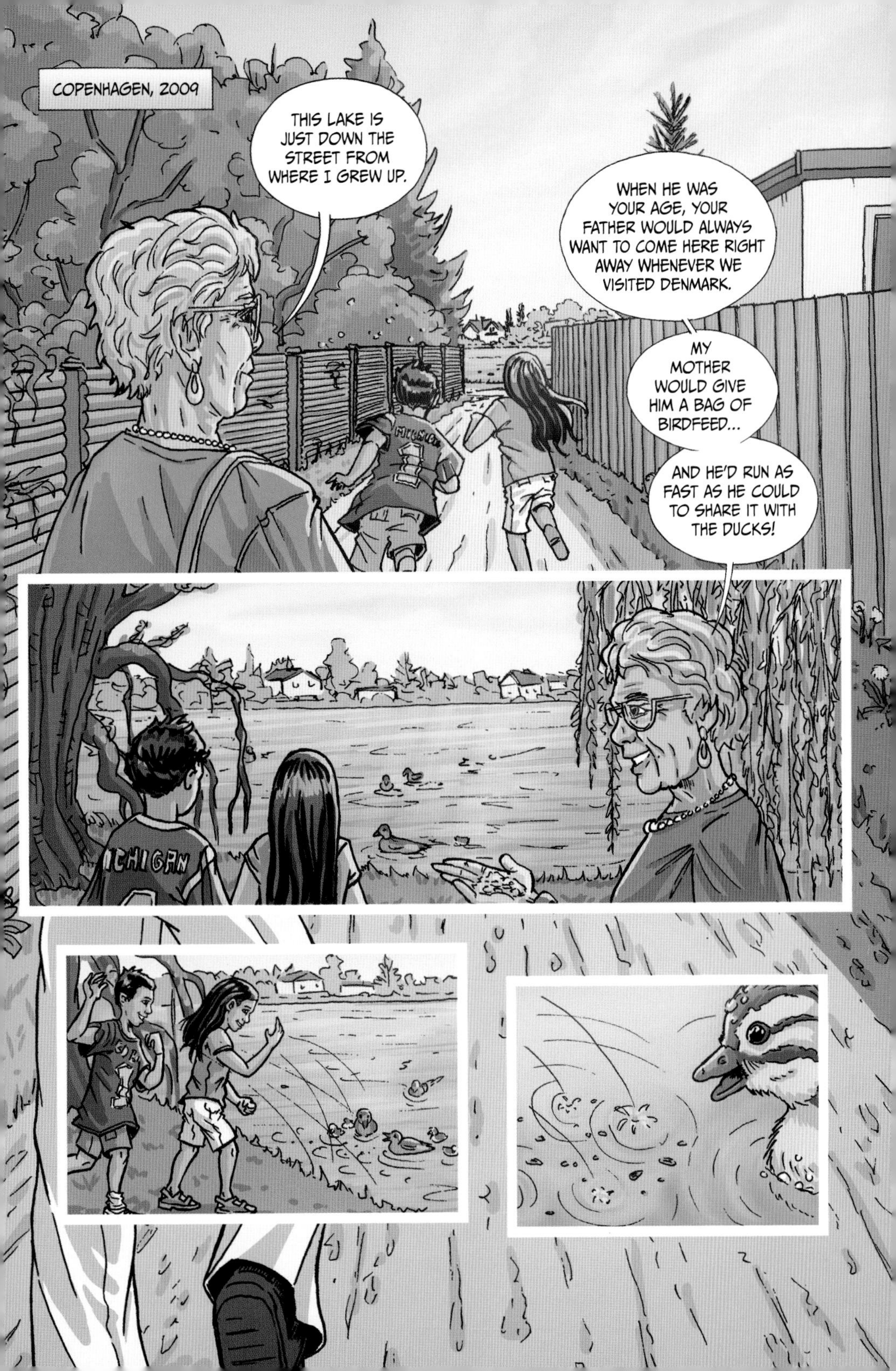
COPENHAGEN, 2009
THIS LAKE IS JUST DOWN THE STREET FROM WHERE I GREW UP.
WHEN HE WAS YOUR AGE, YOUR FATHER WOULD ALWAYS WANT TO COME HERE RIGHT AWAY WHENEVER WE VISITED DENMARK.
MY MOTHER WOULD GIVE HIM A BAG OF BIRDFEED...
AND HE'D RUN AS FAST AS HE COULD TO SHARE IT WITH THE DUCKS!
MICHIGAN

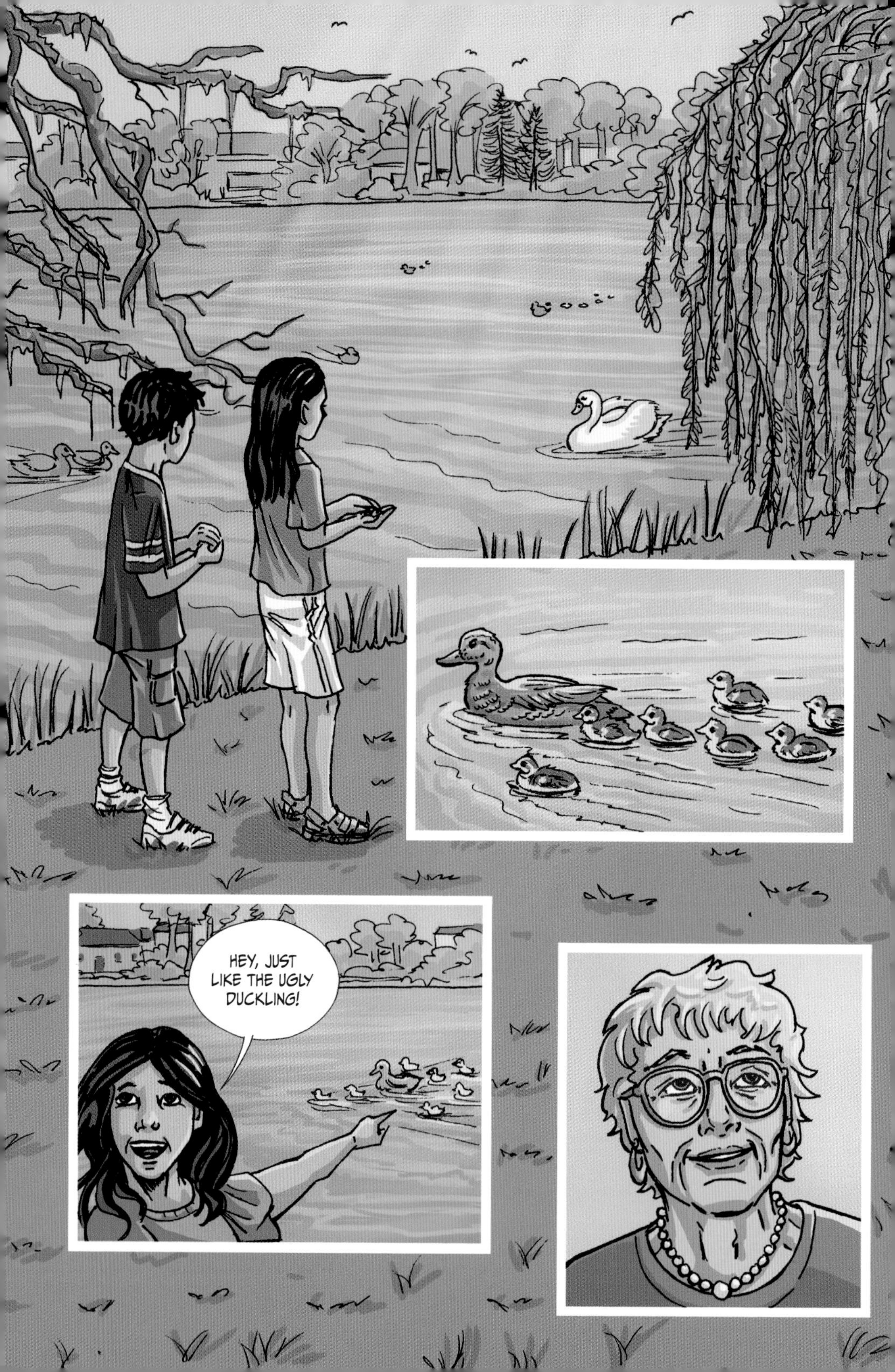
HEY, JUST LIKE THE UGLY DUCKLING!

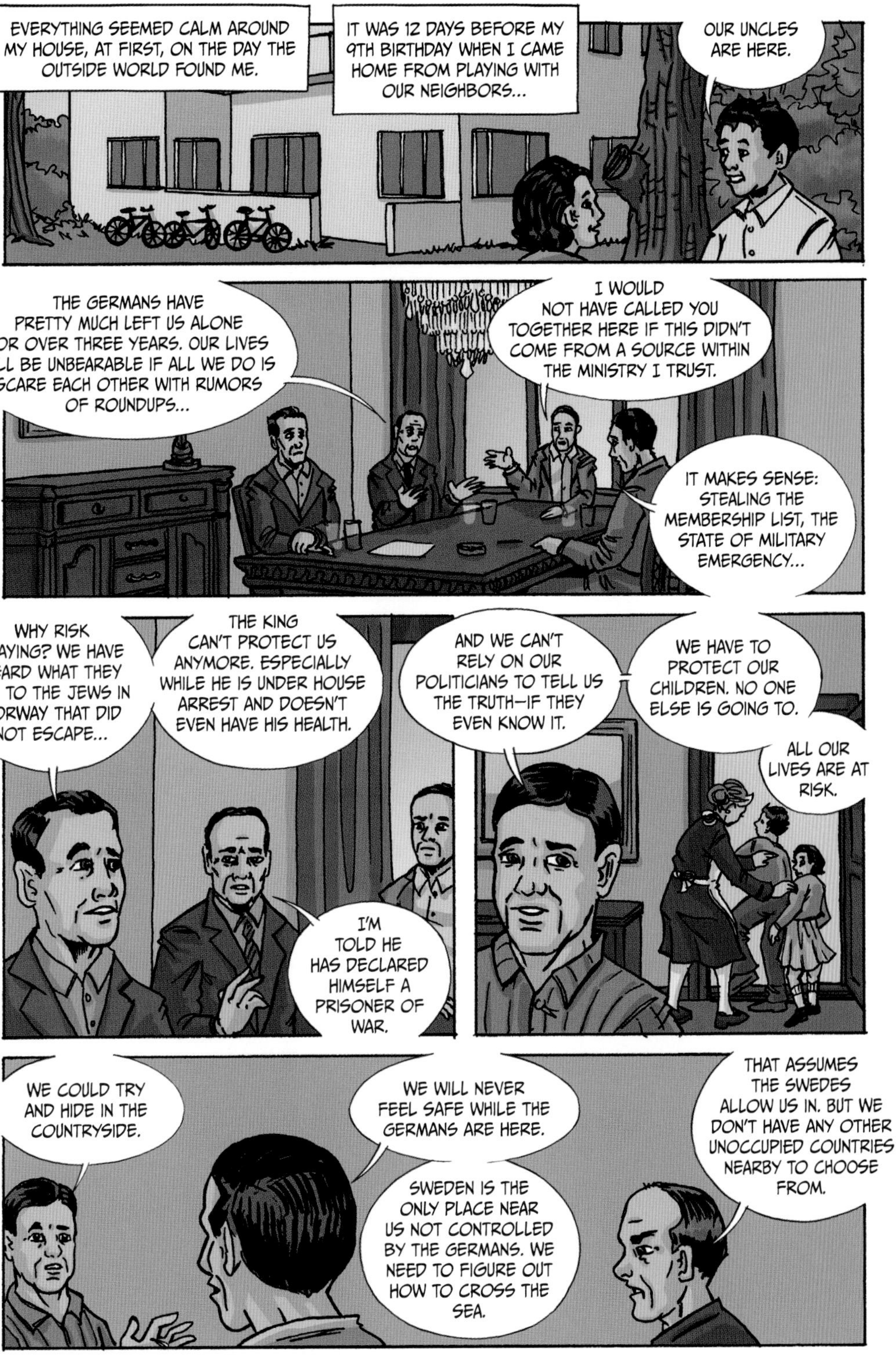
EVERYTHING SEEMED CALM AROUND MY HOUSE, AT FIRST, ON THE DAY THE OUTSIDE WORLD FOUND ME.
IT WAS 12 DAYS BEFORE MY 9TH BIRTHDAY WHEN I CAME HOME FROM PLAYING WITH OUR NEIGHBORS...
OUR UNCLES ARE HERE.
THE GERMANS HAVE PRETTY MUCH LEFT US ALONE FOR OVER THREE YEARS. OUR LIVES WILL BE UNBEARABLE IF ALL WE DO IS SCARE EACH OTHER WITH RUMORS OF ROUNDUPS...
I WOULD NOT HAVE CALLED YOU TOGETHER HERE IF THIS DIDN'T COME FROM A SOURCE WITHIN THE MINISTRY I TRUST.
IT MAKES SENSE: STEALING THE MEMBERSHIP LIST, THE STATE OF MILITARY EMERGENCY...
WHY RISK STAYING? WE HAVE HEARD WHAT THEY DID TO THE JEWS IN NORWAY THAT DID NOT ESCAPE...
THE KING CAN'T PROTECT US ANYMORE. ESPECIALLY WHILE HE IS UNDER HOUSE ARREST AND DOESN'T EVEN HAVE HIS HEALTH.
I'M TOLD HE HAS DECLARED HIMSELF A PRISONER OF WAR.
AND WE CAN'T RELY ON OUR POLITICIANS TO TELL US THE TRUTH—IF THEY EVEN KNOW IT.
WE HAVE TO PROTECT OUR CHILDREN. NO ONE ELSE IS GOING TO.
ALL OUR LIVES ARE AT RISK.
WE COULD TRY AND HIDE IN THE COUNTRYSIDE.
WE WILL NEVER FEEL SAFE WHILE THE GERMANS ARE HERE.
SWEDEN IS THE ONLY PLACE NEAR US NOT CONTROLLED BY THE GERMANS. WE NEED TO FIGURE OUT HOW TO CROSS THE SEA.
THAT ASSUMES THE SWEDES ALLOW US IN. BUT WE DON'T HAVE ANY OTHER UNOCCUPIED COUNTRIES NEARBY TO CHOOSE FROM.

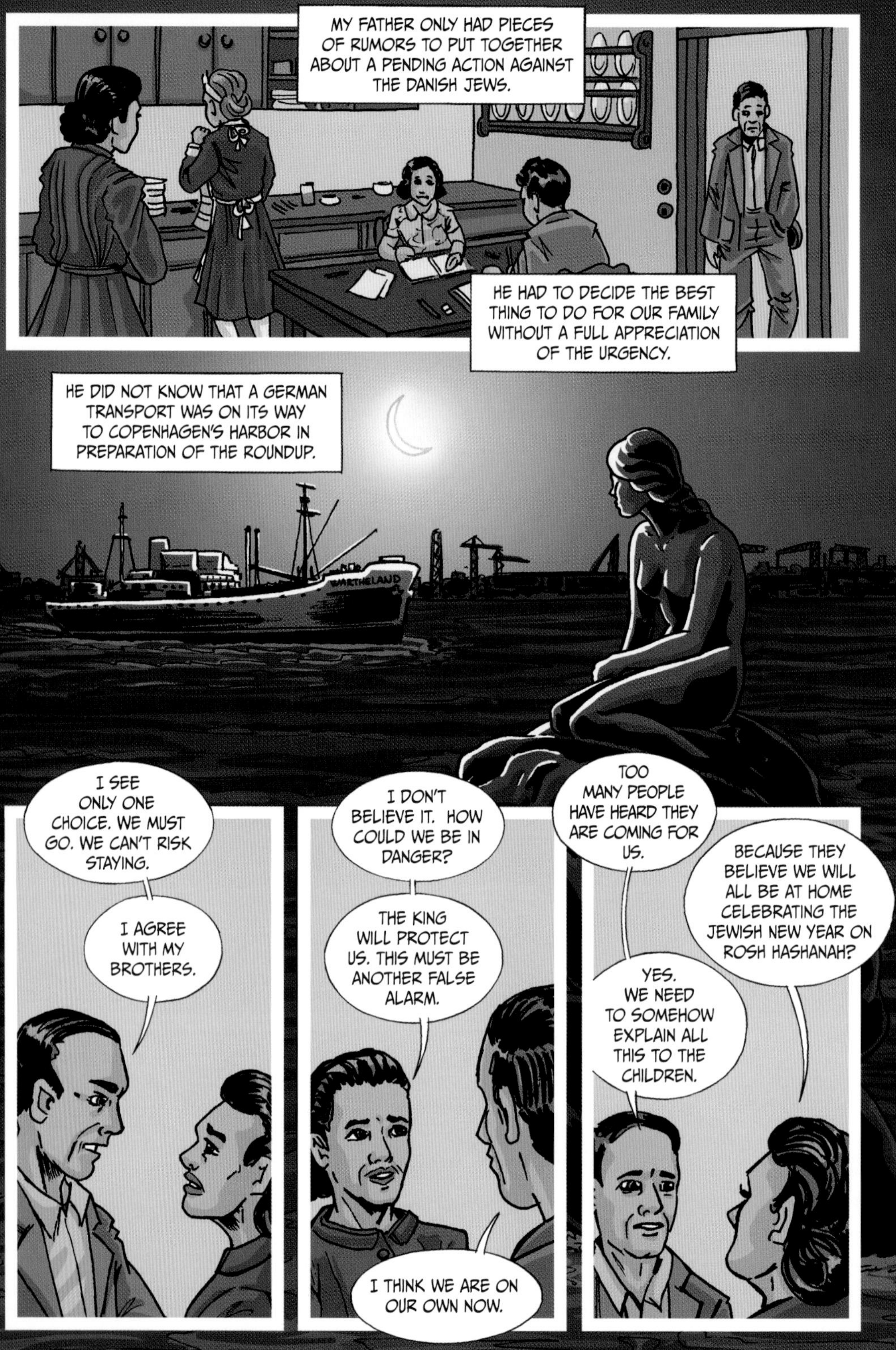
MY FATHER ONLY HAD PIECES OF RUMORS TO PUT TOGETHER ABOUT A PENDING ACTION AGAINST THE DANISH JEWS.
HE HAD TO DECIDE THE BEST THING TO DO FOR OUR FAMILY WITHOUT A FULL APPRECIATION OF THE URGENCY.
HE DID NOT KNOW THAT A GERMAN TRANSPORT WAS ON ITS WAY TO COPENHAGEN'S HARBOR IN PREPARATION OF THE ROUNDUP.
WARTHELAND
I SEE ONLY ONE CHOICE. WE MUST GO. WE CAN'T RISK STAYING.
I AGREE WITH MY BROTHERS.
I DON'T BELIEVE IT. HOW COULD WE BE IN DANGER?
THE KING WILL PROTECT US. THIS MUST BE ANOTHER FALSE ALARM.
I THINK WE ARE ON OUR OWN NOW.
TOO MANY PEOPLE HAVE HEARD THEY ARE COMING FOR US.
BECAUSE THEY BELIEVE WE WILL ALL BE AT HOME CELEBRATING THE JEWISH NEW YEAR ON ROSH HASHANAH?
YES. WE NEED TO SOMEHOW EXPLAIN ALL THIS TO THE CHILDREN.

IT WAS MY FATHER'S BIRTHDAY, AND I DID NOT KNOW WHY WE WERE NOT CELEBRATING THAT NIGHT.

AS HE TOOK ME FOR A WALK, I STARTED TO LEARN ABOUT THE WORLD HE HAD SHIELDED ME FROM EVER SINCE THE NAZI INVASION.

HE DID NOT TALK RIGHT AWAY.

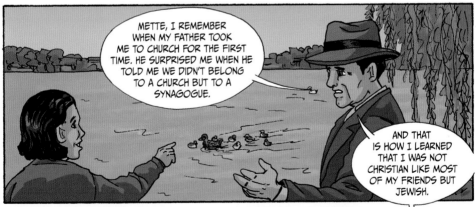

METTE, I REMEMBER WHEN MY FATHER TOOK ME TO CHURCH FOR THE FIRST TIME. HE SURPRISED ME WHEN HE TOLD ME WE DIDN'T BELONG TO A CHURCH BUT TO A SYNAGOGUE.

AND THAT IS HOW I LEARNED THAT I WAS NOT CHRISTIAN LIKE MOST OF MY FRIENDS BUT JEWISH.

I AM JEWISH, AND YOUR MOTHER IS JEWISH, SO THAT MEANS YOU ARE TOO.

DO YOU UNDERSTAND?

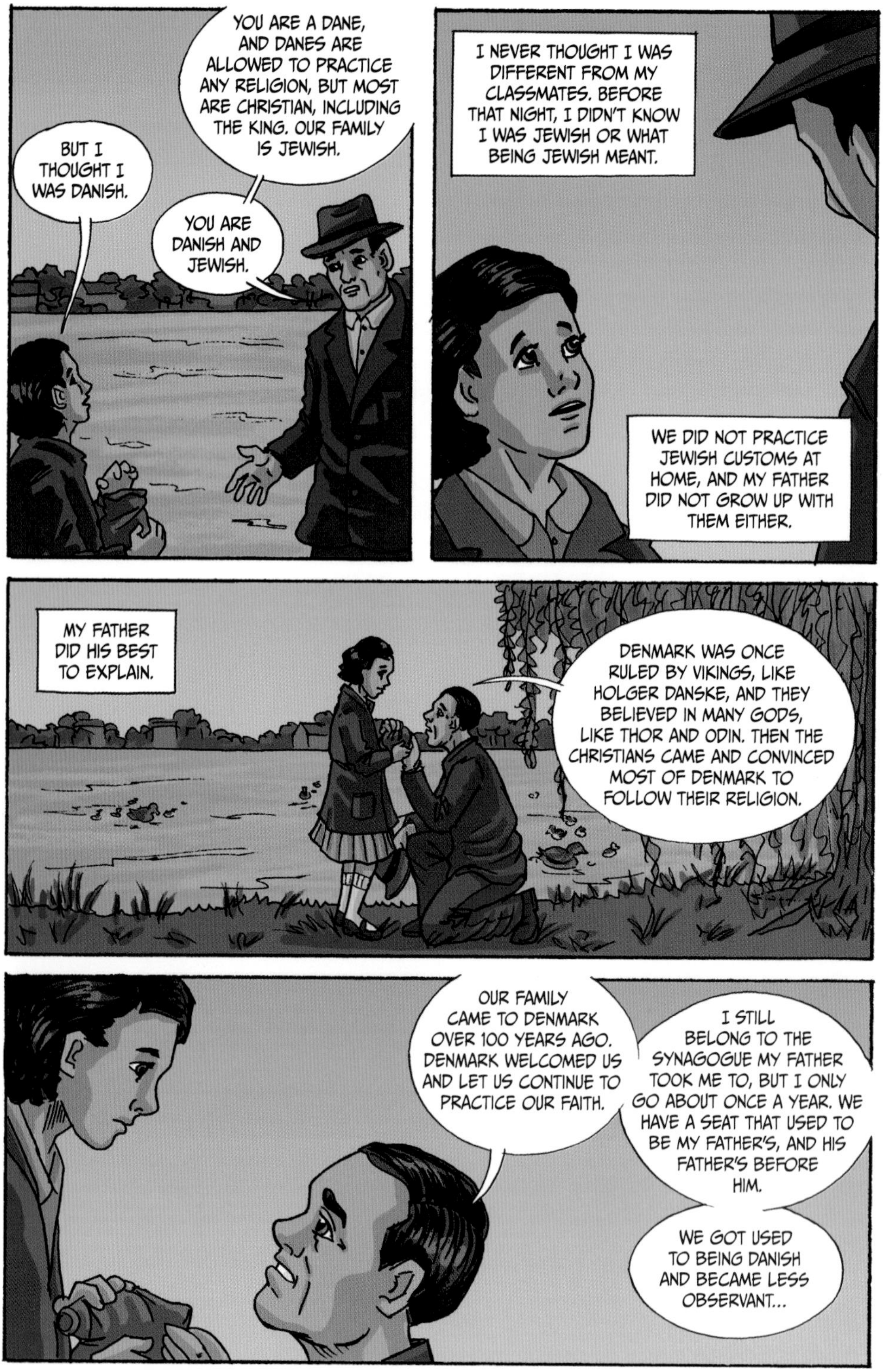
BUT I THOUGHT I WAS DANISH.
YOU ARE A DANE, AND DANES ARE ALLOWED TO PRACTICE ANY RELIGION, BUT MOST ARE CHRISTIAN, INCLUDING THE KING. OUR FAMILY IS JEWISH.
YOU ARE DANISH AND JEWISH.
I NEVER THOUGHT I WAS DIFFERENT FROM MY CLASSMATES. BEFORE THAT NIGHT, I DIDN'T KNOW I WAS JEWISH OR WHAT BEING JEWISH MEANT.
WE DID NOT PRACTICE JEWISH CUSTOMS AT HOME, AND MY FATHER DID NOT GROW UP WITH THEM EITHER.
MY FATHER DID HIS BEST TO EXPLAIN.
DENMARK WAS ONCE RULED BY VIKINGS, LIKE HOLGER DANSKE, AND THEY BELIEVED IN MANY GODS, LIKE THOR AND ODIN. THEN THE CHRISTIANS CAME AND CONVINCED MOST OF DENMARK TO FOLLOW THEIR RELIGION.
OUR FAMILY CAME TO DENMARK OVER 100 YEARS AGO. DENMARK WELCOMED US AND LET US CONTINUE TO PRACTICE OUR FAITH.
I STILL BELONG TO THE SYNAGOGUE MY FATHER TOOK ME TO, BUT I ONLY GO ABOUT ONCE A YEAR. WE HAVE A SEAT THAT USED TO BE MY FATHER'S, AND HIS FATHER'S BEFORE HIM.
WE GOT USED TO BEING DANISH AND BECAME LESS OBSERVANT...

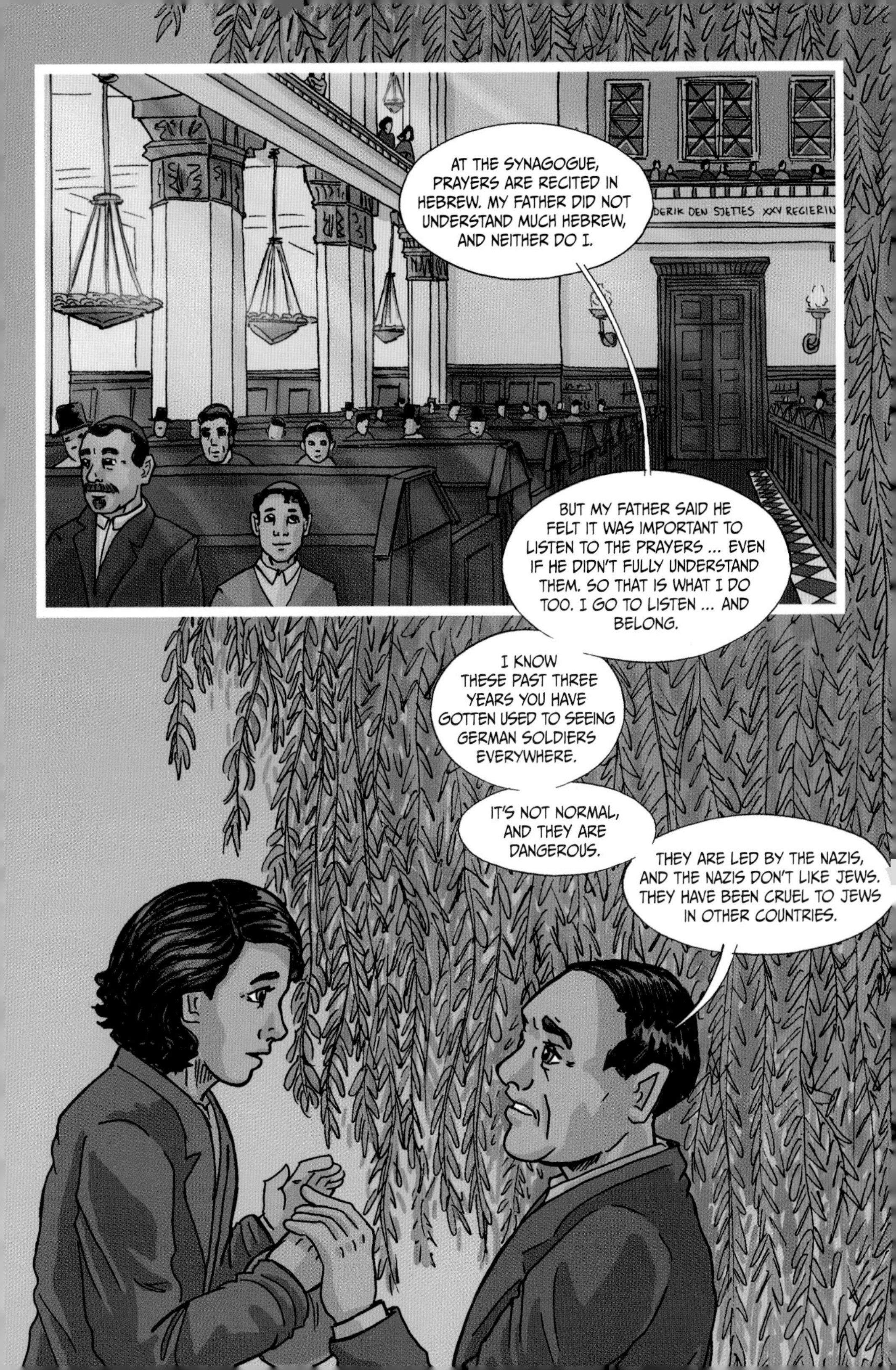
DERIK DEN SJETTES XXV REGIERIN
AT THE SYNAGOGUE, PRAYERS ARE RECITED IN HEBREW. MY FATHER DID NOT UNDERSTAND MUCH HEBREW, AND NEITHER DO I.
BUT MY FATHER SAID HE FELT IT WAS IMPORTANT TO LISTEN TO THE PRAYERS ... EVEN IF HE DIDN'T FULLY UNDERSTAND THEM. SO THAT IS WHAT I DO TOO. I GO TO LISTEN ... AND BELONG.
I KNOW THESE PAST THREE YEARS YOU HAVE GOTTEN USED TO SEEING GERMAN SOLDIERS EVERYWHERE.
IT'S NOT NORMAL, AND THEY ARE DANGEROUS.
THEY ARE LED BY THE NAZIS, AND THE NAZIS DON'T LIKE JEWS. THEY HAVE BEEN CRUEL TO JEWS IN OTHER COUNTRIES.

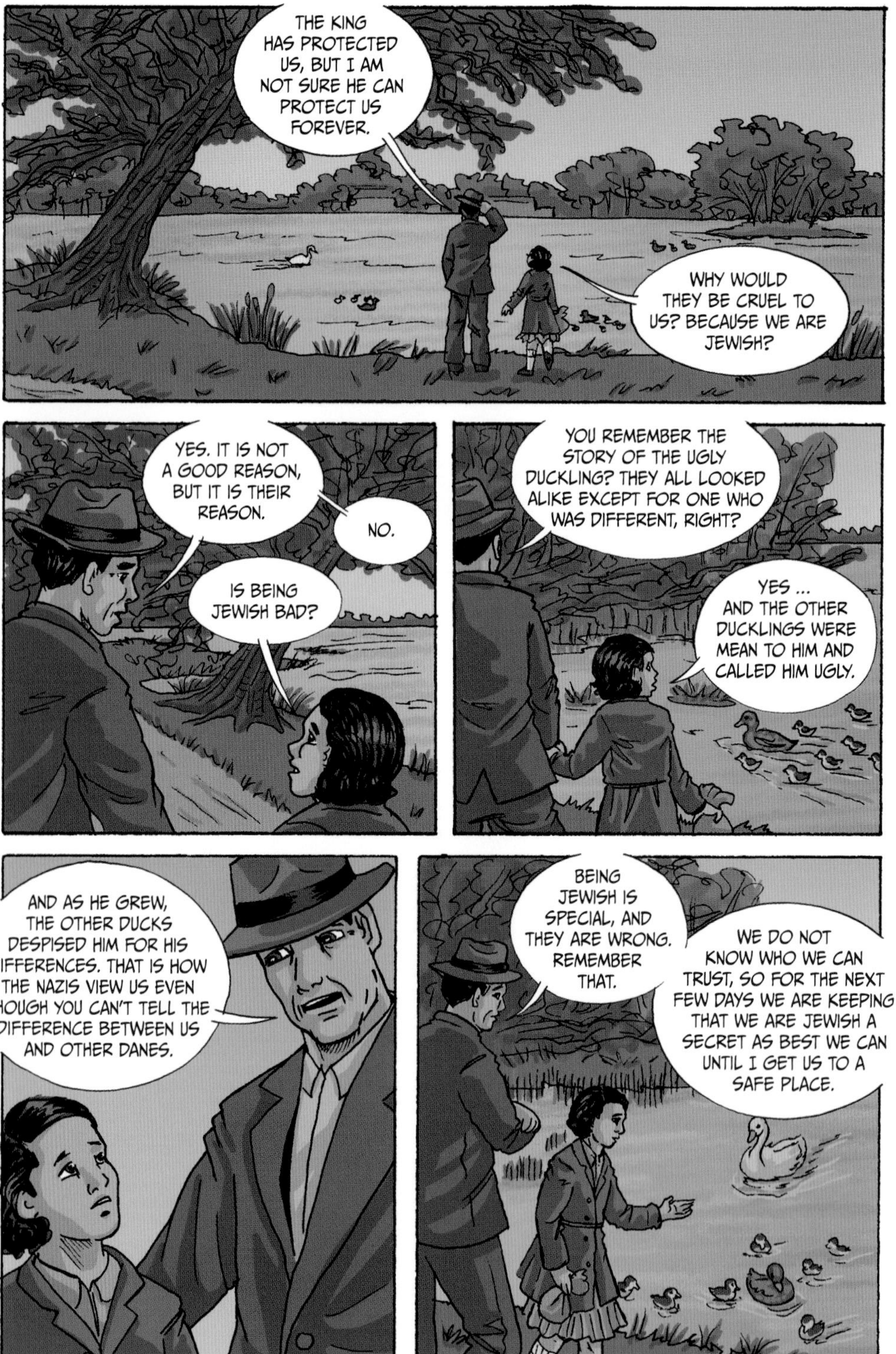
THE KING HAS PROTECTED US, BUT I AM NOT SURE HE CAN PROTECT US FOREVER.
WHY WOULD THEY BE CRUEL TO US? BECAUSE WE ARE JEWISH?
YES. IT IS NOT A GOOD REASON, BUT IT IS THEIR REASON.
NO.
IS BEING JEWISH BAD?
YOU REMEMBER THE STORY OF THE UGLY DUCKLING? THEY ALL LOOKED ALIKE EXCEPT FOR ONE WHO WAS DIFFERENT, RIGHT?
YES ... AND THE OTHER DUCKLINGS WERE MEAN TO HIM AND CALLED HIM UGLY.
AND AS HE GREW, THE OTHER DUCKS DESPISED HIM FOR HIS DIFFERENCES. THAT IS HOW THE NAZIS VIEW US EVEN THOUGH YOU CAN'T TELL THE DIFFERENCE BETWEEN US AND OTHER DANES.
BEING JEWISH IS SPECIAL, AND THEY ARE WRONG. REMEMBER THAT.
WE DO NOT KNOW WHO WE CAN TRUST, SO FOR THE NEXT FEW DAYS WE ARE KEEPING THAT WE ARE JEWISH A SECRET AS BEST WE CAN UNTIL I GET US TO A SAFE PLACE.

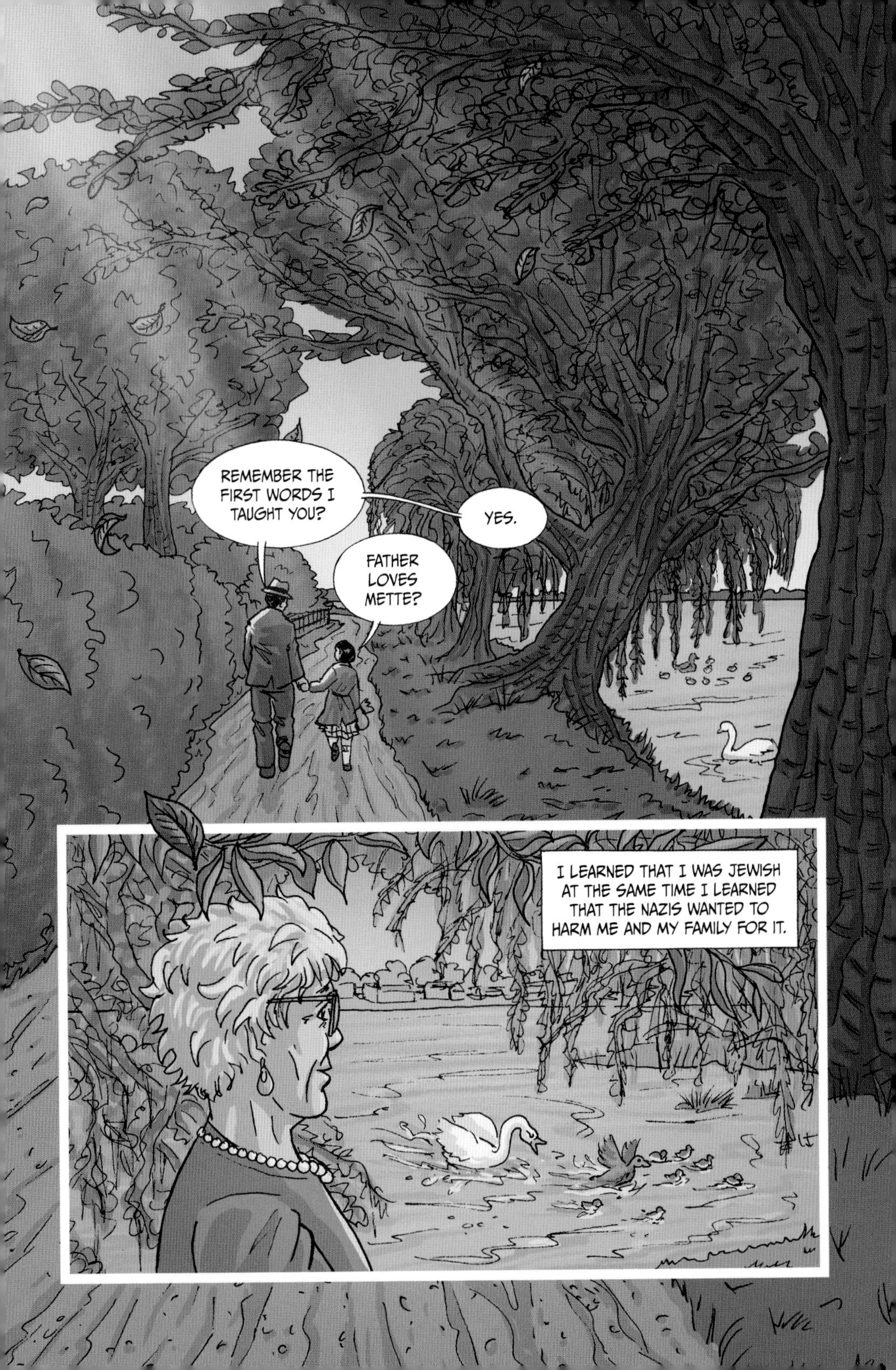
REMEMBER THE FIRST WORDS I TAUGHT YOU?
YES.
FATHER LOVES METTE?
I LEARNED THAT I WAS JEWISH AT THE SAME TIME I LEARNED THAT THE NAZIS WANTED TO HARM ME AND MY FAMILY FOR IT.

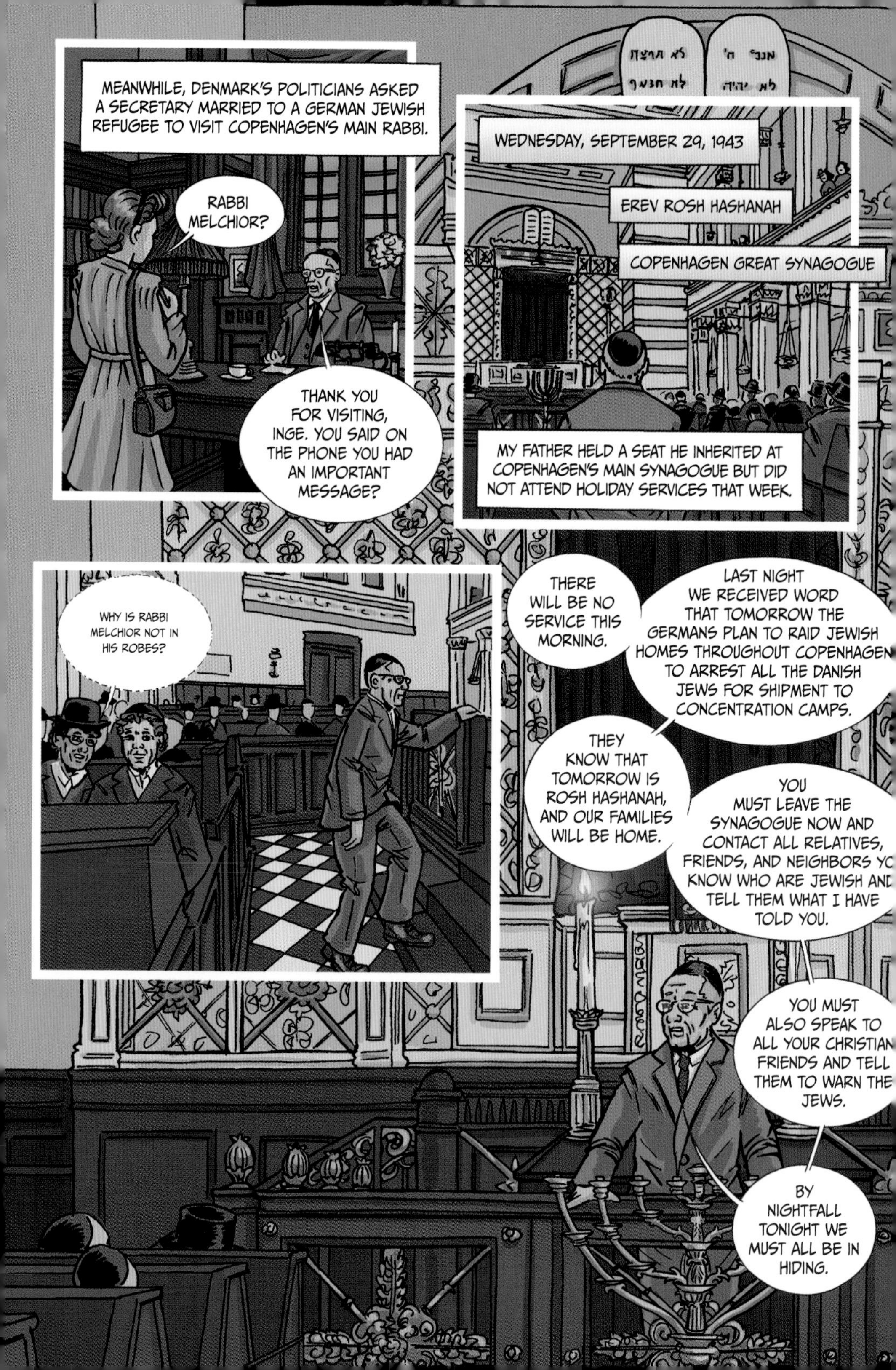
MEANWHILE, DENMARK'S POLITICIANS ASKED A SECRETARY MARRIED TO A GERMAN JEWISH REFUGEE TO VISIT COPENHAGEN'S MAIN RABBI.
RABBI MELCHIOR?
THANK YOU FOR VISITING, INGE. YOU SAID ON THE PHONE YOU HAD AN IMPORTANT MESSAGE?
WEDNESDAY, SEPTEMBER 29, 1943
EREV ROSH HASHANAH
COPENHAGEN GREAT SYNAGOGUE
MY FATHER HELD A SEAT HE INHERITED AT COPENHAGEN'S MAIN SYNAGOGUE BUT DID NOT ATTEND HOLIDAY SERVICES THAT WEEK.
WHY IS RABBI MELCHIOR NOT IN HIS ROBES?
THERE WILL BE NO SERVICE THIS MORNING.
LAST NIGHT WE RECEIVED WORD THAT TOMORROW THE GERMANS PLAN TO RAID JEWISH HOMES THROUGHOUT COPENHAGEN TO ARREST ALL THE DANISH JEWS FOR SHIPMENT TO CONCENTRATION CAMPS.
THEY KNOW THAT TOMORROW IS ROSH HASHANAH, AND OUR FAMILIES WILL BE HOME.
YOU MUST LEAVE THE SYNAGOGUE NOW AND CONTACT ALL RELATIVES, FRIENDS, AND NEIGHBORS YO KNOW WHO ARE JEWISH AND TELL THEM WHAT I HAVE TOLD YOU.
YOU MUST ALSO SPEAK TO ALL YOUR CHRISTIAN FRIENDS AND TELL THEM TO WARN THE JEWS.
BY NIGHTFALL TONIGHT WE MUST ALL BE IN HIDING.

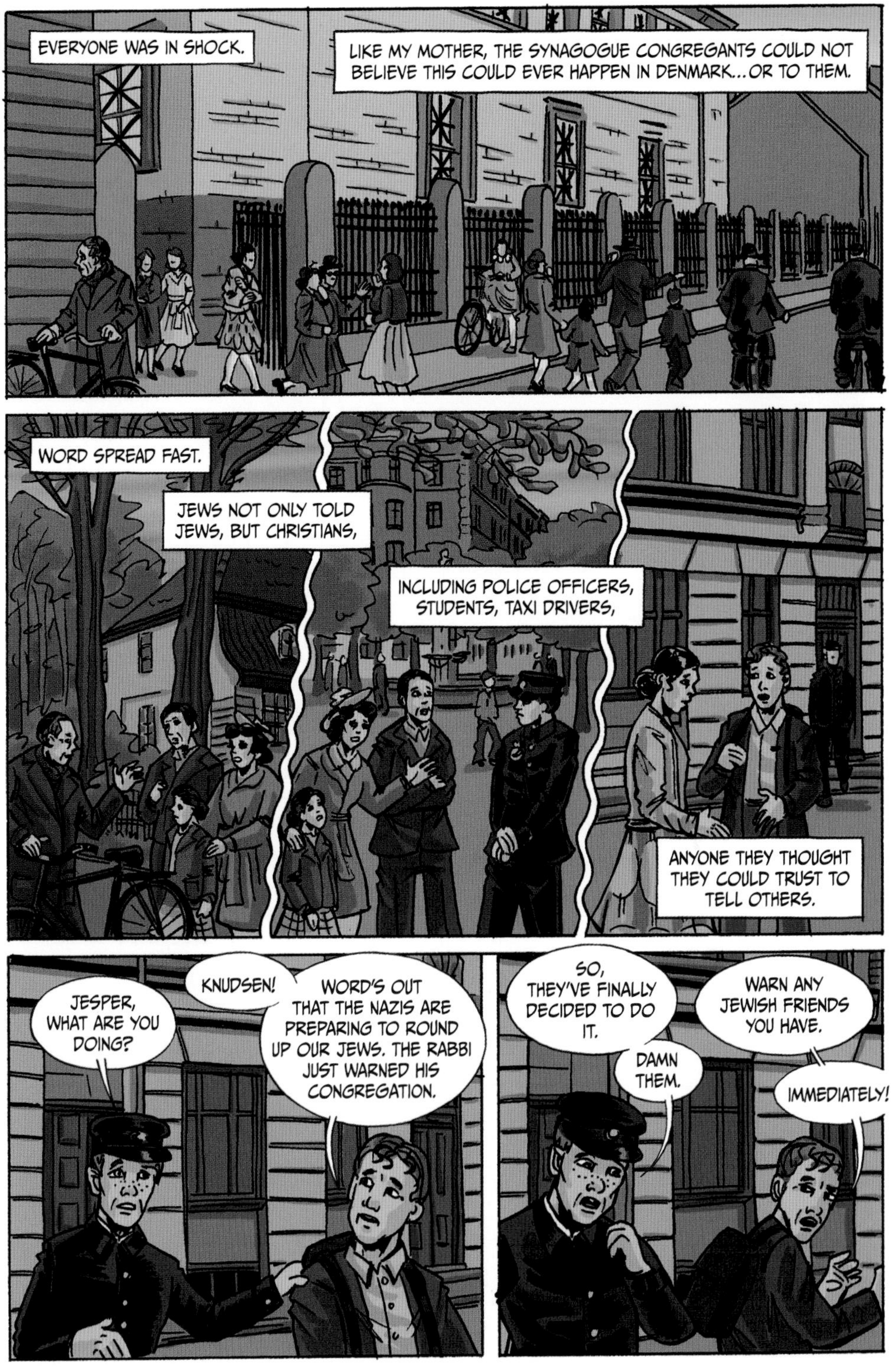
EVERYONE WAS IN SHOCK.
LIKE MY MOTHER, THE SYNAGOGUE CONGREGANTS COULD NOT BELIEVE THIS COULD EVER HAPPEN IN DENMARK...OR TO THEM.
WORD SPREAD FAST.
JEWS NOT ONLY TOLD JEWS, BUT CHRISTIANS,
INCLUDING POLICE OFFICERS, STUDENTS, TAXI DRIVERS,
ANYONE THEY THOUGHT THEY COULD TRUST TO TELL OTHERS.
JESPER, WHAT ARE YOU DOING?
KNUDSEN!
WORD'S OUT THAT THE NAZIS ARE PREPARING TO ROUND UP OUR JEWS. THE RABBI JUST WARNED HIS CONGREGATION.
SO, THEY'VE FINALLY DECIDED TO DO IT.
DAMN THEM.
WARN ANY JEWISH FRIENDS YOU HAVE.
IMMEDIATELY!

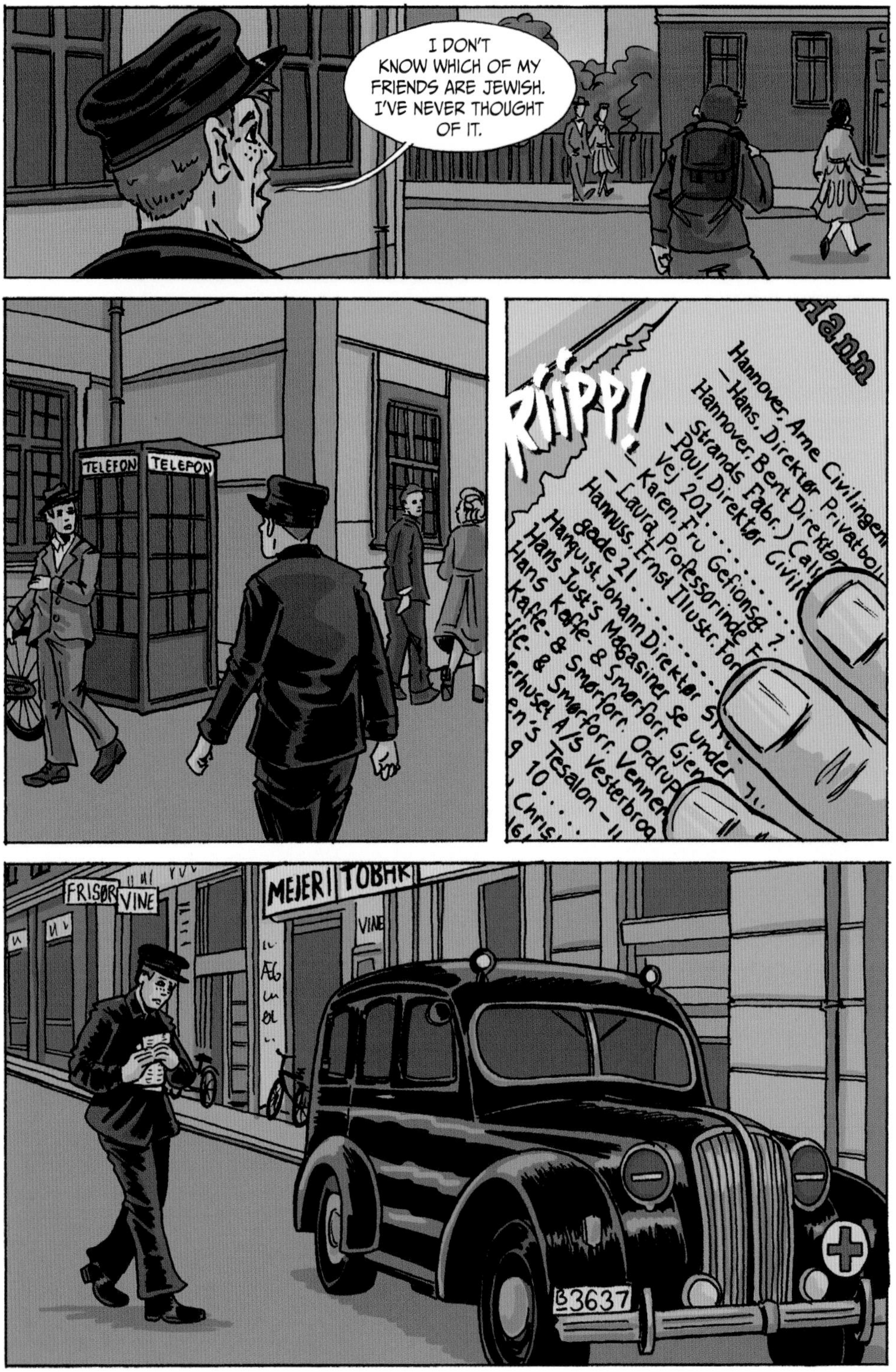
I DON'T KNOW WHICH OF MY FRIENDS ARE JEWISH. I'VE NEVER THOUGHT OF IT.
TELEFON
TELEFON
RIIPP!
Hannover, Arne Civilingen
– Hans, Direktør Privatbol
Hannover, Bent Direktør
– Strands Fabr.) Call
– Poul, Direktør Civil
Vej 201
– Karen, Fru Gefionsg. 7
– Laura, Professorinde F
Hannuss, Ernst Illustr. For
gade 21
Hanquist, Johann Direktør
Hans Just's Magasiner se under
Hans Kaffe- & Smørforr. Gjen
Kaffe- & Smørforr. Ordrup
& Smørforr. Vennem
Tesalon
FRISØR
VINE
MEJERI
TOBAK
VINE
B3637

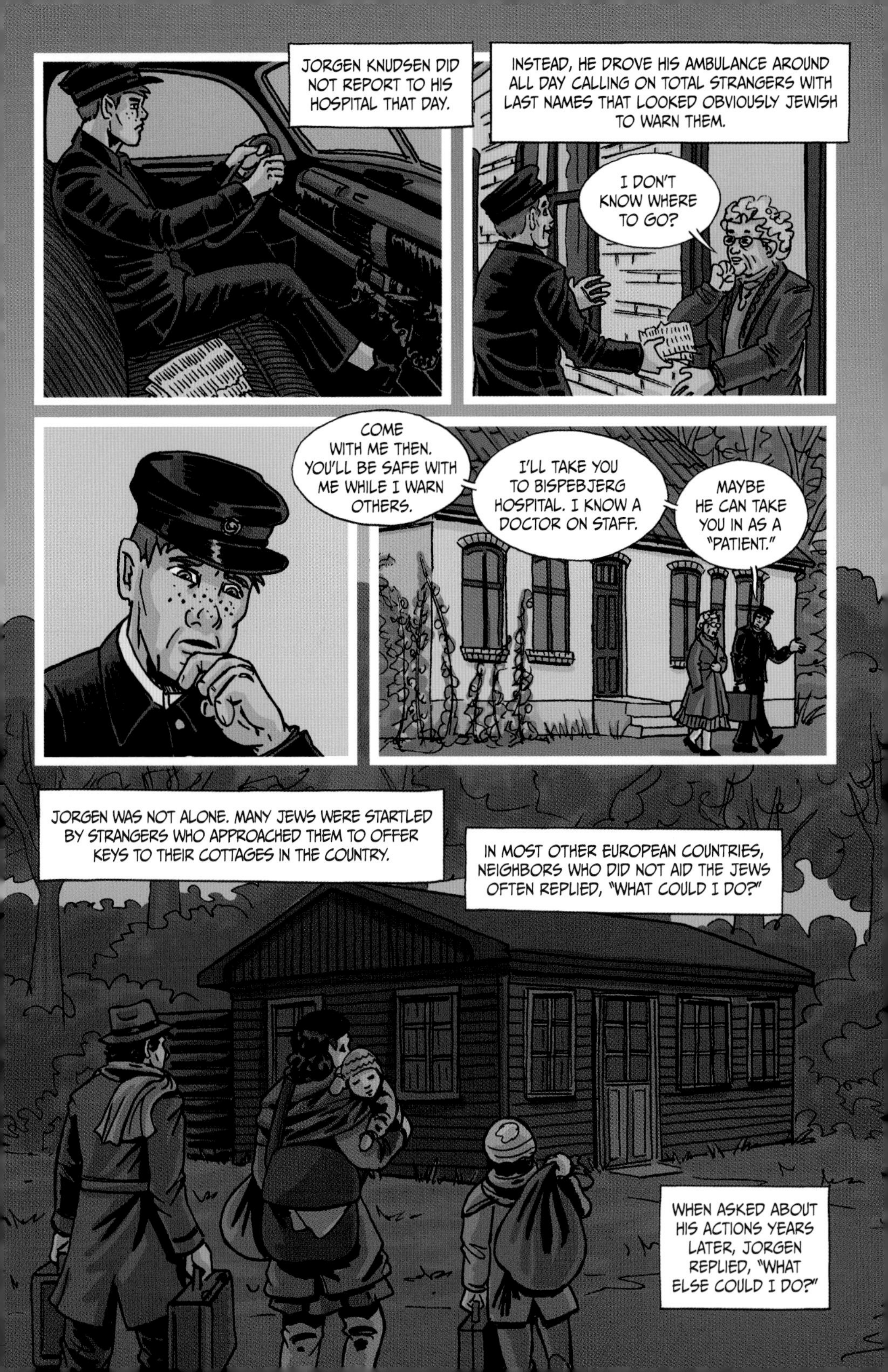
JORGEN KNUDSEN DID NOT REPORT TO HIS HOSPITAL THAT DAY.
INSTEAD, HE DROVE HIS AMBULANCE AROUND ALL DAY CALLING ON TOTAL STRANGERS WITH LAST NAMES THAT LOOKED OBVIOUSLY JEWISH TO WARN THEM.
I DON'T KNOW WHERE TO GO?
COME WITH ME THEN. YOU'LL BE SAFE WITH ME WHILE I WARN OTHERS.
I'LL TAKE YOU TO BISPEBJERG HOSPITAL. I KNOW A DOCTOR ON STAFF.
MAYBE HE CAN TAKE YOU IN AS A "PATIENT."
JORGEN WAS NOT ALONE. MANY JEWS WERE STARTLED BY STRANGERS WHO APPROACHED THEM TO OFFER KEYS TO THEIR COTTAGES IN THE COUNTRY.
IN MOST OTHER EUROPEAN COUNTRIES, NEIGHBORS WHO DID NOT AID THE JEWS OFTEN REPLIED, "WHAT COULD I DO?"
WHEN ASKED ABOUT HIS ACTIONS YEARS LATER, JORGEN REPLIED, "WHAT ELSE COULD I DO?"

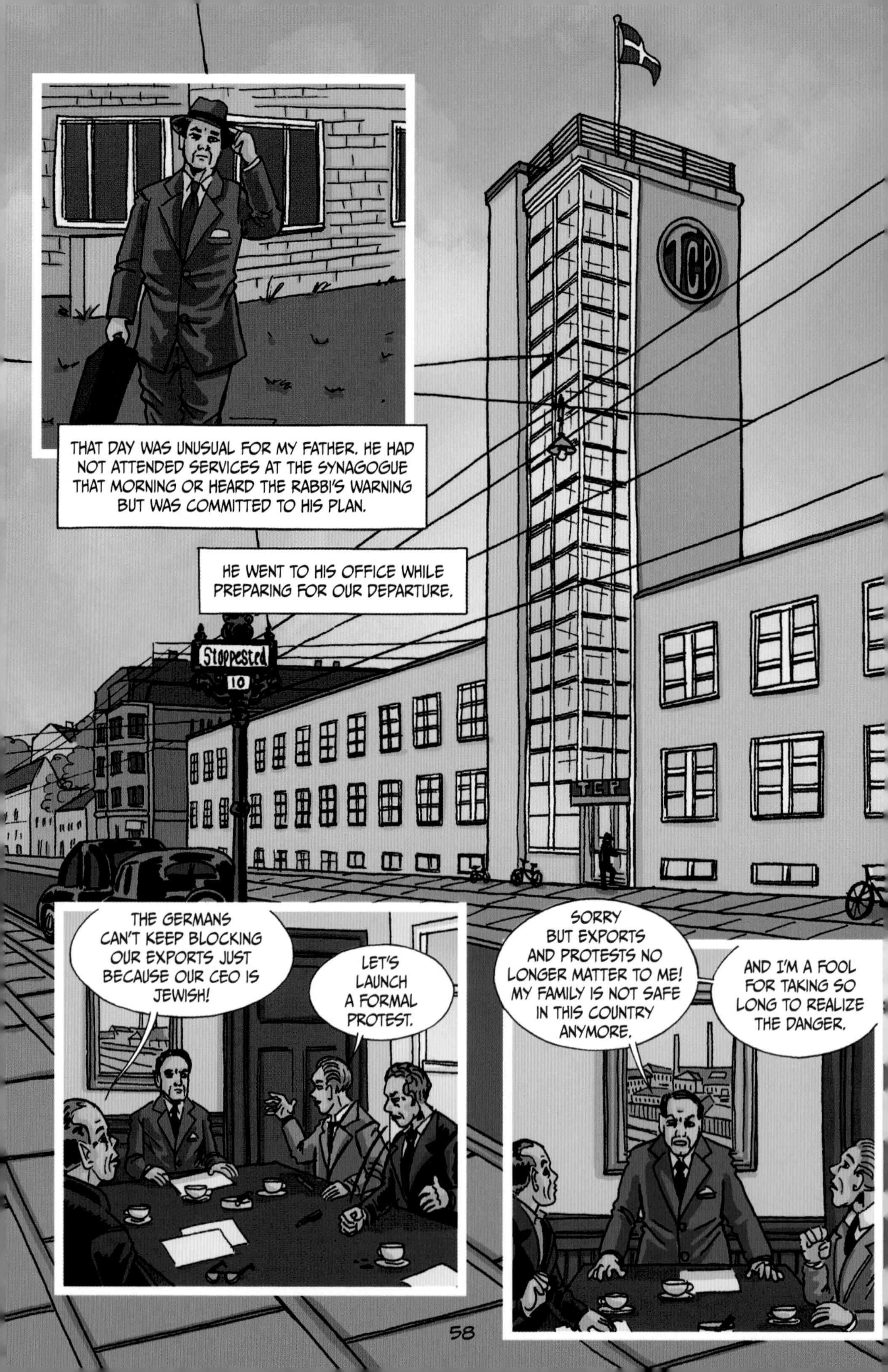

THAT DAY WAS UNUSUAL FOR MY FATHER. HE HAD NOT ATTENDED SERVICES AT THE SYNAGOGUE THAT MORNING OR HEARD THE RABBI'S WARNING BUT WAS COMMITTED TO HIS PLAN.
HE WENT TO HIS OFFICE WHILE PREPARING FOR OUR DEPARTURE.
TCP
Stoppested
10
TCP
THE GERMANS CAN'T KEEP BLOCKING OUR EXPORTS JUST BECAUSE OUR CEO IS JEWISH!
LET'S LAUNCH A FORMAL PROTEST.
SORRY BUT EXPORTS AND PROTESTS NO LONGER MATTER TO ME! MY FAMILY IS NOT SAFE IN THIS COUNTRY ANYMORE.
AND I'M A FOOL FOR TAKING SO LONG TO REALIZE THE DANGER.

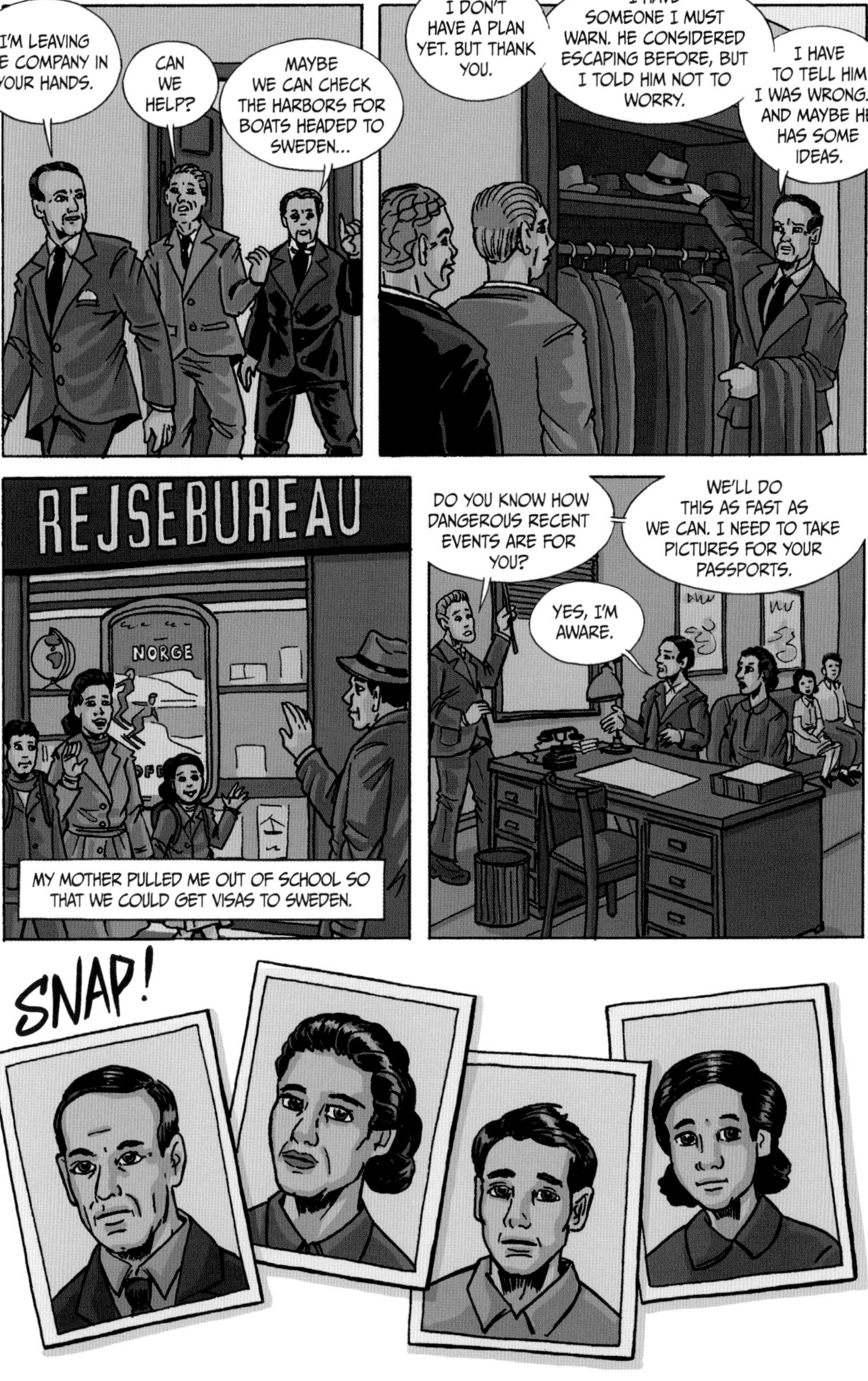
I'M LEAVING THE COMPANY IN YOUR HANDS.
CAN WE HELP?
MAYBE WE CAN CHECK THE HARBORS FOR BOATS HEADED TO SWEDEN...
I DON'T HAVE A PLAN YET. BUT THANK YOU.
I HAVE SOMEONE I MUST WARN. HE CONSIDERED ESCAPING BEFORE, BUT I TOLD HIM NOT TO WORRY.
I HAVE TO TELL HIM I WAS WRONG... AND MAYBE HE HAS SOME IDEAS.
REJSEBUREAU
NORGE
MY MOTHER PULLED ME OUT OF SCHOOL SO THAT WE COULD GET VISAS TO SWEDEN.
DO YOU KNOW HOW DANGEROUS RECENT EVENTS ARE FOR YOU?
WE'LL DO THIS AS FAST AS WE CAN. I NEED TO TAKE PICTURES FOR YOUR PASSPORTS.
YES, I'M AWARE.
SNAP!

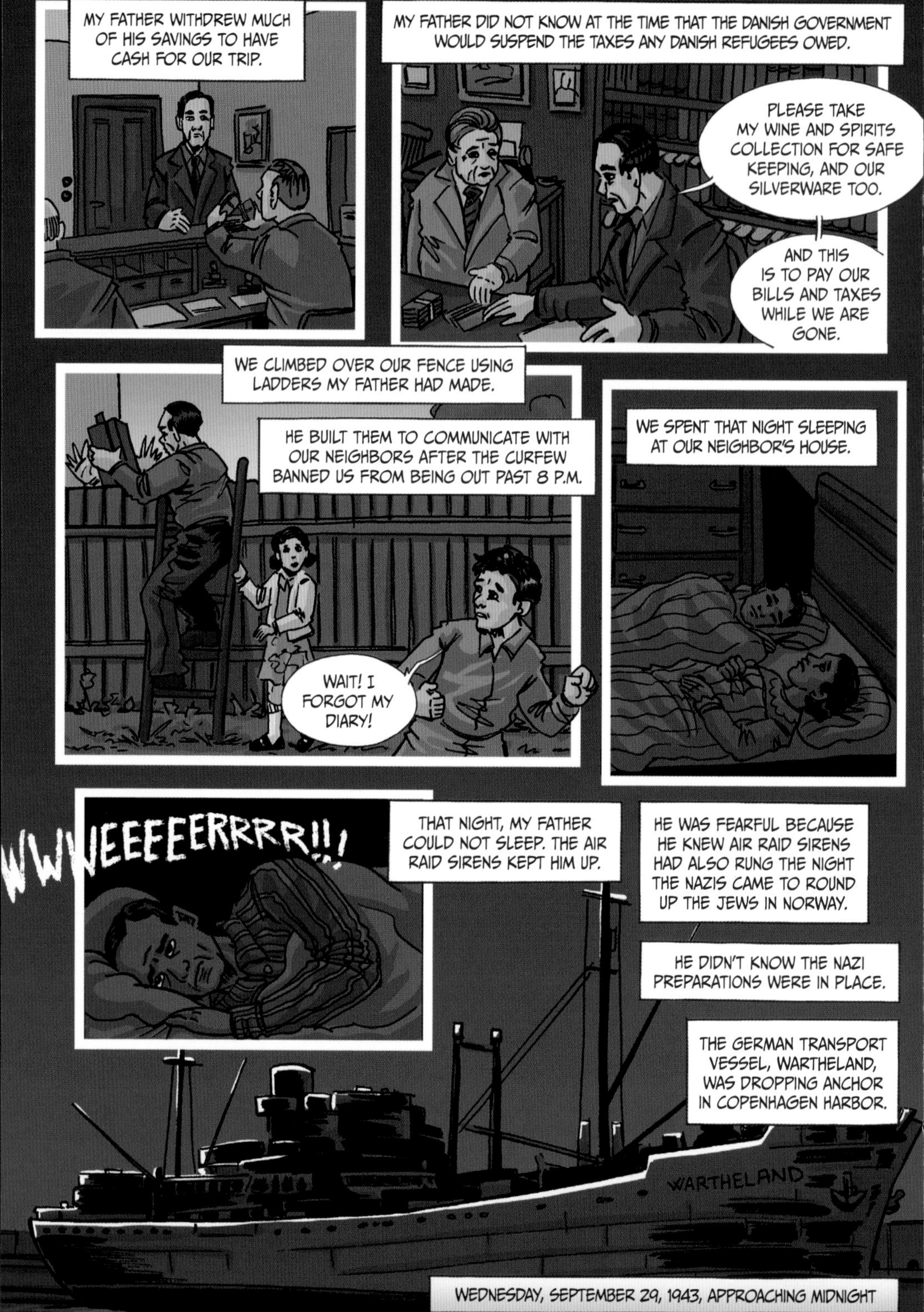
MY FATHER WITHDREW MUCH OF HIS SAVINGS TO HAVE CASH FOR OUR TRIP.
MY FATHER DID NOT KNOW AT THE TIME THAT THE DANISH GOVERNMENT WOULD SUSPEND THE TAXES ANY DANISH REFUGEES OWED.
PLEASE TAKE MY WINE AND SPIRITS COLLECTION FOR SAFE KEEPING, AND OUR SILVERWARE TOO.
AND THIS IS TO PAY OUR BILLS AND TAXES WHILE WE ARE GONE.
WE CLIMBED OVER OUR FENCE USING LADDERS MY FATHER HAD MADE.
HE BUILT THEM TO COMMUNICATE WITH OUR NEIGHBORS AFTER THE CURFEW BANNED US FROM BEING OUT PAST 8 P.M.
WAIT! I FORGOT MY DIARY!
WE SPENT THAT NIGHT SLEEPING AT OUR NEIGHBOR'S HOUSE.
WWWEEEEEERRRRR!!!
THAT NIGHT, MY FATHER COULD NOT SLEEP. THE AIR RAID SIRENS KEPT HIM UP.
HE WAS FEARFUL BECAUSE HE KNEW AIR RAID SIRENS HAD ALSO RUNG THE NIGHT THE NAZIS CAME TO ROUND UP THE JEWS IN NORWAY.
HE DIDN'T KNOW THE NAZI PREPARATIONS WERE IN PLACE.
THE GERMAN TRANSPORT VESSEL, WARTHELAND, WAS DROPPING ANCHOR IN COPENHAGEN HARBOR.
WARTHELAND
WEDNESDAY, SEPTEMBER 29, 1943, APPROACHING MIDNIGHT

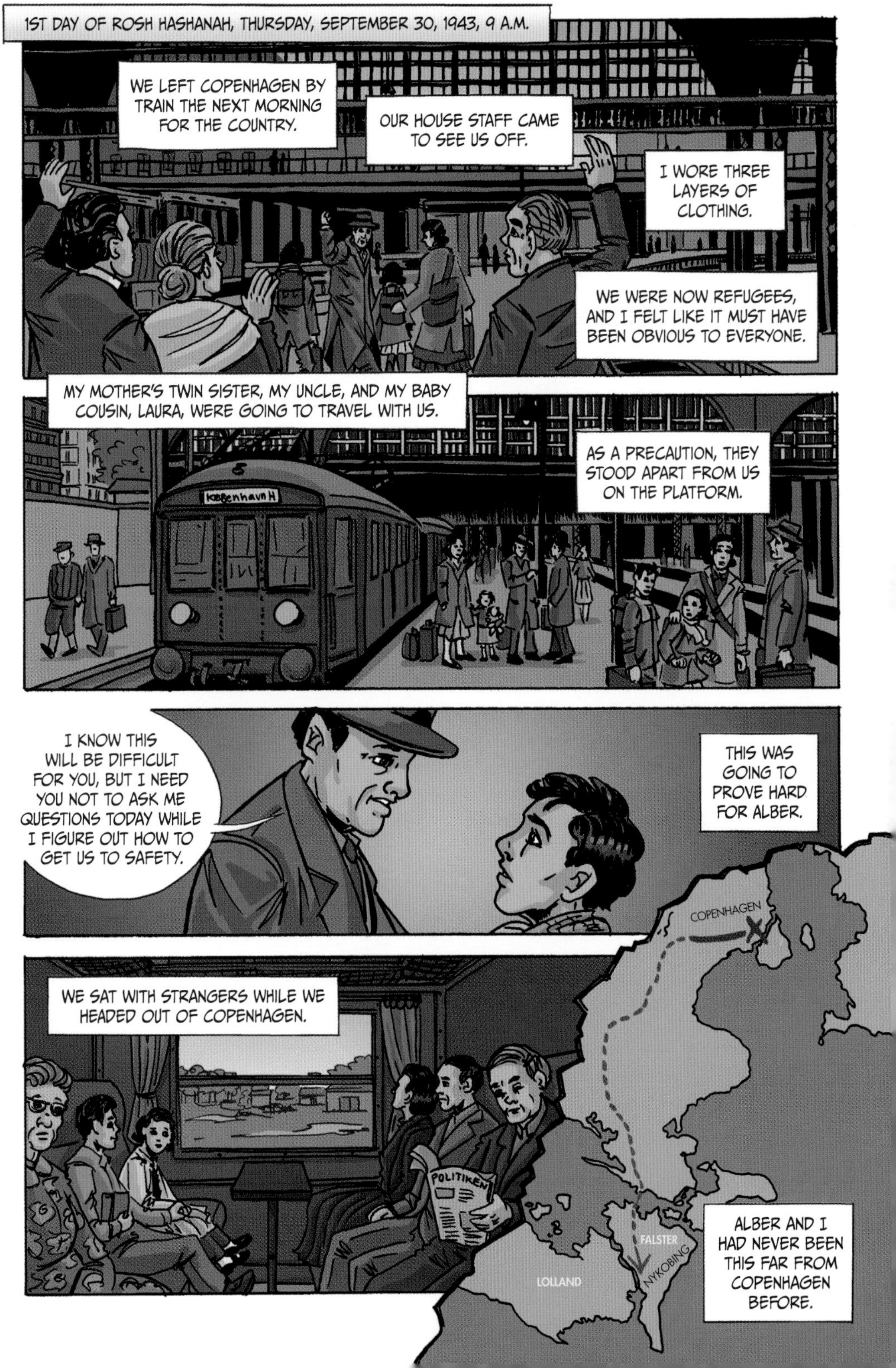

1ST DAY OF ROSH HASHANAH, THURSDAY, SEPTEMBER 30, 1943, 9 A.M.
WE LEFT COPENHAGEN BY TRAIN THE NEXT MORNING FOR THE COUNTRY.
OUR HOUSE STAFF CAME TO SEE US OFF.
I WORE THREE LAYERS OF CLOTHING.
WE WERE NOW REFUGEES, AND I FELT LIKE IT MUST HAVE BEEN OBVIOUS TO EVERYONE.
MY MOTHER'S TWIN SISTER, MY UNCLE, AND MY BABY COUSIN, LAURA, WERE GOING TO TRAVEL WITH US.
København H
AS A PRECAUTION, THEY STOOD APART FROM US ON THE PLATFORM.
I KNOW THIS WILL BE DIFFICULT FOR YOU, BUT I NEED YOU NOT TO ASK ME QUESTIONS TODAY WHILE I FIGURE OUT HOW TO GET US TO SAFETY.
THIS WAS GOING TO PROVE HARD FOR ALBER.
COPENHAGEN
WE SAT WITH STRANGERS WHILE WE HEADED OUT OF COPENHAGEN.
POLITIKEN
FALSTER
NYKOBING
LOLLAND
ALBER AND I HAD NEVER BEEN THIS FAR FROM COPENHAGEN BEFORE.

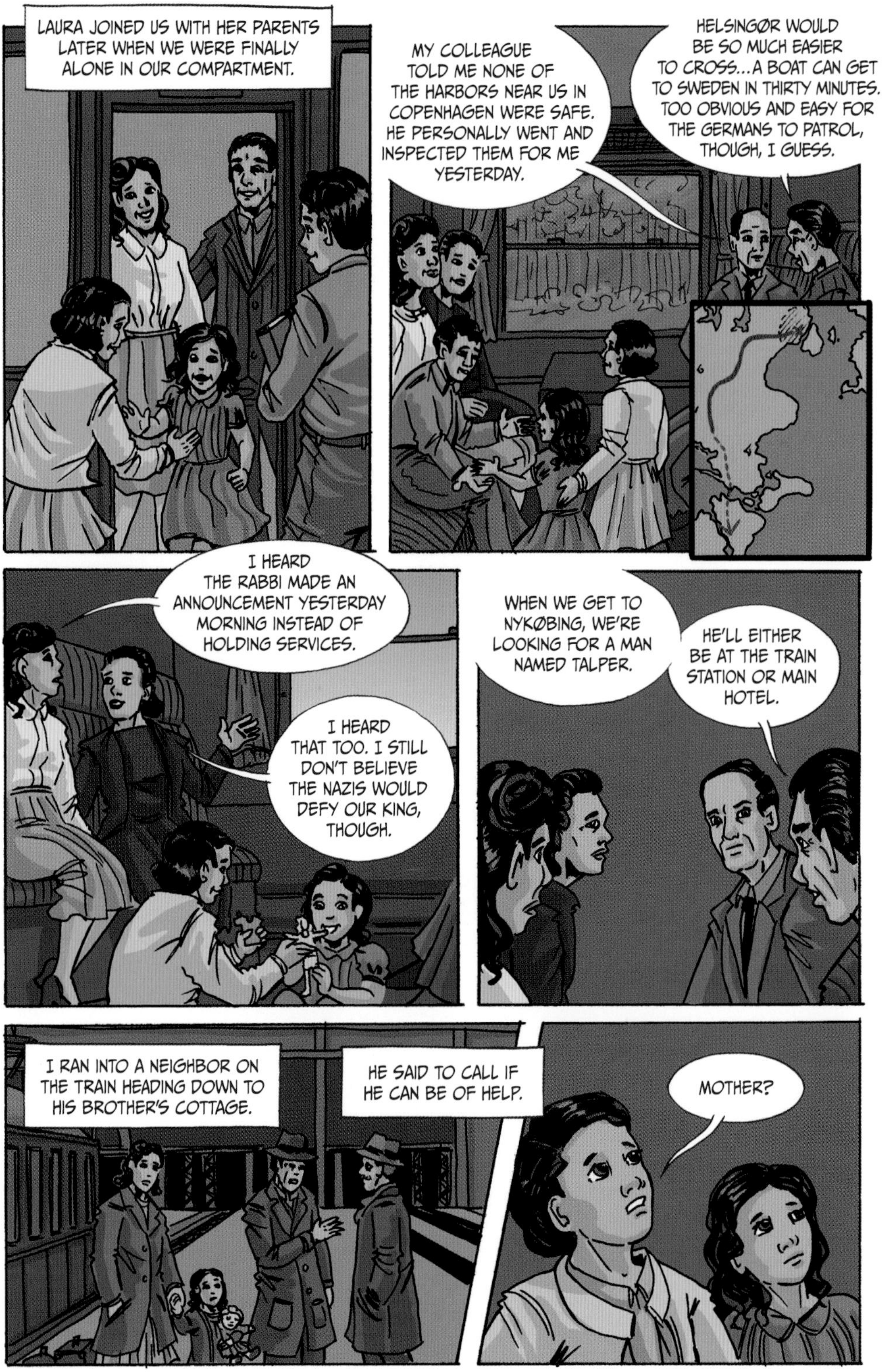
LAURA JOINED US WITH HER PARENTS LATER WHEN WE WERE FINALLY ALONE IN OUR COMPARTMENT.
MY COLLEAGUE TOLD ME NONE OF THE HARBORS NEAR US IN COPENHAGEN WERE SAFE. HE PERSONALLY WENT AND INSPECTED THEM FOR ME YESTERDAY.
HELSINGØR WOULD BE SO MUCH EASIER TO CROSS...A BOAT CAN GET TO SWEDEN IN THIRTY MINUTES. TOO OBVIOUS AND EASY FOR THE GERMANS TO PATROL, THOUGH, I GUESS.
I HEARD THE RABBI MADE AN ANNOUNCEMENT YESTERDAY MORNING INSTEAD OF HOLDING SERVICES.
I HEARD THAT TOO. I STILL DON'T BELIEVE THE NAZIS WOULD DEFY OUR KING, THOUGH.
WHEN WE GET TO NYKØBING, WE'RE LOOKING FOR A MAN NAMED TALPER.
HE'LL EITHER BE AT THE TRAIN STATION OR MAIN HOTEL.
I RAN INTO A NEIGHBOR ON THE TRAIN HEADING DOWN TO HIS BROTHER'S COTTAGE.
HE SAID TO CALL IF HE CAN BE OF HELP.
MOTHER?

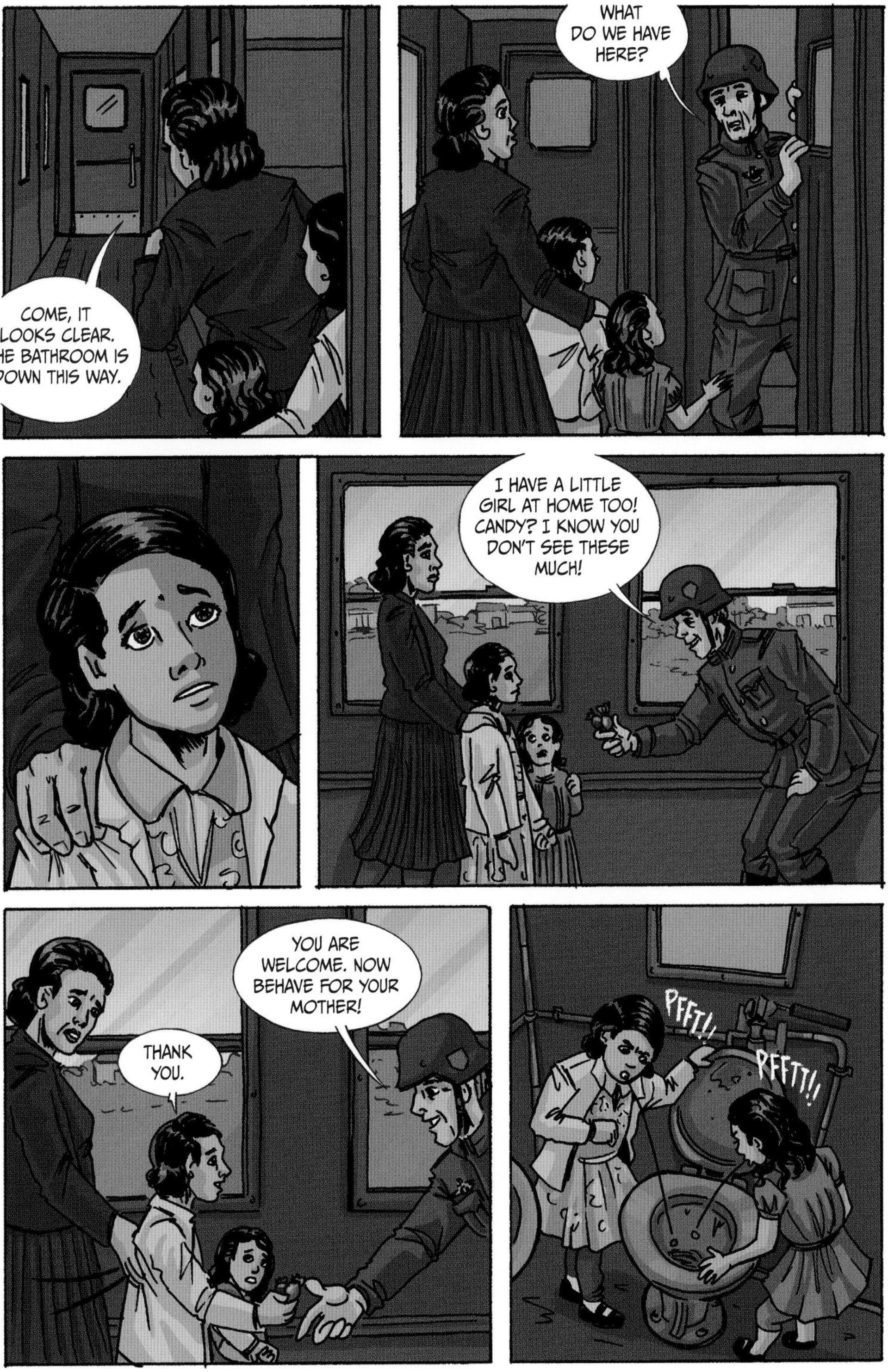
COME, IT LOOKS CLEAR. THE BATHROOM IS DOWN THIS WAY.
WHAT DO WE HAVE HERE?
I HAVE A LITTLE GIRL AT HOME TOO! CANDY? I KNOW YOU DON'T SEE THESE MUCH!
YOU ARE WELCOME. NOW BEHAVE FOR YOUR MOTHER!
THANK YOU.
PFFT!!
PFFTT!!

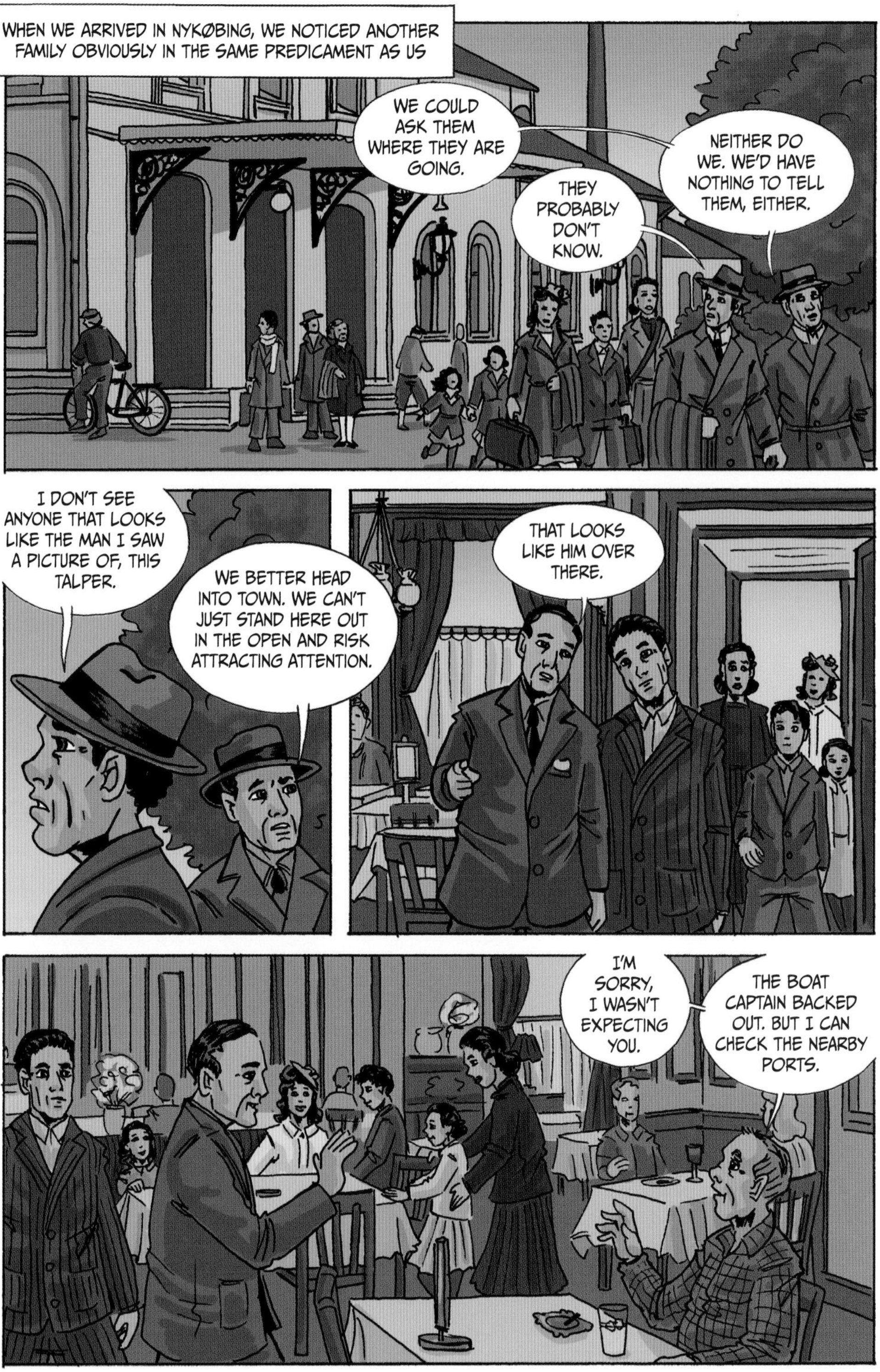
WHEN WE ARRIVED IN NYKØBING, WE NOTICED ANOTHER FAMILY OBVIOUSLY IN THE SAME PREDICAMENT AS US
WE COULD ASK THEM WHERE THEY ARE GOING.
THEY PROBABLY DON'T KNOW.
NEITHER DO WE. WE'D HAVE NOTHING TO TELL THEM, EITHER.
I DON'T SEE ANYONE THAT LOOKS LIKE THE MAN I SAW A PICTURE OF, THIS TALPER.
WE BETTER HEAD INTO TOWN. WE CAN'T JUST STAND HERE OUT IN THE OPEN AND RISK ATTRACTING ATTENTION.
THAT LOOKS LIKE HIM OVER THERE.
I'M SORRY, I WASN'T EXPECTING YOU.
THE BOAT CAPTAIN BACKED OUT. BUT I CAN CHECK THE NEARBY PORTS.

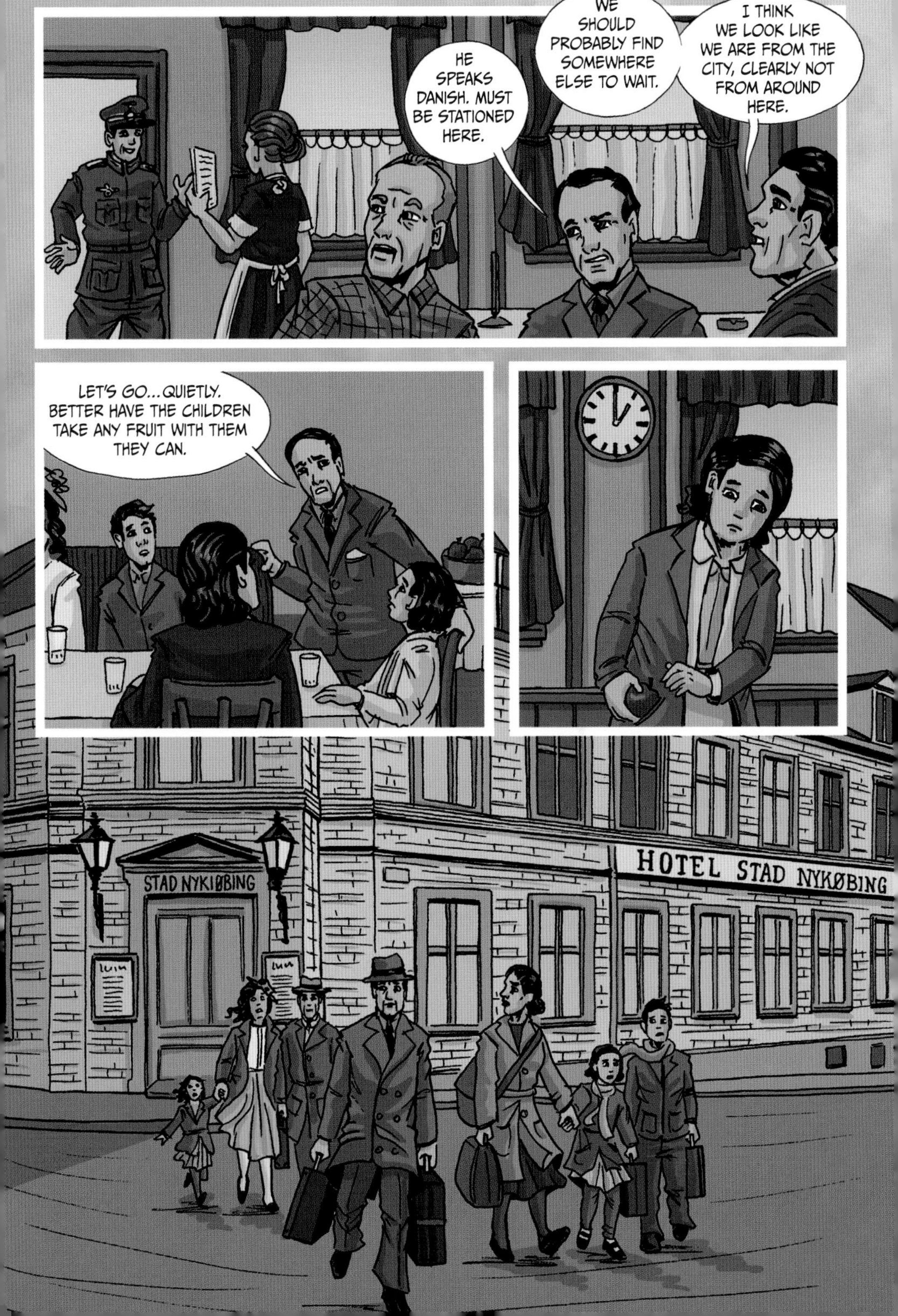
HE SPEAKS DANISH. MUST BE STATIONED HERE.
WE SHOULD PROBABLY FIND SOMEWHERE ELSE TO WAIT.
I THINK WE LOOK LIKE WE ARE FROM THE CITY, CLEARLY NOT FROM AROUND HERE.
LET'S GO...QUIETLY. BETTER HAVE THE CHILDREN TAKE ANY FRUIT WITH THEM THEY CAN.
STAD NYKIØBING
HOTEL STAD NYKØBING

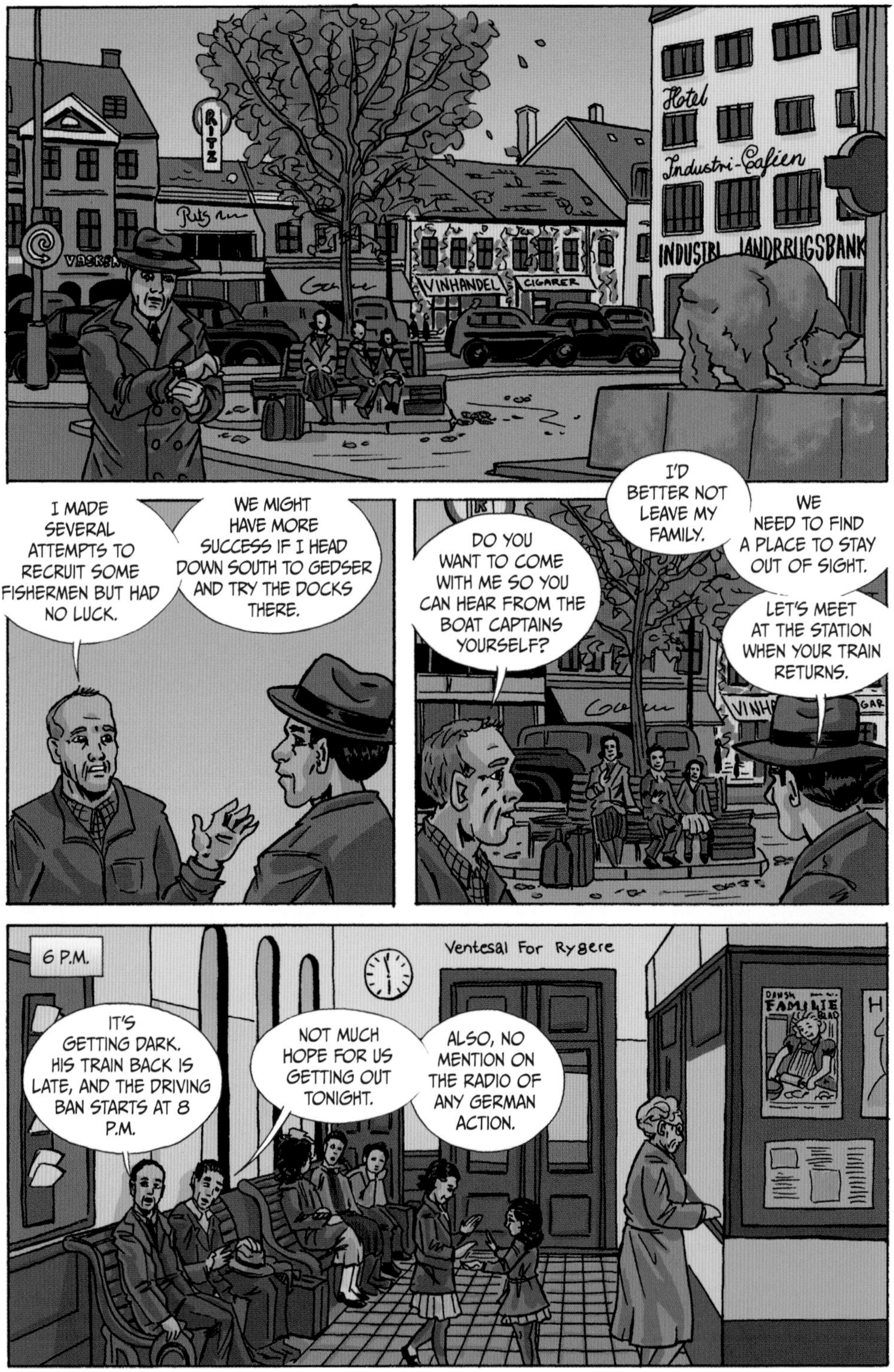
RITZ
Hotel
INDUSTRI LANDBRUGSBANK
VINHANDEL
CIGARER
I MADE SEVERAL ATTEMPTS TO RECRUIT SOME FISHERMEN BUT HAD NO LUCK.
WE MIGHT HAVE MORE SUCCESS IF I HEAD DOWN SOUTH TO GEDSER AND TRY THE DOCKS THERE.
DO YOU WANT TO COME WITH ME SO YOU CAN HEAR FROM THE BOAT CAPTAINS YOURSELF?
I'D BETTER NOT LEAVE MY FAMILY.
WE NEED TO FIND A PLACE TO STAY OUT OF SIGHT.
LET'S MEET AT THE STATION WHEN YOUR TRAIN RETURNS.
6 P.M.
Ventesal For Rygere
IT'S GETTING DARK. HIS TRAIN BACK IS LATE, AND THE DRIVING BAN STARTS AT 8 P.M.
NOT MUCH HOPE FOR US GETTING OUT TONIGHT.
ALSO, NO MENTION ON THE RADIO OF ANY GERMAN ACTION.

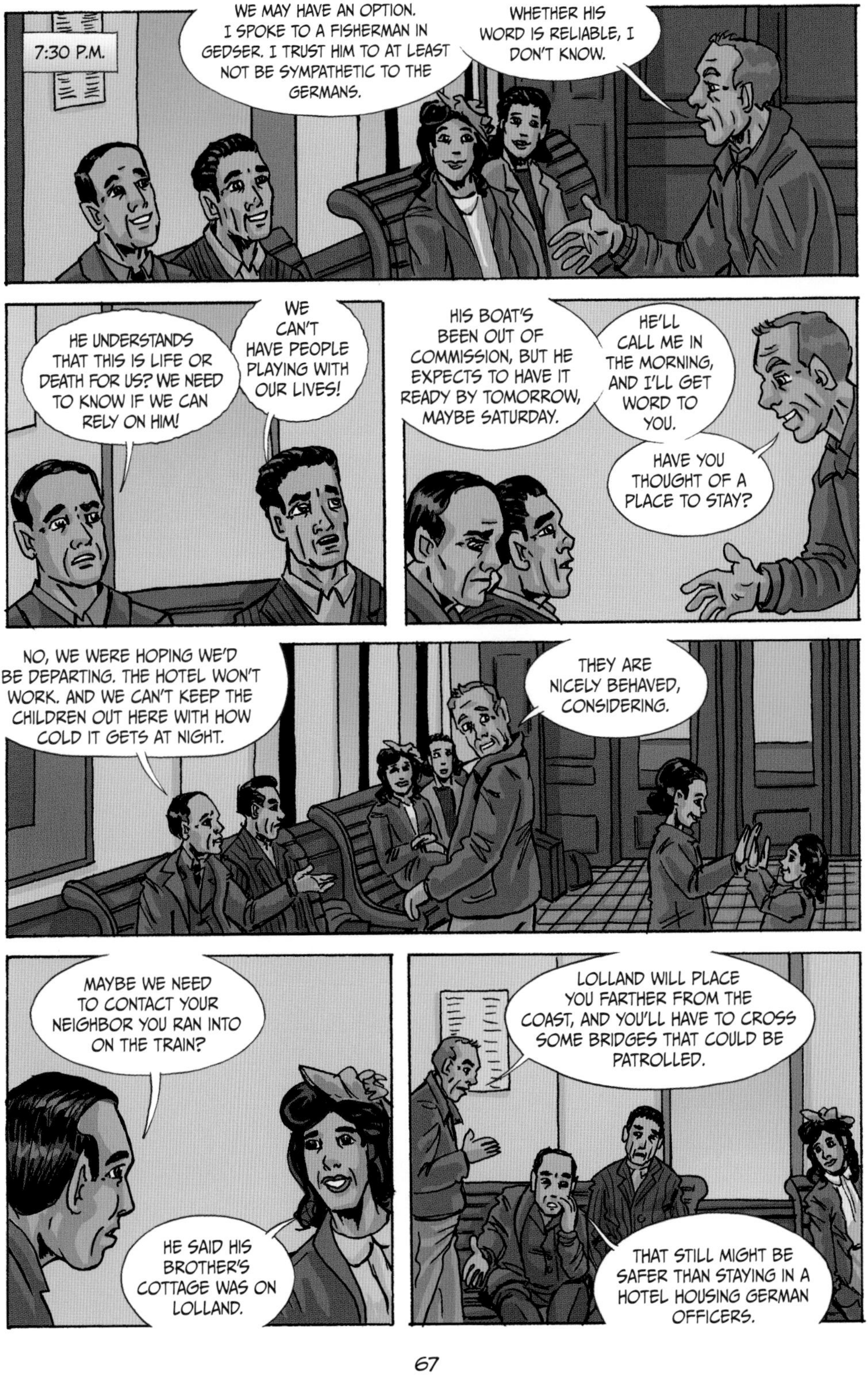
7:30 P.M.
WE MAY HAVE AN OPTION. I SPOKE TO A FISHERMAN IN GEDSER. I TRUST HIM TO AT LEAST NOT BE SYMPATHETIC TO THE GERMANS.
WHETHER HIS WORD IS RELIABLE, I DON'T KNOW.
HE UNDERSTANDS THAT THIS IS LIFE OR DEATH FOR US? WE NEED TO KNOW IF WE CAN RELY ON HIM!
WE CAN'T HAVE PEOPLE PLAYING WITH OUR LIVES!
HIS BOAT'S BEEN OUT OF COMMISSION, BUT HE EXPECTS TO HAVE IT READY BY TOMORROW, MAYBE SATURDAY.
HE'LL CALL ME IN THE MORNING, AND I'LL GET WORD TO YOU.
HAVE YOU THOUGHT OF A PLACE TO STAY?
NO, WE WERE HOPING WE'D BE DEPARTING. THE HOTEL WON'T WORK. AND WE CAN'T KEEP THE CHILDREN OUT HERE WITH HOW COLD IT GETS AT NIGHT.
THEY ARE NICELY BEHAVED, CONSIDERING.
MAYBE WE NEED TO CONTACT YOUR NEIGHBOR YOU RAN INTO ON THE TRAIN?
HE SAID HIS BROTHER'S COTTAGE WAS ON LOLLAND.
LOLLAND WILL PLACE YOU FARTHER FROM THE COAST, AND YOU'LL HAVE TO CROSS SOME BRIDGES THAT COULD BE PATROLLED.
THAT STILL MIGHT BE SAFER THAN STAYING IN A HOTEL HOUSING GERMAN OFFICERS.

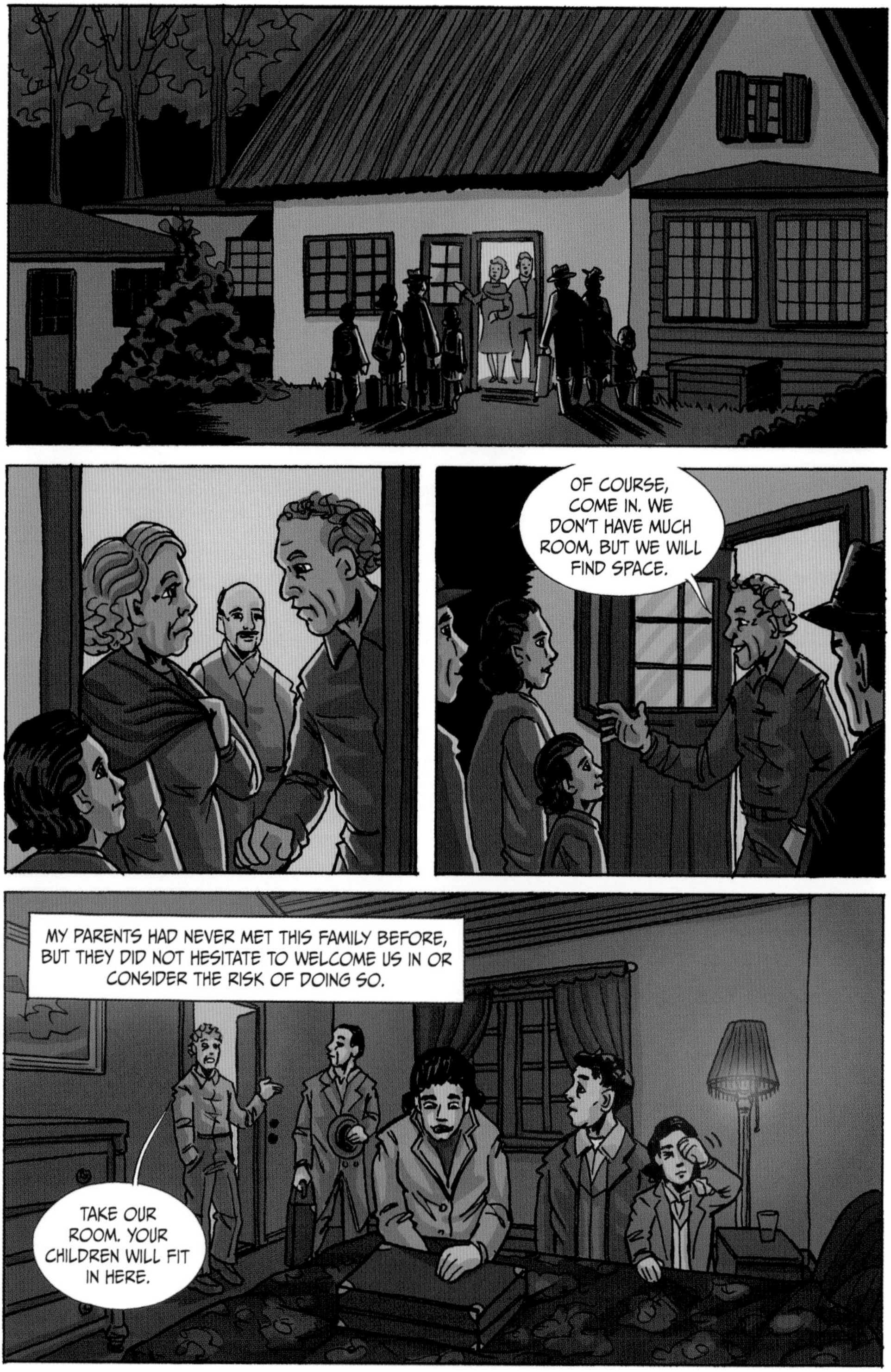
OF COURSE, COME IN. WE DON'T HAVE MUCH ROOM, BUT WE WILL FIND SPACE.
MY PARENTS HAD NEVER MET THIS FAMILY BEFORE, BUT THEY DID NOT HESITATE TO WELCOME US IN OR CONSIDER THE RISK OF DOING SO.
TAKE OUR ROOM. YOUR CHILDREN WILL FIT IN HERE.

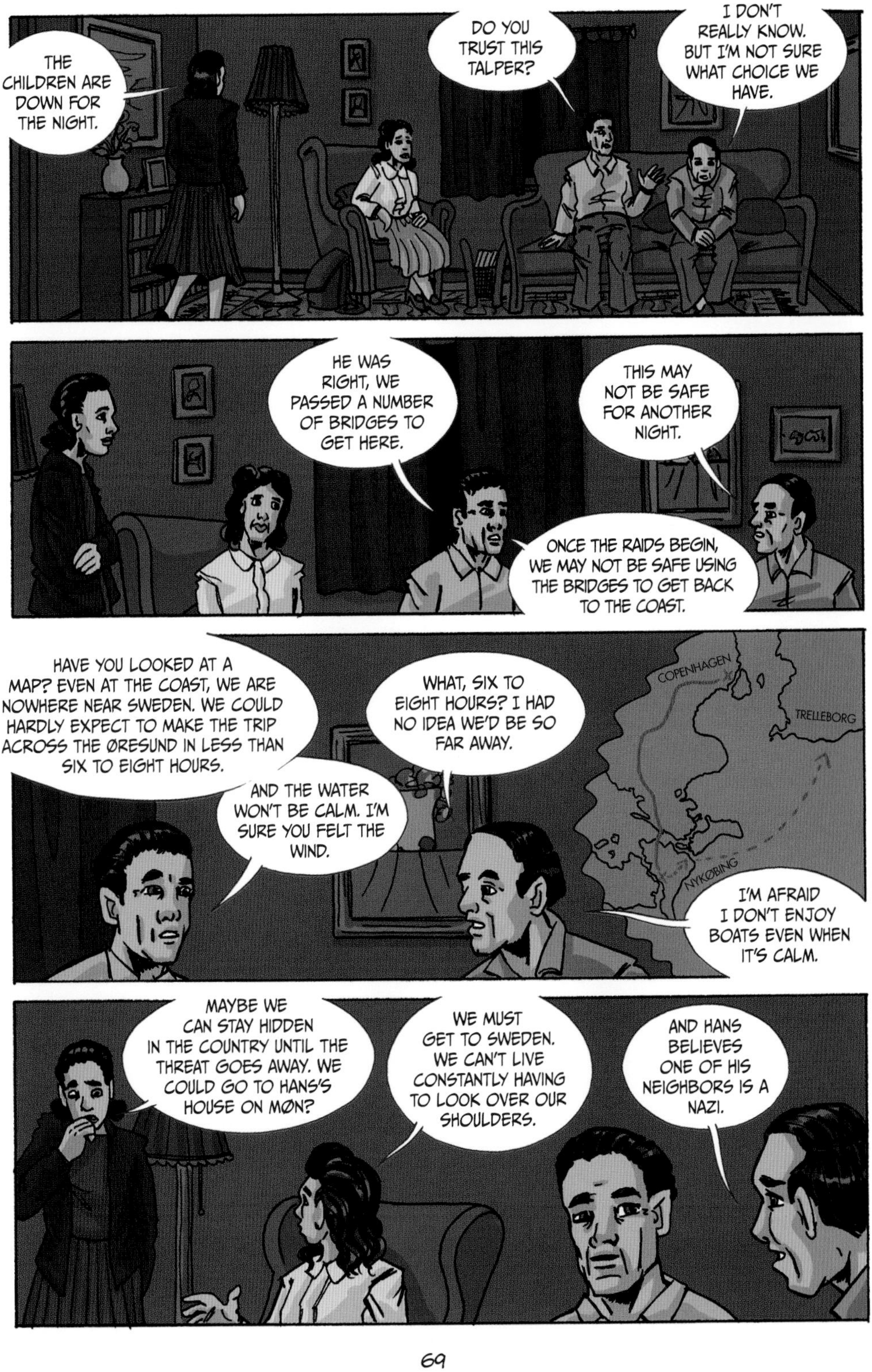
THE CHILDREN ARE DOWN FOR THE NIGHT.
DO YOU TRUST THIS TALPER?
I DON'T REALLY KNOW. BUT I'M NOT SURE WHAT CHOICE WE HAVE.
HE WAS RIGHT, WE PASSED A NUMBER OF BRIDGES TO GET HERE.
THIS MAY NOT BE SAFE FOR ANOTHER NIGHT.
ONCE THE RAIDS BEGIN, WE MAY NOT BE SAFE USING THE BRIDGES TO GET BACK TO THE COAST.
HAVE YOU LOOKED AT A MAP? EVEN AT THE COAST, WE ARE NOWHERE NEAR SWEDEN. WE COULD HARDLY EXPECT TO MAKE THE TRIP ACROSS THE ØRESUND IN LESS THAN SIX TO EIGHT HOURS.
WHAT, SIX TO EIGHT HOURS? I HAD NO IDEA WE'D BE SO FAR AWAY.
AND THE WATER WON'T BE CALM. I'M SURE YOU FELT THE WIND.
COPENHAGEN
TRELLEBORG
NYKØBING
I'M AFRAID I DON'T ENJOY BOATS EVEN WHEN IT'S CALM.
MAYBE WE CAN STAY HIDDEN IN THE COUNTRY UNTIL THE THREAT GOES AWAY. WE COULD GO TO HANS'S HOUSE ON MØN?
WE MUST GET TO SWEDEN. WE CAN'T LIVE CONSTANTLY HAVING TO LOOK OVER OUR SHOULDERS.
AND HANS BELIEVES ONE OF HIS NEIGHBORS IS A NAZI.

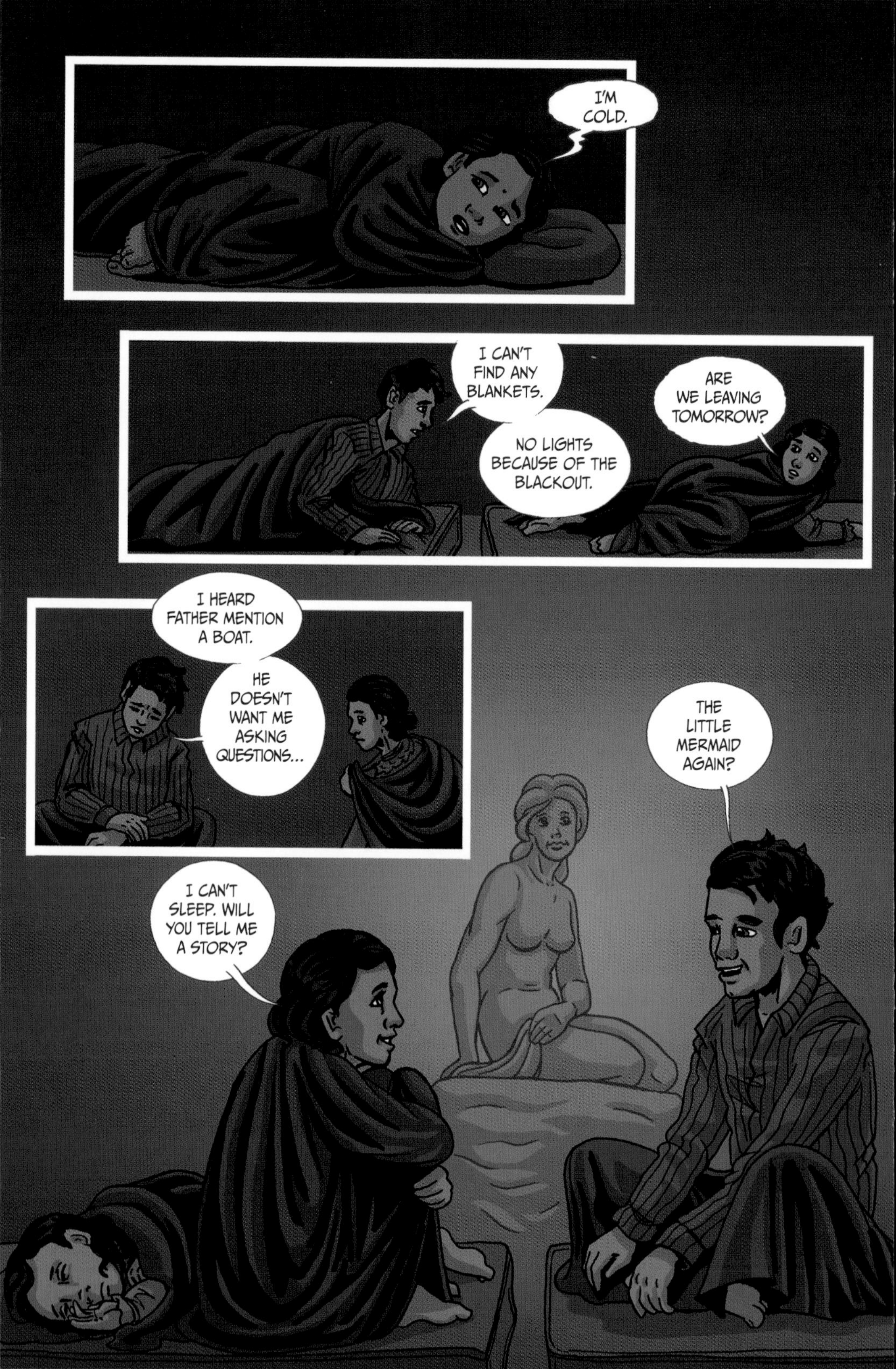
I'M COLD.
I CAN'T FIND ANY BLANKETS.
NO LIGHTS BECAUSE OF THE BLACKOUT.
ARE WE LEAVING TOMORROW?
I HEARD FATHER MENTION A BOAT.
HE DOESN'T WANT ME ASKING QUESTIONS...
THE LITTLE MERMAID AGAIN?
I CAN'T SLEEP. WILL YOU TELL ME A STORY?

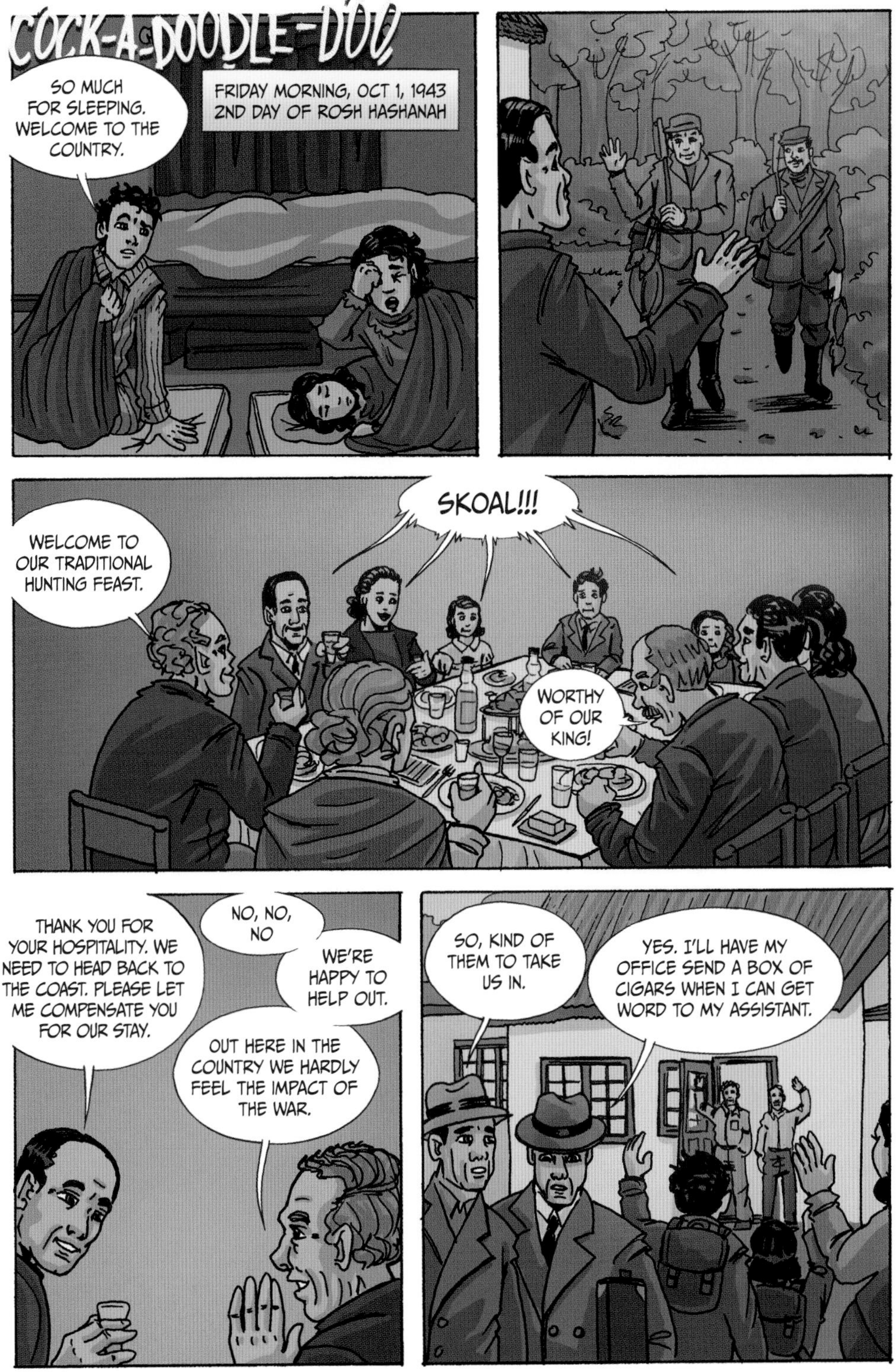
COCK-A-DOODLE-DOO
SO MUCH FOR SLEEPING. WELCOME TO THE COUNTRY.
FRIDAY MORNING, OCT 1, 1943
2ND DAY OF ROSH HASHANAH
SKOAL!!!
WELCOME TO OUR TRADITIONAL HUNTING FEAST.
WORTHY OF OUR KING!
THANK YOU FOR YOUR HOSPITALITY. WE NEED TO HEAD BACK TO THE COAST. PLEASE LET ME COMPENSATE YOU FOR OUR STAY.
NO, NO, NO
WE'RE HAPPY TO HELP OUT.
OUT HERE IN THE COUNTRY WE HARDLY FEEL THE IMPACT OF THE WAR.
SO, KIND OF THEM TO TAKE US IN.
YES. I'LL HAVE MY OFFICE SEND A BOX OF CIGARS WHEN I CAN GET WORD TO MY ASSISTANT.

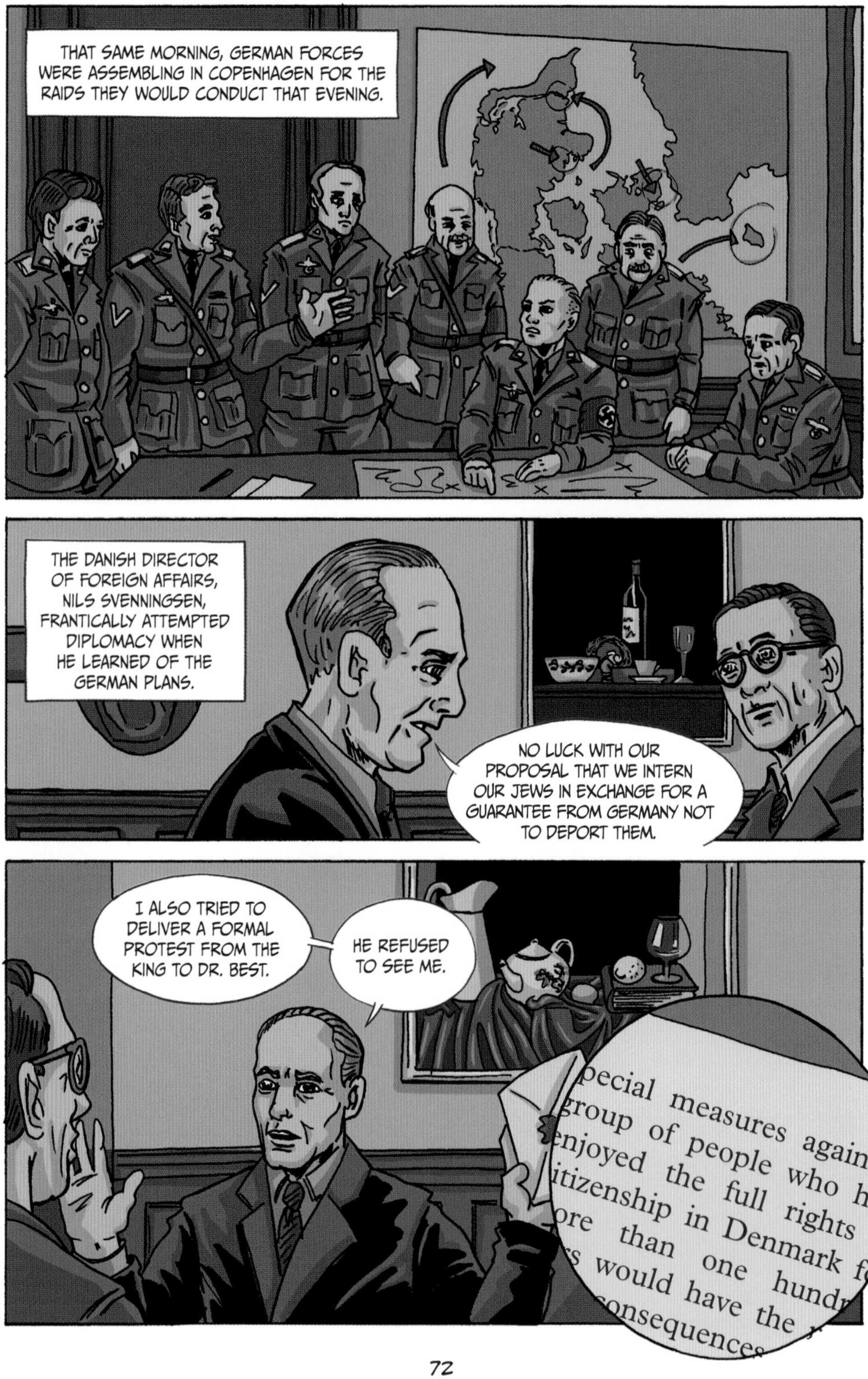
THAT SAME MORNING, GERMAN FORCES WERE ASSEMBLING IN COPENHAGEN FOR THE RAIDS THEY WOULD CONDUCT THAT EVENING.
THE DANISH DIRECTOR OF FOREIGN AFFAIRS, NILS SVENNINGSEN, FRANTICALLY ATTEMPTED DIPLOMACY WHEN HE LEARNED OF THE GERMAN PLANS.
NO LUCK WITH OUR PROPOSAL THAT WE INTERN OUR JEWS IN EXCHANGE FOR A GUARANTEE FROM GERMANY NOT TO DEPORT THEM.
I ALSO TRIED TO DELIVER A FORMAL PROTEST FROM THE KING TO DR. BEST.
HE REFUSED TO SEE ME.
pecial measures against
group of people who hav
enjoyed the full rights
itizenship in Denmark f
ore than one hundr
s would have the
onsequences

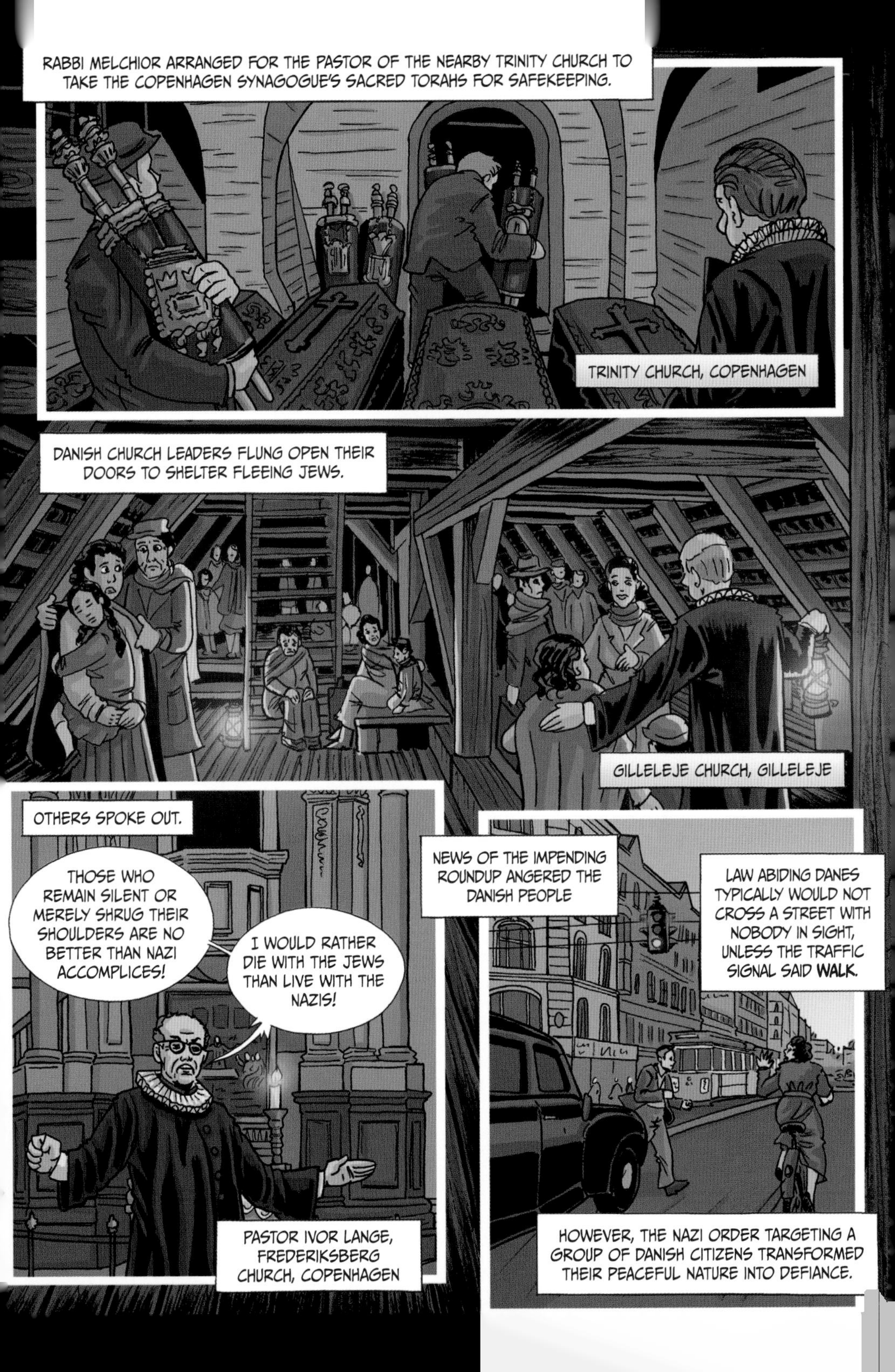

RABBI MELCHIOR ARRANGED FOR THE PASTOR OF THE NEARBY TRINITY CHURCH TO TAKE THE COPENHAGEN SYNAGOGUE'S SACRED TORAHS FOR SAFEKEEPING.
TRINITY CHURCH, COPENHAGEN
DANISH CHURCH LEADERS FLUNG OPEN THEIR DOORS TO SHELTER FLEEING JEWS.
GILLELEJE CHURCH, GILLELEJE
OTHERS SPOKE OUT.
THOSE WHO REMAIN SILENT OR MERELY SHRUG THEIR SHOULDERS ARE NO BETTER THAN NAZI ACCOMPLICES!
I WOULD RATHER DIE WITH THE JEWS THAN LIVE WITH THE NAZIS!
PASTOR IVOR LANGE, FREDERIKSBERG CHURCH, COPENHAGEN
NEWS OF THE IMPENDING ROUNDUP ANGERED THE DANISH PEOPLE
LAW ABIDING DANES TYPICALLY WOULD NOT CROSS A STREET WITH NOBODY IN SIGHT, UNLESS THE TRAFFIC SIGNAL SAID **WALK**.
HOWEVER, THE NAZI ORDER TARGETING A GROUP OF DANISH CITIZENS TRANSFORMED THEIR PEACEFUL NATURE INTO DEFIANCE.

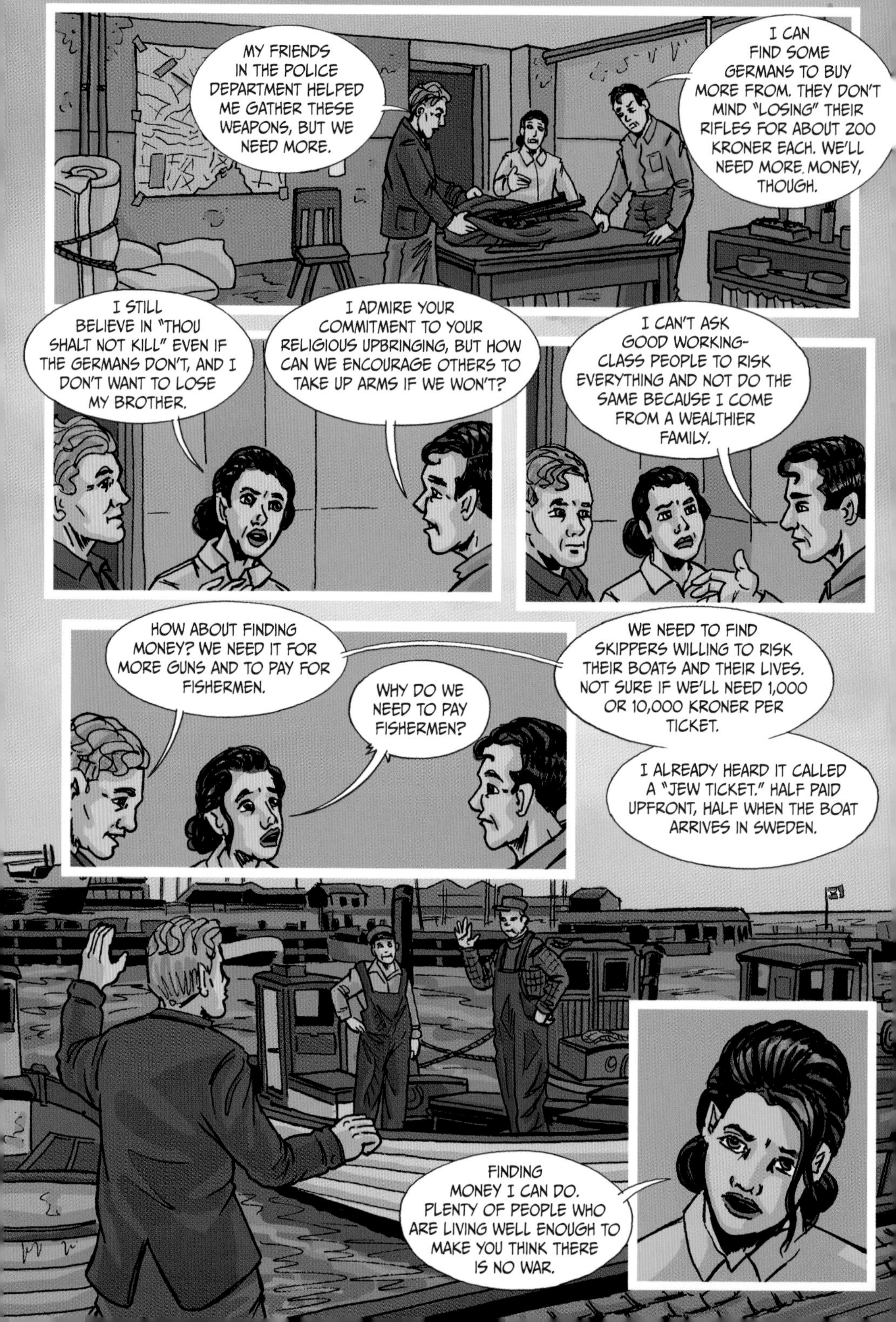
MY FRIENDS IN THE POLICE DEPARTMENT HELPED ME GATHER THESE WEAPONS, BUT WE NEED MORE.
I CAN FIND SOME GERMANS TO BUY MORE FROM. THEY DON'T MIND "LOSING" THEIR RIFLES FOR ABOUT 200 KRONER EACH. WE'LL NEED MORE MONEY, THOUGH.
I STILL BELIEVE IN "THOU SHALT NOT KILL" EVEN IF THE GERMANS DON'T, AND I DON'T WANT TO LOSE MY BROTHER.
I ADMIRE YOUR COMMITMENT TO YOUR RELIGIOUS UPBRINGING, BUT HOW CAN WE ENCOURAGE OTHERS TO TAKE UP ARMS IF WE WON'T?
I CAN'T ASK GOOD WORKING-CLASS PEOPLE TO RISK EVERYTHING AND NOT DO THE SAME BECAUSE I COME FROM A WEALTHIER FAMILY.
HOW ABOUT FINDING MONEY? WE NEED IT FOR MORE GUNS AND TO PAY FOR FISHERMEN.
WHY DO WE NEED TO PAY FISHERMEN?
WE NEED TO FIND SKIPPERS WILLING TO RISK THEIR BOATS AND THEIR LIVES. NOT SURE IF WE'LL NEED 1,000 OR 10,000 KRONER PER TICKET.
I ALREADY HEARD IT CALLED A "JEW TICKET." HALF PAID UPFRONT, HALF WHEN THE BOAT ARRIVES IN SWEDEN.
FINDING MONEY I CAN DO. PLENTY OF PEOPLE WHO ARE LIVING WELL ENOUGH TO MAKE YOU THINK THERE IS NO WAR.

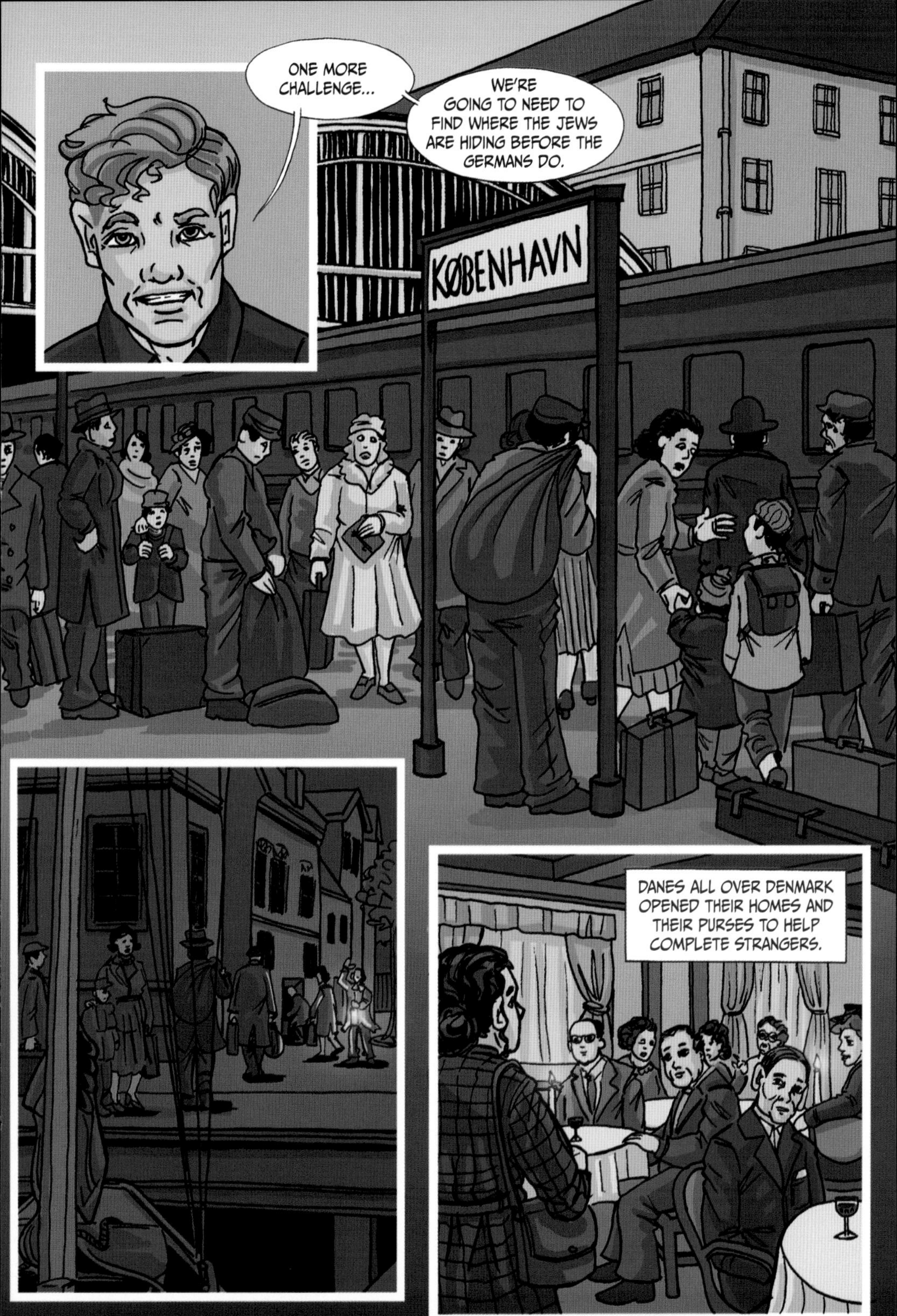
ONE MORE CHALLENGE...
WE'RE GOING TO NEED TO FIND WHERE THE JEWS ARE HIDING BEFORE THE GERMANS DO.
KØBENHAVN
DANES ALL OVER DENMARK OPENED THEIR HOMES AND THEIR PURSES TO HELP COMPLETE STRANGERS.

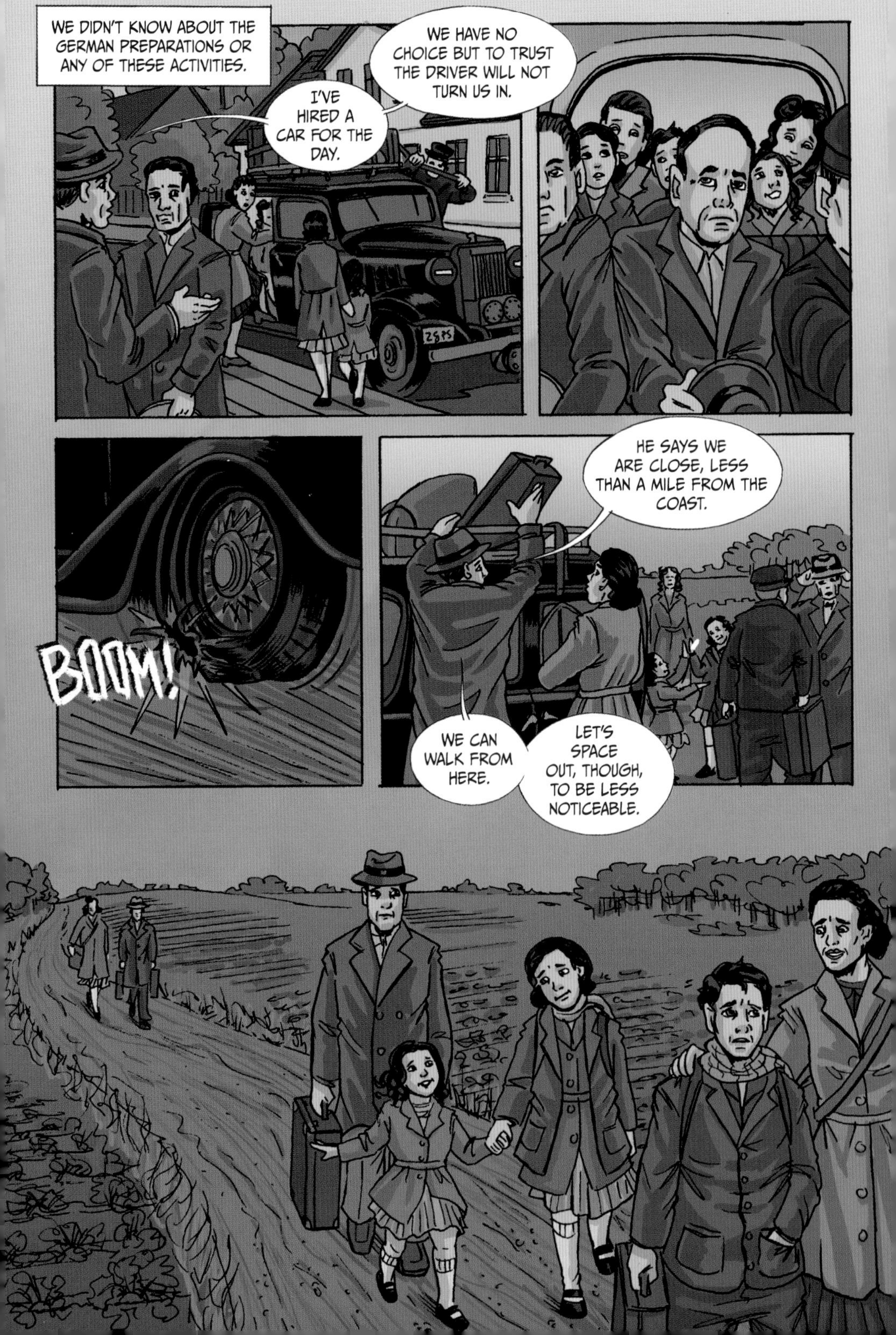
WE DIDN'T KNOW ABOUT THE GERMAN PREPARATIONS OR ANY OF THESE ACTIVITIES.
I'VE HIRED A CAR FOR THE DAY.
WE HAVE NO CHOICE BUT TO TRUST THE DRIVER WILL NOT TURN US IN.
BOOM!
HE SAYS WE ARE CLOSE, LESS THAN A MILE FROM THE COAST.
WE CAN WALK FROM HERE.
LET'S SPACE OUT, THOUGH, TO BE LESS NOTICEABLE.

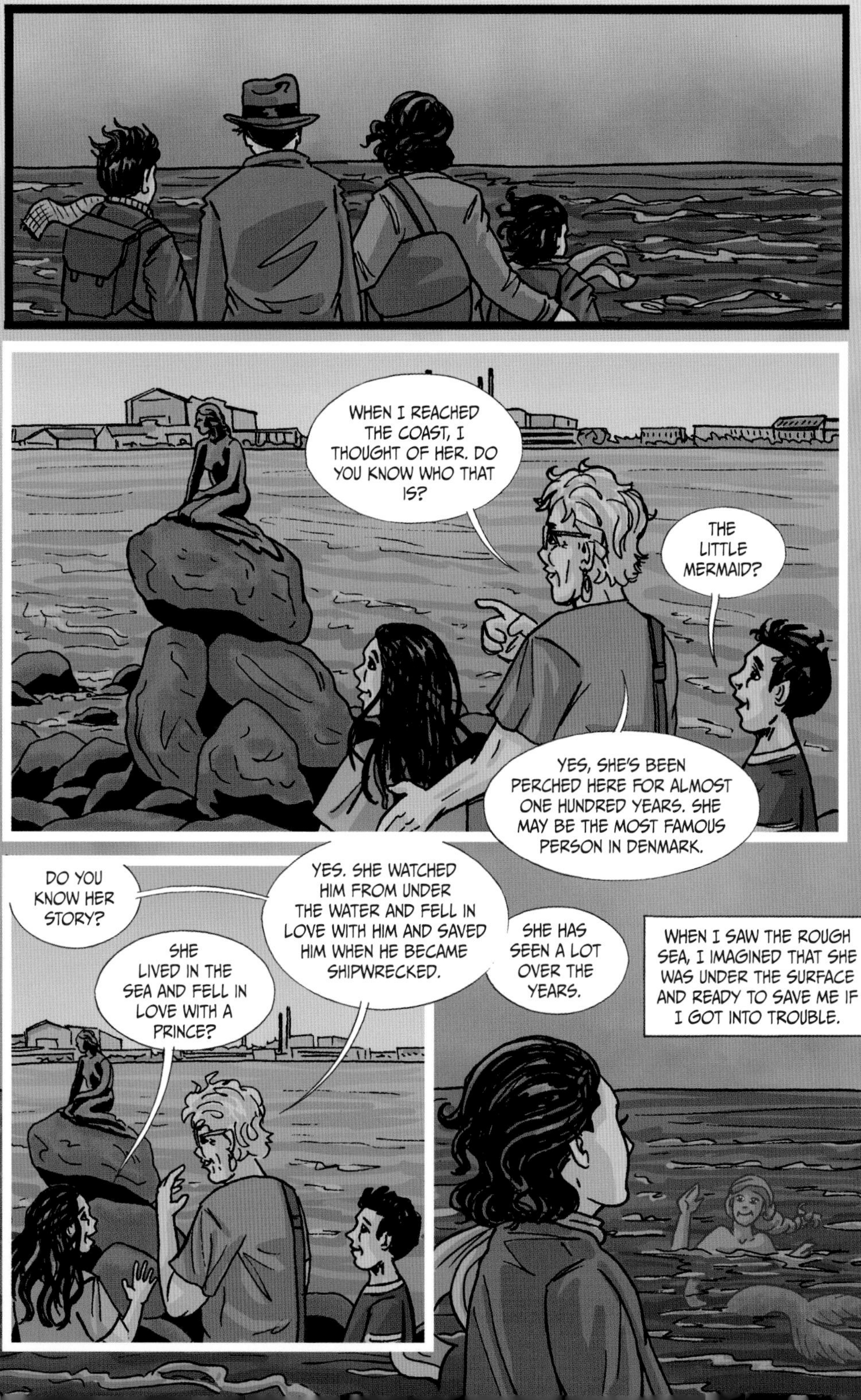
WHEN I REACHED THE COAST, I THOUGHT OF HER. DO YOU KNOW WHO THAT IS?
THE LITTLE MERMAID?
YES, SHE'S BEEN PERCHED HERE FOR ALMOST ONE HUNDRED YEARS. SHE MAY BE THE MOST FAMOUS PERSON IN DENMARK.
DO YOU KNOW HER STORY?
SHE LIVED IN THE SEA AND FELL IN LOVE WITH A PRINCE?
YES. SHE WATCHED HIM FROM UNDER THE WATER AND FELL IN LOVE WITH HIM AND SAVED HIM WHEN HE BECAME SHIPWRECKED.
SHE HAS SEEN A LOT OVER THE YEARS.
WHEN I SAW THE ROUGH SEA, I IMAGINED THAT SHE WAS UNDER THE SURFACE AND READY TO SAVE ME IF I GOT INTO TROUBLE.

FALSTER COASTLINE AT GRØNSUND, 6 P.M.

THE SKIPPER CONTACTED ME LAST MINUTE, SAID HE HAD AGGRAVATED A HERNIA THIS MORNING COMPLETING A CHORE.

HE INSISTED ON VISITING HIS DOCTOR.

WE NEED TO WAIT FOR A MESSAGE. I'M HOPING TO HEAR FROM HIM BY 7:30.

HARD TO IMAGINE SOMEONE MAKING A STORY LIKE THAT UP!

ALMOST MAKES IT SOUND BELIEVABLE!

SO, WE JUST WAIT?

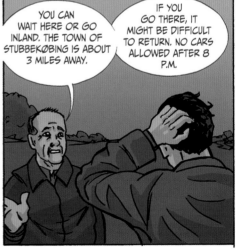

YOU CAN WAIT HERE OR GO INLAND. THE TOWN OF STUBBEKØBING IS ABOUT 3 MILES AWAY.

IF YOU GO THERE, IT MIGHT BE DIFFICULT TO RETURN. NO CARS ALLOWED AFTER 8 P.M.

78

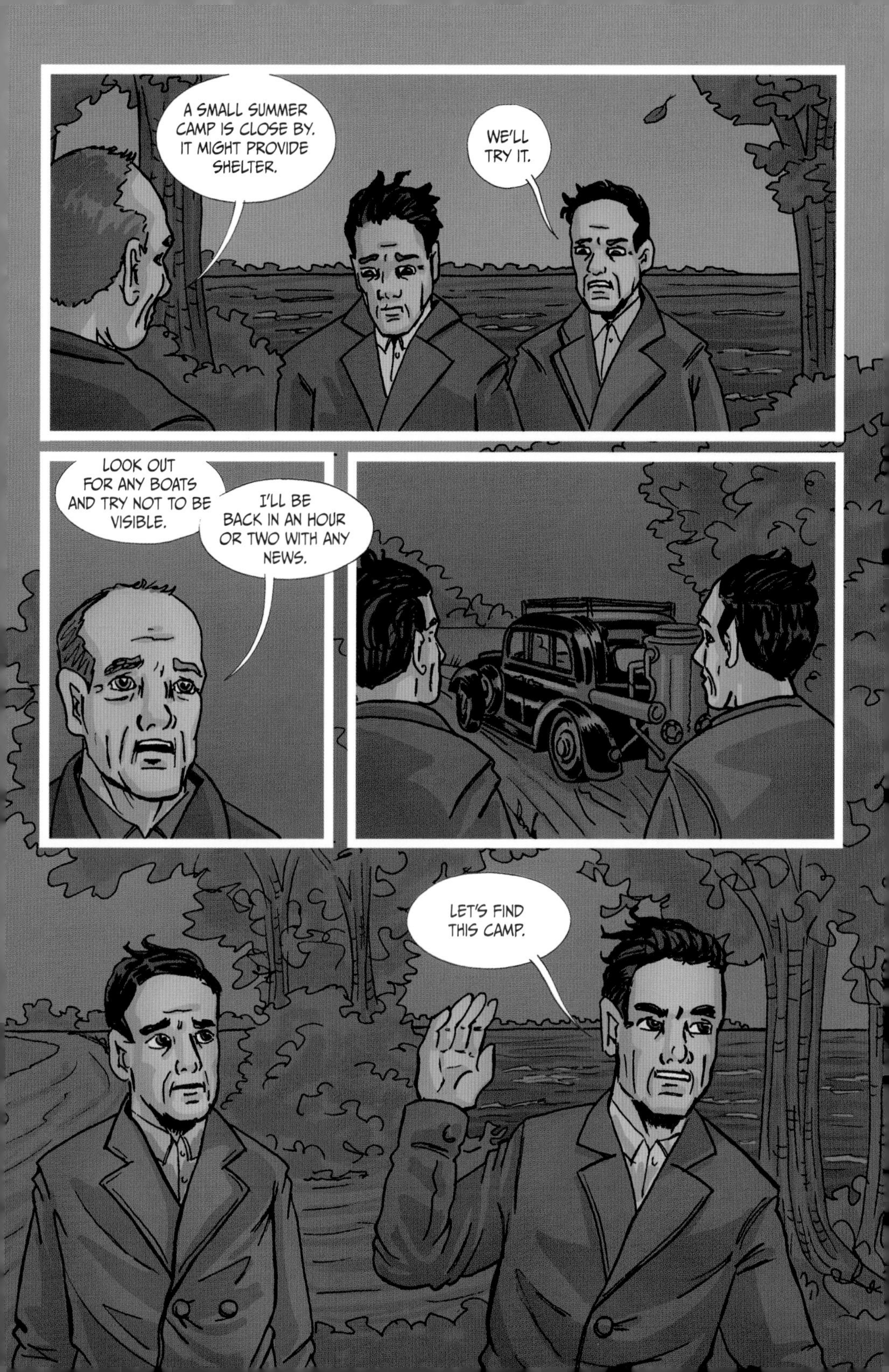
A SMALL SUMMER CAMP IS CLOSE BY. IT MIGHT PROVIDE SHELTER.
WE'LL TRY IT.
LOOK OUT FOR ANY BOATS AND TRY NOT TO BE VISIBLE.
I'LL BE BACK IN AN HOUR OR TWO WITH ANY NEWS.
LET'S FIND THIS CAMP.

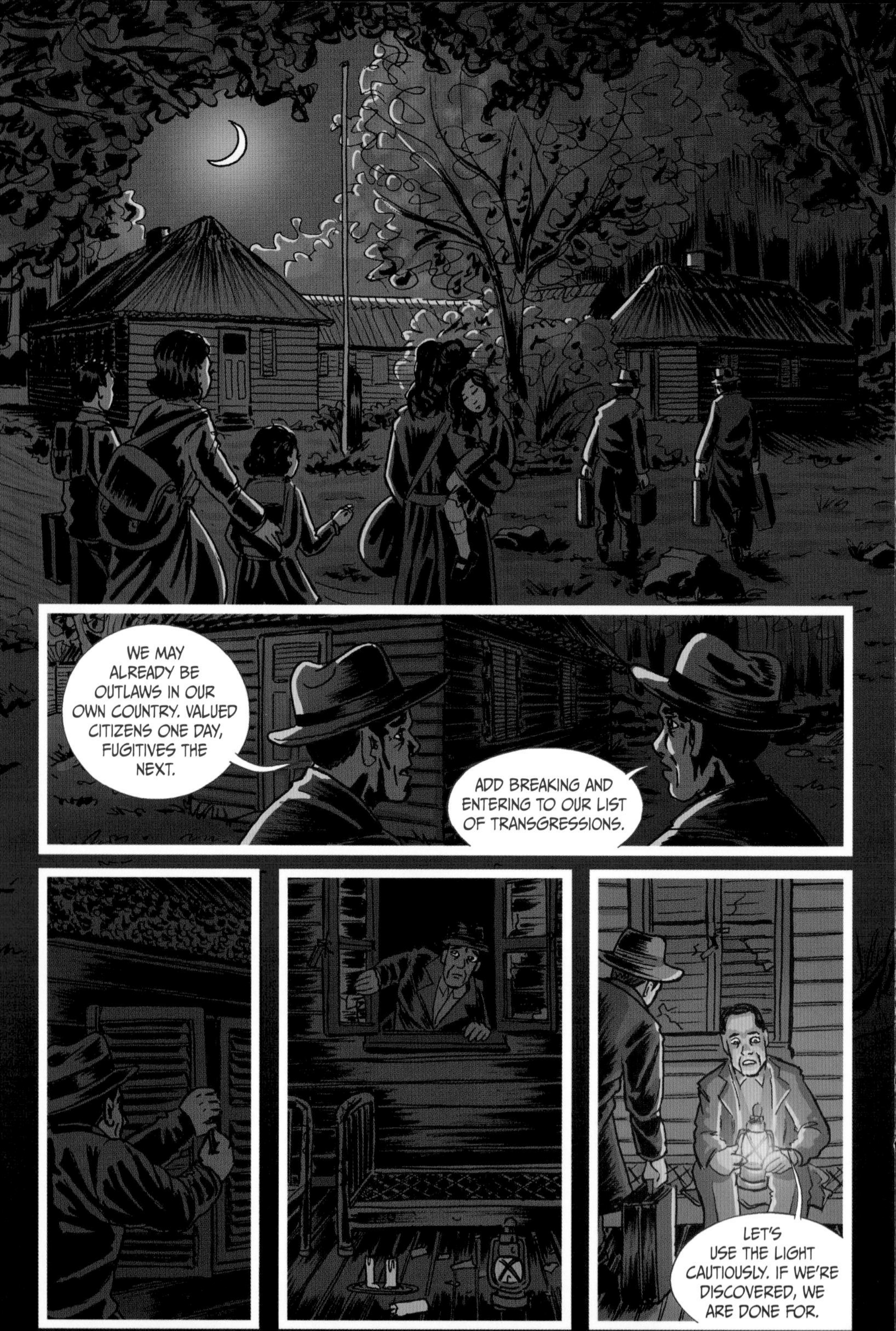
WE MAY ALREADY BE OUTLAWS IN OUR OWN COUNTRY. VALUED CITIZENS ONE DAY, FUGITIVES THE NEXT.
ADD BREAKING AND ENTERING TO OUR LIST OF TRANSGRESSIONS.
LET'S USE THE LIGHT CAUTIOUSLY. IF WE'RE DISCOVERED, WE ARE DONE FOR.

THIS SHOULD MAKE THE CHILDREN MORE COMFORTABLE.

WE DON'T HAVE MUCH TO FEED THEM. JUST THE LITTLE THAT'S LEFT OF THE SANDWICHES FROM THIS MORNING AND THE FRUIT THEY TOOK YESTERDAY.

NOTHING TO DRINK.

8 P.M.

I'M AFRAID I HAVE HEARD NOTHING YET.

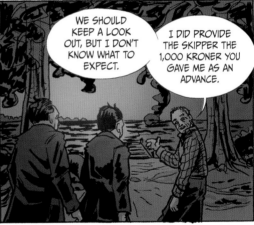

WE SHOULD KEEP A LOOK OUT, BUT I DON'T KNOW WHAT TO EXPECT.

I DID PROVIDE THE SKIPPER THE 1,000 KRONER YOU GAVE ME AS AN ADVANCE.

HOW ARE YOUR FAMILIES HOLDING UP?

EVERYONE'S A LITTLE TIRED AND ON EDGE. THANK YOU FOR GIVING MY WIFE YOUR COAT.

IF THE NAZIS ARE OUT HUNTING US NOW, FEWER PEOPLE MAY BE WILLING TO HELP US.

AND IF WE DO GET A BOAT, I WONDER IF THE CHILDREN CAN HANDLE THE CROSSING.

NOT KNOWING IS THE WORST PART... AND THE WAITING.

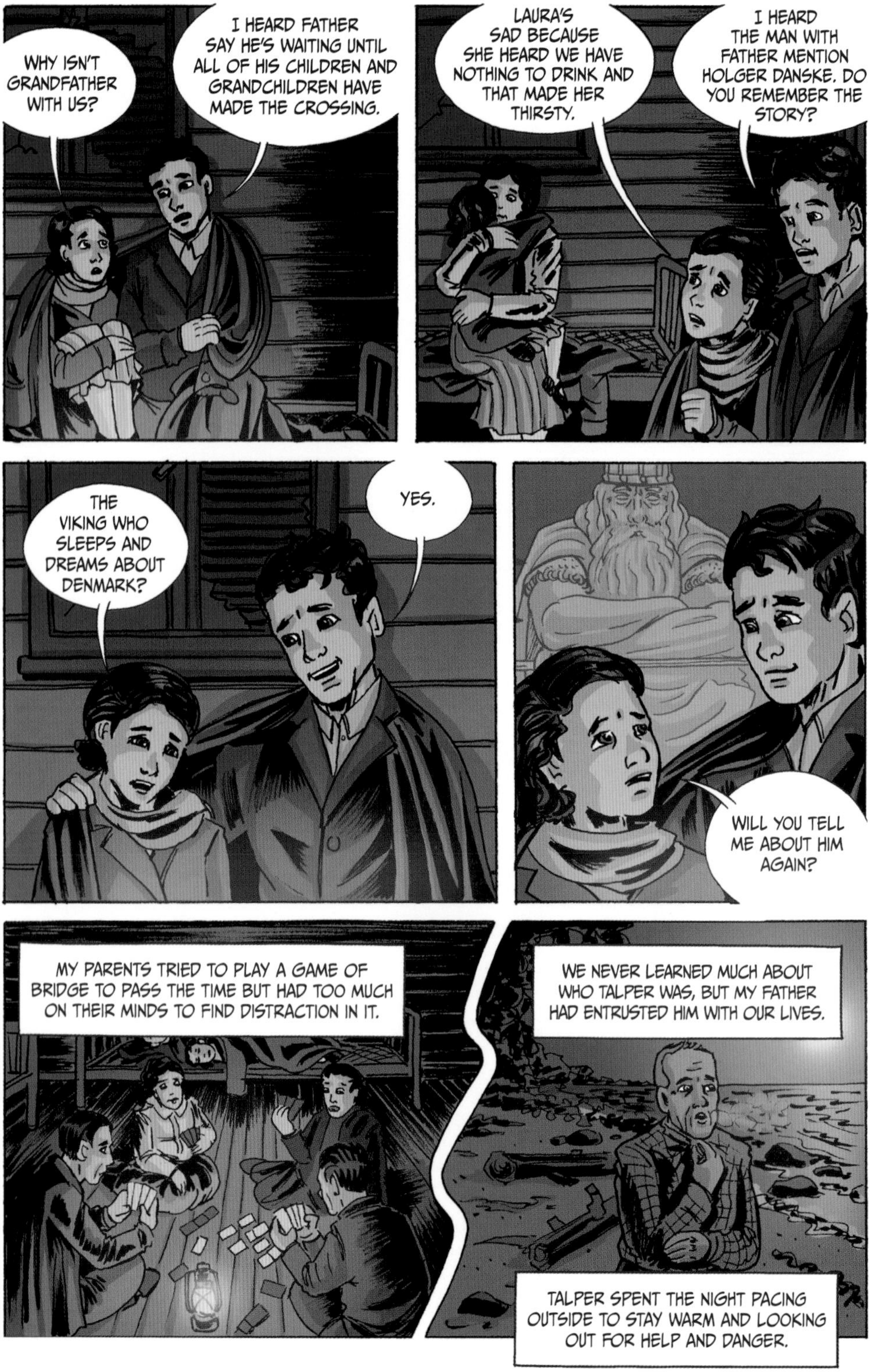
WHY ISN'T GRANDFATHER WITH US?
I HEARD FATHER SAY HE'S WAITING UNTIL ALL OF HIS CHILDREN AND GRANDCHILDREN HAVE MADE THE CROSSING.
LAURA'S SAD BECAUSE SHE HEARD WE HAVE NOTHING TO DRINK AND THAT MADE HER THIRSTY.
I HEARD THE MAN WITH FATHER MENTION HOLGER DANSKE. DO YOU REMEMBER THE STORY?
THE VIKING WHO SLEEPS AND DREAMS ABOUT DENMARK?
YES.
WILL YOU TELL ME ABOUT HIM AGAIN?
MY PARENTS TRIED TO PLAY A GAME OF BRIDGE TO PASS THE TIME BUT HAD TOO MUCH ON THEIR MINDS TO FIND DISTRACTION IN IT.
WE NEVER LEARNED MUCH ABOUT WHO TALPER WAS, BUT MY FATHER HAD ENTRUSTED HIM WITH OUR LIVES.
TALPER SPENT THE NIGHT PACING OUTSIDE TO STAY WARM AND LOOKING OUT FOR HELP AND DANGER.

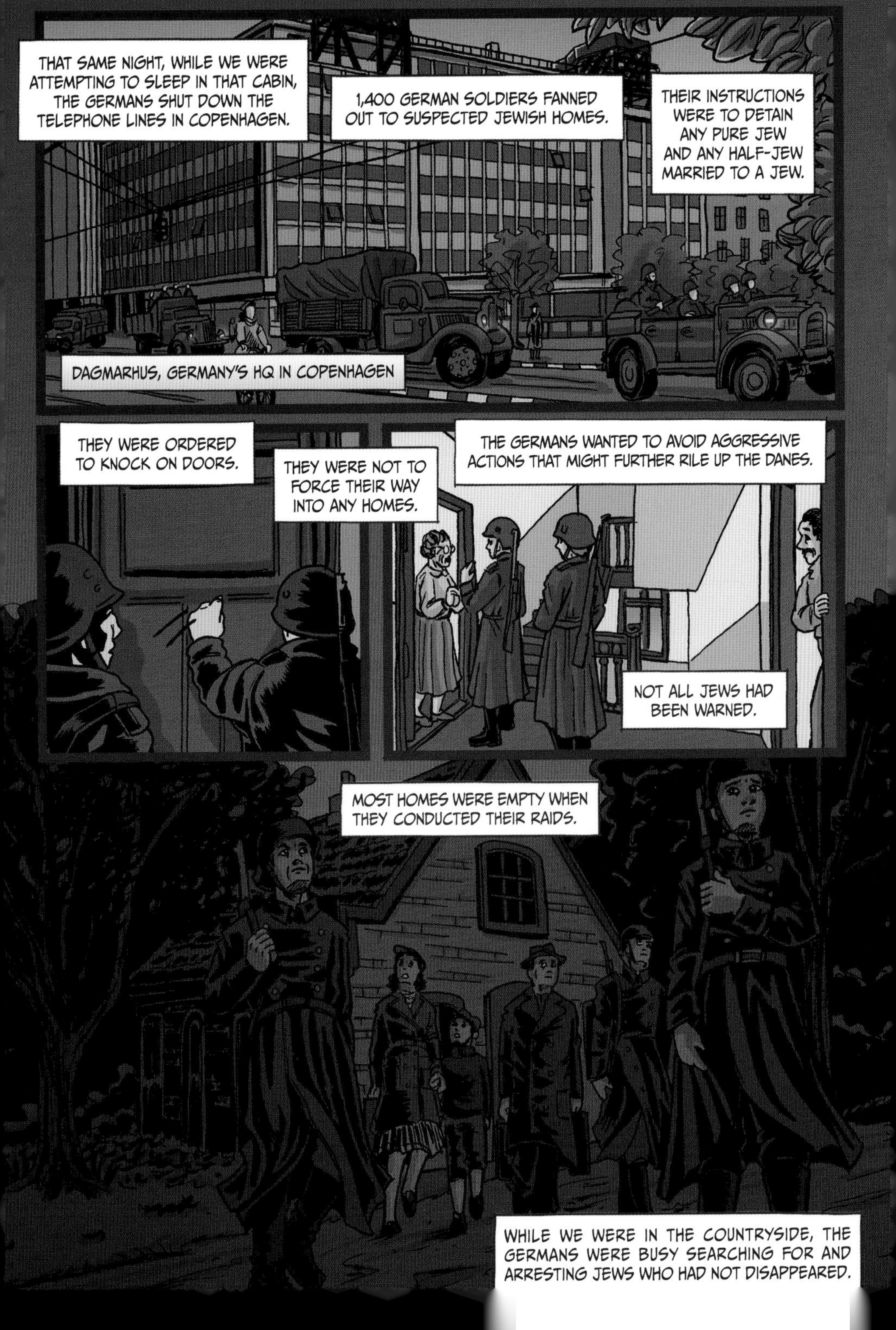
THAT SAME NIGHT, WHILE WE WERE ATTEMPTING TO SLEEP IN THAT CABIN, THE GERMANS SHUT DOWN THE TELEPHONE LINES IN COPENHAGEN.
1,400 GERMAN SOLDIERS FANNED OUT TO SUSPECTED JEWISH HOMES.
THEIR INSTRUCTIONS WERE TO DETAIN ANY PURE JEW AND ANY HALF-JEW MARRIED TO A JEW.
DAGMARHUS, GERMANY'S HQ IN COPENHAGEN
THEY WERE ORDERED TO KNOCK ON DOORS.
THEY WERE NOT TO FORCE THEIR WAY INTO ANY HOMES.
THE GERMANS WANTED TO AVOID AGGRESSIVE ACTIONS THAT MIGHT FURTHER RILE UP THE DANES.
NOT ALL JEWS HAD BEEN WARNED.
MOST HOMES WERE EMPTY WHEN THEY CONDUCTED THEIR RAIDS.
WHILE WE WERE IN THE COUNTRYSIDE, THE GERMANS WERE BUSY SEARCHING FOR AND ARRESTING JEWS WHO HAD NOT DISAPPEARED.

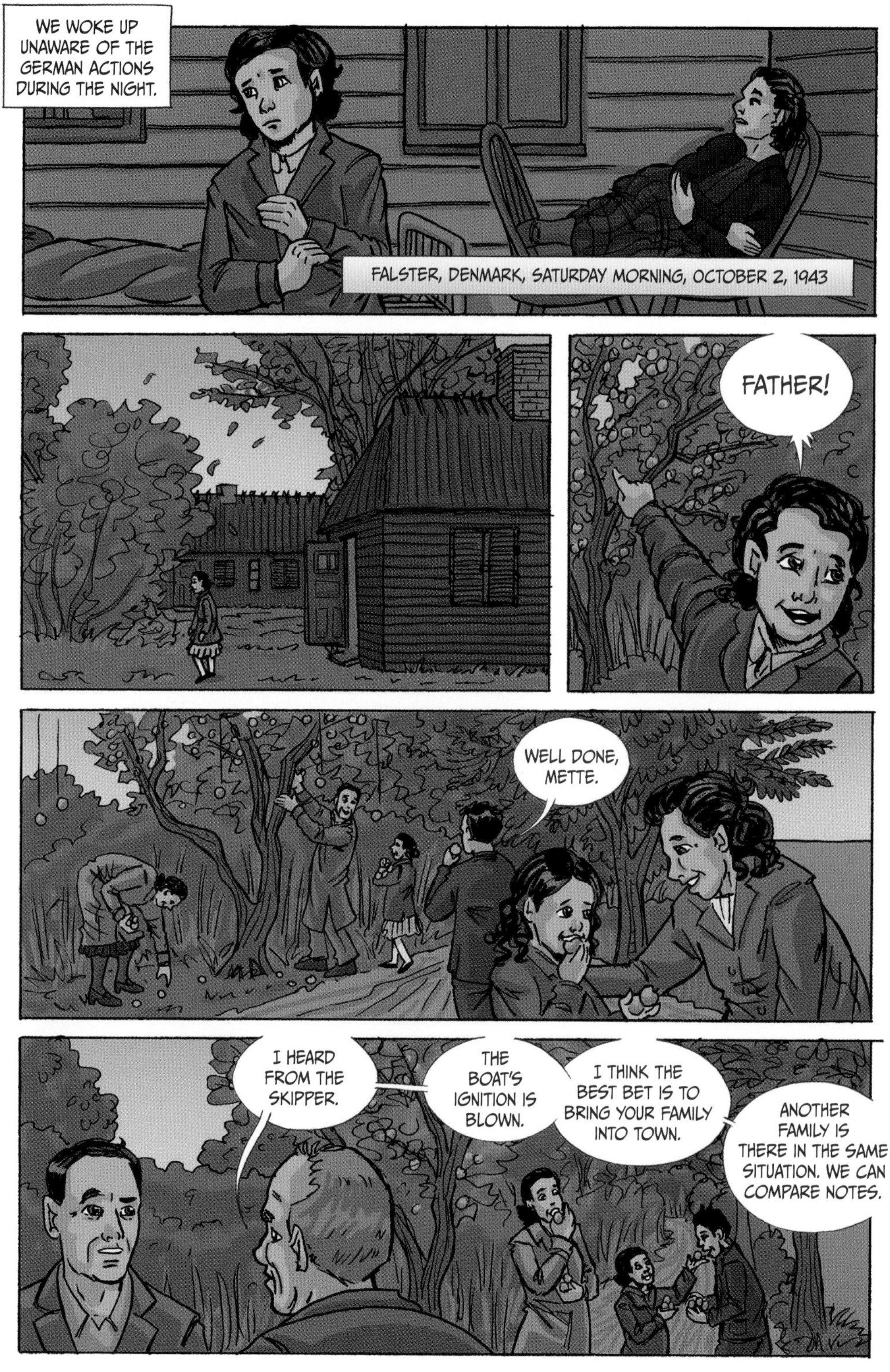
WE WOKE UP UNAWARE OF THE GERMAN ACTIONS DURING THE NIGHT.
FALSTER, DENMARK, SATURDAY MORNING, OCTOBER 2, 1943
FATHER!
WELL DONE, METTE.
I HEARD FROM THE SKIPPER.
THE BOAT'S IGNITION IS BLOWN.
I THINK THE BEST BET IS TO BRING YOUR FAMILY INTO TOWN.
ANOTHER FAMILY IS THERE IN THE SAME SITUATION. WE CAN COMPARE NOTES.

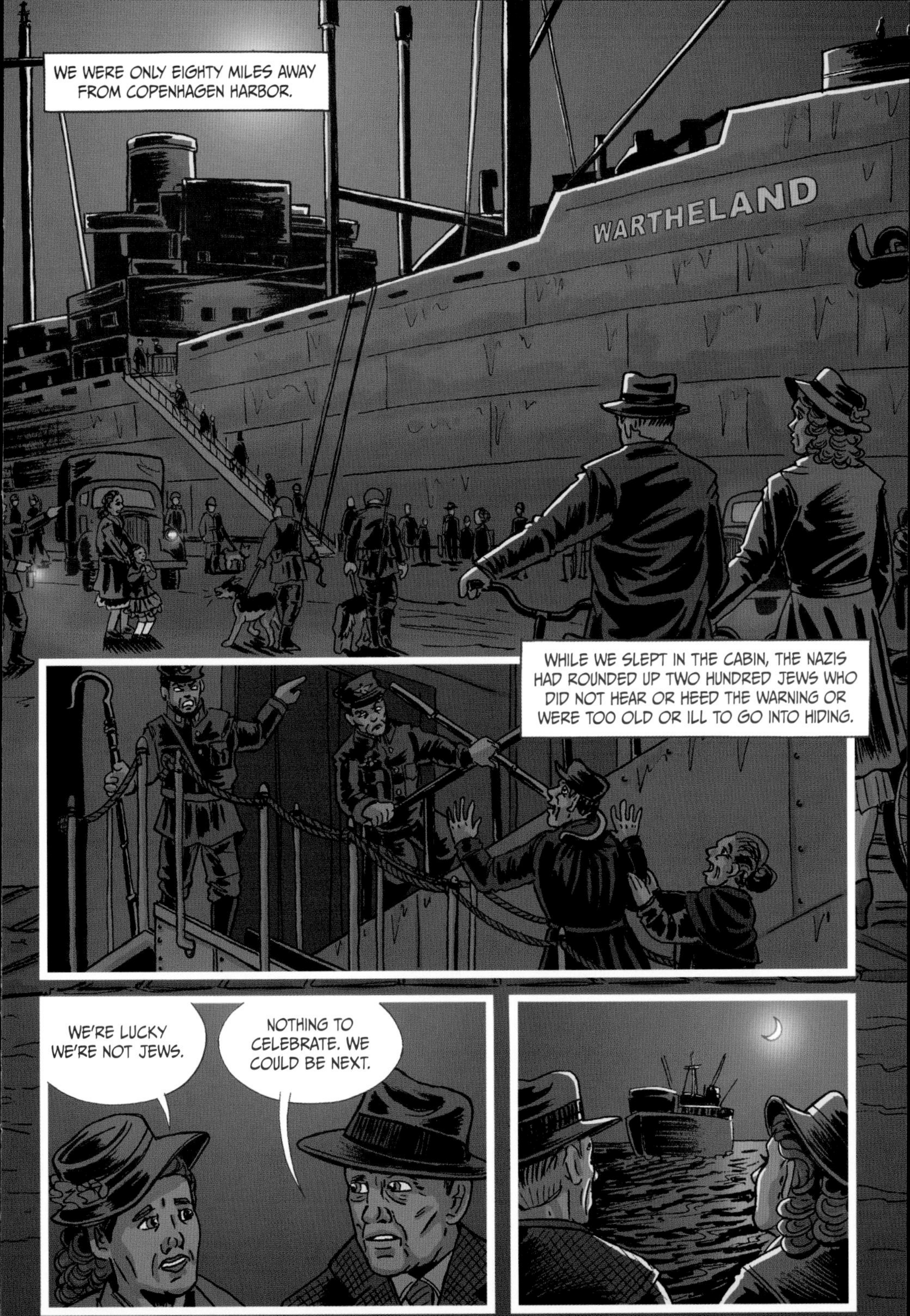
WE WERE ONLY EIGHTY MILES AWAY FROM COPENHAGEN HARBOR.
WARTHELAND
WHILE WE SLEPT IN THE CABIN, THE NAZIS HAD ROUNDED UP TWO HUNDRED JEWS WHO DID NOT HEAR OR HEED THE WARNING OR WERE TOO OLD OR ILL TO GO INTO HIDING.
WE'RE LUCKY WE'RE NOT JEWS.
NOTHING TO CELEBRATE. WE COULD BE NEXT.

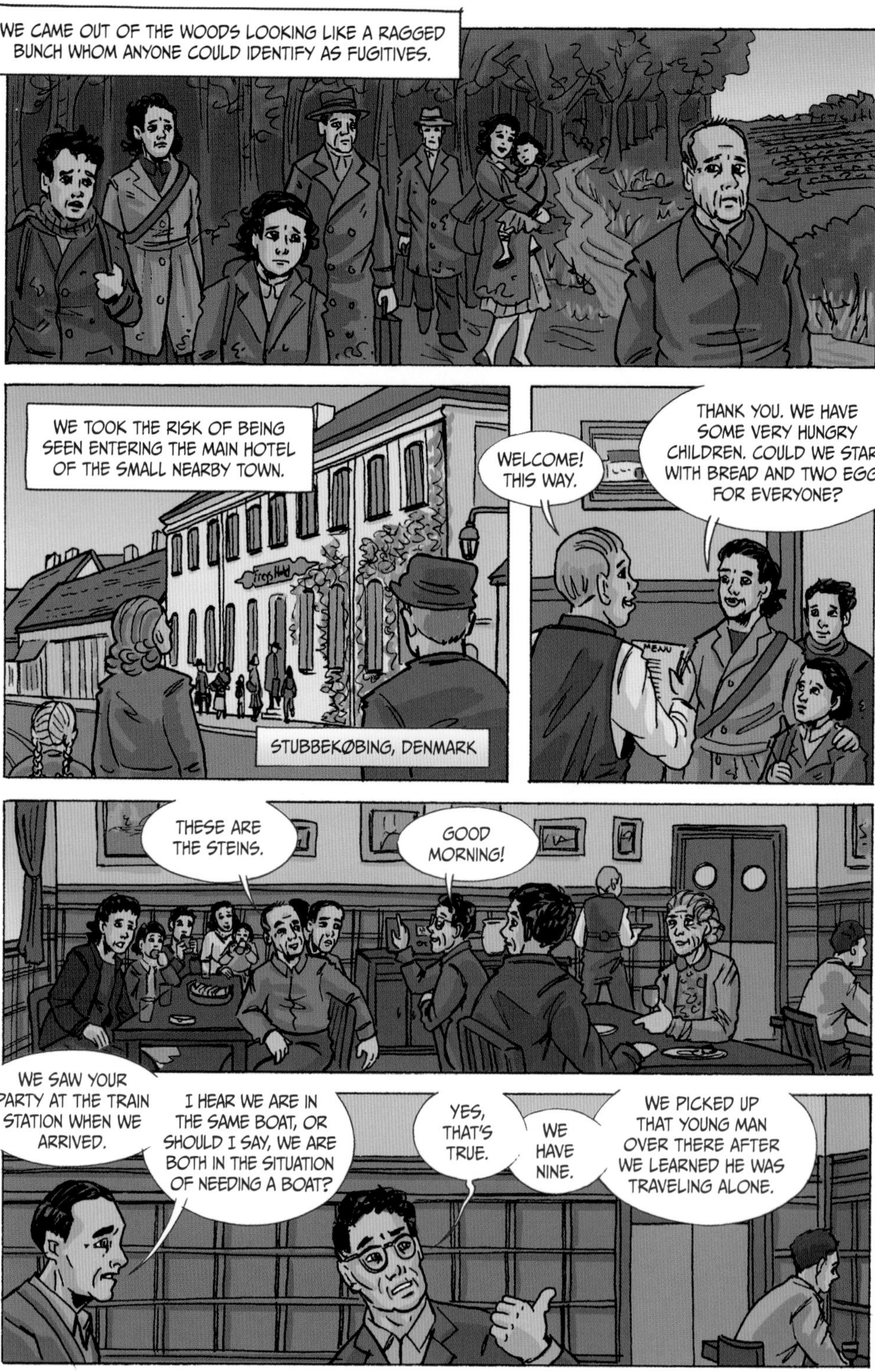

WE CAME OUT OF THE WOODS LOOKING LIKE A RAGGED BUNCH WHOM ANYONE COULD IDENTIFY AS FUGITIVES.
WE TOOK THE RISK OF BEING SEEN ENTERING THE MAIN HOTEL OF THE SMALL NEARBY TOWN.
STUBBEKØBING, DENMARK
WELCOME! THIS WAY.
THANK YOU. WE HAVE SOME VERY HUNGRY CHILDREN. COULD WE START WITH BREAD AND TWO EGGS FOR EVERYONE?
THESE ARE THE STEINS.
GOOD MORNING!
WE SAW YOUR PARTY AT THE TRAIN STATION WHEN WE ARRIVED.
I HEAR WE ARE IN THE SAME BOAT, OR SHOULD I SAY, WE ARE BOTH IN THE SITUATION OF NEEDING A BOAT?
YES, THAT'S TRUE.
WE HAVE NINE.
WE PICKED UP THAT YOUNG MAN OVER THERE AFTER WE LEARNED HE WAS TRAVELING ALONE.

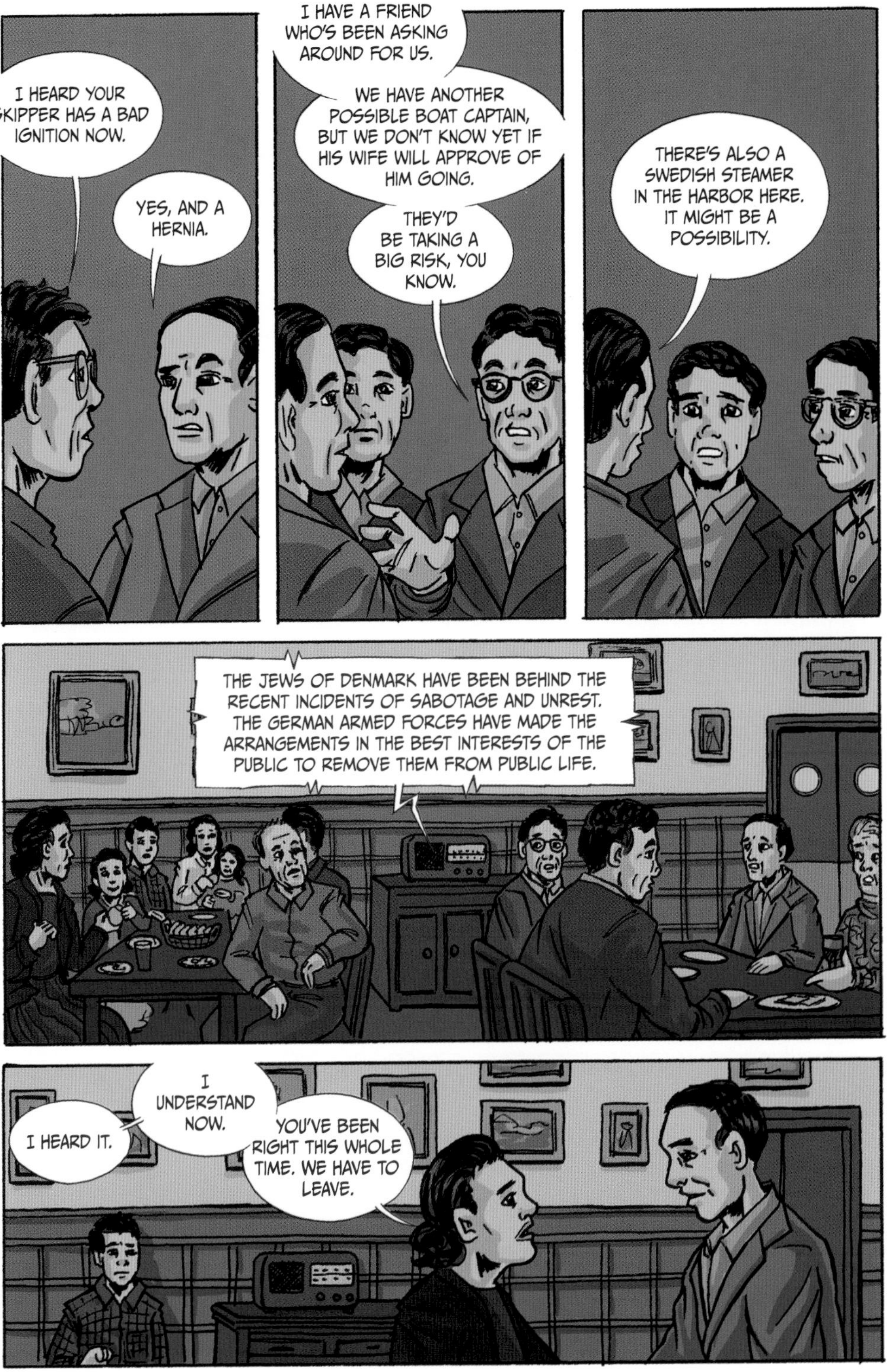
I HEARD YOUR SKIPPER HAS A BAD IGNITION NOW.
YES, AND A HERNIA.
I HAVE A FRIEND WHO'S BEEN ASKING AROUND FOR US.
WE HAVE ANOTHER POSSIBLE BOAT CAPTAIN, BUT WE DON'T KNOW YET IF HIS WIFE WILL APPROVE OF HIM GOING.
THEY'D BE TAKING A BIG RISK, YOU KNOW.
THERE'S ALSO A SWEDISH STEAMER IN THE HARBOR HERE. IT MIGHT BE A POSSIBILITY.
THE JEWS OF DENMARK HAVE BEEN BEHIND THE RECENT INCIDENTS OF SABOTAGE AND UNREST. THE GERMAN ARMED FORCES HAVE MADE THE ARRANGEMENTS IN THE BEST INTERESTS OF THE PUBLIC TO REMOVE THEM FROM PUBLIC LIFE.
I HEARD IT.
I UNDERSTAND NOW.
YOU'VE BEEN RIGHT THIS WHOLE TIME. WE HAVE TO LEAVE.

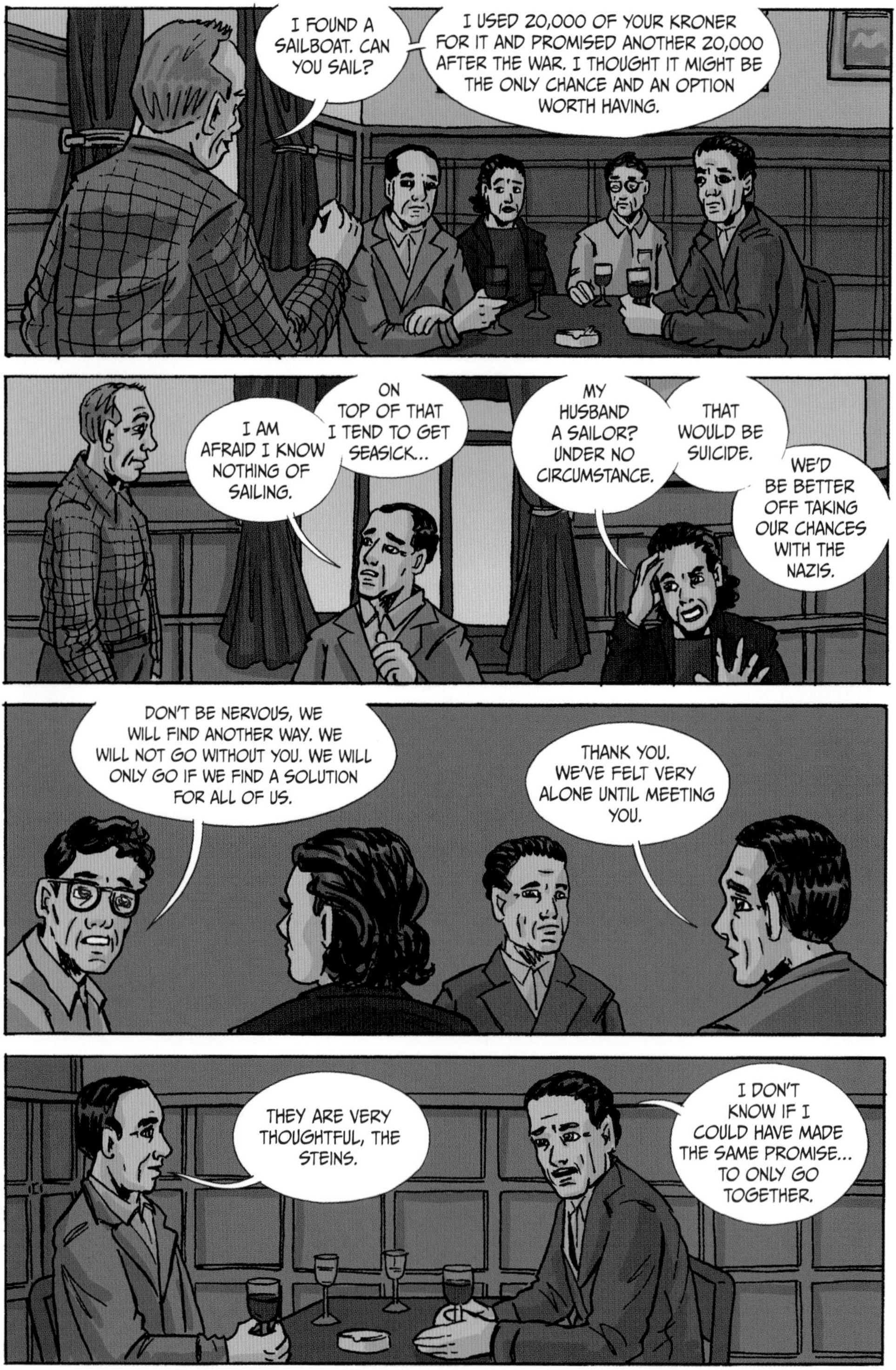
I FOUND A SAILBOAT. CAN YOU SAIL?
I USED 20,000 OF YOUR KRONER FOR IT AND PROMISED ANOTHER 20,000 AFTER THE WAR. I THOUGHT IT MIGHT BE THE ONLY CHANCE AND AN OPTION WORTH HAVING.
I AM AFRAID I KNOW NOTHING OF SAILING.
ON TOP OF THAT I TEND TO GET SEASICK...
MY HUSBAND A SAILOR? UNDER NO CIRCUMSTANCE.
THAT WOULD BE SUICIDE.
WE'D BE BETTER OFF TAKING OUR CHANCES WITH THE NAZIS.
DON'T BE NERVOUS, WE WILL FIND ANOTHER WAY. WE WILL NOT GO WITHOUT YOU. WE WILL ONLY GO IF WE FIND A SOLUTION FOR ALL OF US.
THANK YOU. WE'VE FELT VERY ALONE UNTIL MEETING YOU.
THEY ARE VERY THOUGHTFUL, THE STEINS.
I DON'T KNOW IF I COULD HAVE MADE THE SAME PROMISE... TO ONLY GO TOGETHER.

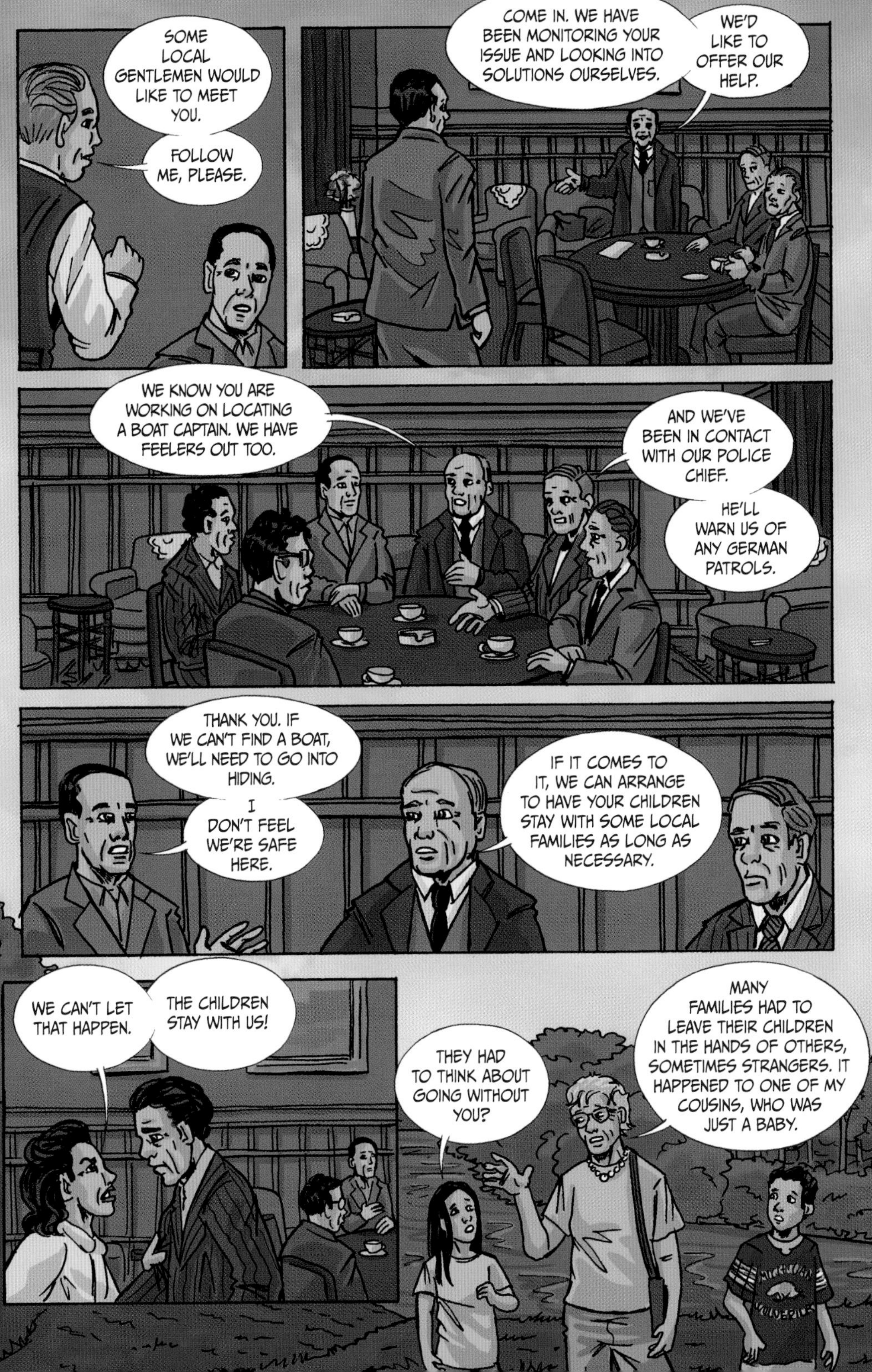

SOME LOCAL GENTLEMEN WOULD LIKE TO MEET YOU.
FOLLOW ME, PLEASE.
COME IN. WE HAVE BEEN MONITORING YOUR ISSUE AND LOOKING INTO SOLUTIONS OURSELVES.
WE'D LIKE TO OFFER OUR HELP.
WE KNOW YOU ARE WORKING ON LOCATING A BOAT CAPTAIN. WE HAVE FEELERS OUT TOO.
AND WE'VE BEEN IN CONTACT WITH OUR POLICE CHIEF.
HE'LL WARN US OF ANY GERMAN PATROLS.
THANK YOU. IF WE CAN'T FIND A BOAT, WE'LL NEED TO GO INTO HIDING.
I DON'T FEEL WE'RE SAFE HERE.
IF IT COMES TO IT, WE CAN ARRANGE TO HAVE YOUR CHILDREN STAY WITH SOME LOCAL FAMILIES AS LONG AS NECESSARY.
WE CAN'T LET THAT HAPPEN.
THE CHILDREN STAY WITH US!
THEY HAD TO THINK ABOUT GOING WITHOUT YOU?
MANY FAMILIES HAD TO LEAVE THEIR CHILDREN IN THE HANDS OF OTHERS, SOMETIMES STRANGERS. IT HAPPENED TO ONE OF MY COUSINS, WHO WAS JUST A BABY.

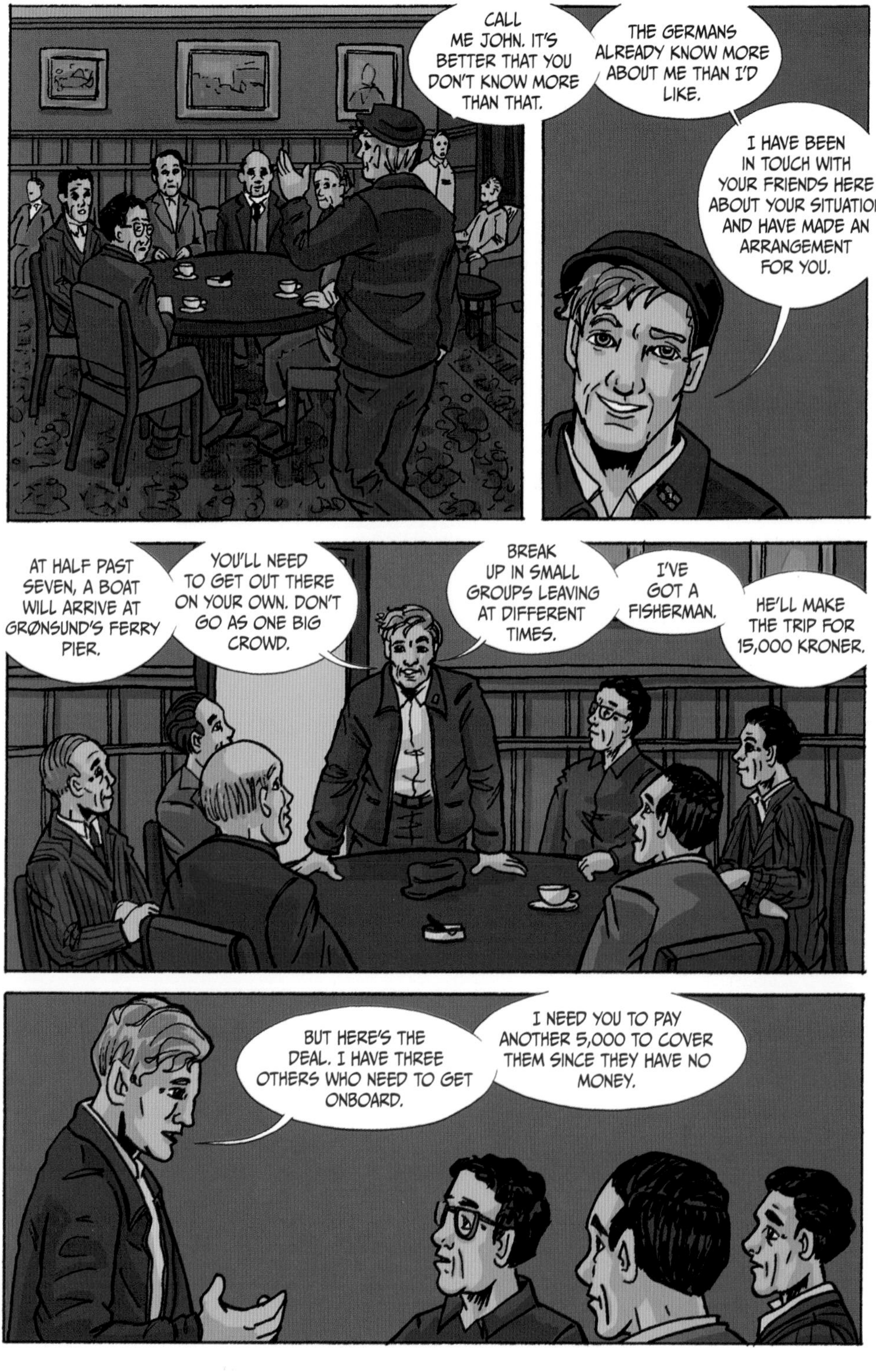
CALL ME JOHN. IT'S BETTER THAT YOU DON'T KNOW MORE THAN THAT.
THE GERMANS ALREADY KNOW MORE ABOUT ME THAN I'D LIKE.
I HAVE BEEN IN TOUCH WITH YOUR FRIENDS HERE ABOUT YOUR SITUATION AND HAVE MADE AN ARRANGEMENT FOR YOU.
AT HALF PAST SEVEN, A BOAT WILL ARRIVE AT GRØNSUND'S FERRY PIER.
YOU'LL NEED TO GET OUT THERE ON YOUR OWN. DON'T GO AS ONE BIG CROWD.
BREAK UP IN SMALL GROUPS LEAVING AT DIFFERENT TIMES.
I'VE GOT A FISHERMAN.
HE'LL MAKE THE TRIP FOR 15,000 KRONER.
BUT HERE'S THE DEAL. I HAVE THREE OTHERS WHO NEED TO GET ONBOARD.
I NEED YOU TO PAY ANOTHER 5,000 TO COVER THEM SINCE THEY HAVE NO MONEY.

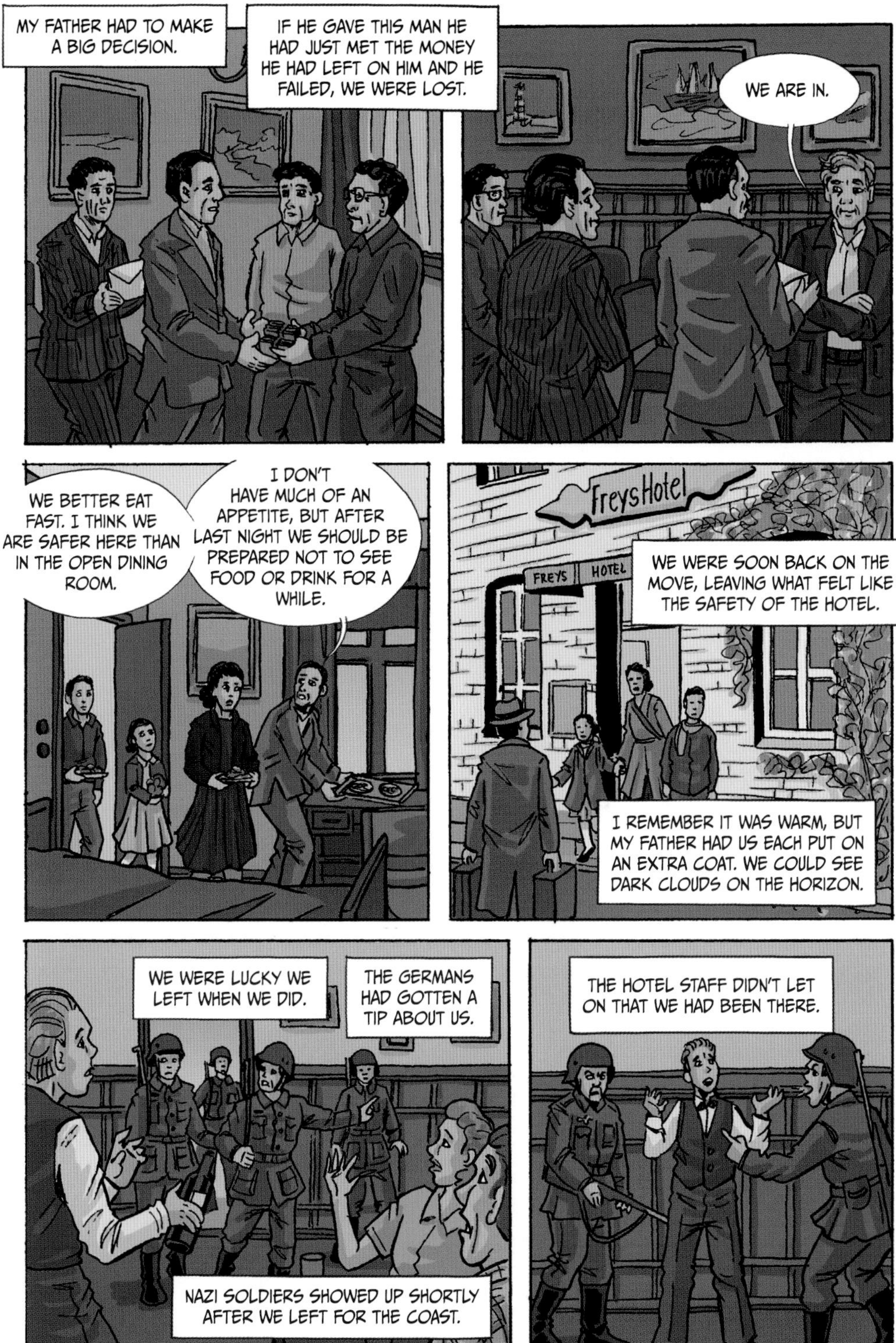
MY FATHER HAD TO MAKE A BIG DECISION.
IF HE GAVE THIS MAN HE HAD JUST MET THE MONEY HE HAD LEFT ON HIM AND HE FAILED, WE WERE LOST.
WE ARE IN.
WE BETTER EAT FAST. I THINK WE ARE SAFER HERE THAN IN THE OPEN DINING ROOM.
I DON'T HAVE MUCH OF AN APPETITE, BUT AFTER LAST NIGHT WE SHOULD BE PREPARED NOT TO SEE FOOD OR DRINK FOR A WHILE.
FreysHotel
FREYS HOTEL
WE WERE SOON BACK ON THE MOVE, LEAVING WHAT FELT LIKE THE SAFETY OF THE HOTEL.
I REMEMBER IT WAS WARM, BUT MY FATHER HAD US EACH PUT ON AN EXTRA COAT. WE COULD SEE DARK CLOUDS ON THE HORIZON.
WE WERE LUCKY WE LEFT WHEN WE DID.
THE GERMANS HAD GOTTEN A TIP ABOUT US.
NAZI SOLDIERS SHOWED UP SHORTLY AFTER WE LEFT FOR THE COAST.
THE HOTEL STAFF DIDN'T LET ON THAT WE HAD BEEN THERE.

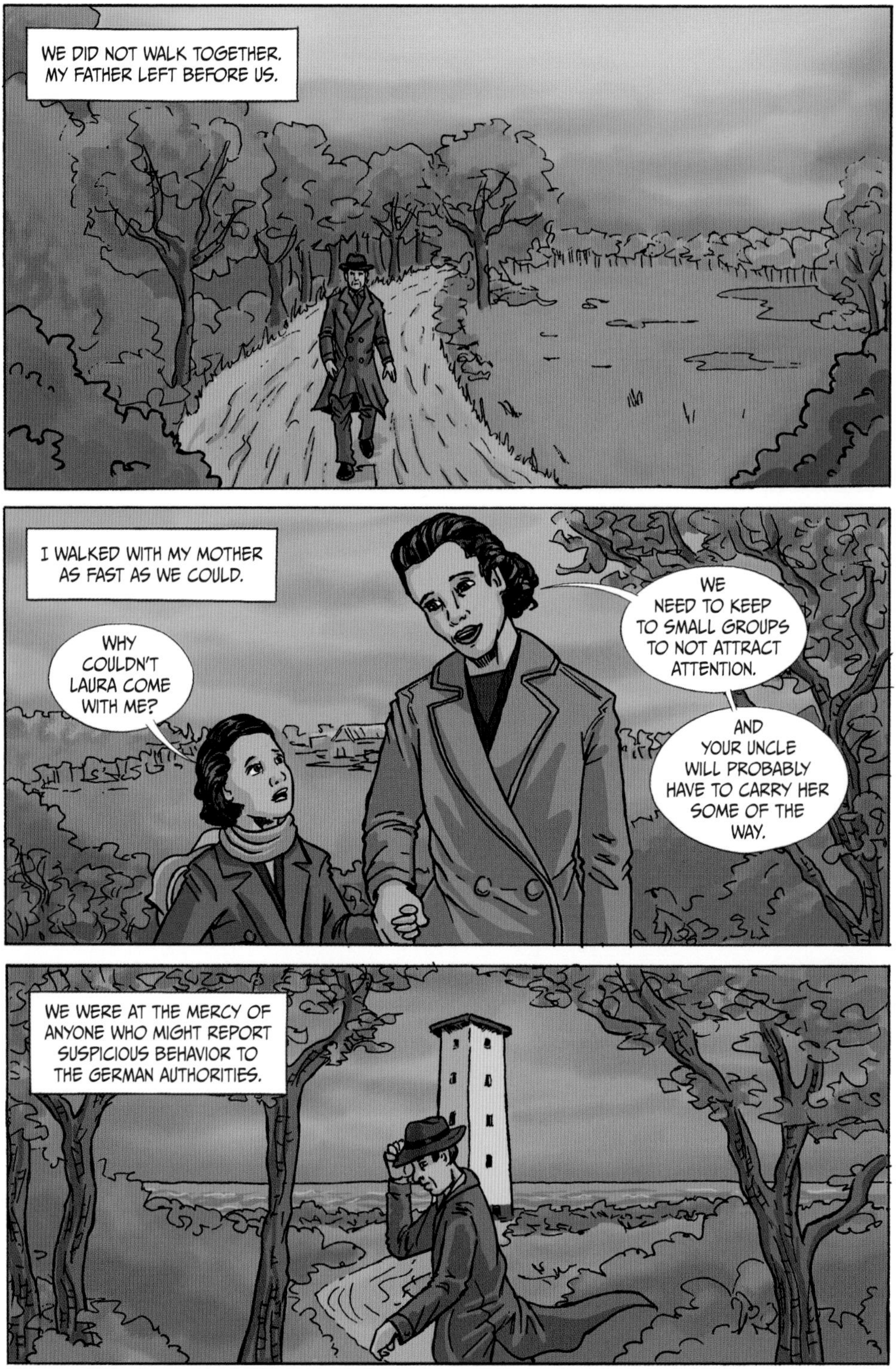
WE DID NOT WALK TOGETHER. MY FATHER LEFT BEFORE US.
I WALKED WITH MY MOTHER AS FAST AS WE COULD.
WHY COULDN'T LAURA COME WITH ME?
WE NEED TO KEEP TO SMALL GROUPS TO NOT ATTRACT ATTENTION.
AND YOUR UNCLE WILL PROBABLY HAVE TO CARRY HER SOME OF THE WAY.
WE WERE AT THE MERCY OF ANYONE WHO MIGHT REPORT SUSPICIOUS BEHAVIOR TO THE GERMAN AUTHORITIES.

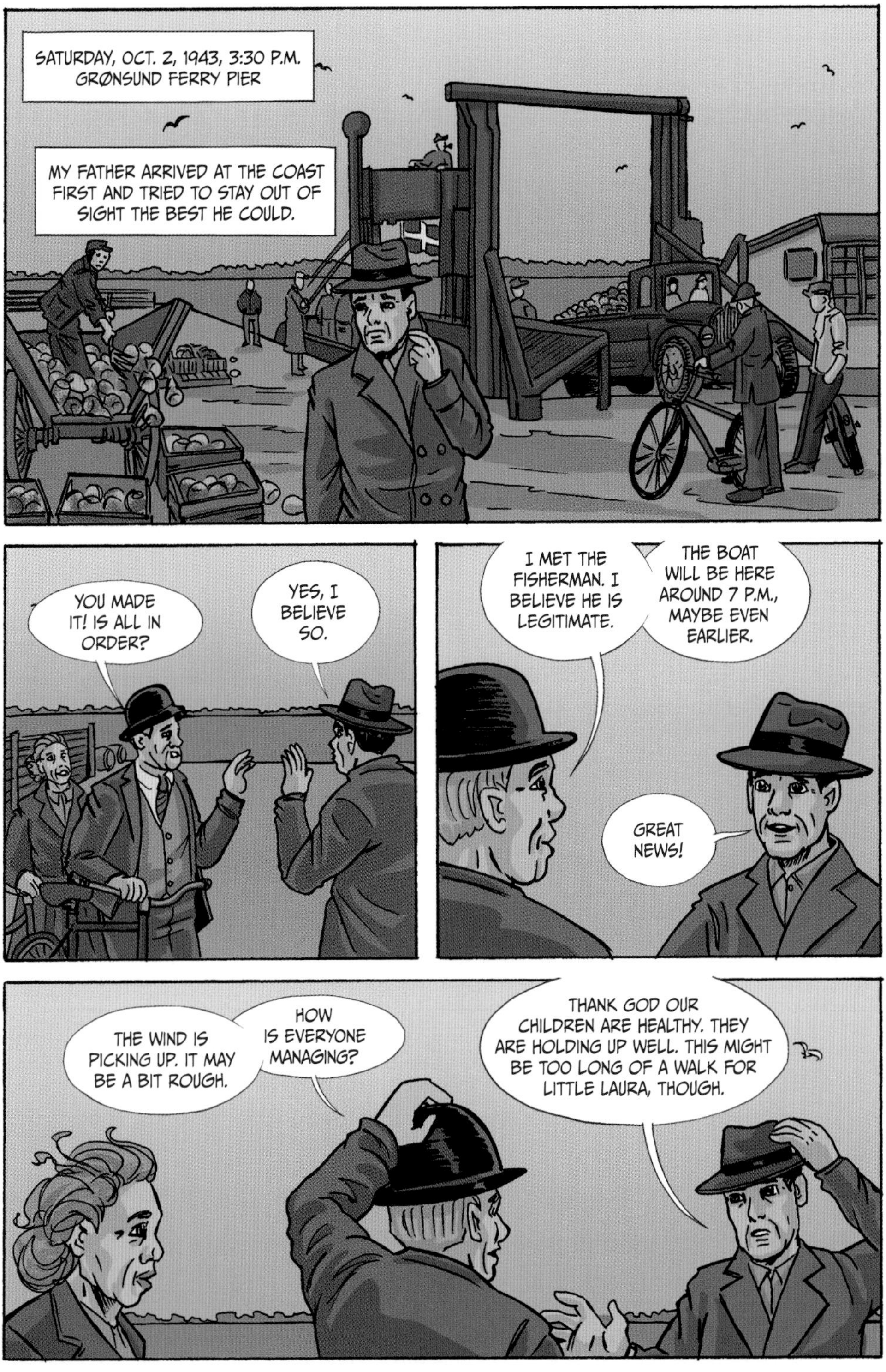
SATURDAY, OCT. 2, 1943, 3:30 P.M.
GRØNSUND FERRY PIER
MY FATHER ARRIVED AT THE COAST FIRST AND TRIED TO STAY OUT OF SIGHT THE BEST HE COULD.
YOU MADE IT! IS ALL IN ORDER?
YES, I BELIEVE SO.
I MET THE FISHERMAN. I BELIEVE HE IS LEGITIMATE.
THE BOAT WILL BE HERE AROUND 7 P.M., MAYBE EVEN EARLIER.
GREAT NEWS!
THE WIND IS PICKING UP. IT MAY BE A BIT ROUGH.
HOW IS EVERYONE MANAGING?
THANK GOD OUR CHILDREN ARE HEALTHY. THEY ARE HOLDING UP WELL. THIS MIGHT BE TOO LONG OF A WALK FOR LITTLE LAURA, THOUGH.

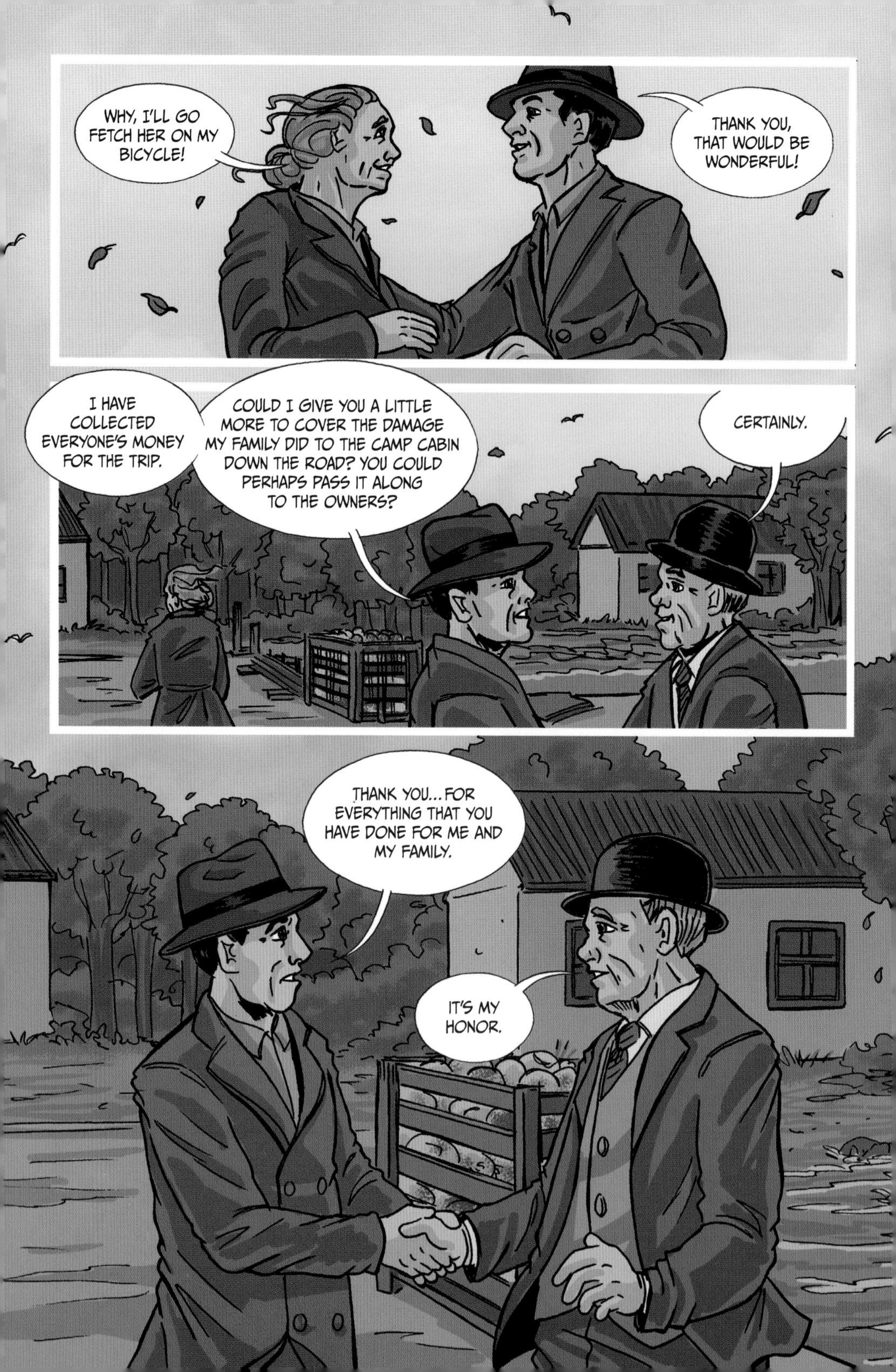
WHY, I'LL GO FETCH HER ON MY BICYCLE!
THANK YOU, THAT WOULD BE WONDERFUL!
I HAVE COLLECTED EVERYONE'S MONEY FOR THE TRIP.
COULD I GIVE YOU A LITTLE MORE TO COVER THE DAMAGE MY FAMILY DID TO THE CAMP CABIN DOWN THE ROAD? YOU COULD PERHAPS PASS IT ALONG TO THE OWNERS?
CERTAINLY.
THANK YOU...FOR EVERYTHING THAT YOU HAVE DONE FOR ME AND MY FAMILY.
IT'S MY HONOR.

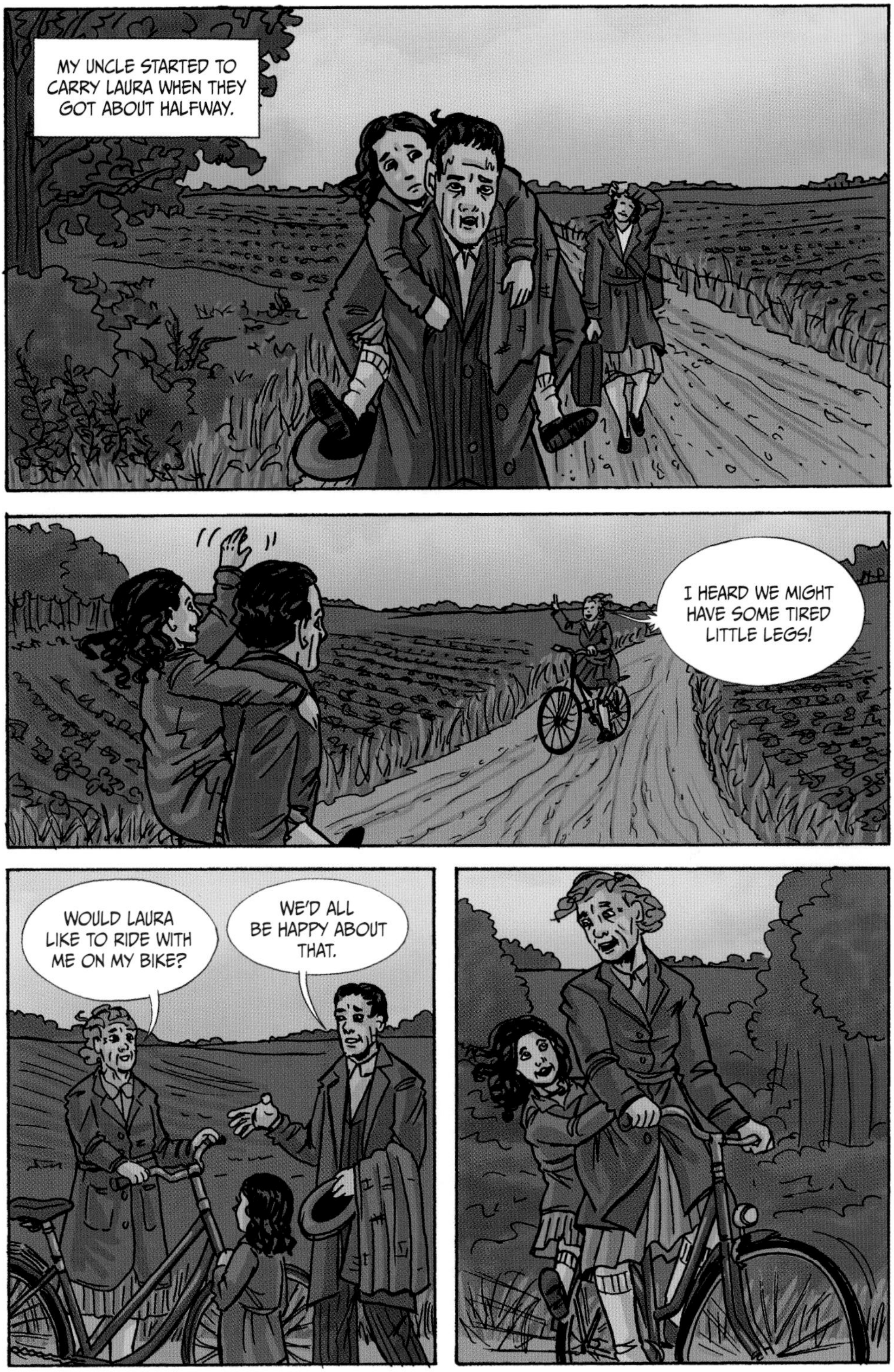
MY UNCLE STARTED TO CARRY LAURA WHEN THEY GOT ABOUT HALFWAY.
I HEARD WE MIGHT HAVE SOME TIRED LITTLE LEGS!
WOULD LAURA LIKE TO RIDE WITH ME ON MY BIKE?
WE'D ALL BE HAPPY ABOUT THAT.

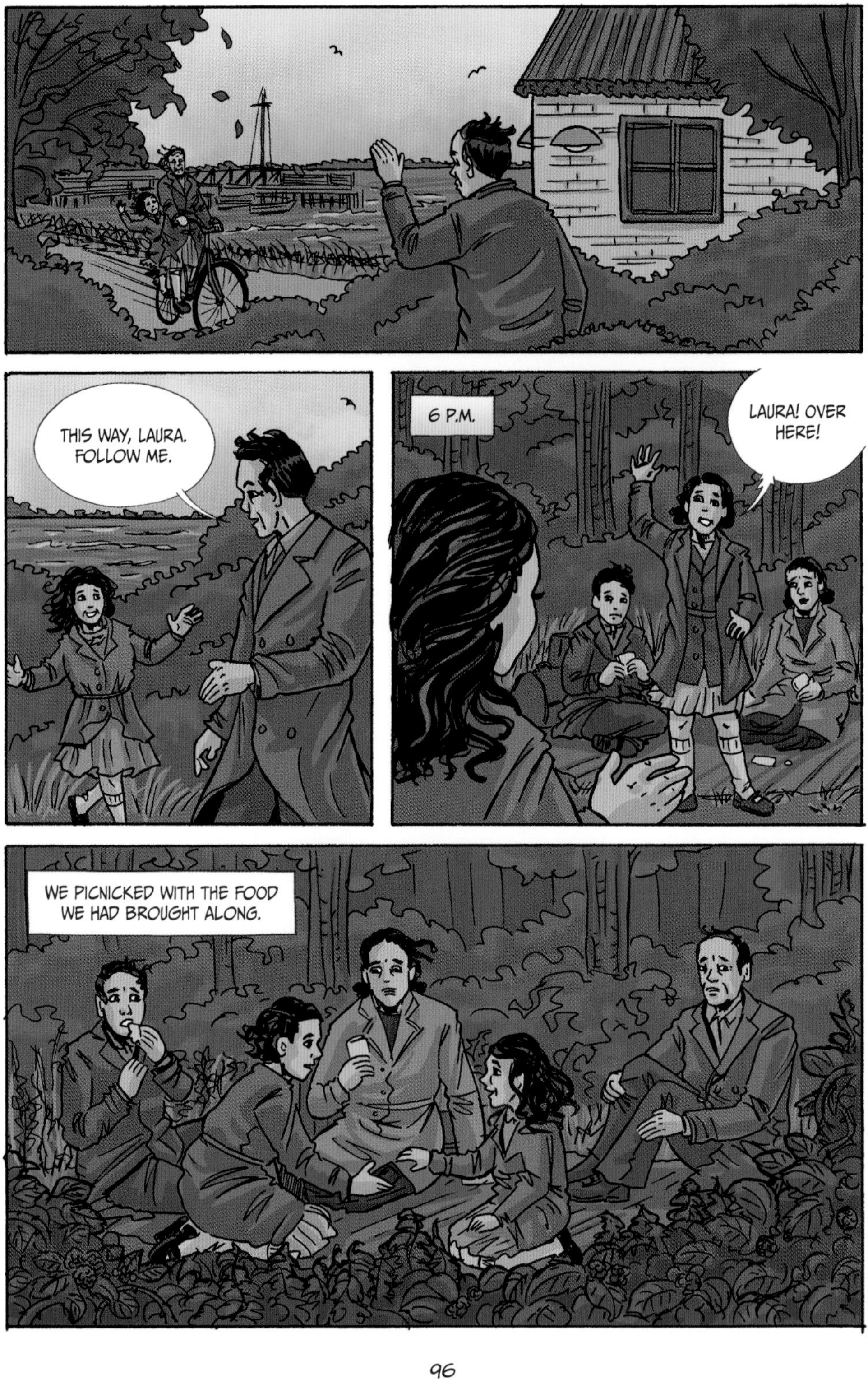
THIS WAY, LAURA. FOLLOW ME.
6 P.M.
LAURA! OVER HERE!
WE PICNICKED WITH THE FOOD WE HAD BROUGHT ALONG.

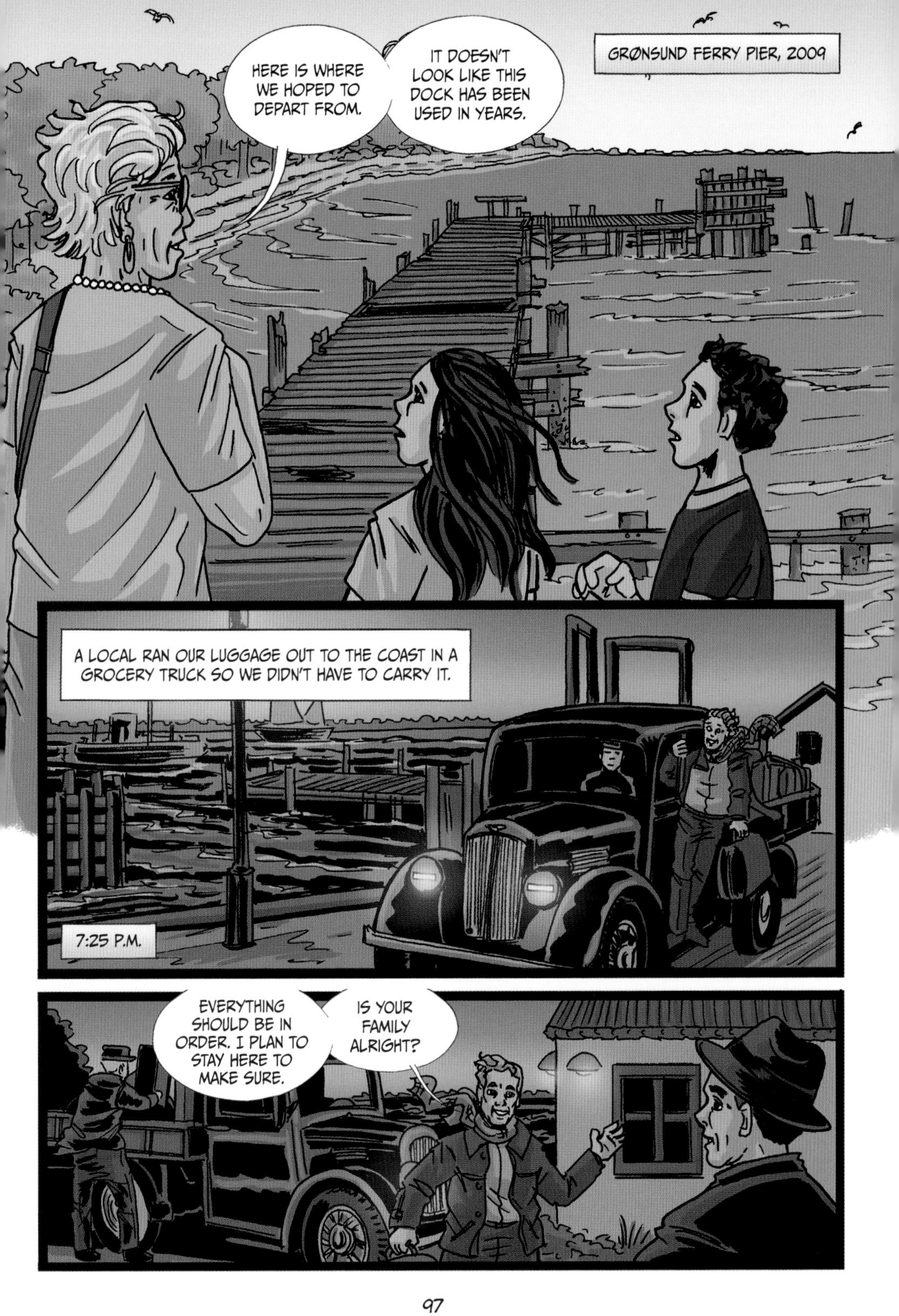
GRØNSUND FERRY PIER, 2009
HERE IS WHERE WE HOPED TO DEPART FROM.
IT DOESN'T LOOK LIKE THIS DOCK HAS BEEN USED IN YEARS.
A LOCAL RAN OUR LUGGAGE OUT TO THE COAST IN A GROCERY TRUCK SO WE DIDN'T HAVE TO CARRY IT.
7:25 P.M.
EVERYTHING SHOULD BE IN ORDER. I PLAN TO STAY HERE TO MAKE SURE.
IS YOUR FAMILY ALRIGHT?

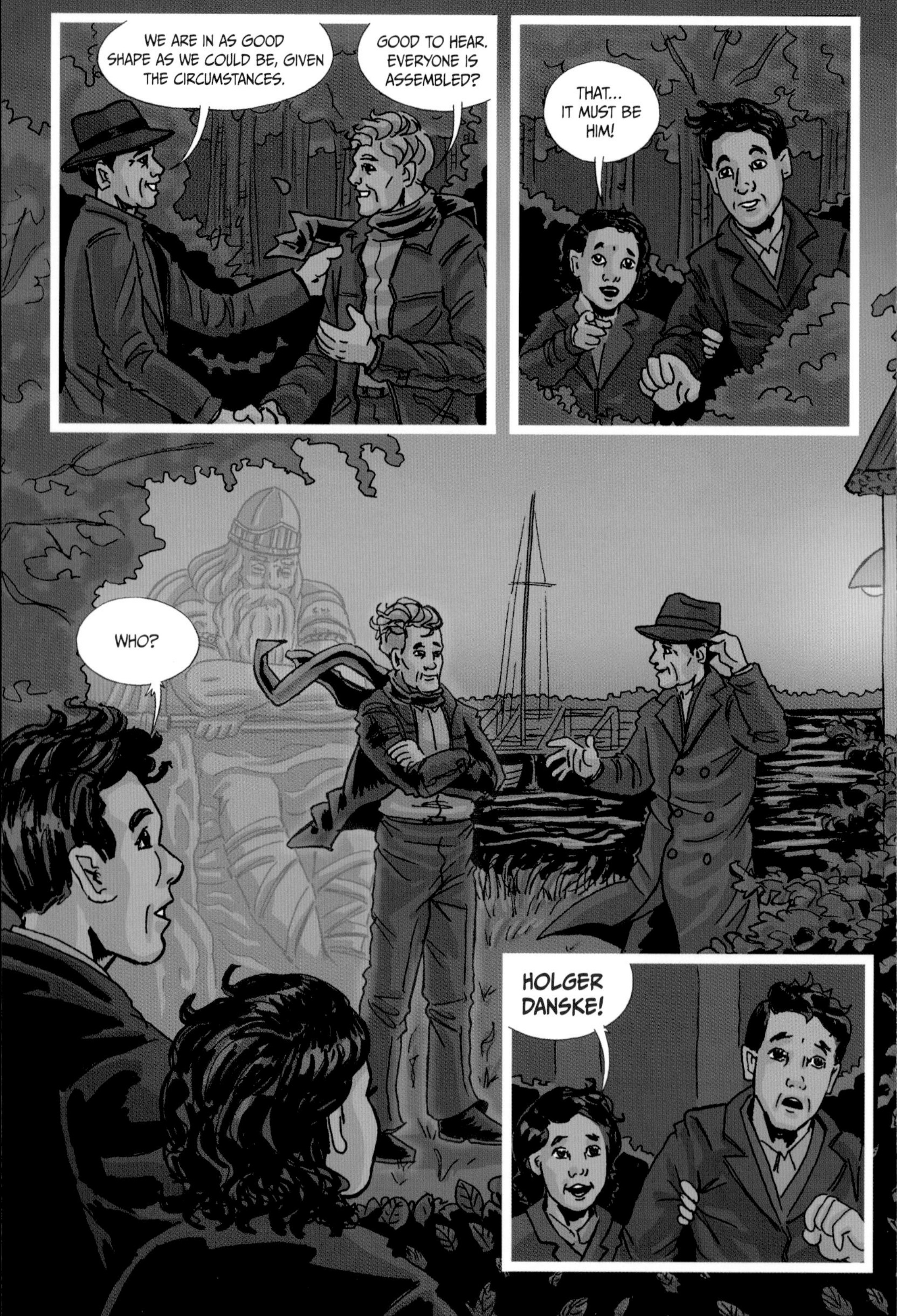
WE ARE IN AS GOOD SHAPE AS WE COULD BE, GIVEN THE CIRCUMSTANCES.
GOOD TO HEAR. EVERYONE IS ASSEMBLED?
THAT... IT MUST BE HIM!
WHO?
HOLGER DANSKE!

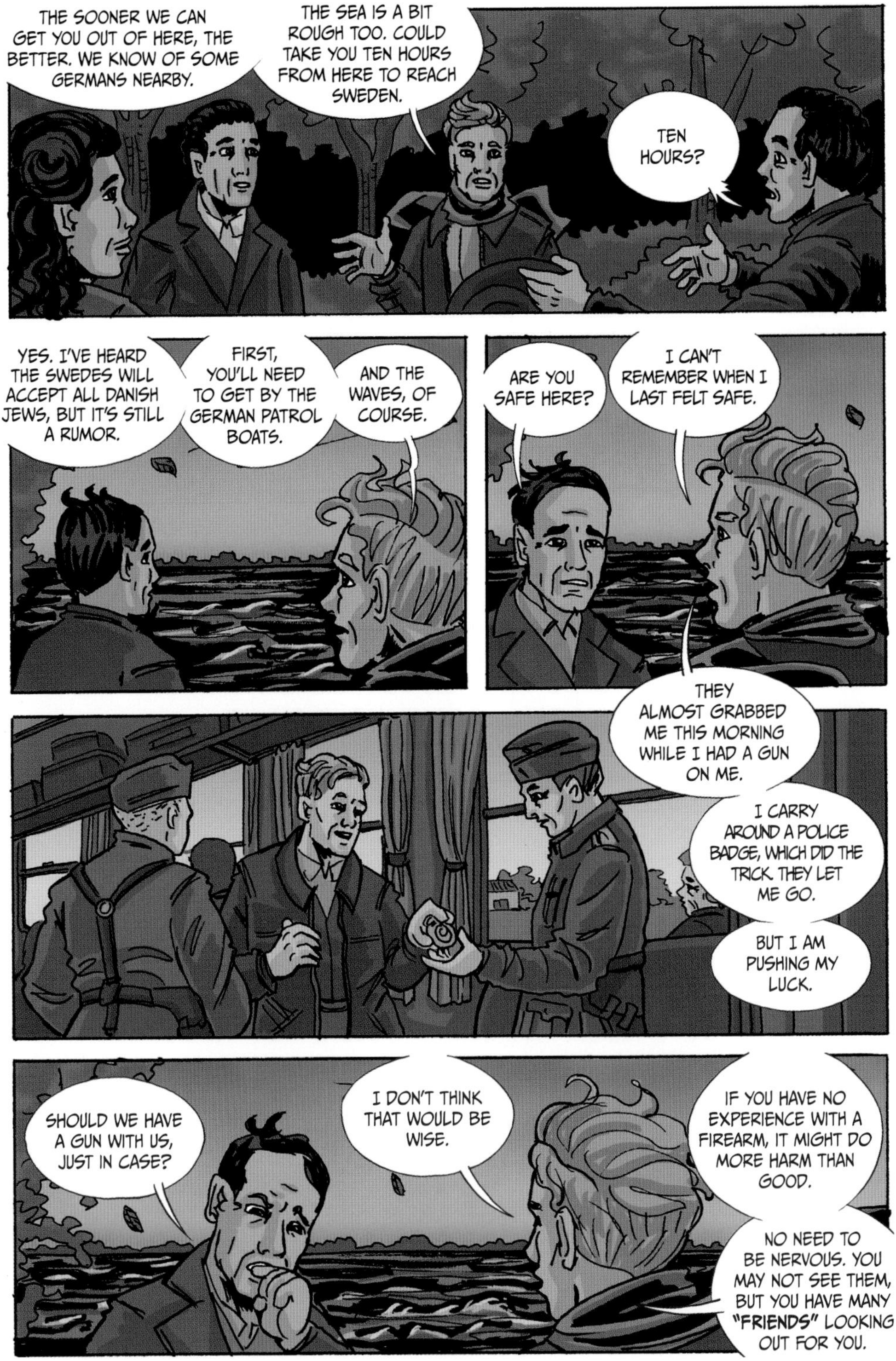
THE SOONER WE CAN GET YOU OUT OF HERE, THE BETTER. WE KNOW OF SOME GERMANS NEARBY.
THE SEA IS A BIT ROUGH TOO. COULD TAKE YOU TEN HOURS FROM HERE TO REACH SWEDEN.
TEN HOURS?
YES. I'VE HEARD THE SWEDES WILL ACCEPT ALL DANISH JEWS, BUT IT'S STILL A RUMOR.
FIRST, YOU'LL NEED TO GET BY THE GERMAN PATROL BOATS.
AND THE WAVES, OF COURSE.
ARE YOU SAFE HERE?
I CAN'T REMEMBER WHEN I LAST FELT SAFE.
THEY ALMOST GRABBED ME THIS MORNING WHILE I HAD A GUN ON ME.
I CARRY AROUND A POLICE BADGE, WHICH DID THE TRICK. THEY LET ME GO.
BUT I AM PUSHING MY LUCK.
SHOULD WE HAVE A GUN WITH US, JUST IN CASE?
I DON'T THINK THAT WOULD BE WISE.
IF YOU HAVE NO EXPERIENCE WITH A FIREARM, IT MIGHT DO MORE HARM THAN GOOD.
NO NEED TO BE NERVOUS. YOU MAY NOT SEE THEM, BUT YOU HAVE MANY "FRIENDS" LOOKING OUT FOR YOU.

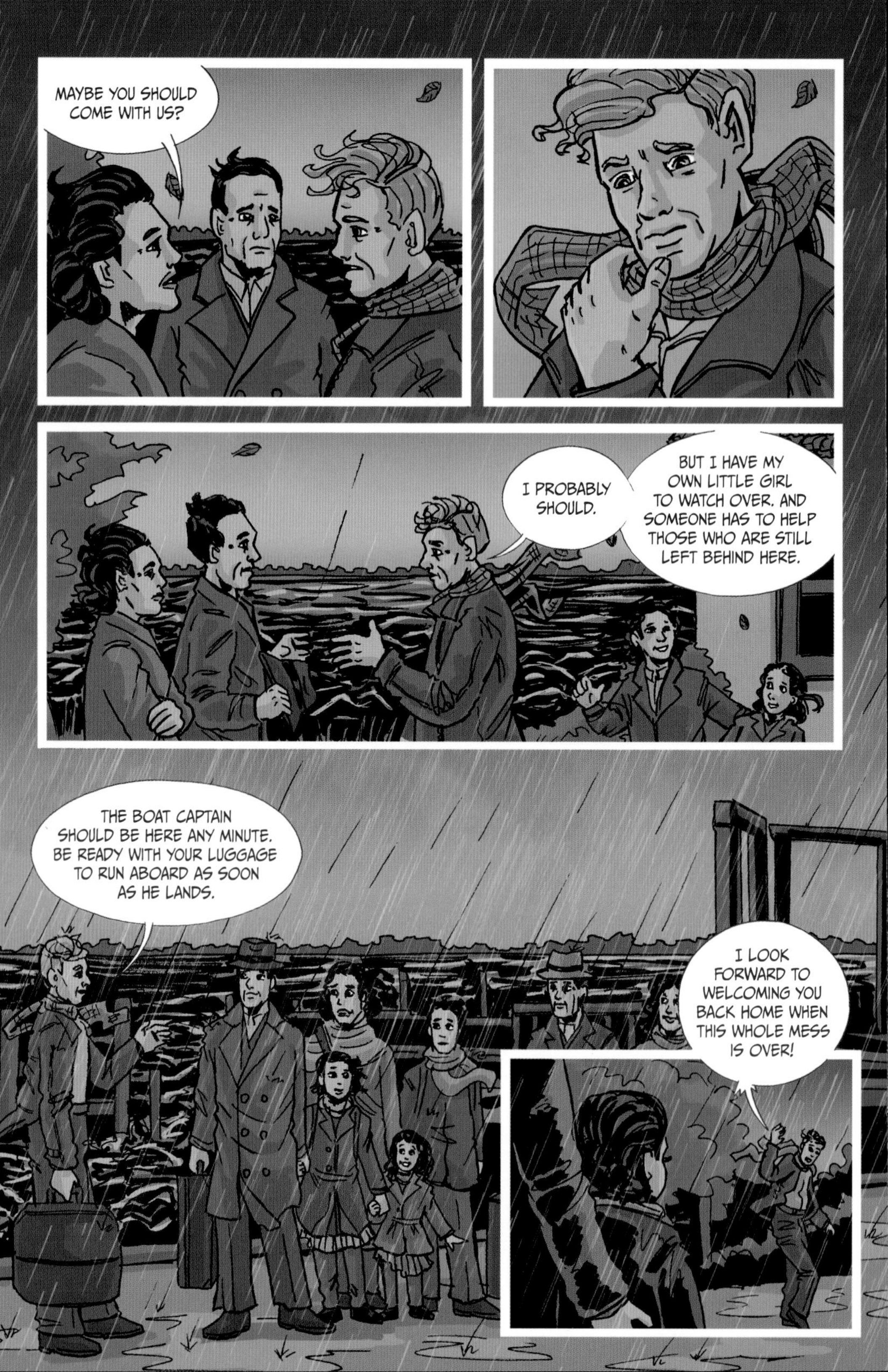
MAYBE YOU SHOULD COME WITH US?
I PROBABLY SHOULD.
BUT I HAVE MY OWN LITTLE GIRL TO WATCH OVER. AND SOMEONE HAS TO HELP THOSE WHO ARE STILL LEFT BEHIND HERE.
THE BOAT CAPTAIN SHOULD BE HERE ANY MINUTE. BE READY WITH YOUR LUGGAGE TO RUN ABOARD AS SOON AS HE LANDS.
I LOOK FORWARD TO WELCOMING YOU BACK HOME WHEN THIS WHOLE MESS IS OVER!

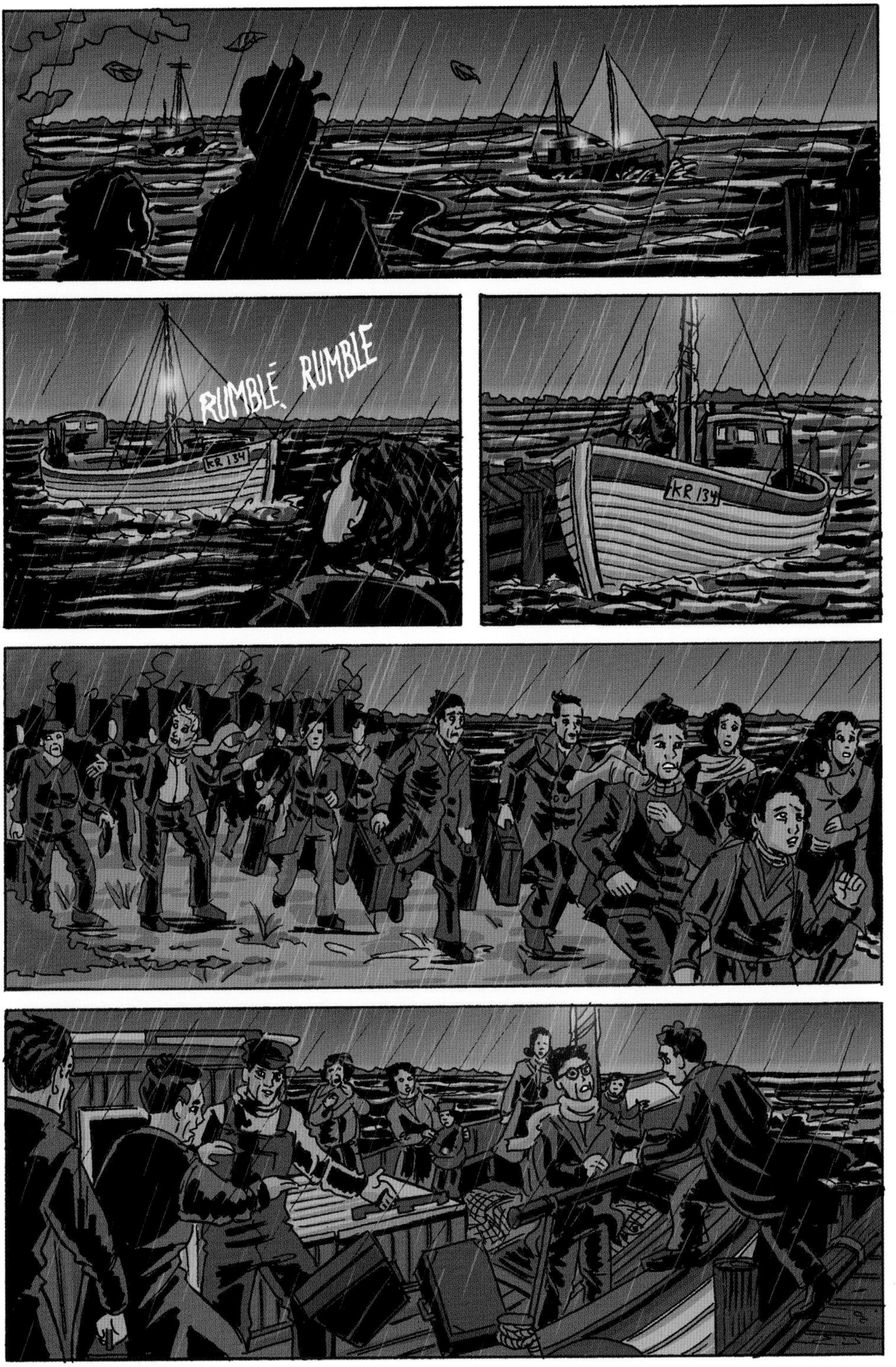
RUMBLE, RUMBLE
KR 134

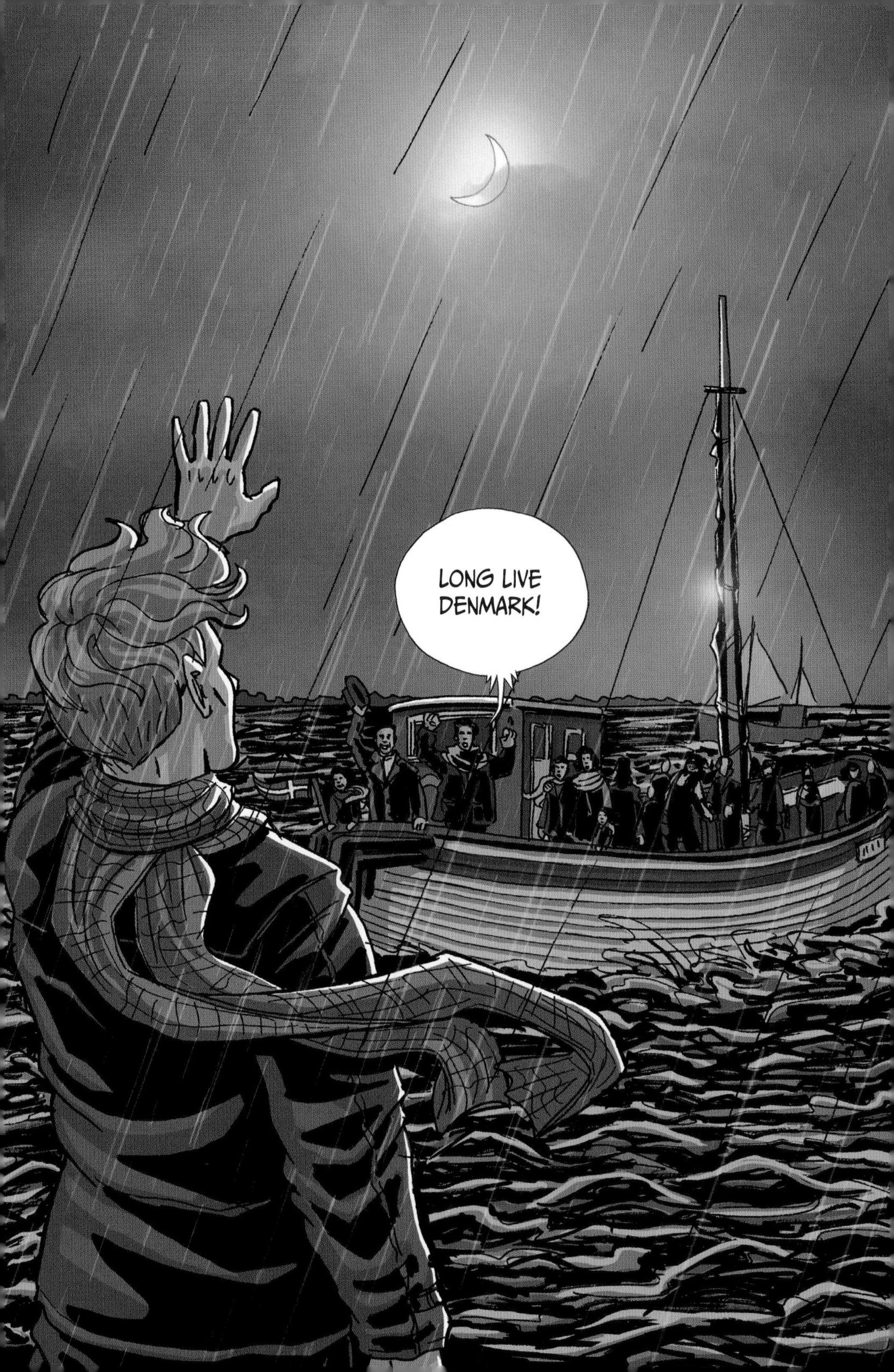
LONG LIVE DENMARK!

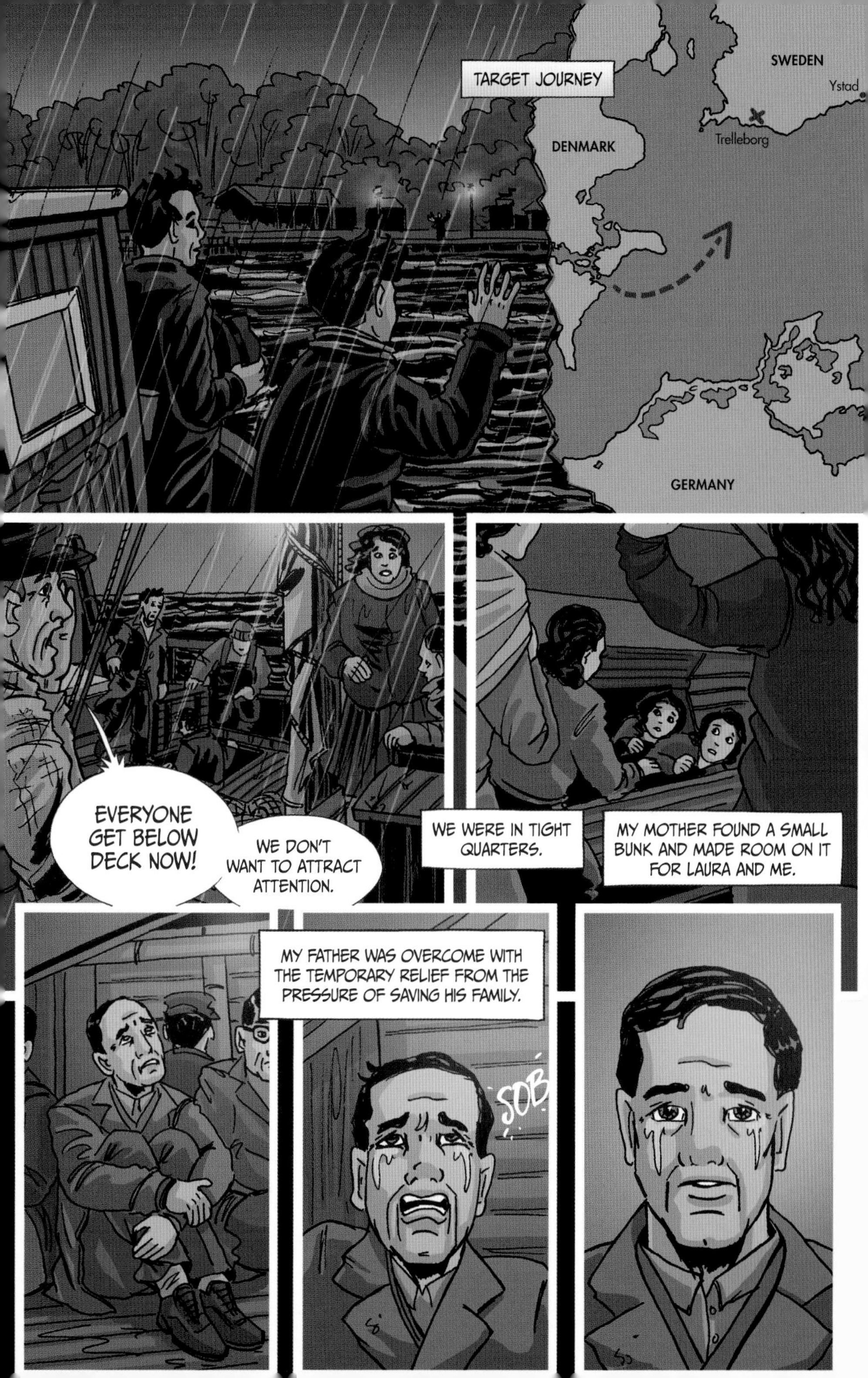
TARGET JOURNEY
SWEDEN
Ystad
Trelleborg
DENMARK
GERMANY
EVERYONE GET BELOW DECK NOW!
WE DON'T WANT TO ATTRACT ATTENTION.
WE WERE IN TIGHT QUARTERS.
MY MOTHER FOUND A SMALL BUNK AND MADE ROOM ON IT FOR LAURA AND ME.
MY FATHER WAS OVERCOME WITH THE TEMPORARY RELIEF FROM THE PRESSURE OF SAVING HIS FAMILY.
SOB

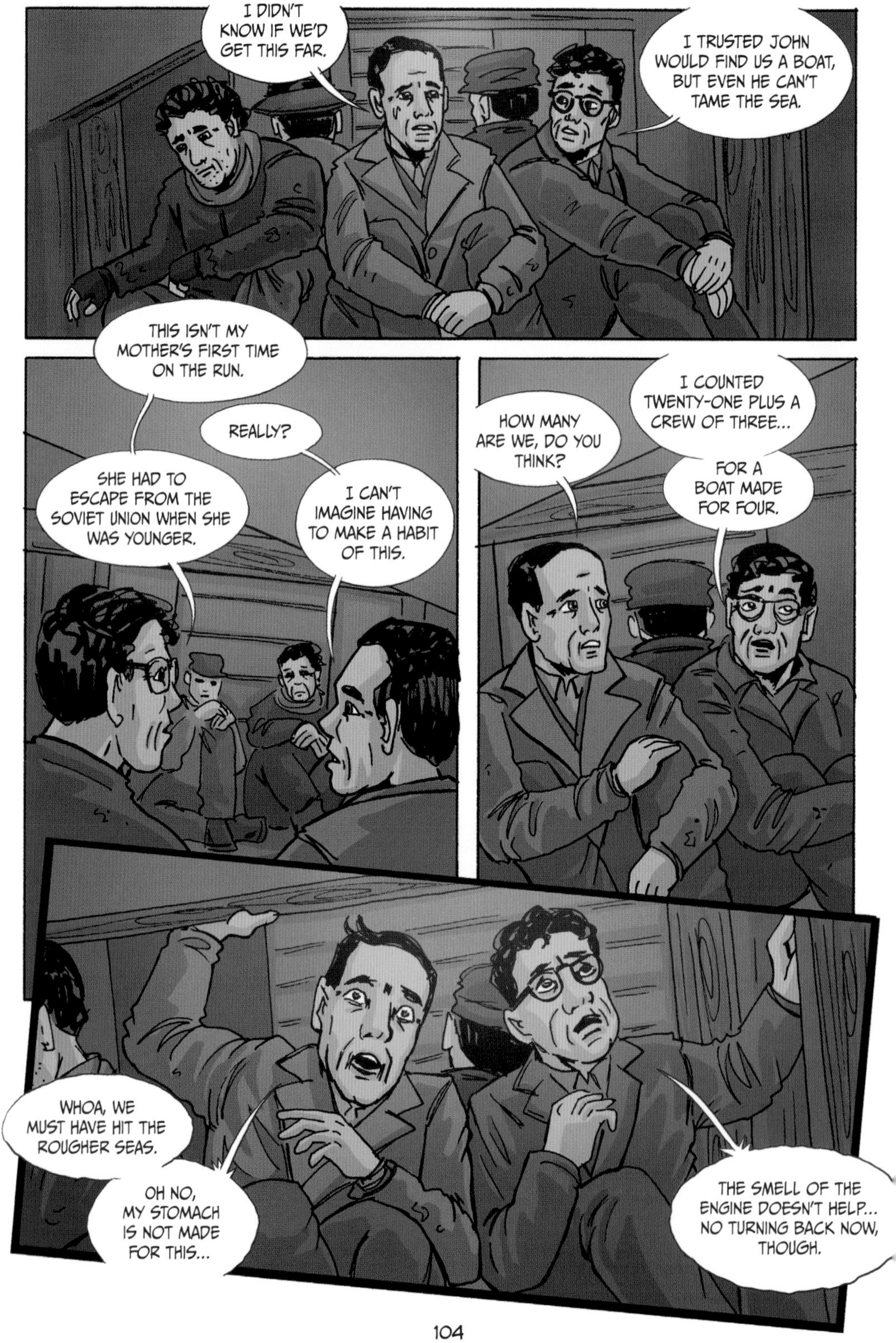
I DIDN'T KNOW IF WE'D GET THIS FAR.
I TRUSTED JOHN WOULD FIND US A BOAT, BUT EVEN HE CAN'T TAME THE SEA.
THIS ISN'T MY MOTHER'S FIRST TIME ON THE RUN.
REALLY?
SHE HAD TO ESCAPE FROM THE SOVIET UNION WHEN SHE WAS YOUNGER.
I CAN'T IMAGINE HAVING TO MAKE A HABIT OF THIS.
HOW MANY ARE WE, DO YOU THINK?
I COUNTED TWENTY-ONE PLUS A CREW OF THREE...
FOR A BOAT MADE FOR FOUR.
WHOA, WE MUST HAVE HIT THE ROUGHER SEAS.
OH NO, MY STOMACH IS NOT MADE FOR THIS...
THE SMELL OF THE ENGINE DOESN'T HELP... NO TURNING BACK NOW, THOUGH.

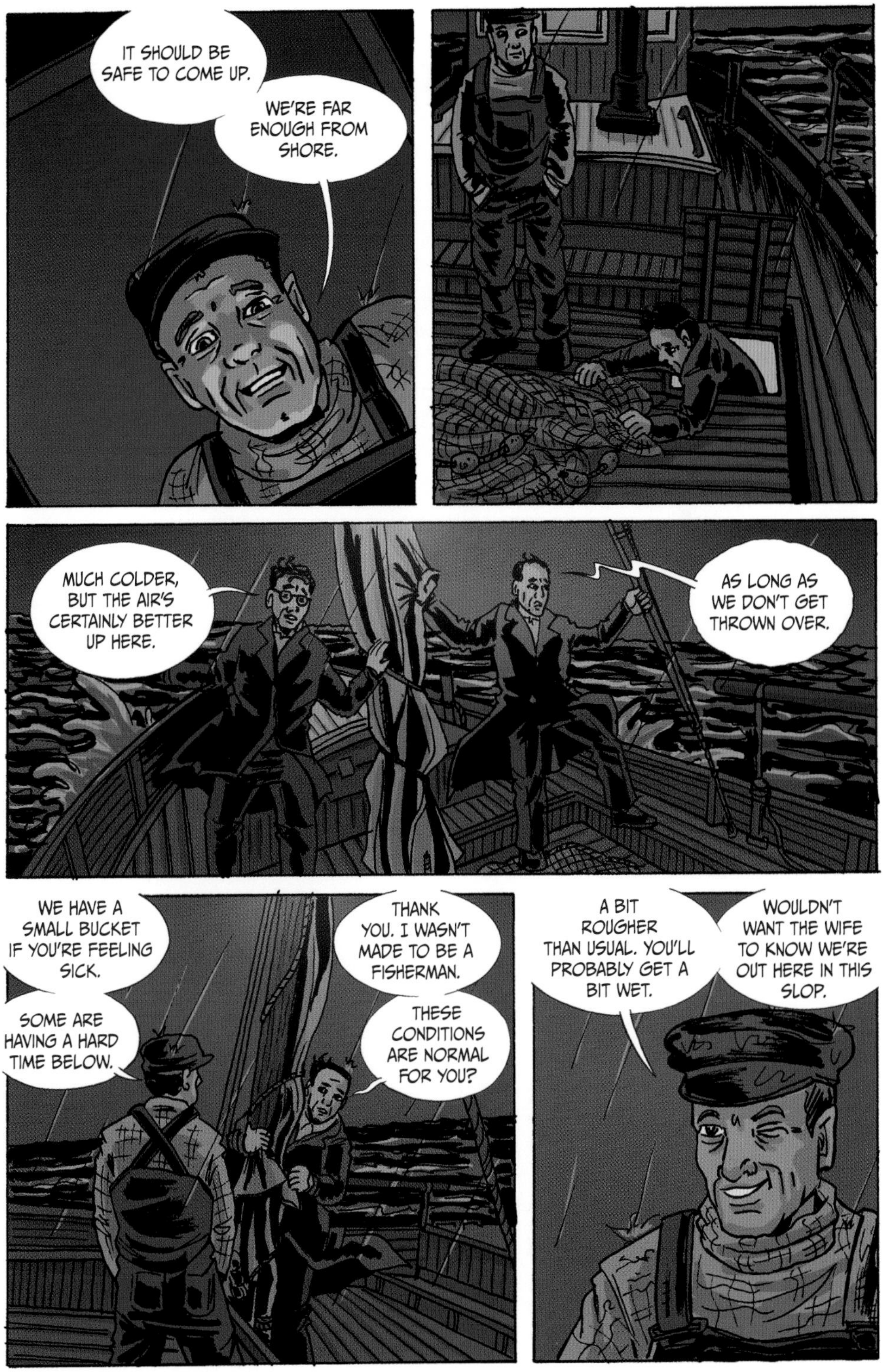
IT SHOULD BE SAFE TO COME UP.
WE'RE FAR ENOUGH FROM SHORE.
MUCH COLDER, BUT THE AIR'S CERTAINLY BETTER UP HERE.
AS LONG AS WE DON'T GET THROWN OVER.
WE HAVE A SMALL BUCKET IF YOU'RE FEELING SICK.
SOME ARE HAVING A HARD TIME BELOW.
THANK YOU. I WASN'T MADE TO BE A FISHERMAN.
THESE CONDITIONS ARE NORMAL FOR YOU?
A BIT ROUGHER THAN USUAL. YOU'LL PROBABLY GET A BIT WET.
WOULDN'T WANT THE WIFE TO KNOW WE'RE OUT HERE IN THIS SLOP.

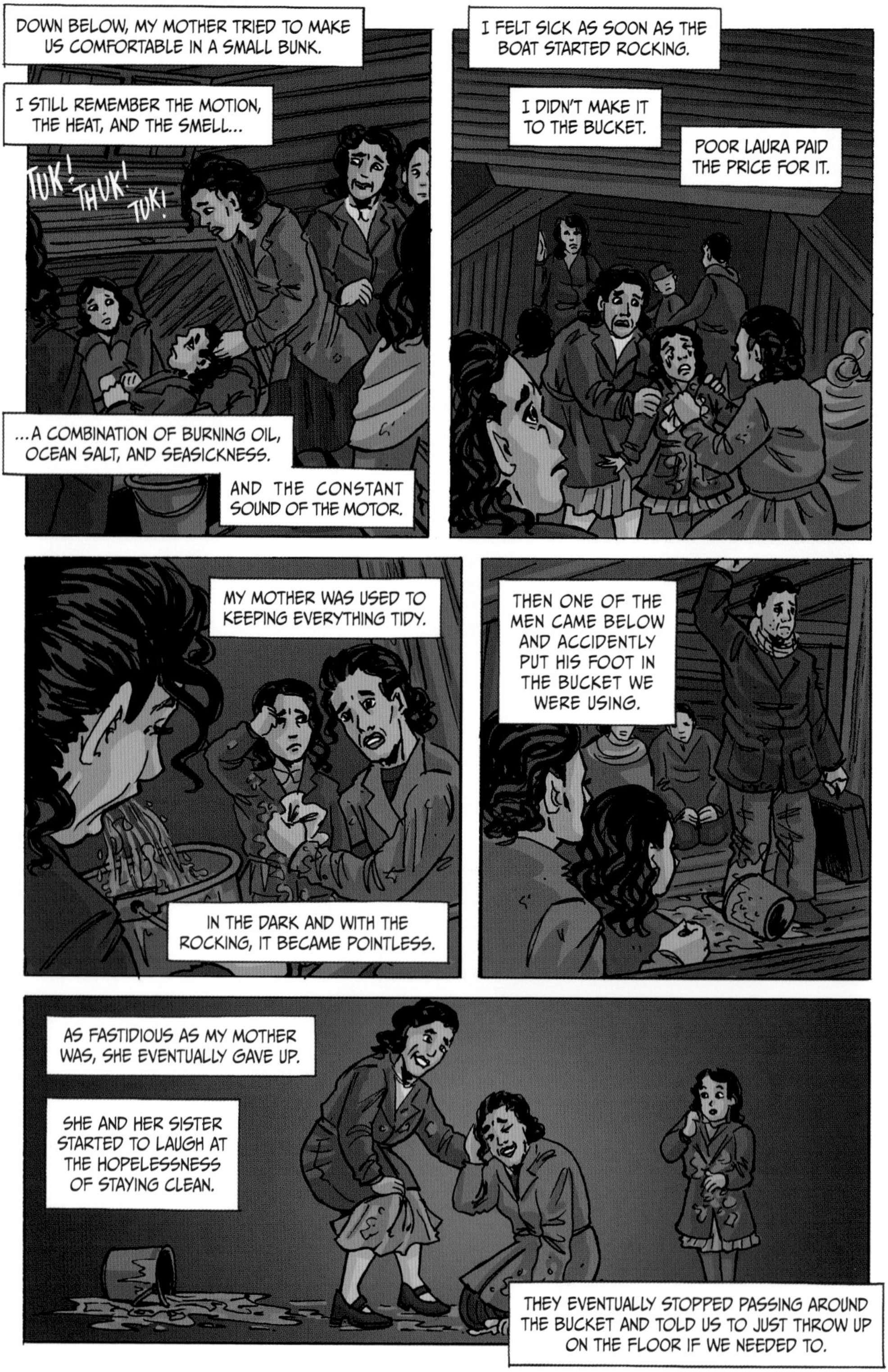
DOWN BELOW, MY MOTHER TRIED TO MAKE US COMFORTABLE IN A SMALL BUNK.
I STILL REMEMBER THE MOTION, THE HEAT, AND THE SMELL...
TUK! THUK! TUK!
...A COMBINATION OF BURNING OIL, OCEAN SALT, AND SEASICKNESS.
AND THE CONSTANT SOUND OF THE MOTOR.
I FELT SICK AS SOON AS THE BOAT STARTED ROCKING.
I DIDN'T MAKE IT TO THE BUCKET.
POOR LAURA PAID THE PRICE FOR IT.
MY MOTHER WAS USED TO KEEPING EVERYTHING TIDY.
IN THE DARK AND WITH THE ROCKING, IT BECAME POINTLESS.
THEN ONE OF THE MEN CAME BELOW AND ACCIDENTLY PUT HIS FOOT IN THE BUCKET WE WERE USING.
AS FASTIDIOUS AS MY MOTHER WAS, SHE EVENTUALLY GAVE UP.
SHE AND HER SISTER STARTED TO LAUGH AT THE HOPELESSNESS OF STAYING CLEAN.
THEY EVENTUALLY STOPPED PASSING AROUND THE BUCKET AND TOLD US TO JUST THROW UP ON THE FLOOR IF WE NEEDED TO.

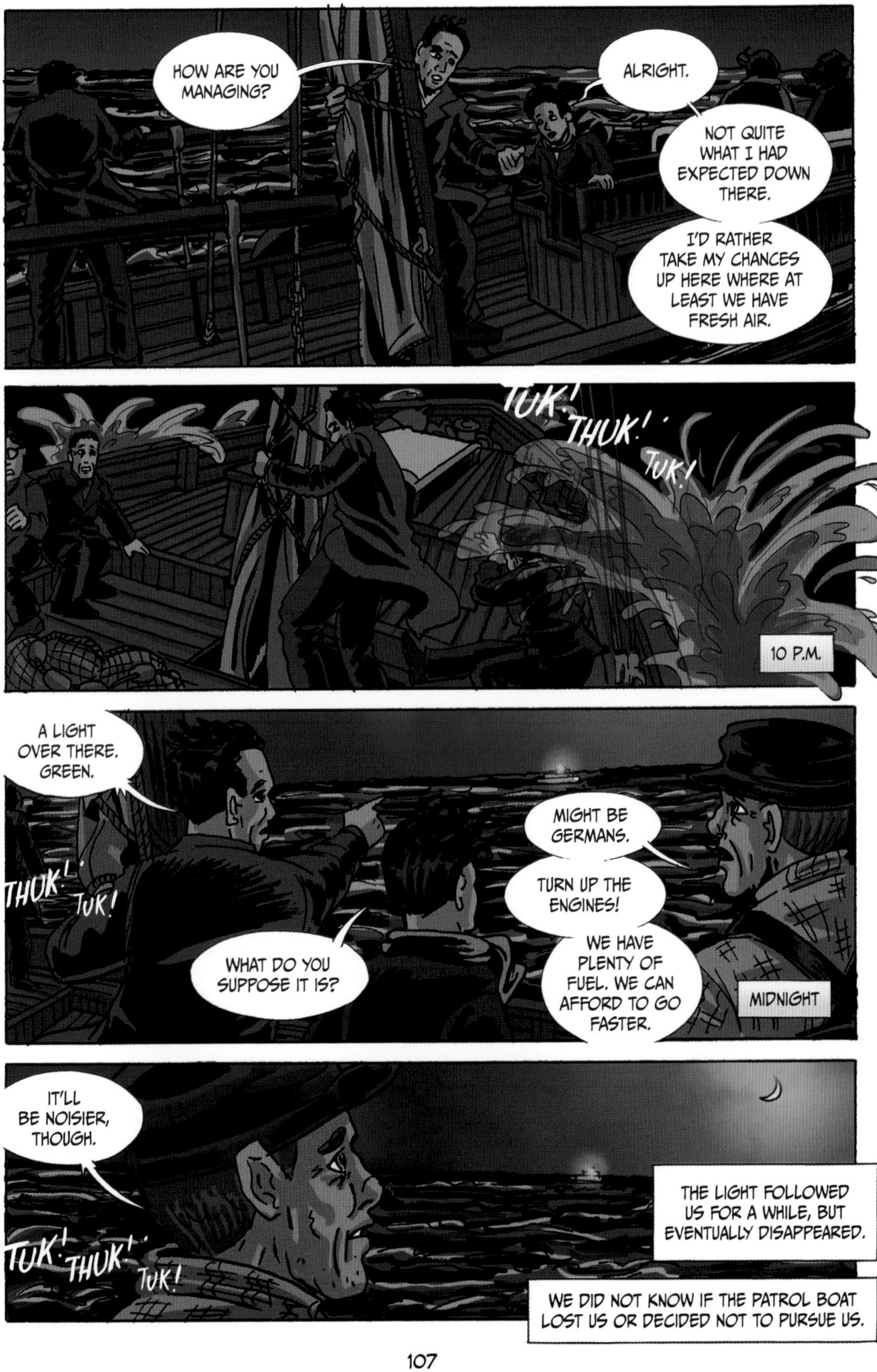
HOW ARE YOU MANAGING?
ALRIGHT.
NOT QUITE WHAT I HAD EXPECTED DOWN THERE.
I'D RATHER TAKE MY CHANCES UP HERE WHERE AT LEAST WE HAVE FRESH AIR.
TUK! THUK! TUK!
10 P.M.
A LIGHT OVER THERE. GREEN.
THUK! TUK!
WHAT DO YOU SUPPOSE IT IS?
MIGHT BE GERMANS.
TURN UP THE ENGINES!
WE HAVE PLENTY OF FUEL. WE CAN AFFORD TO GO FASTER.
MIDNIGHT
IT'LL BE NOISIER, THOUGH.
TUK! THUK! TUK!
THE LIGHT FOLLOWED US FOR A WHILE, BUT EVENTUALLY DISAPPEARED.
WE DID NOT KNOW IF THE PATROL BOAT LOST US OR DECIDED NOT TO PURSUE US.

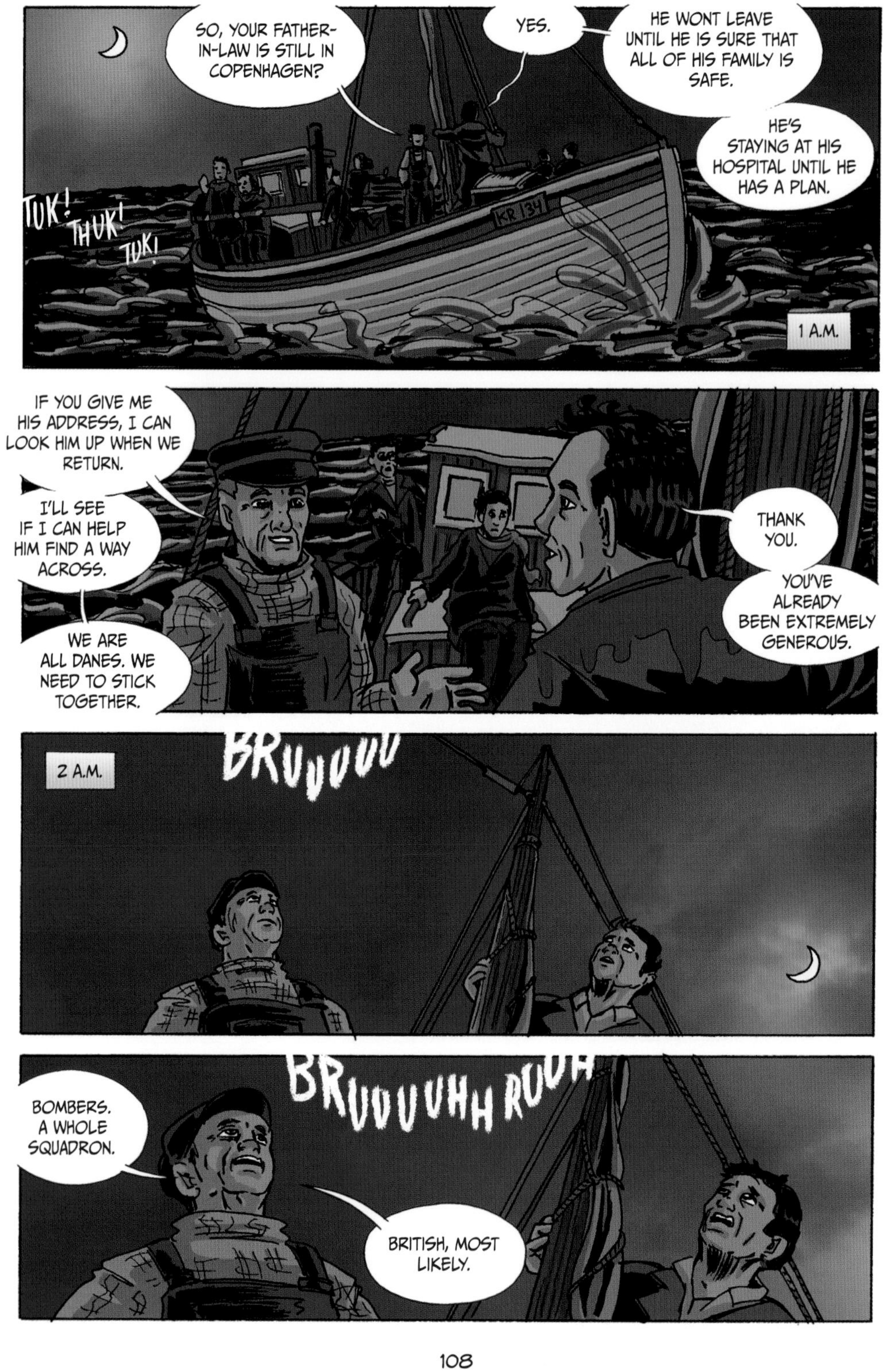

SO, YOUR FATHER-IN-LAW IS STILL IN COPENHAGEN?
YES.
HE WONT LEAVE UNTIL HE IS SURE THAT ALL OF HIS FAMILY IS SAFE.
HE'S STAYING AT HIS HOSPITAL UNTIL HE HAS A PLAN.
TUK! THUK! TUK!
1 A.M.
IF YOU GIVE ME HIS ADDRESS, I CAN LOOK HIM UP WHEN WE RETURN.
I'LL SEE IF I CAN HELP HIM FIND A WAY ACROSS.
WE ARE ALL DANES. WE NEED TO STICK TOGETHER.
THANK YOU.
YOU'VE ALREADY BEEN EXTREMELY GENEROUS.
2 A.M.
BRUUUUU
BRUUUUHH RUUH
BOMBERS. A WHOLE SQUADRON.
BRITISH, MOST LIKELY.

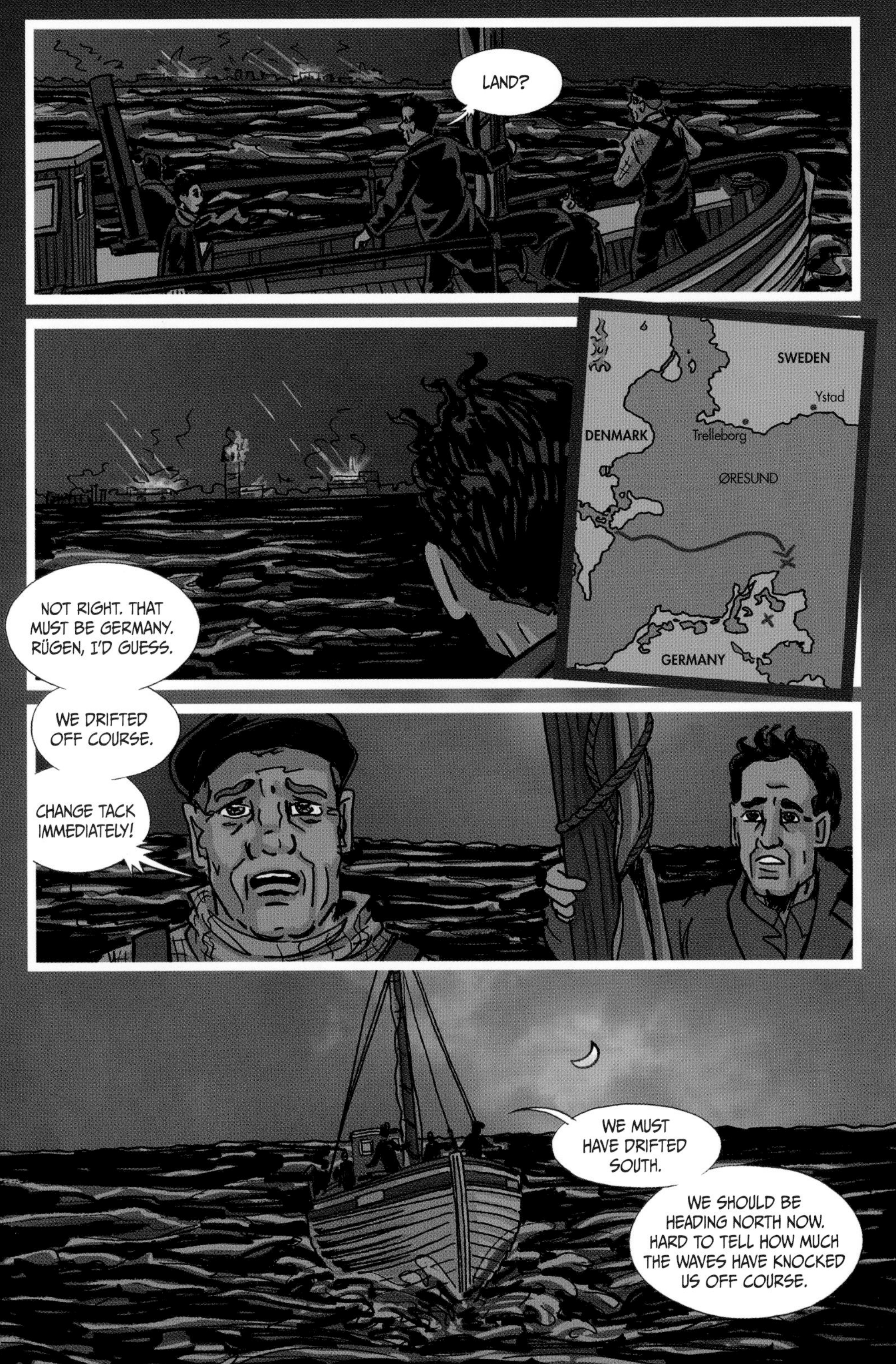
LAND?
SWEDEN
Ystad
DENMARK
Trelleborg
ØRESUND
GERMANY
NOT RIGHT. THAT MUST BE GERMANY. RÜGEN, I'D GUESS.
WE DRIFTED OFF COURSE.
CHANGE TACK IMMEDIATELY!
WE MUST HAVE DRIFTED SOUTH.
WE SHOULD BE HEADING NORTH NOW. HARD TO TELL HOW MUCH THE WAVES HAVE KNOCKED US OFF COURSE.

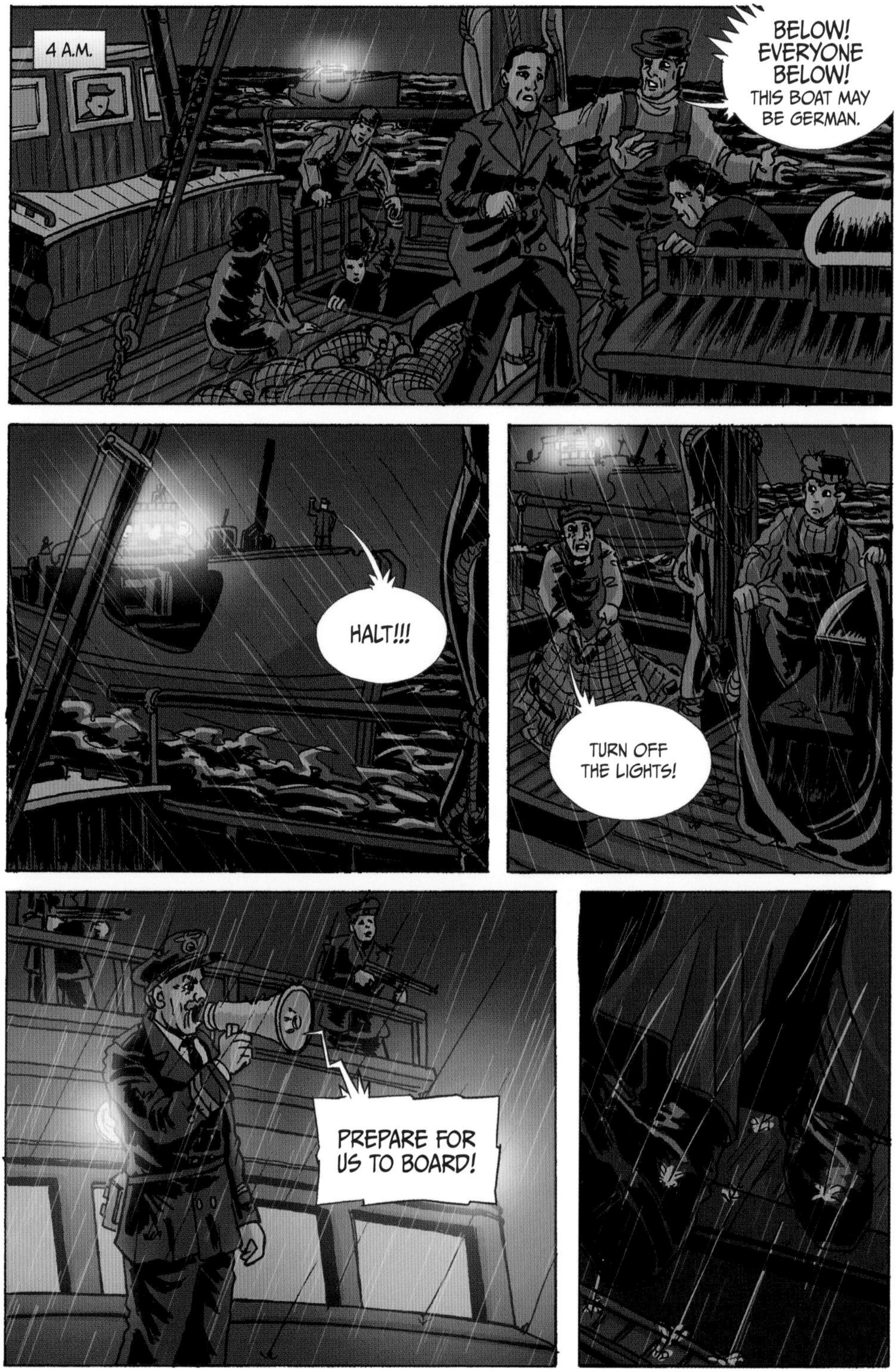
4 A.M.
BELOW! EVERYONE BELOW! THIS BOAT MAY BE GERMAN.
HALT!!!
TURN OFF THE LIGHTS!
PREPARE FOR US TO BOARD!

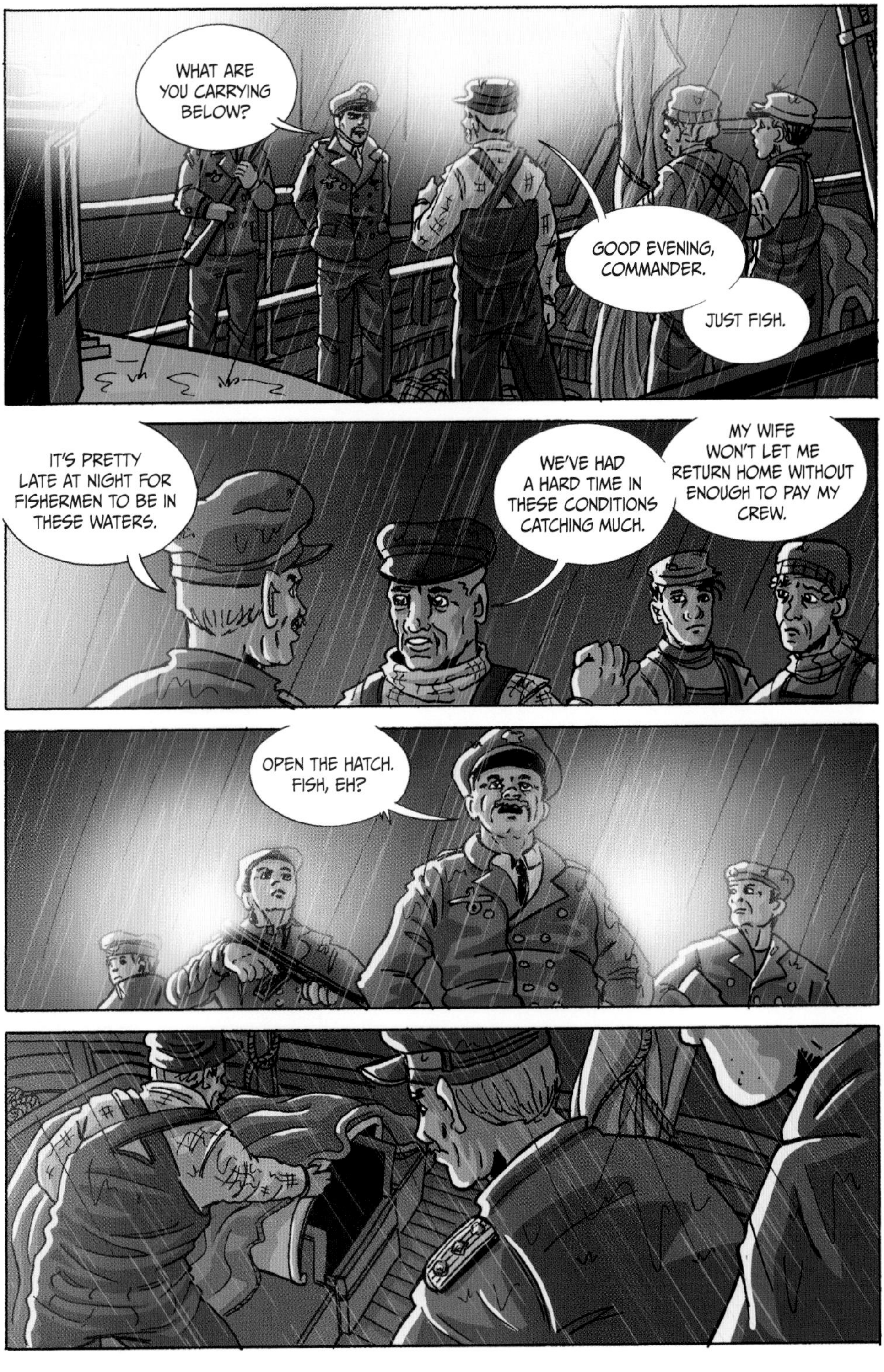
WHAT ARE YOU CARRYING BELOW?
GOOD EVENING, COMMANDER.
JUST FISH.
IT'S PRETTY LATE AT NIGHT FOR FISHERMEN TO BE IN THESE WATERS.
WE'VE HAD A HARD TIME IN THESE CONDITIONS CATCHING MUCH.
MY WIFE WON'T LET ME RETURN HOME WITHOUT ENOUGH TO PAY MY CREW.
OPEN THE HATCH. FISH, EH?

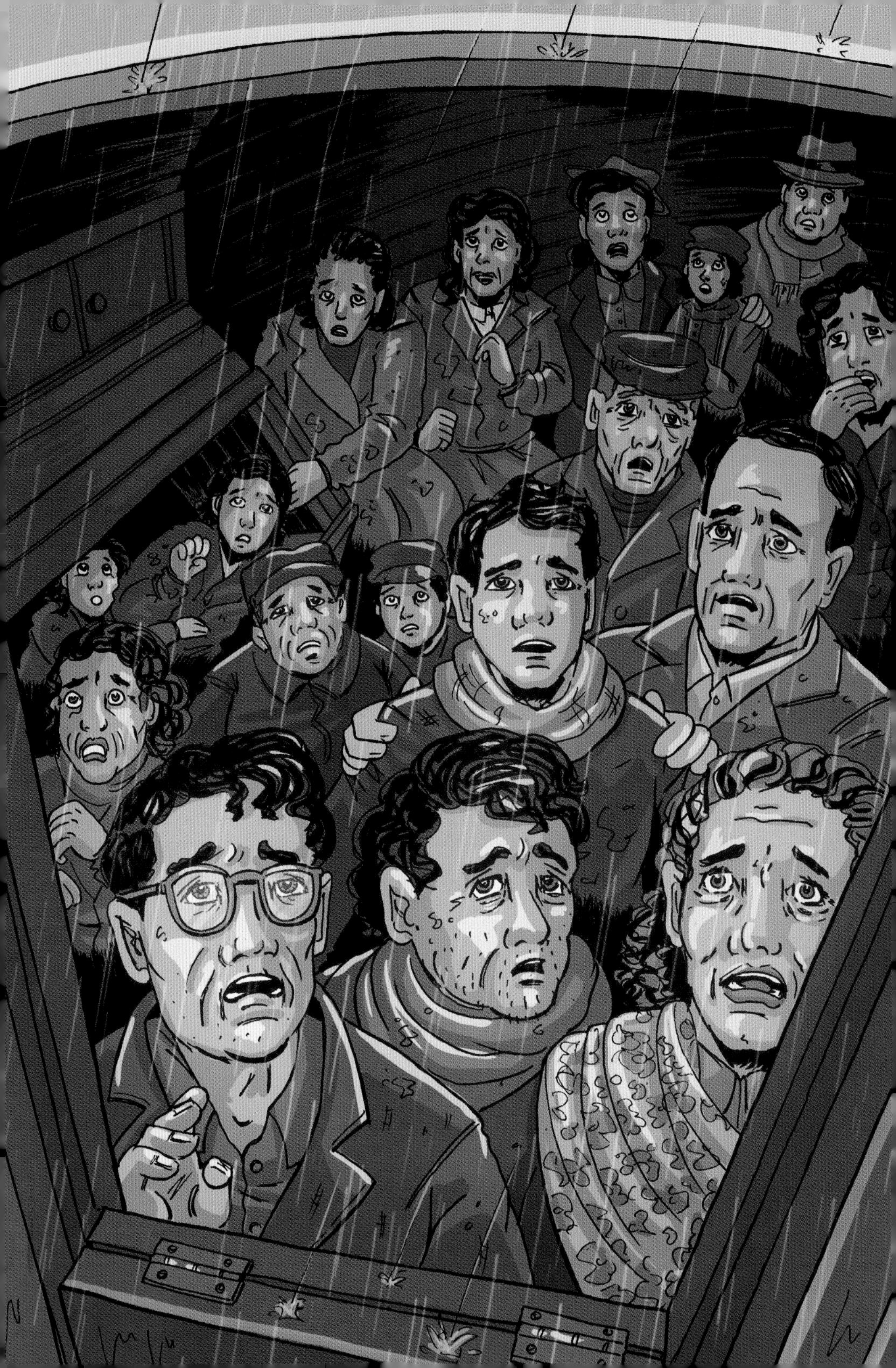

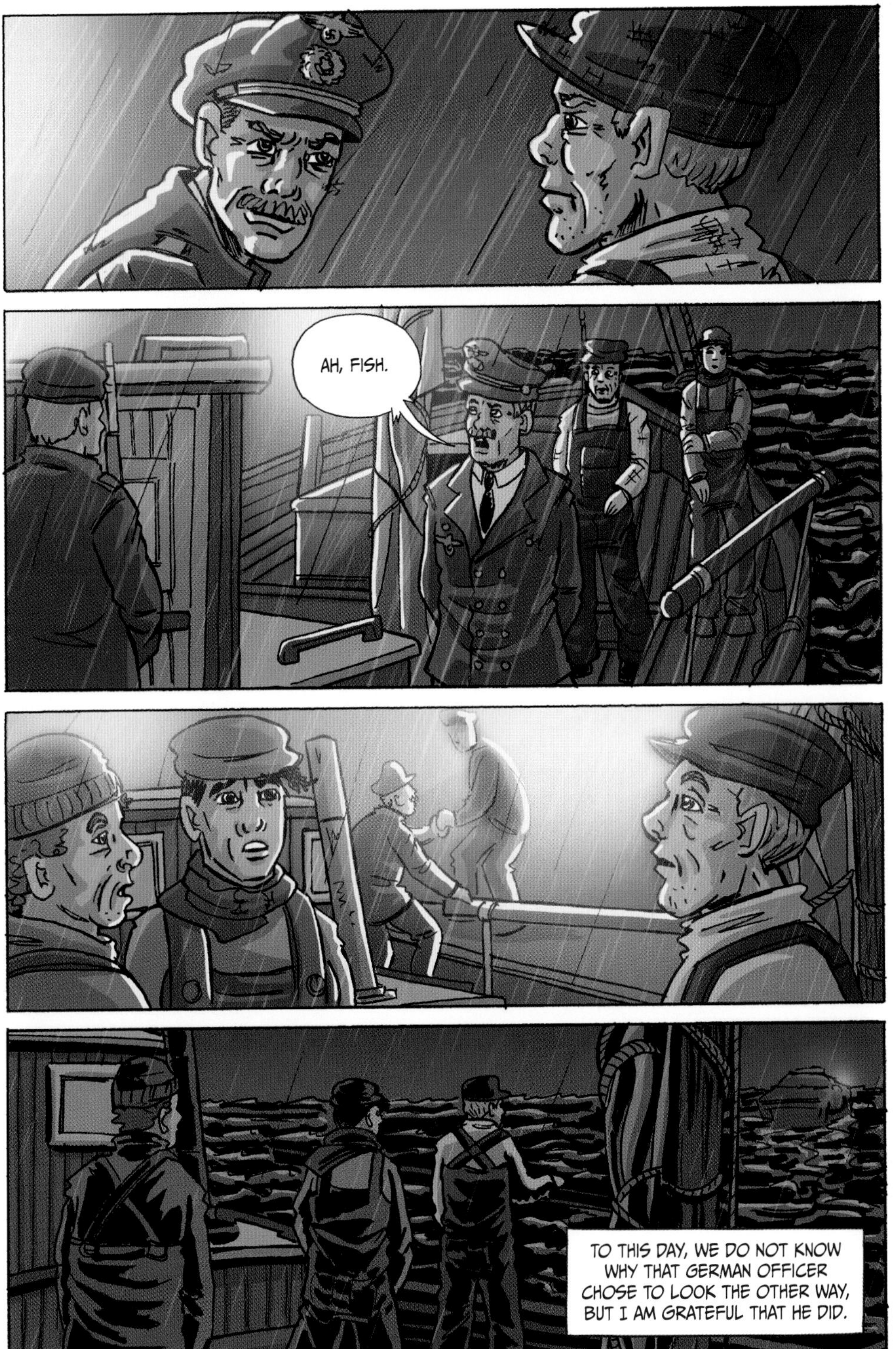
AH, FISH.
TO THIS DAY, WE DO NOT KNOW WHY THAT GERMAN OFFICER CHOSE TO LOOK THE OTHER WAY, BUT I AM GRATEFUL THAT HE DID.

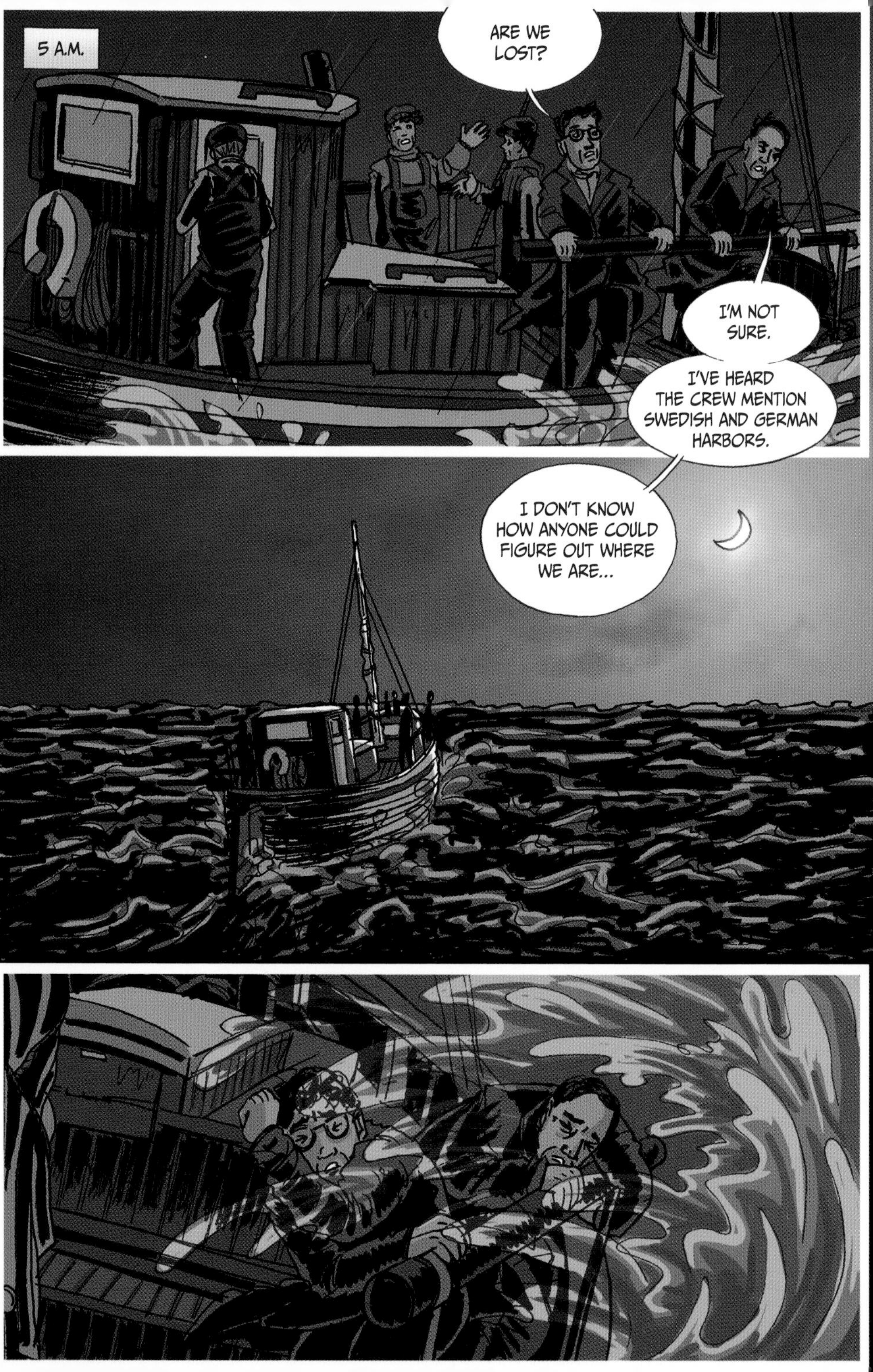
5 A.M.
ARE WE LOST?
I'M NOT SURE.
I'VE HEARD THE CREW MENTION SWEDISH AND GERMAN HARBORS.
I DON'T KNOW HOW ANYONE COULD FIGURE OUT WHERE WE ARE...

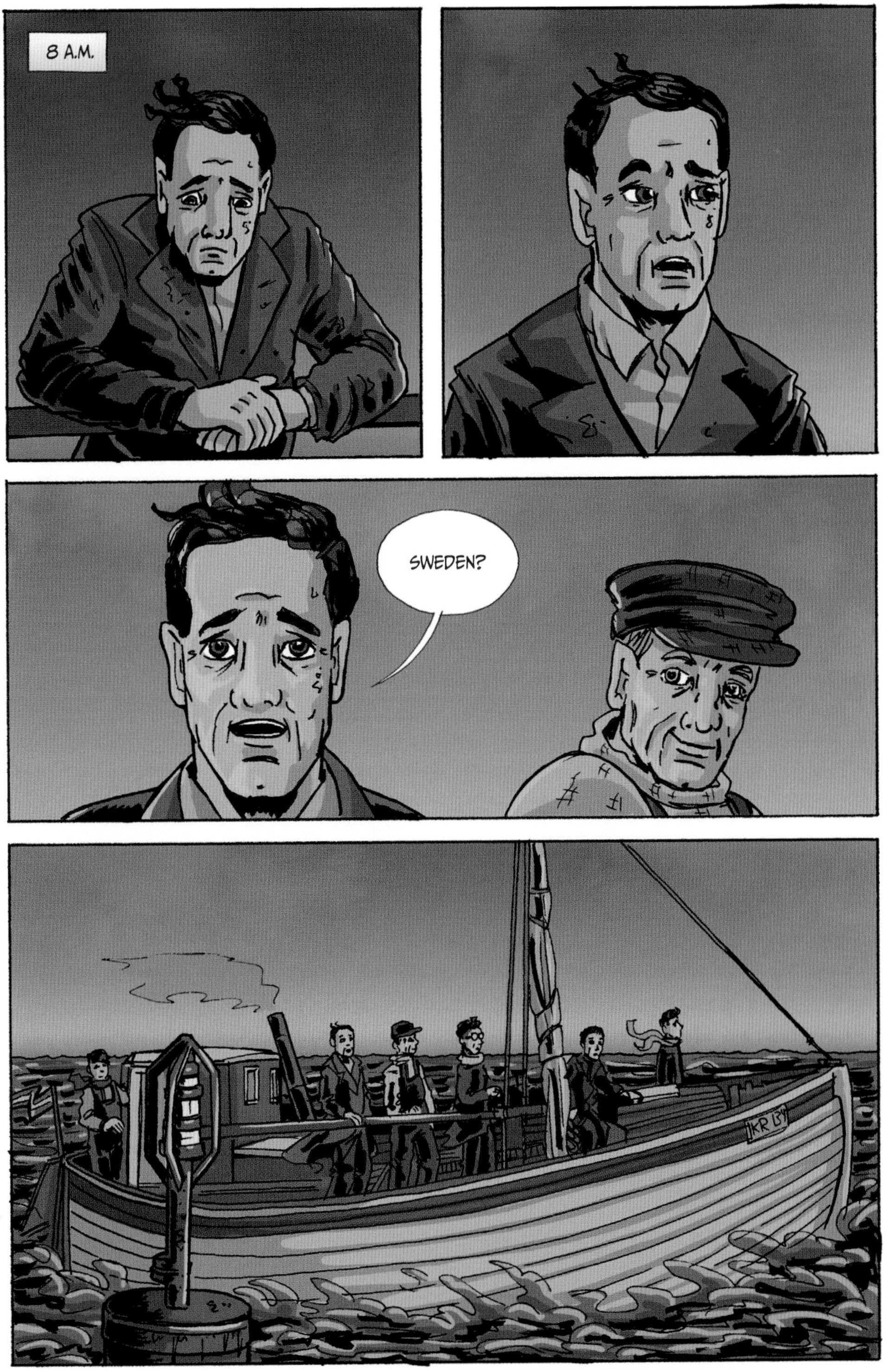
8 A.M.
SWEDEN?

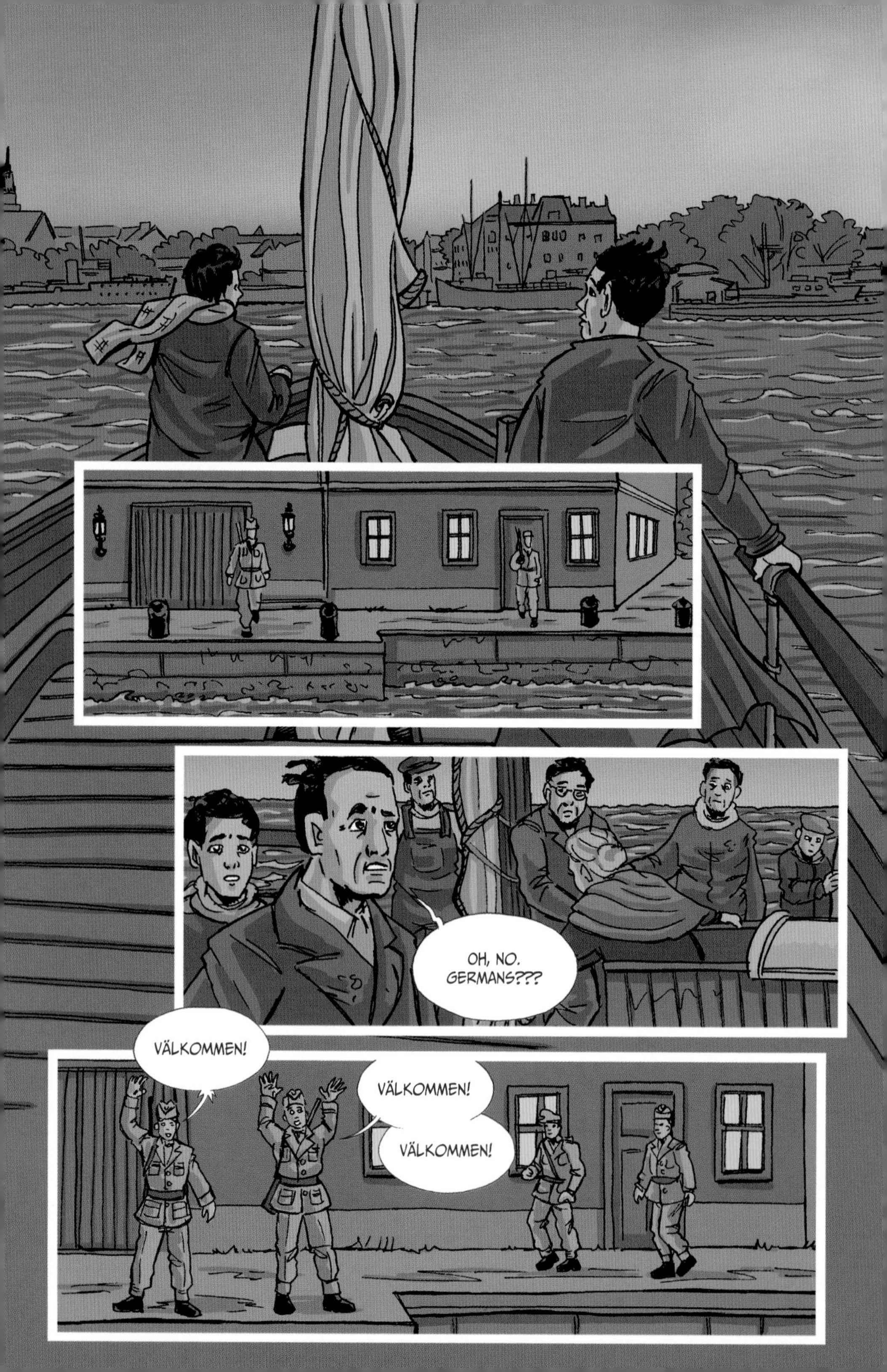
OH, NO.
GERMANS???
VÄLKOMMEN!
VÄLKOMMEN!
VÄLKOMMEN!

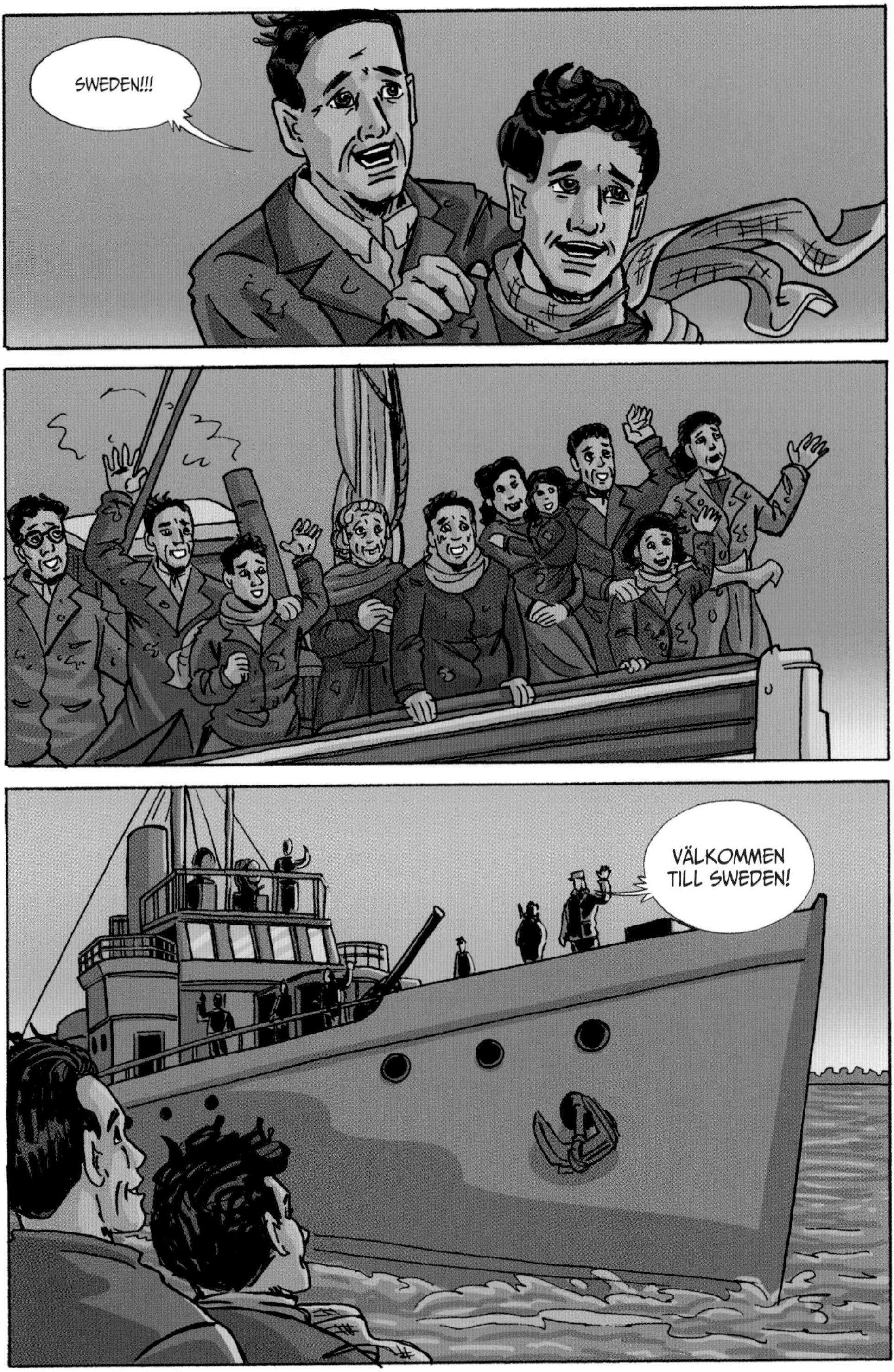
SWEDEN!!!
VÄLKOMMEN TILL SWEDEN!

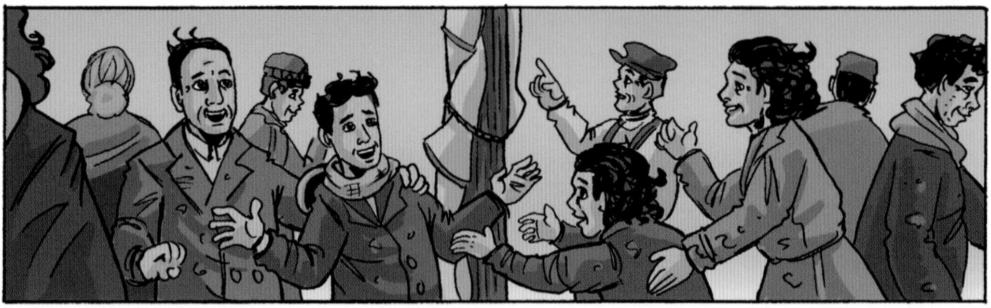

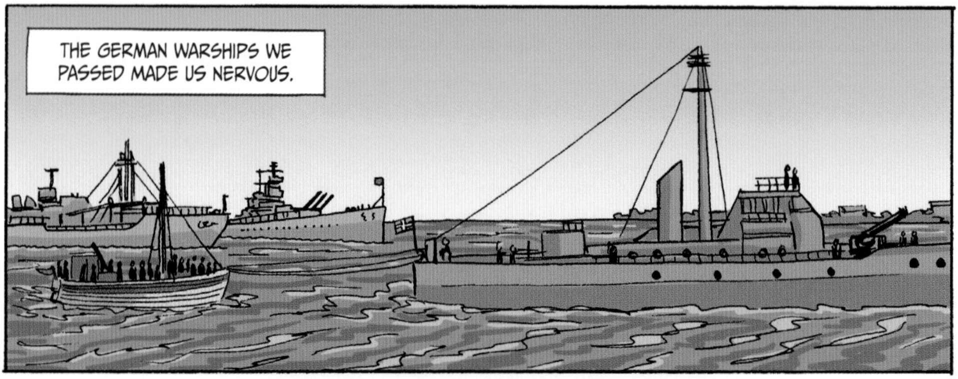
THE GERMAN WARSHIPS WE PASSED MADE US NERVOUS.

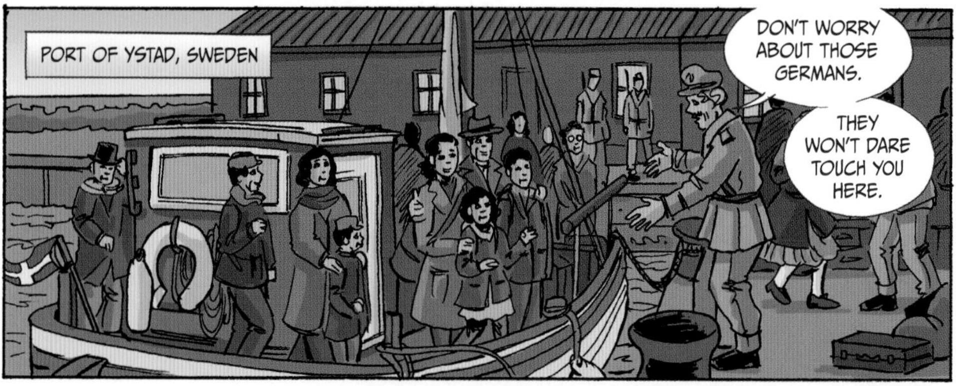
PORT OF YSTAD, SWEDEN
DON'T WORRY ABOUT THOSE GERMANS.
THEY WON'T DARE TOUCH YOU HERE.

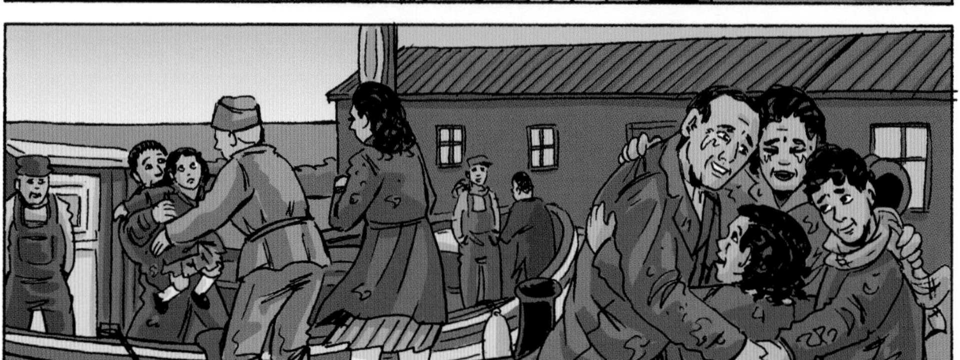

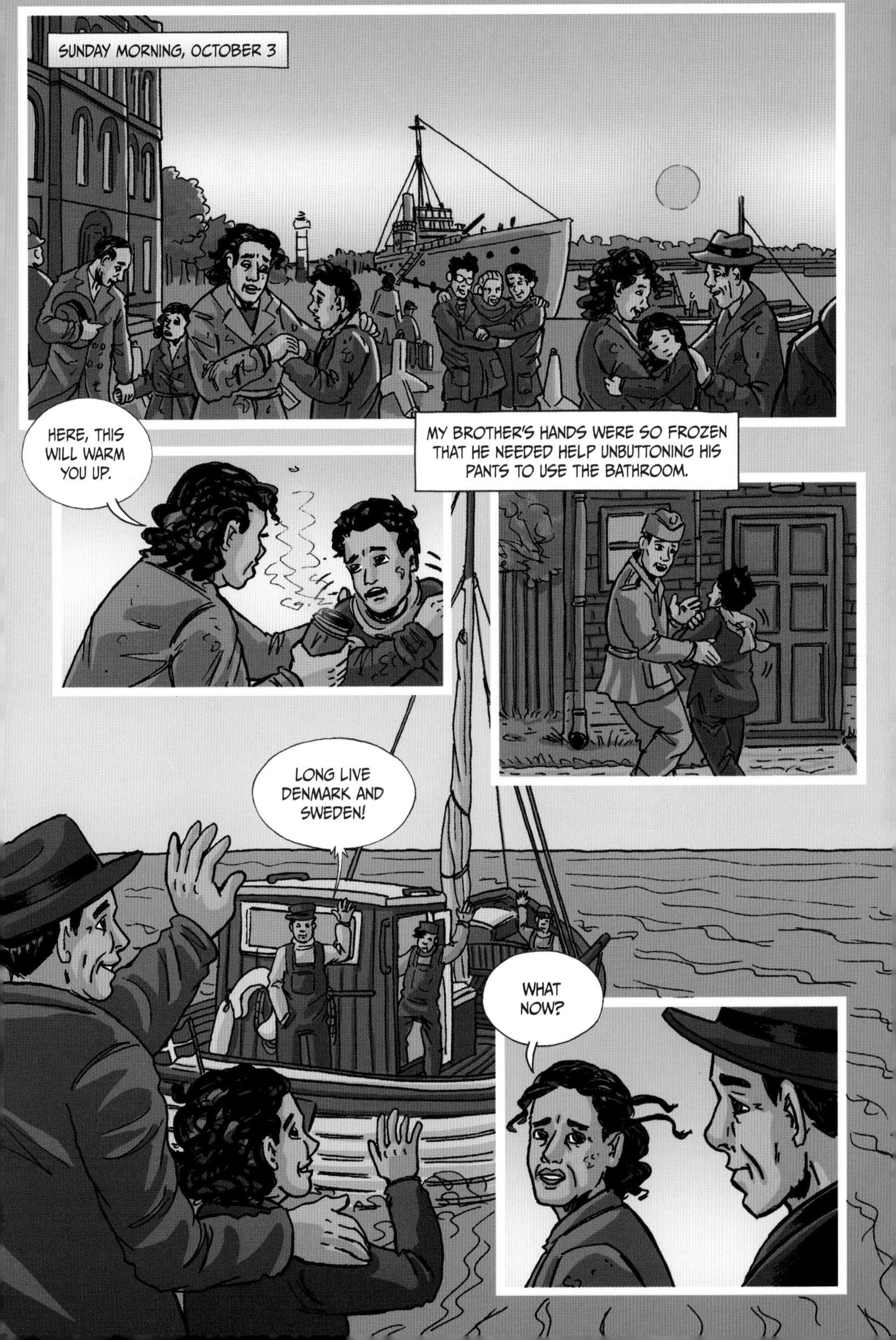
SUNDAY MORNING, OCTOBER 3
HERE, THIS WILL WARM YOU UP.
MY BROTHER'S HANDS WERE SO FROZEN THAT HE NEEDED HELP UNBUTTONING HIS PANTS TO USE THE BATHROOM.
LONG LIVE DENMARK AND SWEDEN!
WHAT NOW?

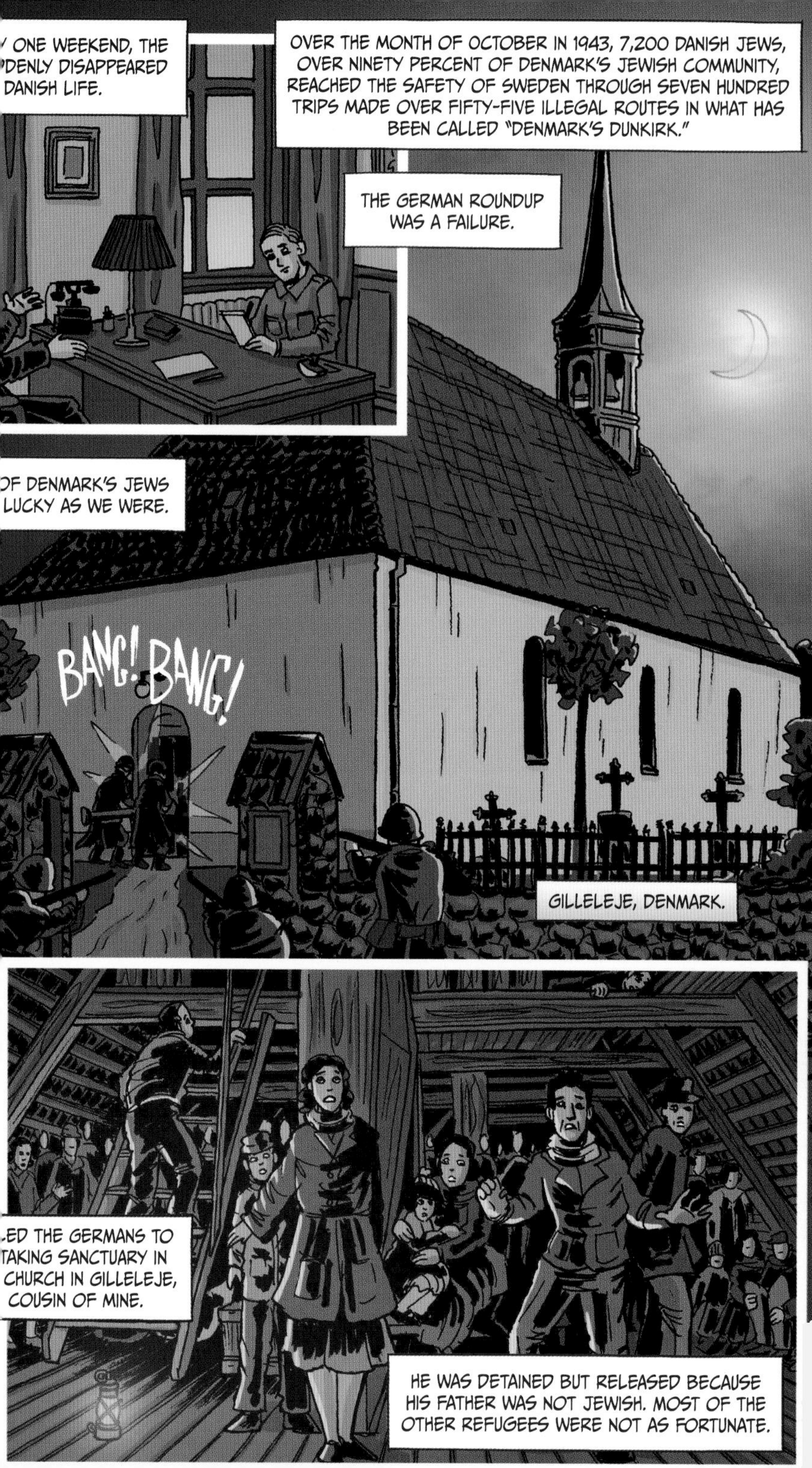
ONE WEEKEND, THE
DENLY DISAPPEARED
DANISH LIFE.
OVER THE MONTH OF OCTOBER IN 1943, 7,200 DANISH JEWS, OVER NINETY PERCENT OF DENMARK'S JEWISH COMMUNITY, REACHED THE SAFETY OF SWEDEN THROUGH SEVEN HUNDRED TRIPS MADE OVER FIFTY-FIVE ILLEGAL ROUTES IN WHAT HAS BEEN CALLED "DENMARK'S DUNKIRK."
THE GERMAN ROUNDUP WAS A FAILURE.
OF DENMARK'S JEWS
LUCKY AS WE WERE.
BANG! BANG!
GILLELEJE, DENMARK.
ED THE GERMANS TO
TAKING SANCTUARY IN
CHURCH IN GILLELEJE,
COUSIN OF MINE.
HE WAS DETAINED BUT RELEASED BECAUSE HIS FATHER WAS NOT JEWISH. MOST OF THE OTHER REFUGEES WERE NOT AS FORTUNATE.

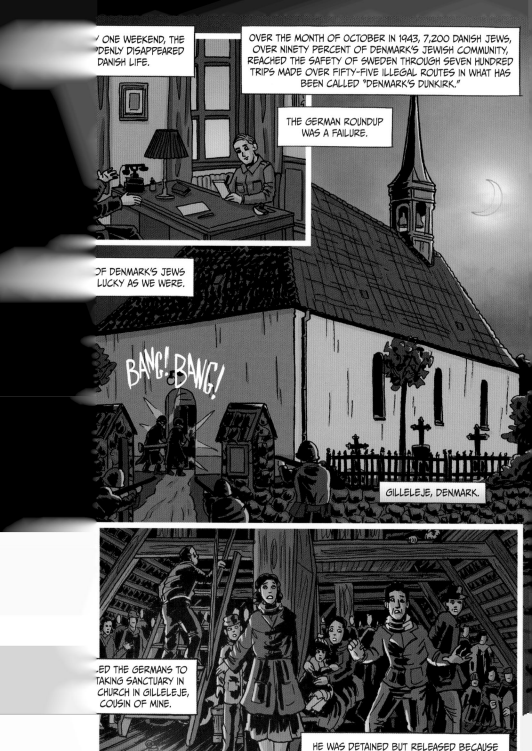

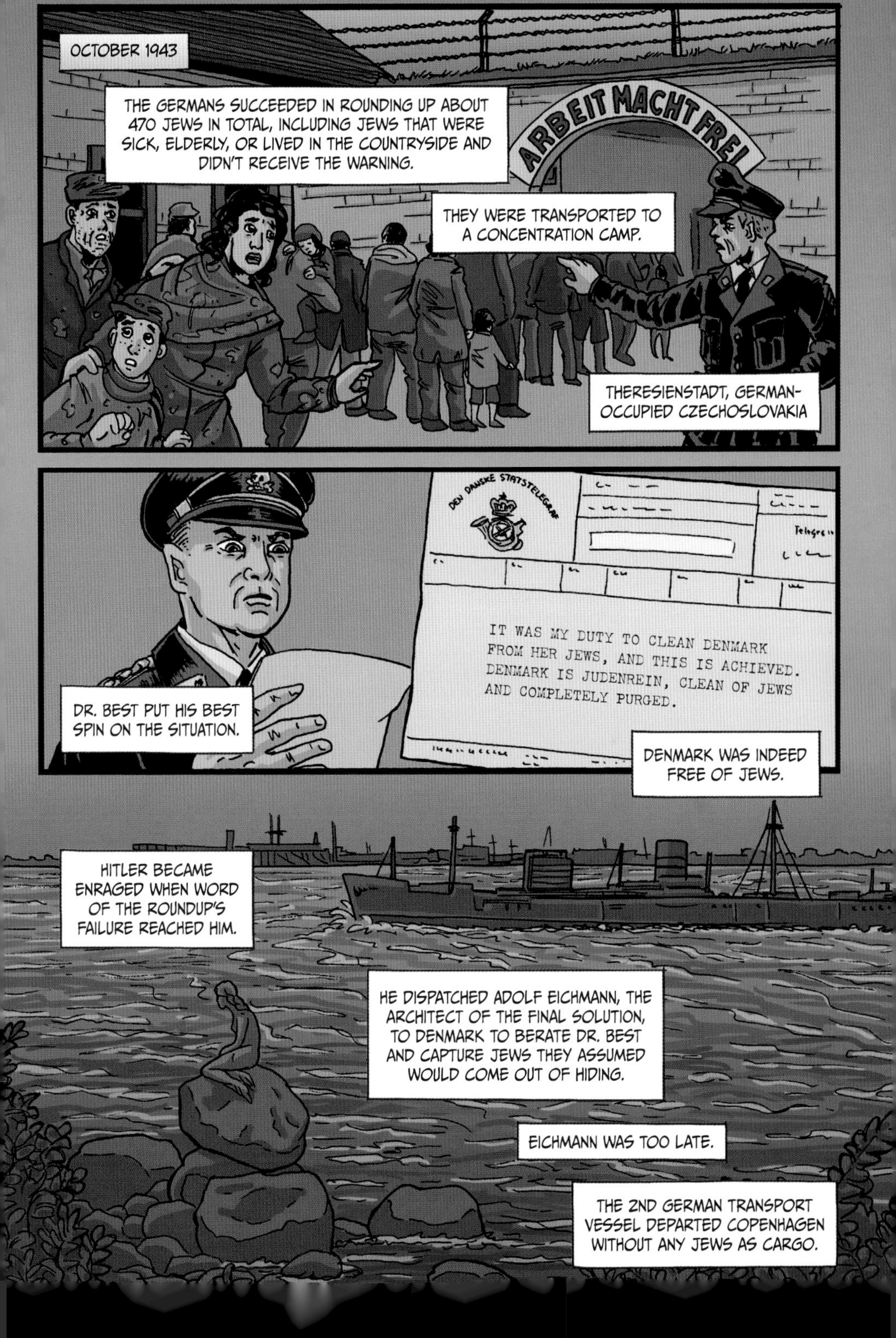
OCTOBER 1943
THE GERMANS SUCCEEDED IN ROUNDING UP ABOUT 470 JEWS IN TOTAL, INCLUDING JEWS THAT WERE SICK, ELDERLY, OR LIVED IN THE COUNTRYSIDE AND DIDN'T RECEIVE THE WARNING.
ARBEIT MACHT FREI
THEY WERE TRANSPORTED TO A CONCENTRATION CAMP.
THERESIENSTADT, GERMAN-OCCUPIED CZECHOSLOVAKIA
DEN DANSKE STATSTELEGRAF
IT WAS MY DUTY TO CLEAN DENMARK FROM HER JEWS, AND THIS IS ACHIEVED. DENMARK IS JUDENREIN, CLEAN OF JEWS AND COMPLETELY PURGED.
DR. BEST PUT HIS BEST SPIN ON THE SITUATION.
DENMARK WAS INDEED FREE OF JEWS.
HITLER BECAME ENRAGED WHEN WORD OF THE ROUNDUP'S FAILURE REACHED HIM.
HE DISPATCHED ADOLF EICHMANN, THE ARCHITECT OF THE FINAL SOLUTION, TO DENMARK TO BERATE DR. BEST AND CAPTURE JEWS THEY ASSUMED WOULD COME OUT OF HIDING.
EICHMANN WAS TOO LATE.
THE 2ND GERMAN TRANSPORT VESSEL DEPARTED COPENHAGEN WITHOUT ANY JEWS AS CARGO.

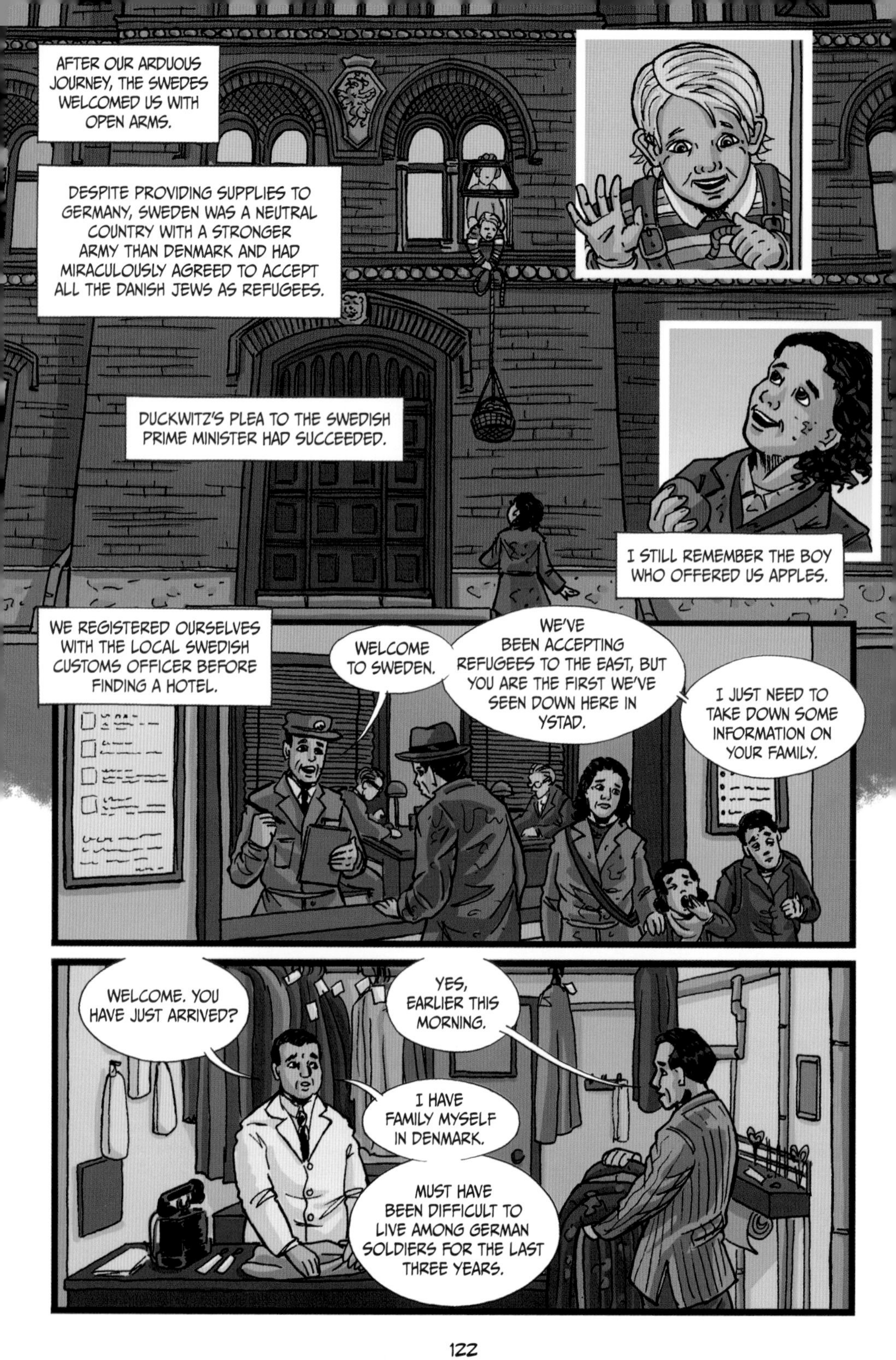
AFTER OUR ARDUOUS JOURNEY, THE SWEDES WELCOMED US WITH OPEN ARMS.
DESPITE PROVIDING SUPPLIES TO GERMANY, SWEDEN WAS A NEUTRAL COUNTRY WITH A STRONGER ARMY THAN DENMARK AND HAD MIRACULOUSLY AGREED TO ACCEPT ALL THE DANISH JEWS AS REFUGEES.
DUCKWITZ'S PLEA TO THE SWEDISH PRIME MINISTER HAD SUCCEEDED.
I STILL REMEMBER THE BOY WHO OFFERED US APPLES.
WE REGISTERED OURSELVES WITH THE LOCAL SWEDISH CUSTOMS OFFICER BEFORE FINDING A HOTEL.
WELCOME TO SWEDEN.
WE'VE BEEN ACCEPTING REFUGEES TO THE EAST, BUT YOU ARE THE FIRST WE'VE SEEN DOWN HERE IN YSTAD.
I JUST NEED TO TAKE DOWN SOME INFORMATION ON YOUR FAMILY.
WELCOME. YOU HAVE JUST ARRIVED?
YES, EARLIER THIS MORNING.
I HAVE FAMILY MYSELF IN DENMARK.
MUST HAVE BEEN DIFFICULT TO LIVE AMONG GERMAN SOLDIERS FOR THE LAST THREE YEARS.

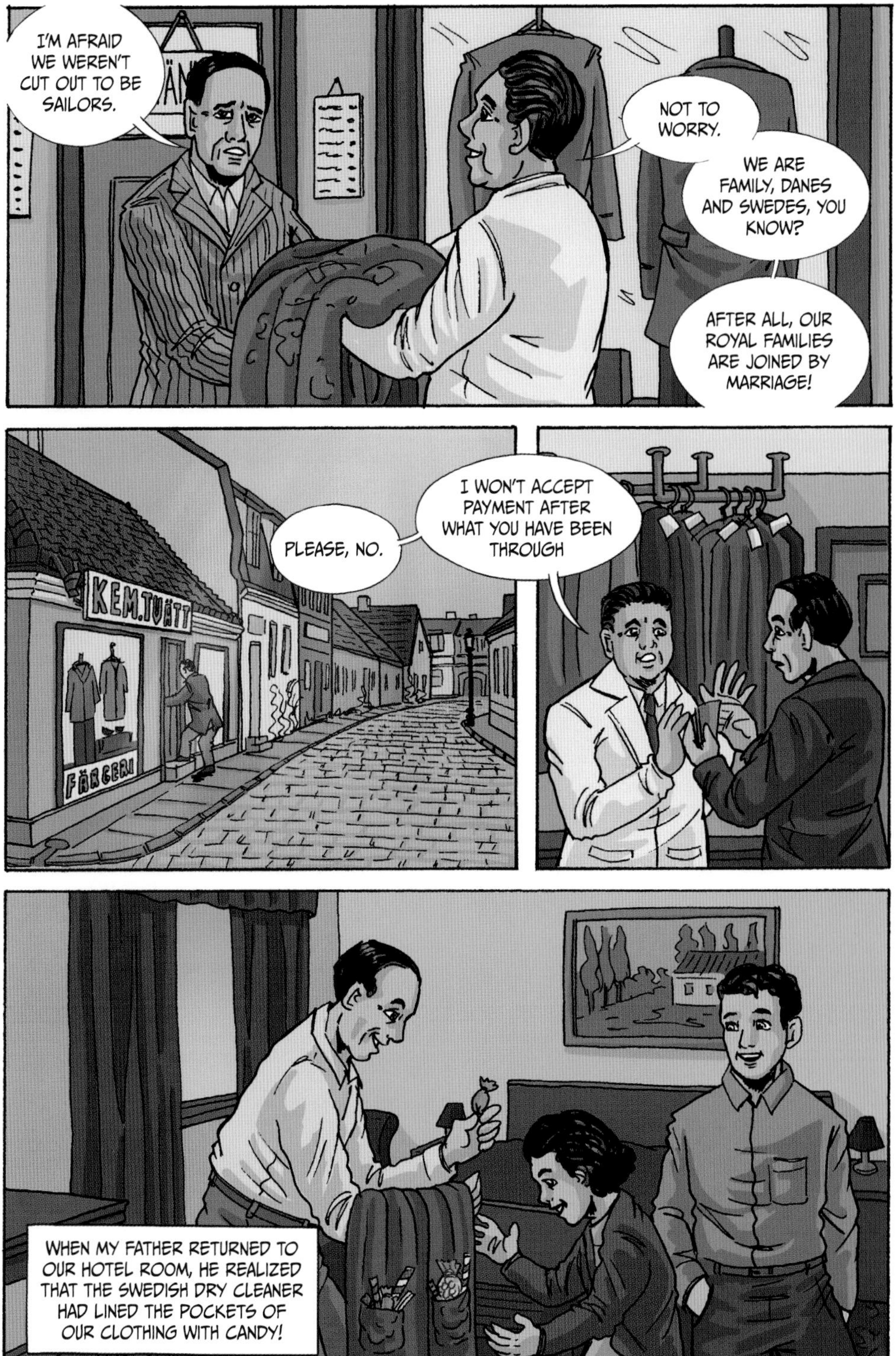
I'M AFRAID WE WEREN'T CUT OUT TO BE SAILORS.
NOT TO WORRY.
WE ARE FAMILY, DANES AND SWEDES, YOU KNOW?
AFTER ALL, OUR ROYAL FAMILIES ARE JOINED BY MARRIAGE!
KEM.TVÄTT
FÄRGERI
PLEASE, NO.
I WON'T ACCEPT PAYMENT AFTER WHAT YOU HAVE BEEN THROUGH
WHEN MY FATHER RETURNED TO OUR HOTEL ROOM, HE REALIZED THAT THE SWEDISH DRY CLEANER HAD LINED THE POCKETS OF OUR CLOTHING WITH CANDY!

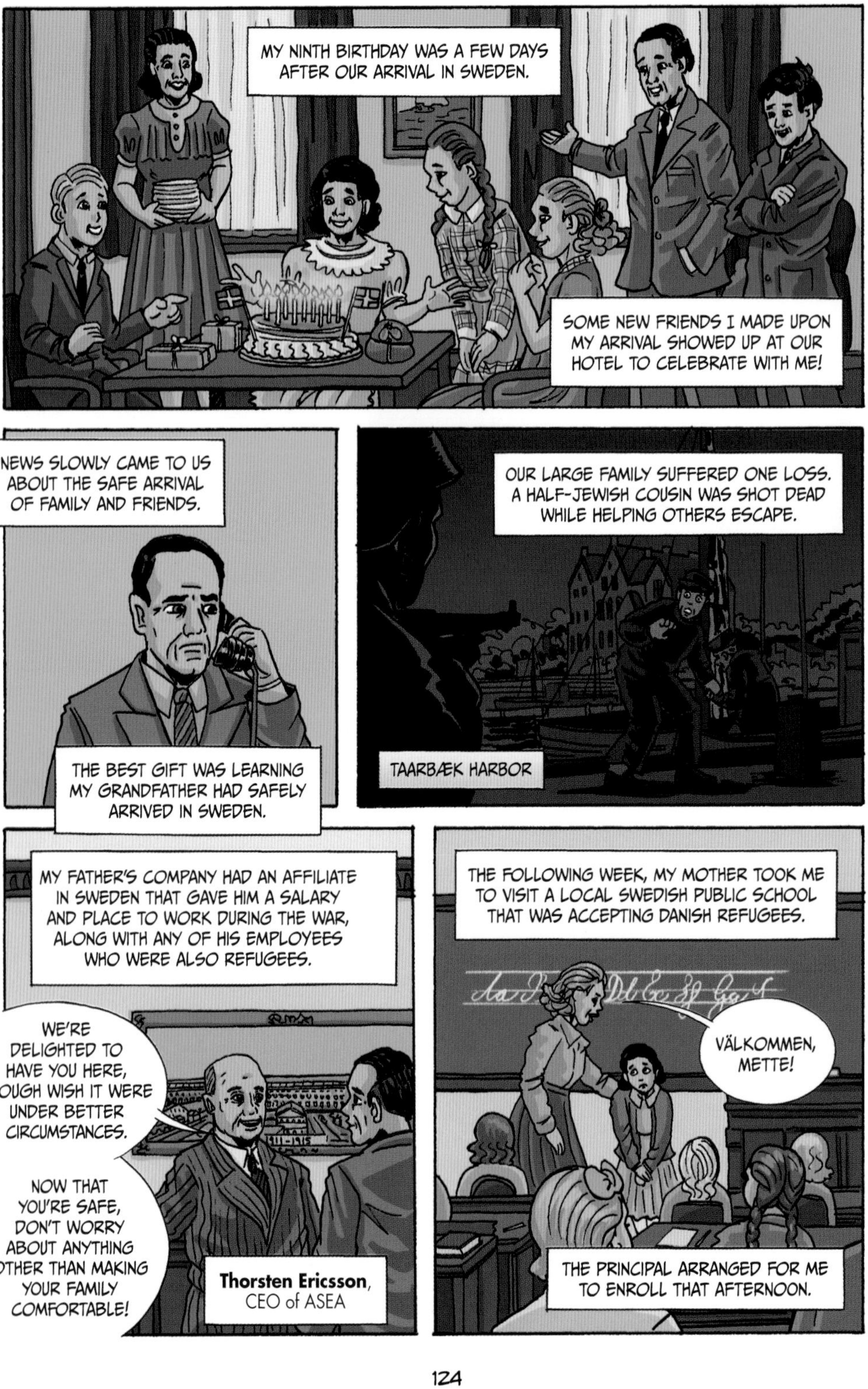

MY NINTH BIRTHDAY WAS A FEW DAYS AFTER OUR ARRIVAL IN SWEDEN.
SOME NEW FRIENDS I MADE UPON MY ARRIVAL SHOWED UP AT OUR HOTEL TO CELEBRATE WITH ME!
NEWS SLOWLY CAME TO US ABOUT THE SAFE ARRIVAL OF FAMILY AND FRIENDS.
THE BEST GIFT WAS LEARNING MY GRANDFATHER HAD SAFELY ARRIVED IN SWEDEN.
OUR LARGE FAMILY SUFFERED ONE LOSS. A HALF-JEWISH COUSIN WAS SHOT DEAD WHILE HELPING OTHERS ESCAPE.
TAARBÆK HARBOR
MY FATHER'S COMPANY HAD AN AFFILIATE IN SWEDEN THAT GAVE HIM A SALARY AND PLACE TO WORK DURING THE WAR, ALONG WITH ANY OF HIS EMPLOYEES WHO WERE ALSO REFUGEES.
WE'RE DELIGHTED TO HAVE YOU HERE, THOUGH WISH IT WERE UNDER BETTER CIRCUMSTANCES.
NOW THAT YOU'RE SAFE, DON'T WORRY ABOUT ANYTHING OTHER THAN MAKING YOUR FAMILY COMFORTABLE!
Thorsten Ericsson, CEO of ASEA
THE FOLLOWING WEEK, MY MOTHER TOOK ME TO VISIT A LOCAL SWEDISH PUBLIC SCHOOL THAT WAS ACCEPTING DANISH REFUGEES.
VÄLKOMMEN, METTE!
THE PRINCIPAL ARRANGED FOR ME TO ENROLL THAT AFTERNOON.

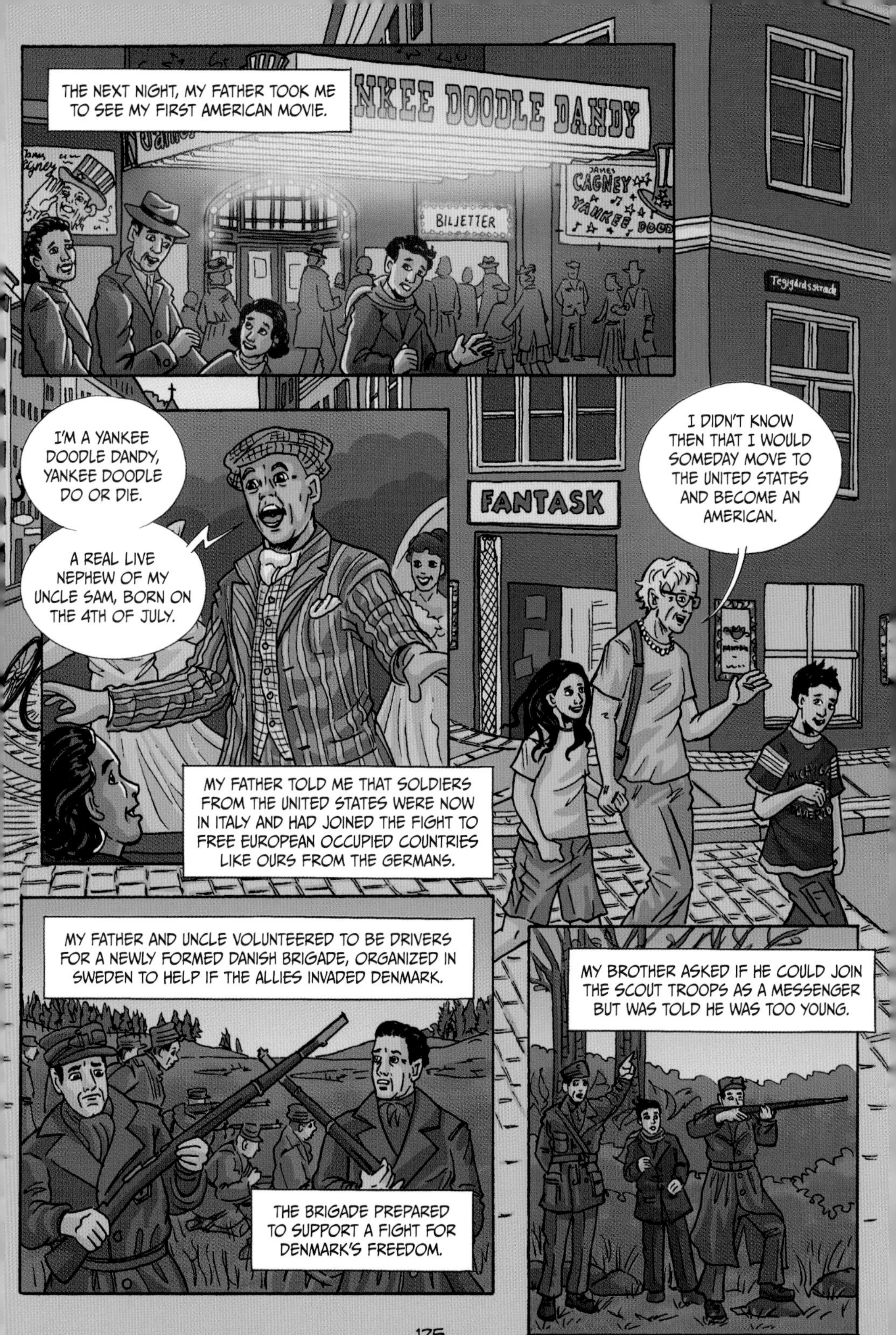
THE NEXT NIGHT, MY FATHER TOOK ME TO SEE MY FIRST AMERICAN MOVIE.
NKEE DOODLE DANDY
JAMES CAGNEY YANKEE DOOD
BILJETTER
Tegigårdsstræde
I'M A YANKEE DOODLE DANDY, YANKEE DOODLE DO OR DIE.
A REAL LIVE NEPHEW OF MY UNCLE SAM, BORN ON THE 4TH OF JULY.
FANTASK
I DIDN'T KNOW THEN THAT I WOULD SOMEDAY MOVE TO THE UNITED STATES AND BECOME AN AMERICAN.
MY FATHER TOLD ME THAT SOLDIERS FROM THE UNITED STATES WERE NOW IN ITALY AND HAD JOINED THE FIGHT TO FREE EUROPEAN OCCUPIED COUNTRIES LIKE OURS FROM THE GERMANS.
MY FATHER AND UNCLE VOLUNTEERED TO BE DRIVERS FOR A NEWLY FORMED DANISH BRIGADE, ORGANIZED IN SWEDEN TO HELP IF THE ALLIES INVADED DENMARK.
THE BRIGADE PREPARED TO SUPPORT A FIGHT FOR DENMARK'S FREEDOM.
MY BROTHER ASKED IF HE COULD JOIN THE SCOUT TROOPS AS A MESSENGER BUT WAS TOLD HE WAS TOO YOUNG.

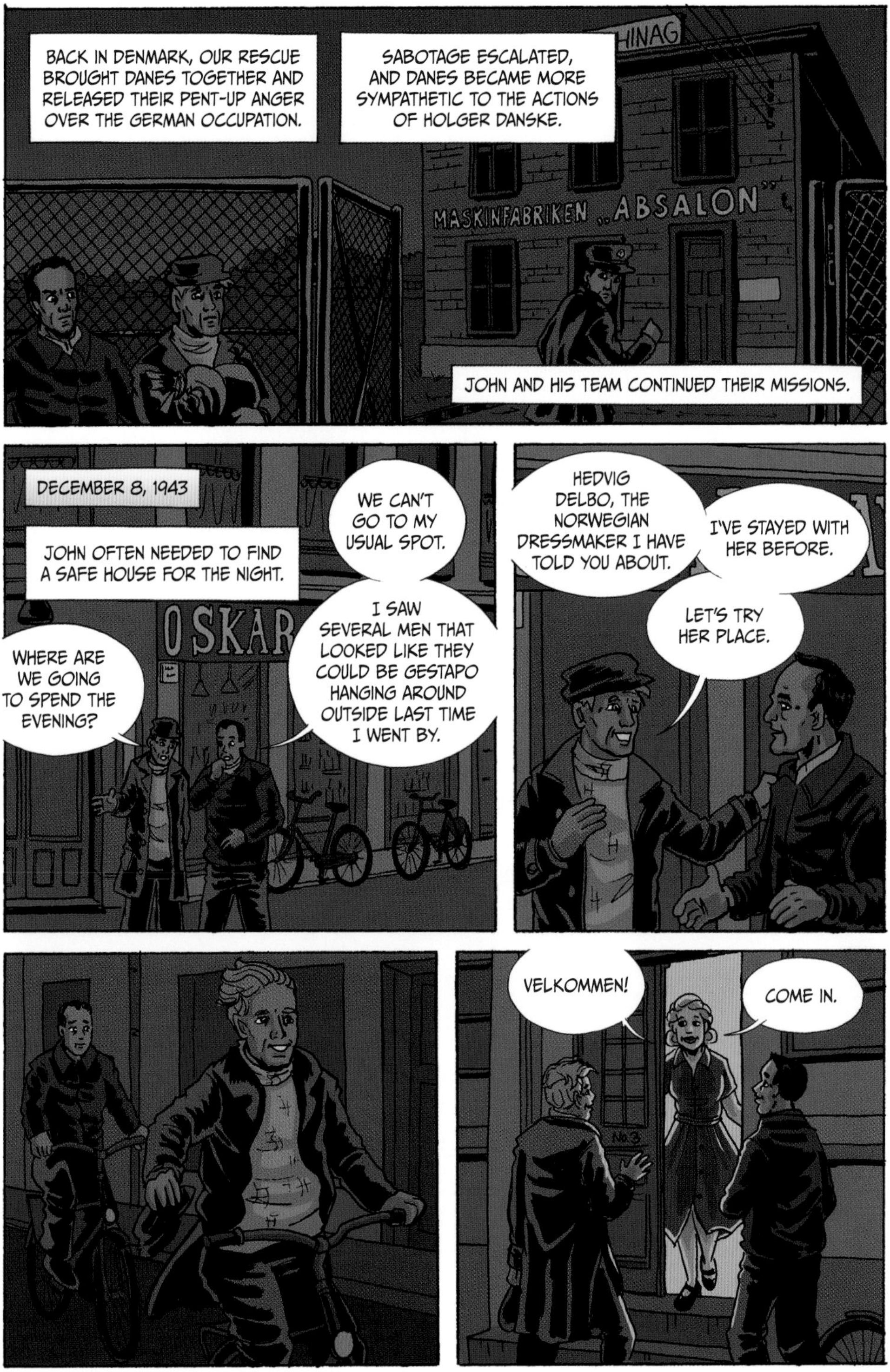
BACK IN DENMARK, OUR RESCUE BROUGHT DANES TOGETHER AND RELEASED THEIR PENT-UP ANGER OVER THE GERMAN OCCUPATION.
SABOTAGE ESCALATED, AND DANES BECAME MORE SYMPATHETIC TO THE ACTIONS OF HOLGER DANSKE.
HINAG
MASKINFABRIKEN „ABSALON"
JOHN AND HIS TEAM CONTINUED THEIR MISSIONS.
DECEMBER 8, 1943
JOHN OFTEN NEEDED TO FIND A SAFE HOUSE FOR THE NIGHT.
OSKAR
WHERE ARE WE GOING TO SPEND THE EVENING?
WE CAN'T GO TO MY USUAL SPOT.
I SAW SEVERAL MEN THAT LOOKED LIKE THEY COULD BE GESTAPO HANGING AROUND OUTSIDE LAST TIME I WENT BY.
HEDVIG DELBO, THE NORWEGIAN DRESSMAKER I HAVE TOLD YOU ABOUT.
I'VE STAYED WITH HER BEFORE.
LET'S TRY HER PLACE.
VELKOMMEN!
COME IN.

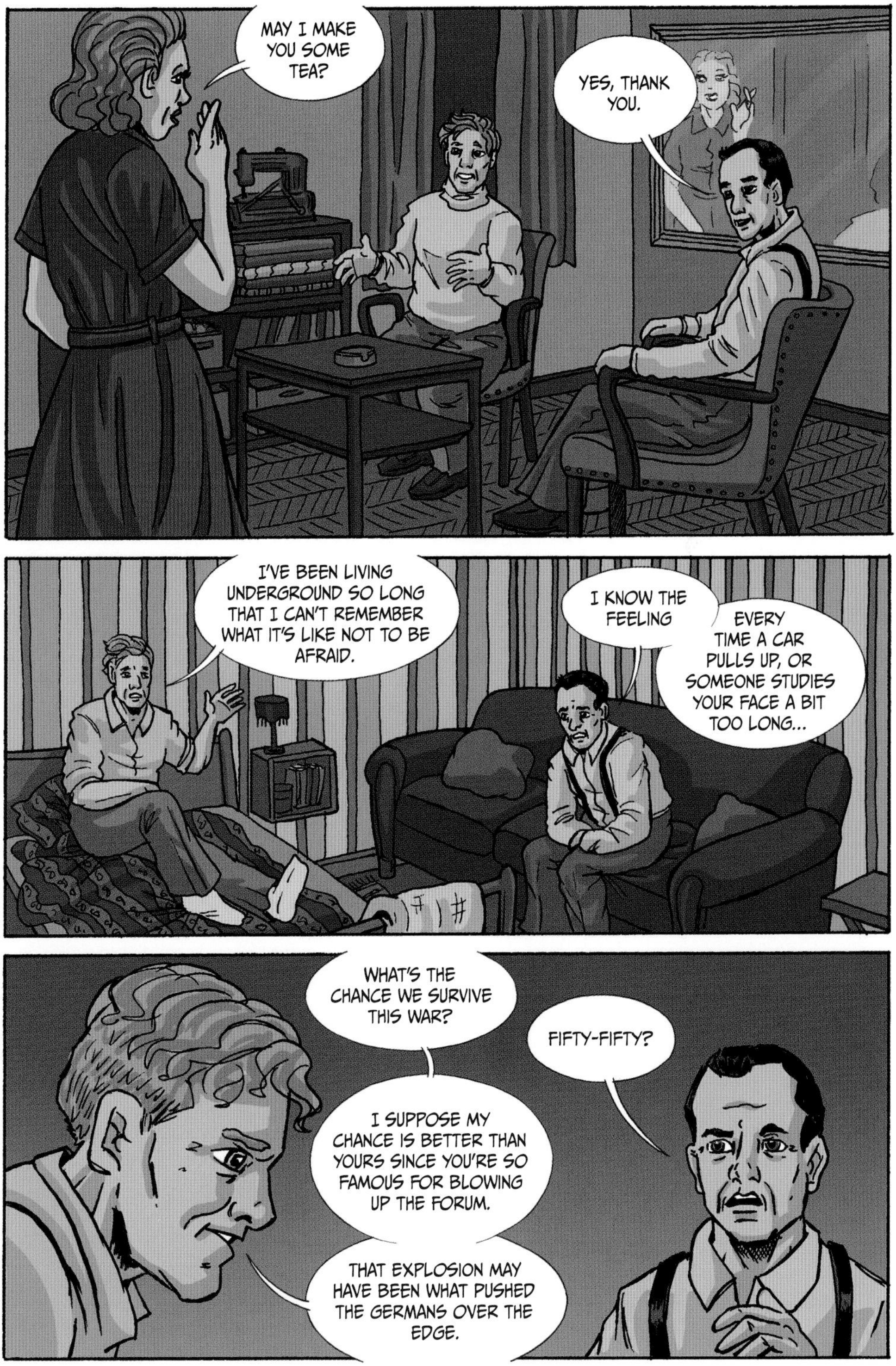
MAY I MAKE YOU SOME TEA?
YES, THANK YOU.
I'VE BEEN LIVING UNDERGROUND SO LONG THAT I CAN'T REMEMBER WHAT IT'S LIKE NOT TO BE AFRAID.
I KNOW THE FEELING
EVERY TIME A CAR PULLS UP, OR SOMEONE STUDIES YOUR FACE A BIT TOO LONG...
WHAT'S THE CHANCE WE SURVIVE THIS WAR?
FIFTY-FIFTY?
I SUPPOSE MY CHANCE IS BETTER THAN YOURS SINCE YOU'RE SO FAMOUS FOR BLOWING UP THE FORUM.
THAT EXPLOSION MAY HAVE BEEN WHAT PUSHED THE GERMANS OVER THE EDGE.

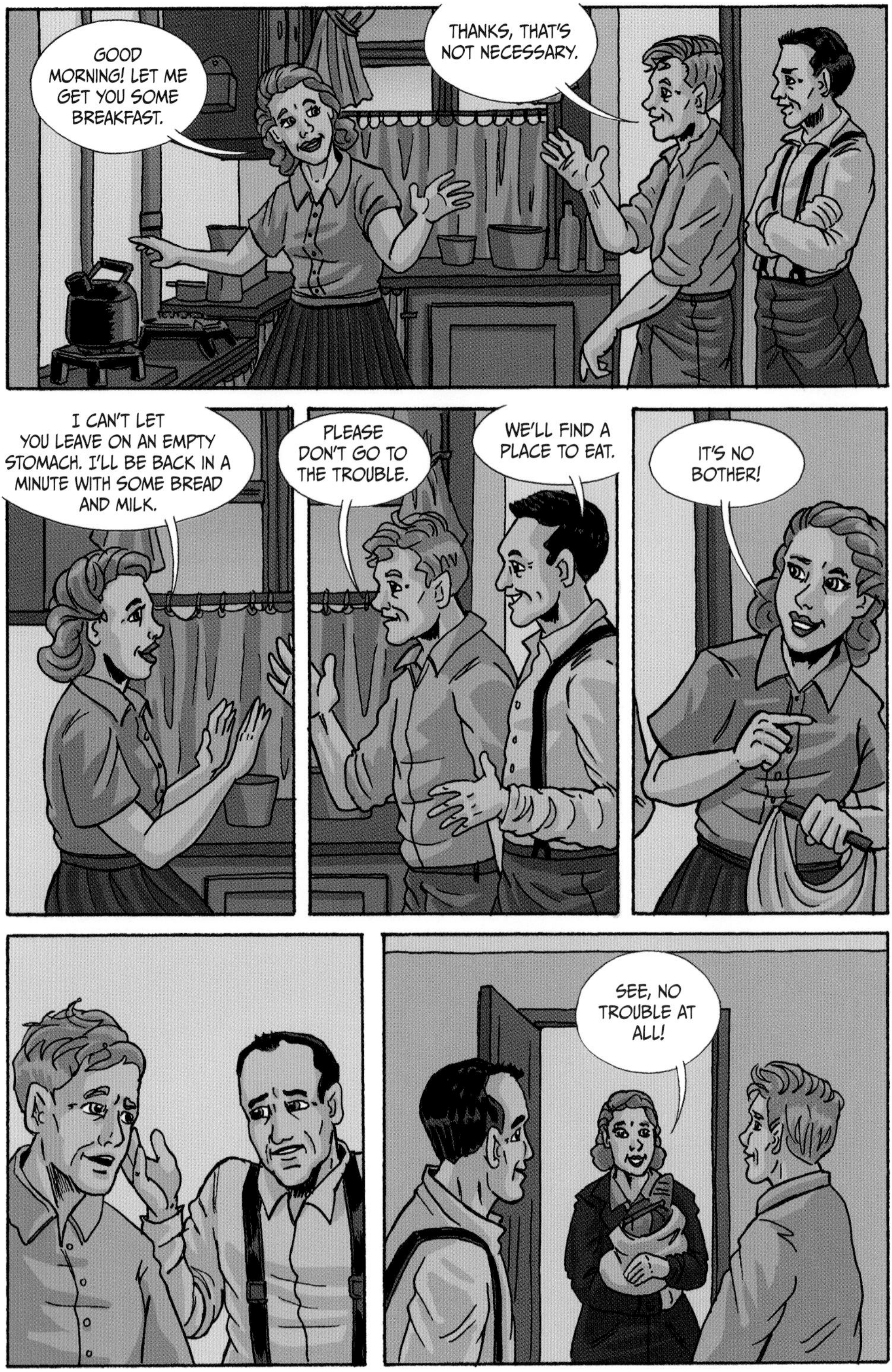
GOOD MORNING! LET ME GET YOU SOME BREAKFAST.
THANKS, THAT'S NOT NECESSARY.
I CAN'T LET YOU LEAVE ON AN EMPTY STOMACH. I'LL BE BACK IN A MINUTE WITH SOME BREAD AND MILK.
PLEASE DON'T GO TO THE TROUBLE.
WE'LL FIND A PLACE TO EAT.
IT'S NO BOTHER!
SEE, NO TROUBLE AT ALL!

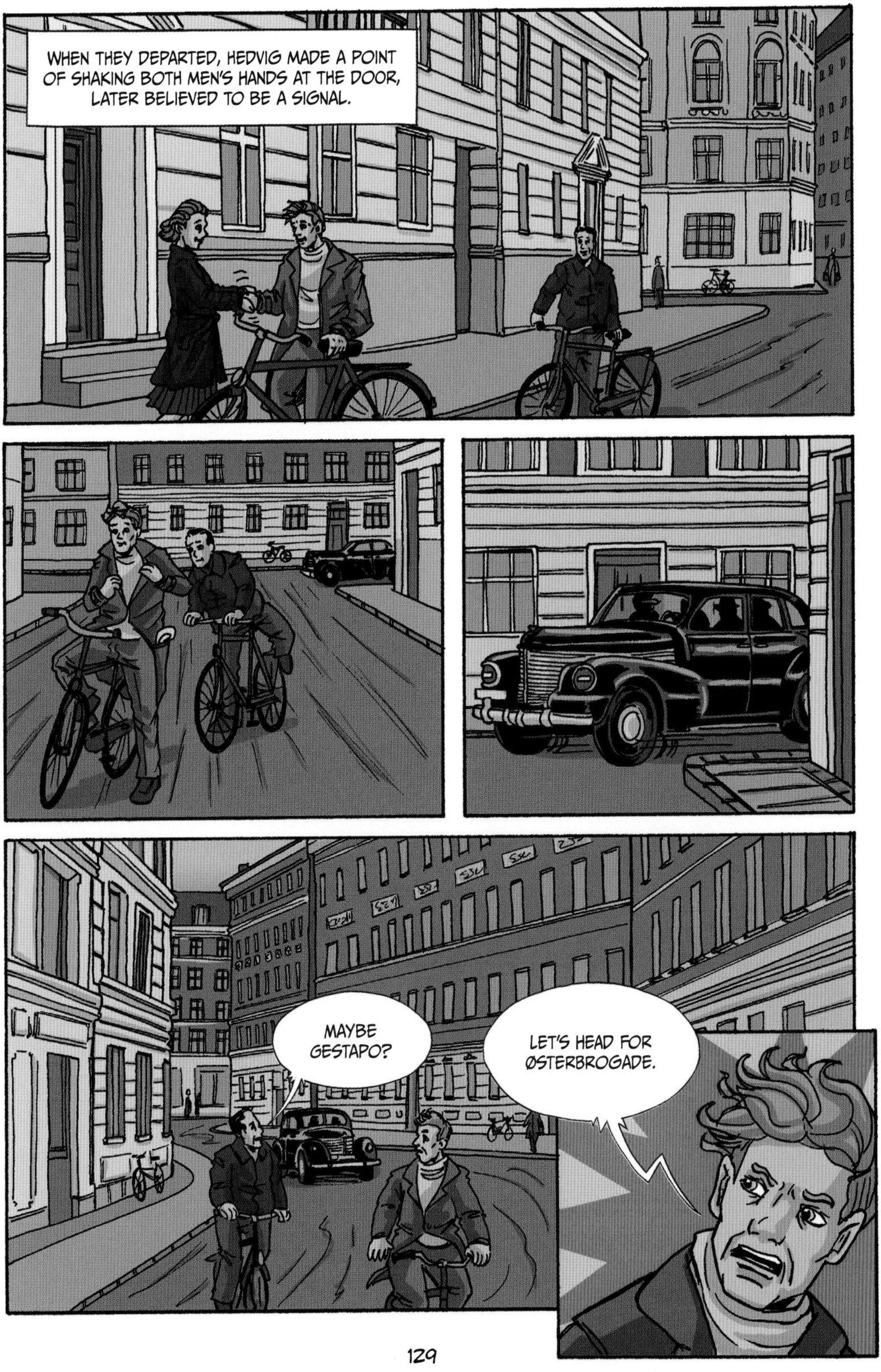

WHEN THEY DEPARTED, HEDVIG MADE A POINT OF SHAKING BOTH MEN'S HANDS AT THE DOOR, LATER BELIEVED TO BE A SIGNAL.
MAYBE GESTAPO?
LET'S HEAD FOR ØSTERBROGADE.

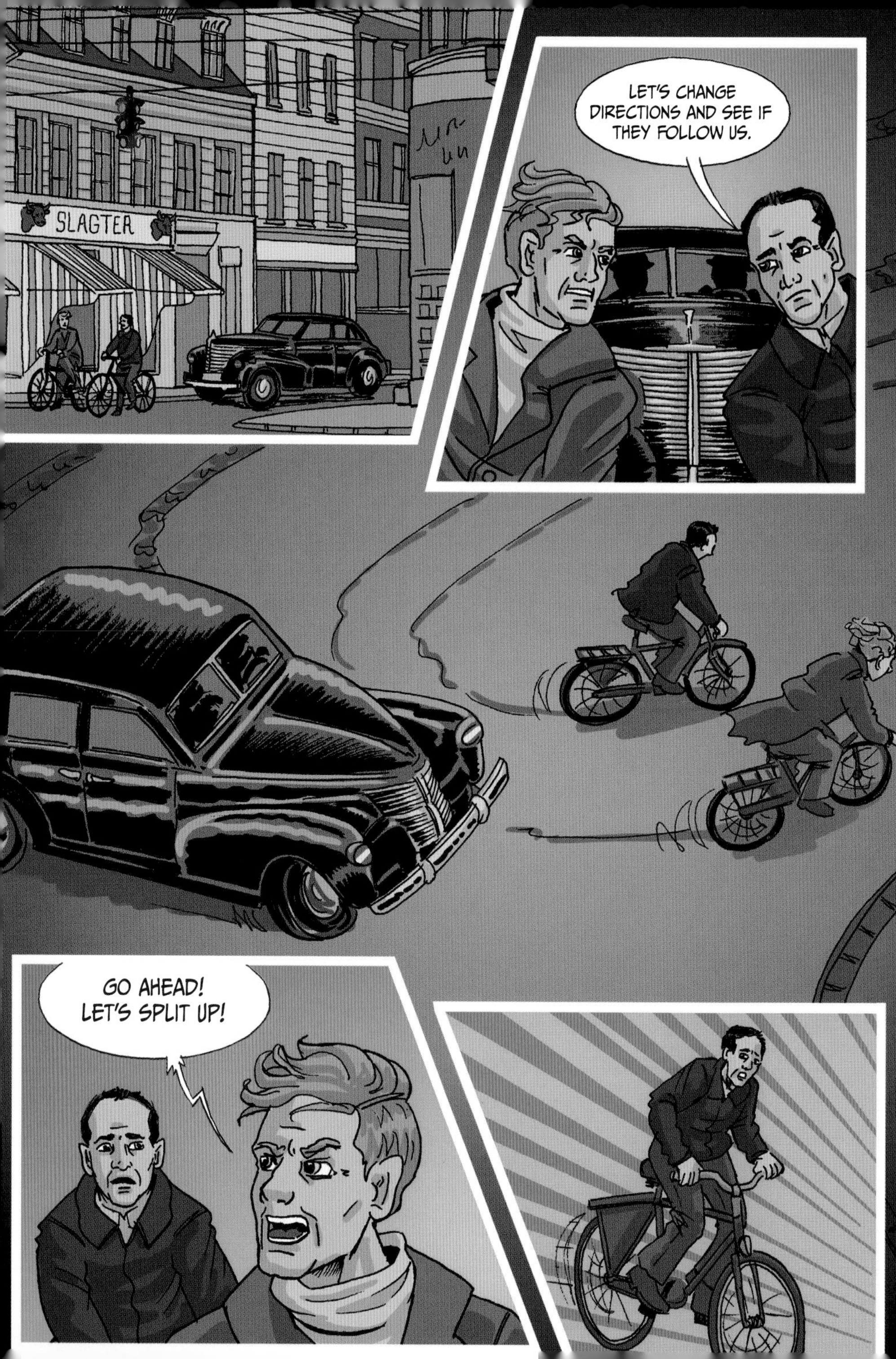
SLAGTER
LET'S CHANGE DIRECTIONS AND SEE IF THEY FOLLOW US.
GO AHEAD! LET'S SPLIT UP!

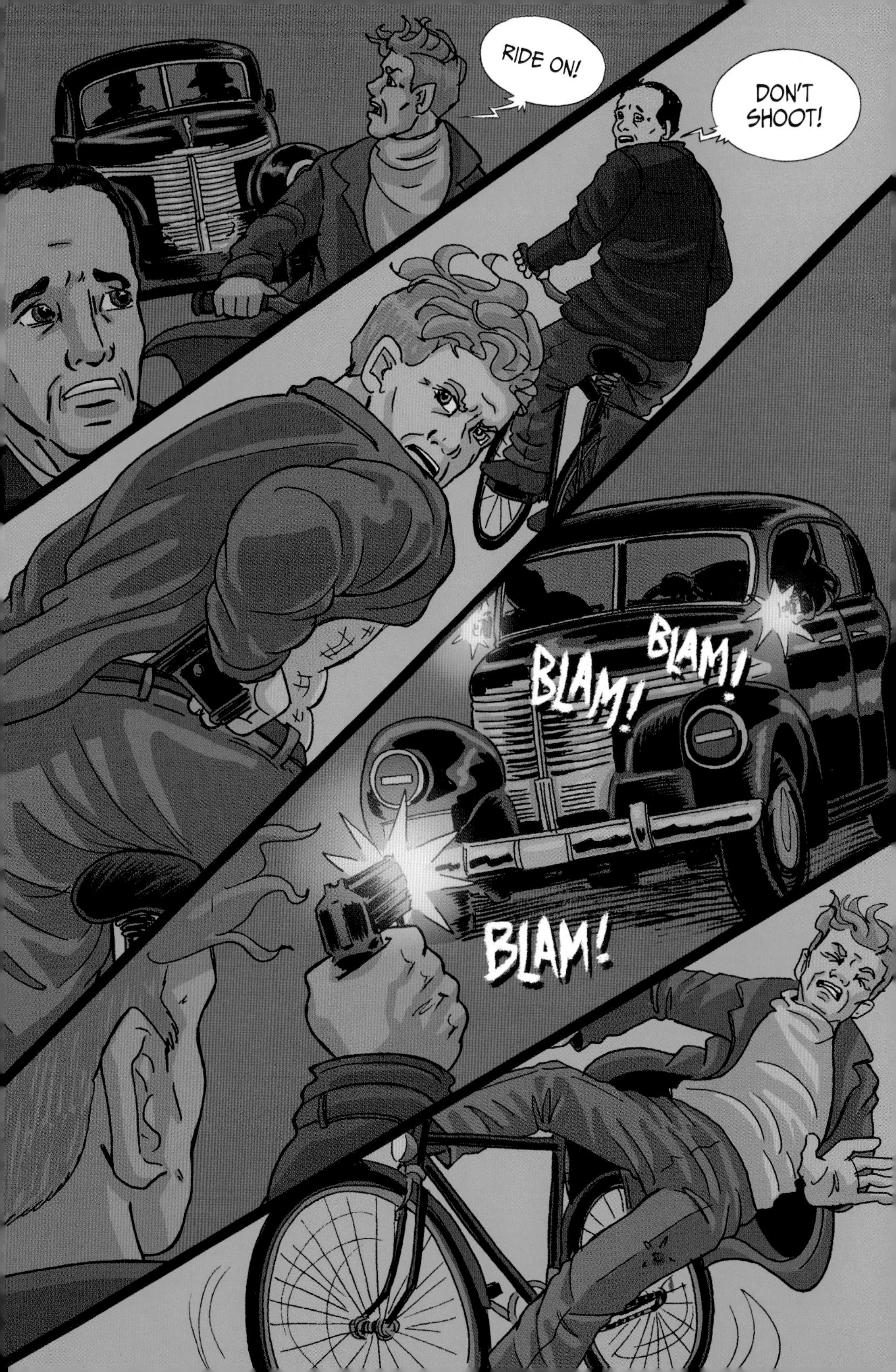
RIDE ON!
DON'T SHOOT!
BLAM!
BLAM!
BLAM!

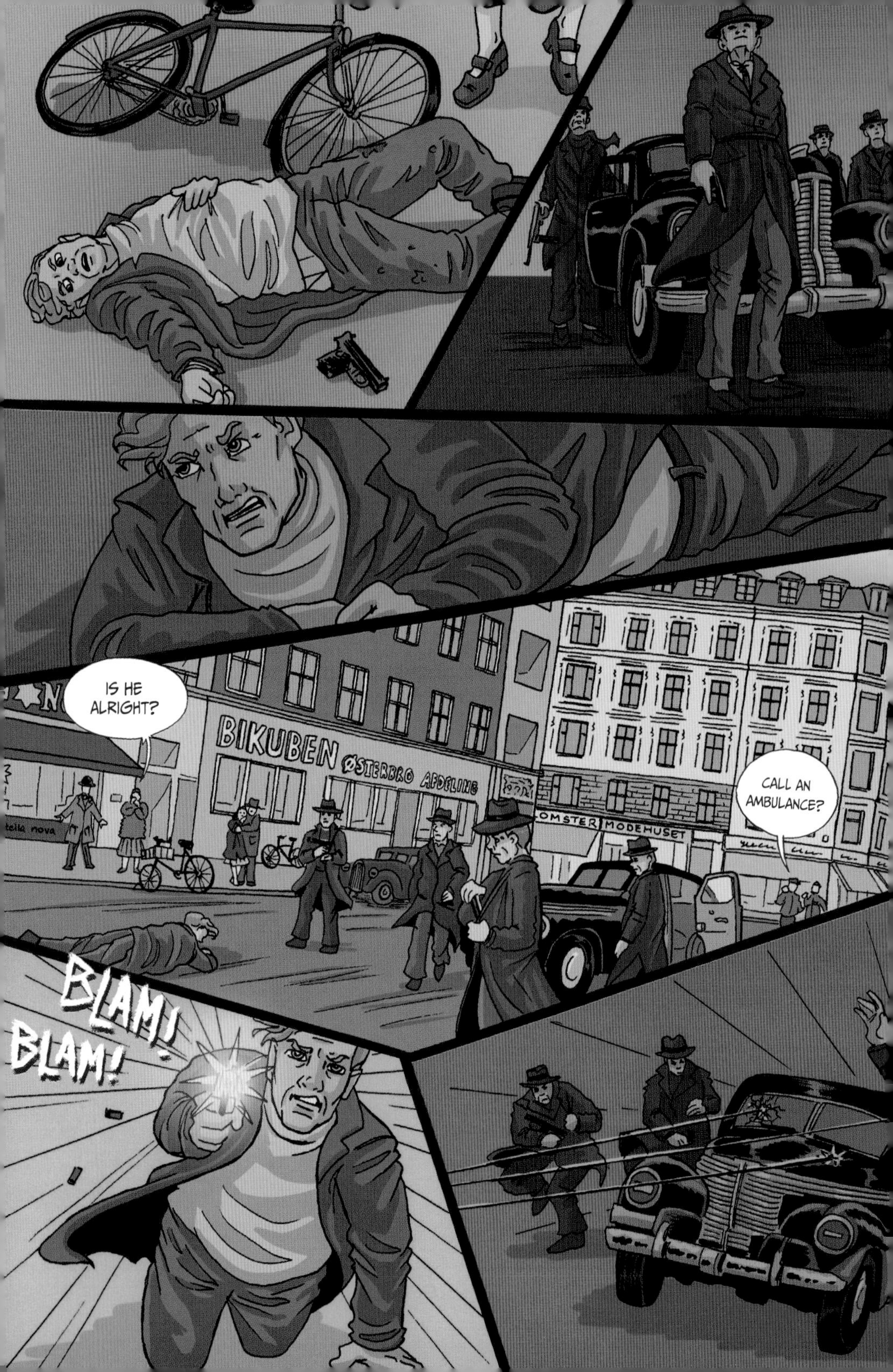
IS HE ALRIGHT?
CALL AN AMBULANCE?
BIKUBEN ØSTERBRO AFDELING
MODEHUSET
BLAM!
BLAM!

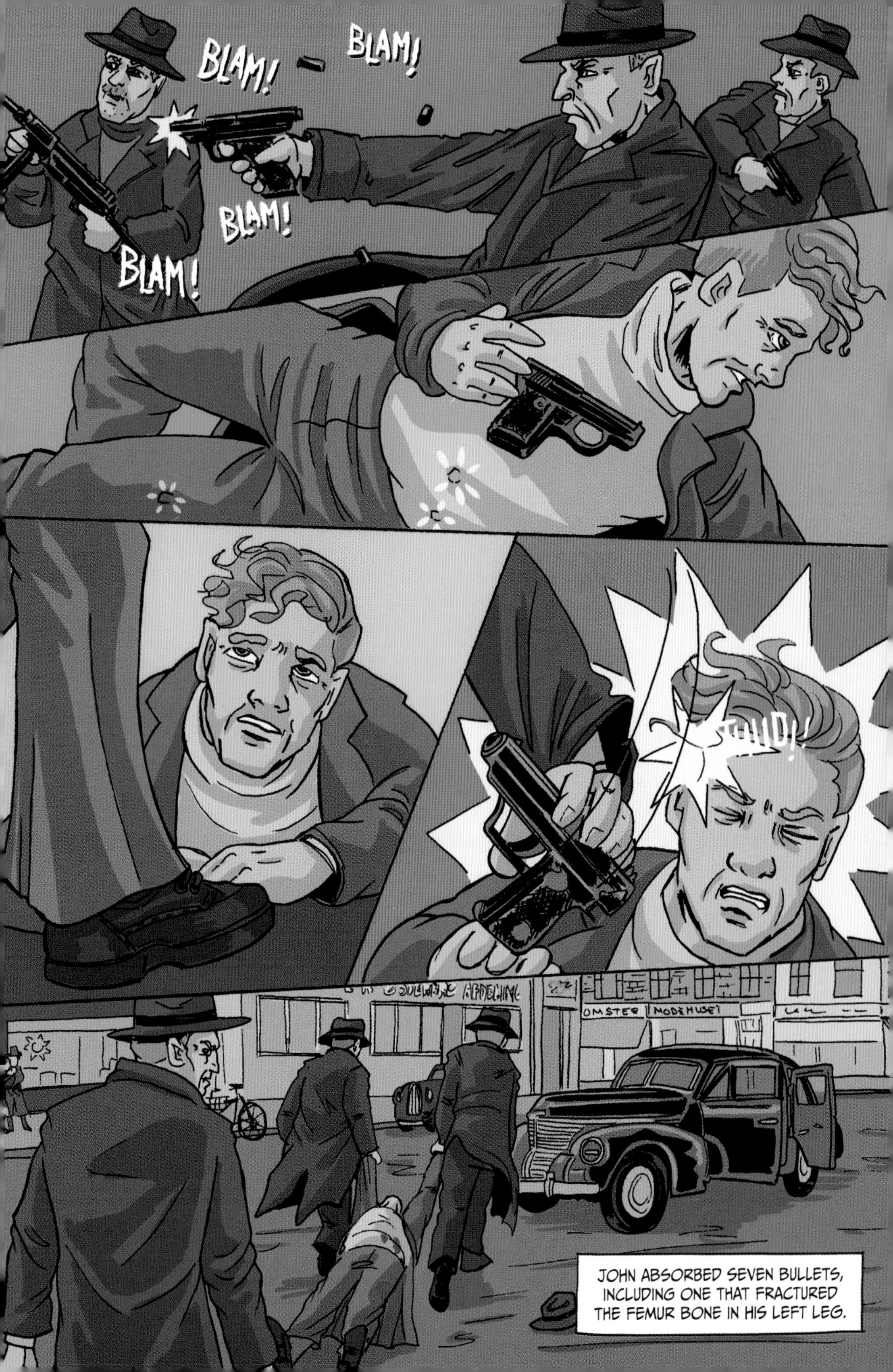
BLAM!
BLAM!
BLAM!
BLAM!
OMSTER
MODEHUSET
JOHN ABSORBED SEVEN BULLETS, INCLUDING ONE THAT FRACTURED THE FEMUR BONE IN HIS LEFT LEG.

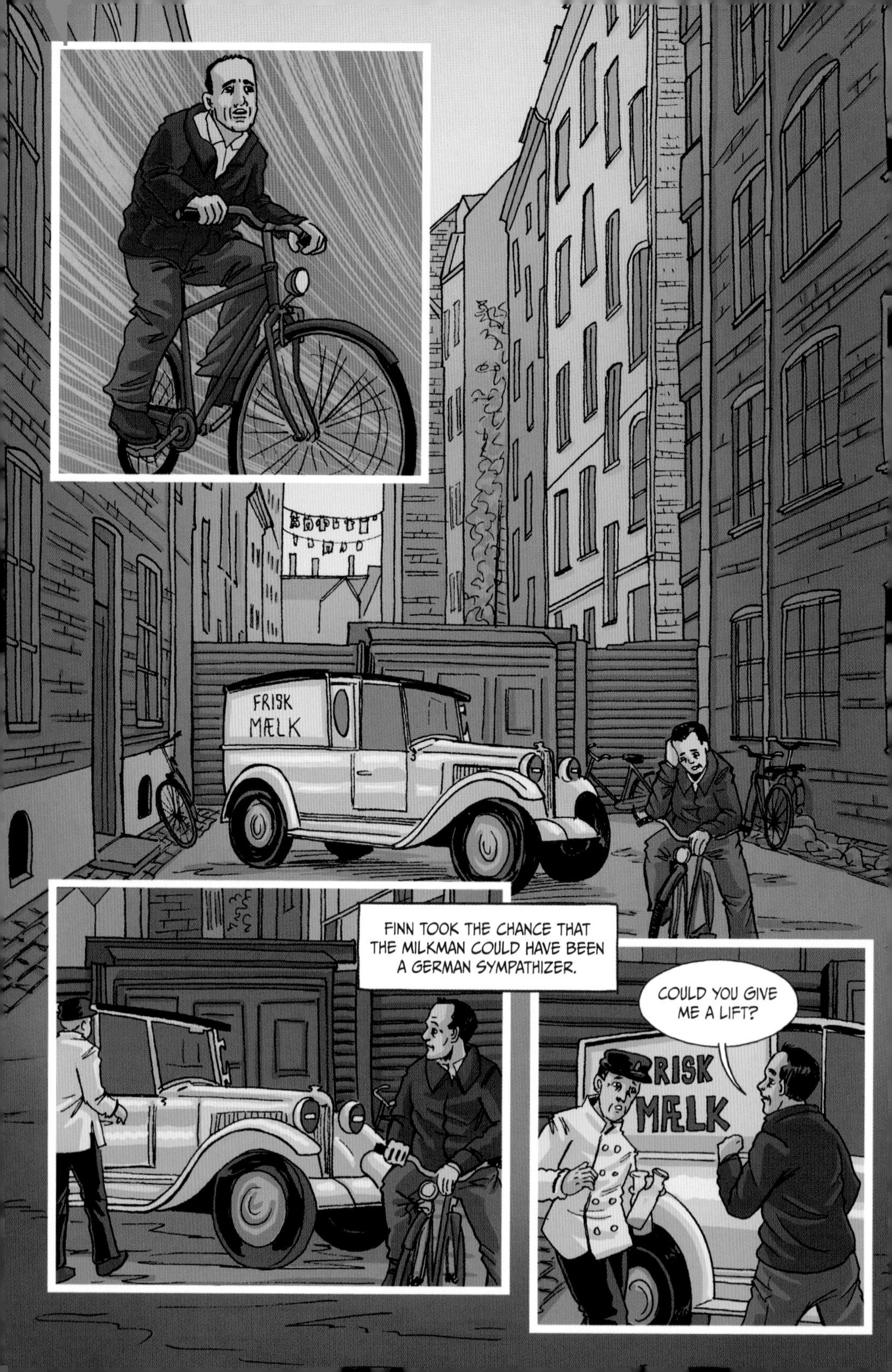
FRISK
MÆLK
FINN TOOK THE CHANCE THAT THE MILKMAN COULD HAVE BEEN A GERMAN SYMPATHIZER.
COULD YOU GIVE ME A LIFT?
RISK
MÆLK

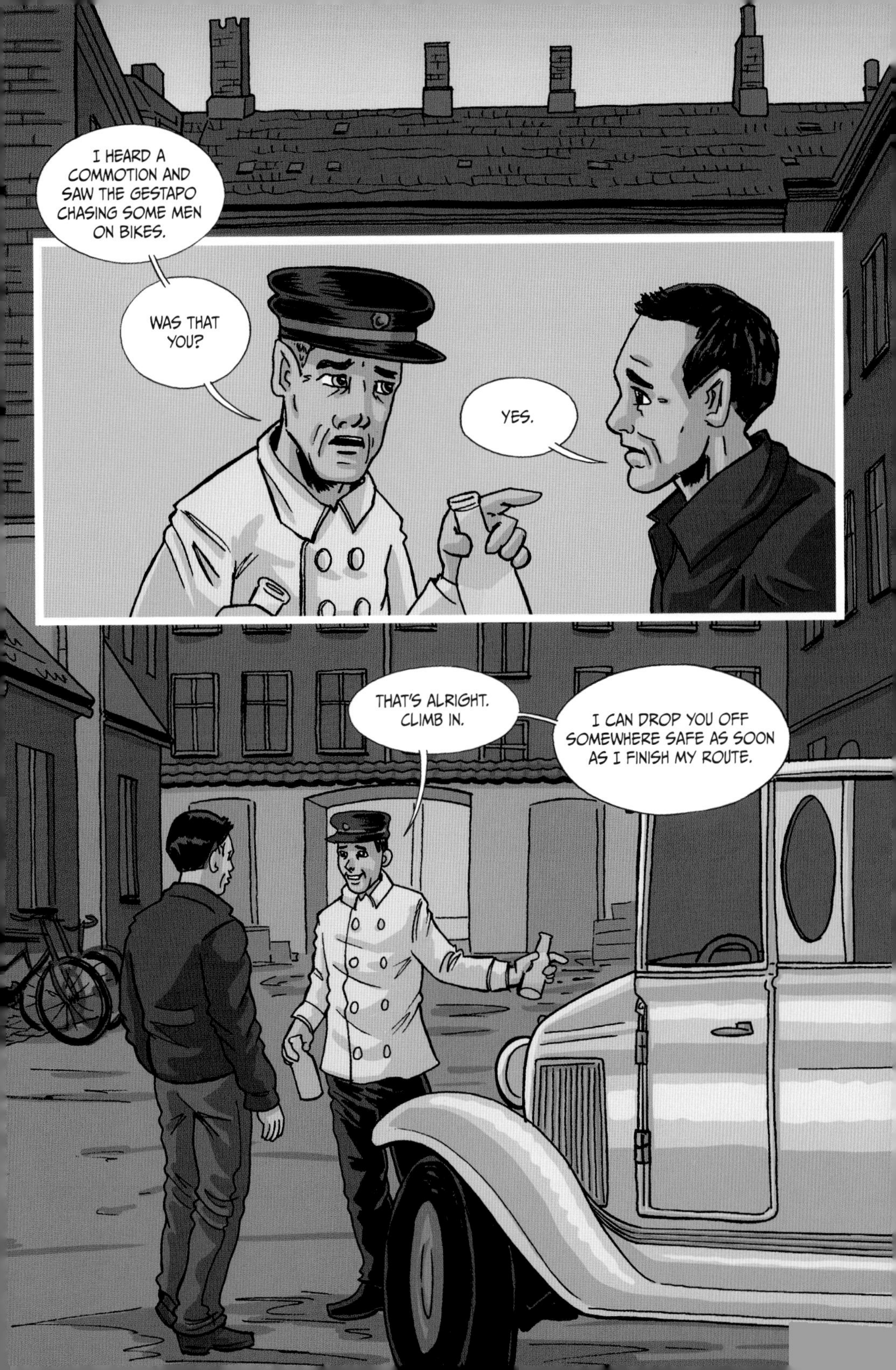
I HEARD A COMMOTION AND SAW THE GESTAPO CHASING SOME MEN ON BIKES.
WAS THAT YOU?
YES.
THAT'S ALRIGHT. CLIMB IN.
I CAN DROP YOU OFF SOMEWHERE SAFE AS SOON AS I FINISH MY ROUTE.

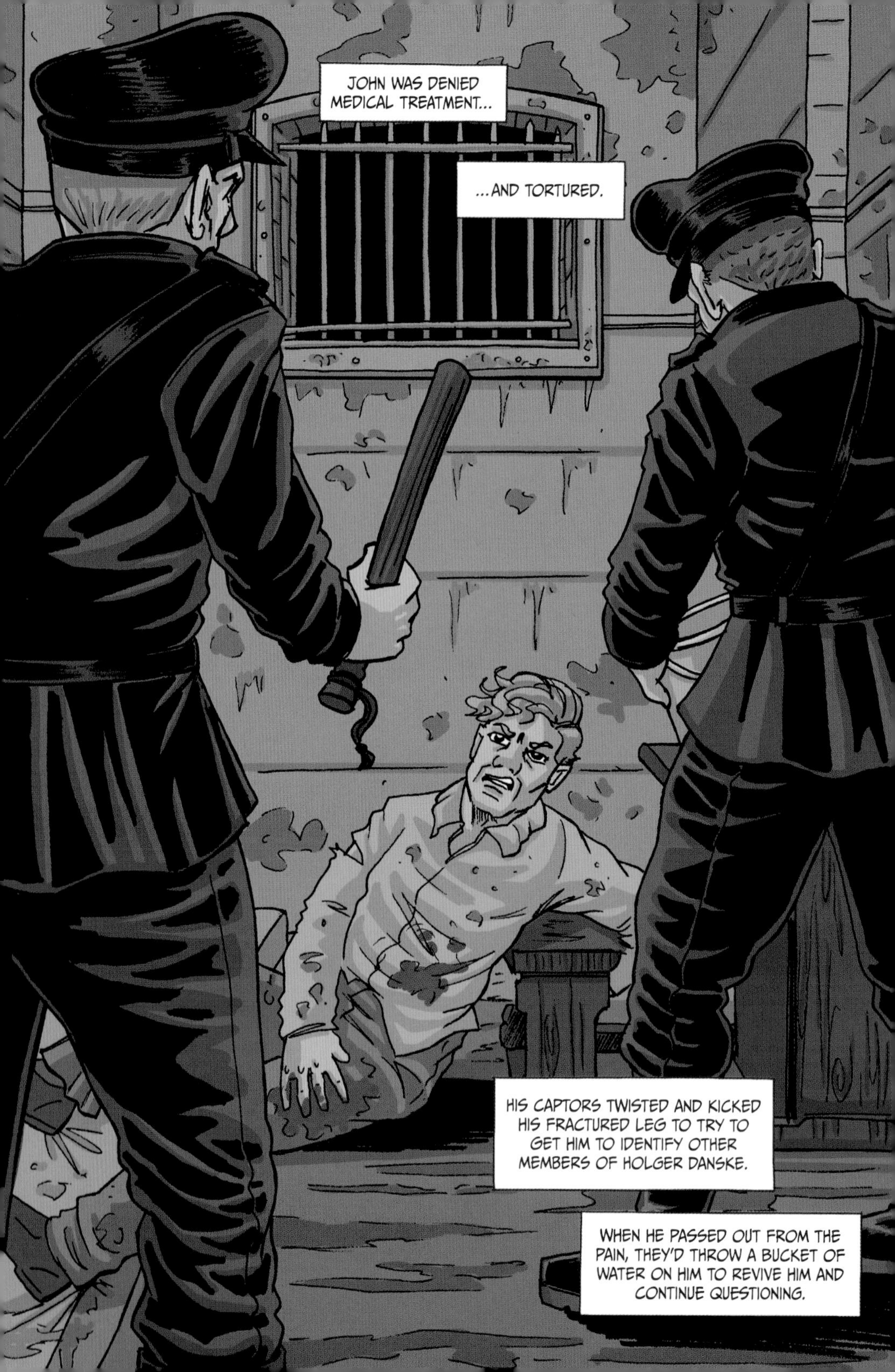
JOHN WAS DENIED MEDICAL TREATMENT...
...AND TORTURED.
HIS CAPTORS TWISTED AND KICKED HIS FRACTURED LEG TO TRY TO GET HIM TO IDENTIFY OTHER MEMBERS OF HOLGER DANSKE.
WHEN HE PASSED OUT FROM THE PAIN, THEY'D THROW A BUCKET OF WATER ON HIM TO REVIVE HIM AND CONTINUE QUESTIONING.

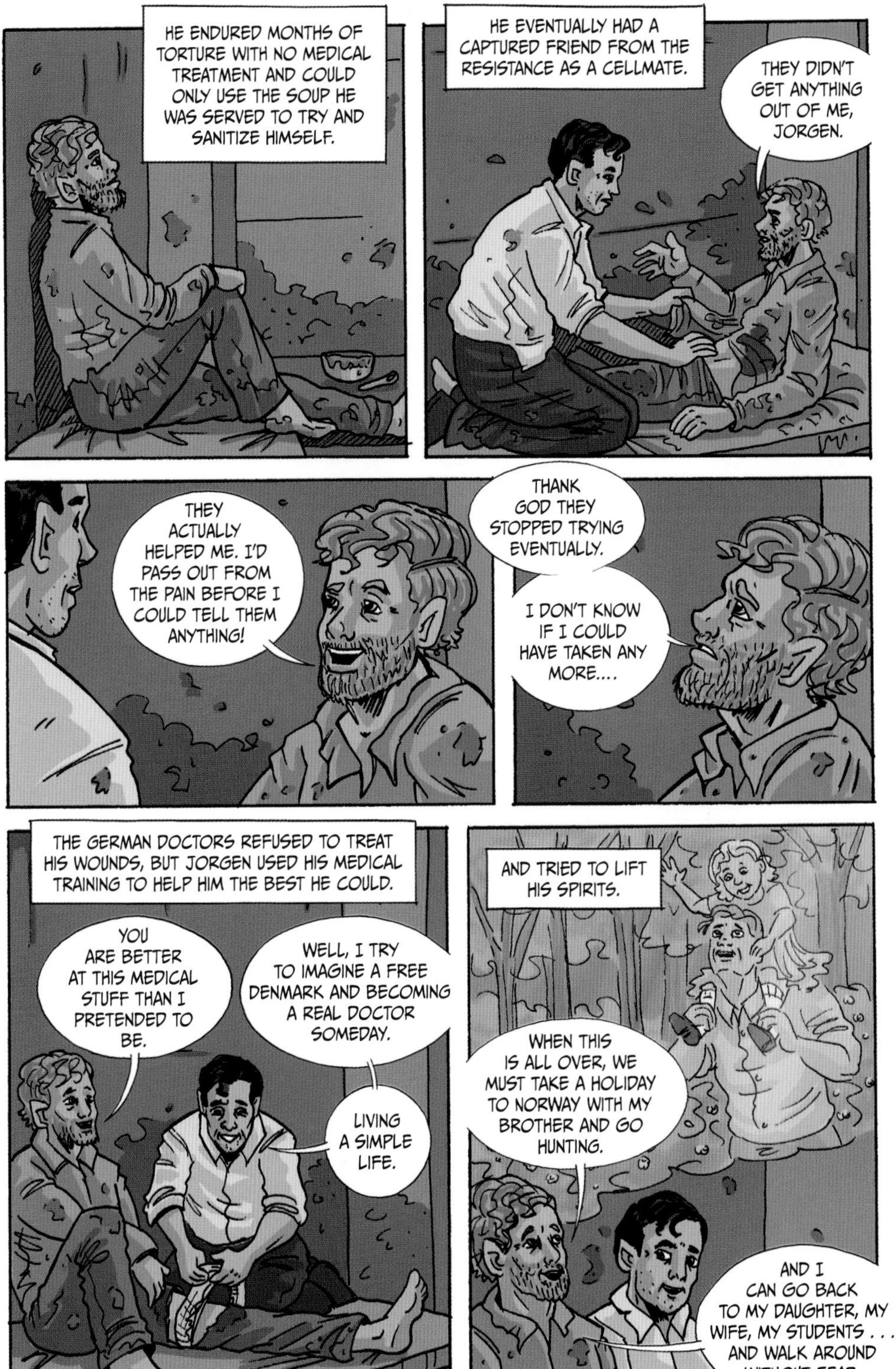
HE ENDURED MONTHS OF TORTURE WITH NO MEDICAL TREATMENT AND COULD ONLY USE THE SOUP HE WAS SERVED TO TRY AND SANITIZE HIMSELF.
HE EVENTUALLY HAD A CAPTURED FRIEND FROM THE RESISTANCE AS A CELLMATE.
THEY DIDN'T GET ANYTHING OUT OF ME, JORGEN.
THEY ACTUALLY HELPED ME. I'D PASS OUT FROM THE PAIN BEFORE I COULD TELL THEM ANYTHING!
THANK GOD THEY STOPPED TRYING EVENTUALLY.
I DON'T KNOW IF I COULD HAVE TAKEN ANY MORE....
THE GERMAN DOCTORS REFUSED TO TREAT HIS WOUNDS, BUT JORGEN USED HIS MEDICAL TRAINING TO HELP HIM THE BEST HE COULD.
YOU ARE BETTER AT THIS MEDICAL STUFF THAN I PRETENDED TO BE.
WELL, I TRY TO IMAGINE A FREE DENMARK AND BECOMING A REAL DOCTOR SOMEDAY.
LIVING A SIMPLE LIFE.
AND TRIED TO LIFT HIS SPIRITS.
WHEN THIS IS ALL OVER, WE MUST TAKE A HOLIDAY TO NORWAY WITH MY BROTHER AND GO HUNTING.
AND I CAN GO BACK TO MY DAUGHTER, MY WIFE, MY STUDENTS . . . AND WALK AROUND WITHOUT FEAR.

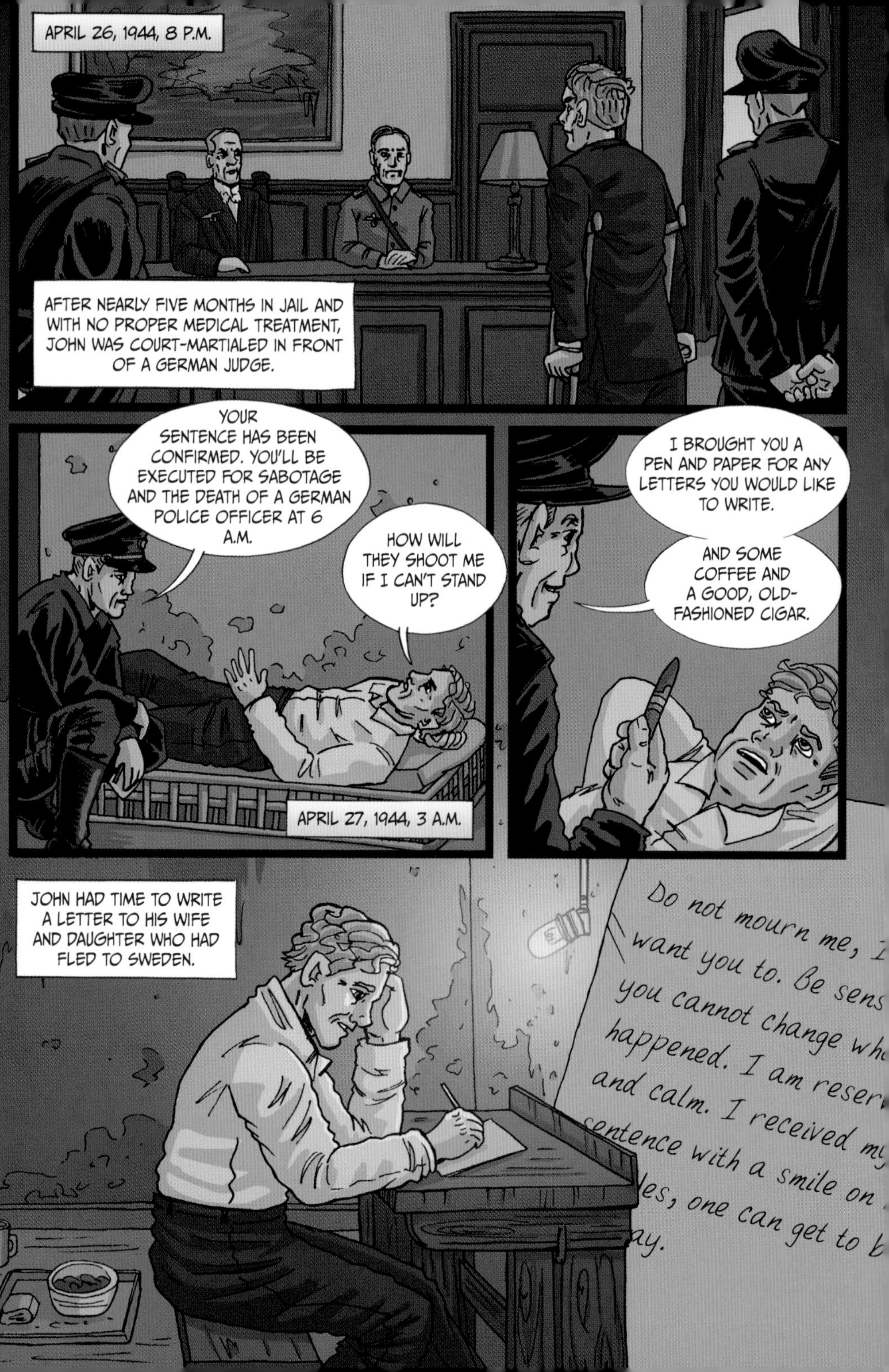
APRIL 26, 1944, 8 P.M.
AFTER NEARLY FIVE MONTHS IN JAIL AND WITH NO PROPER MEDICAL TREATMENT, JOHN WAS COURT-MARTIALED IN FRONT OF A GERMAN JUDGE.
YOUR SENTENCE HAS BEEN CONFIRMED. YOU'LL BE EXECUTED FOR SABOTAGE AND THE DEATH OF A GERMAN POLICE OFFICER AT 6 A.M.
HOW WILL THEY SHOOT ME IF I CAN'T STAND UP?
APRIL 27, 1944, 3 A.M.
I BROUGHT YOU A PEN AND PAPER FOR ANY LETTERS YOU WOULD LIKE TO WRITE.
AND SOME COFFEE AND A GOOD, OLD-FASHIONED CIGAR.
JOHN HAD TIME TO WRITE A LETTER TO HIS WIFE AND DAUGHTER WHO HAD FLED TO SWEDEN.
Do not mourn me,
want you to. Be sens
you cannot change wh
happened. I am reser
and calm. I received m
entence with a smile on
es, one can get to b
ay.

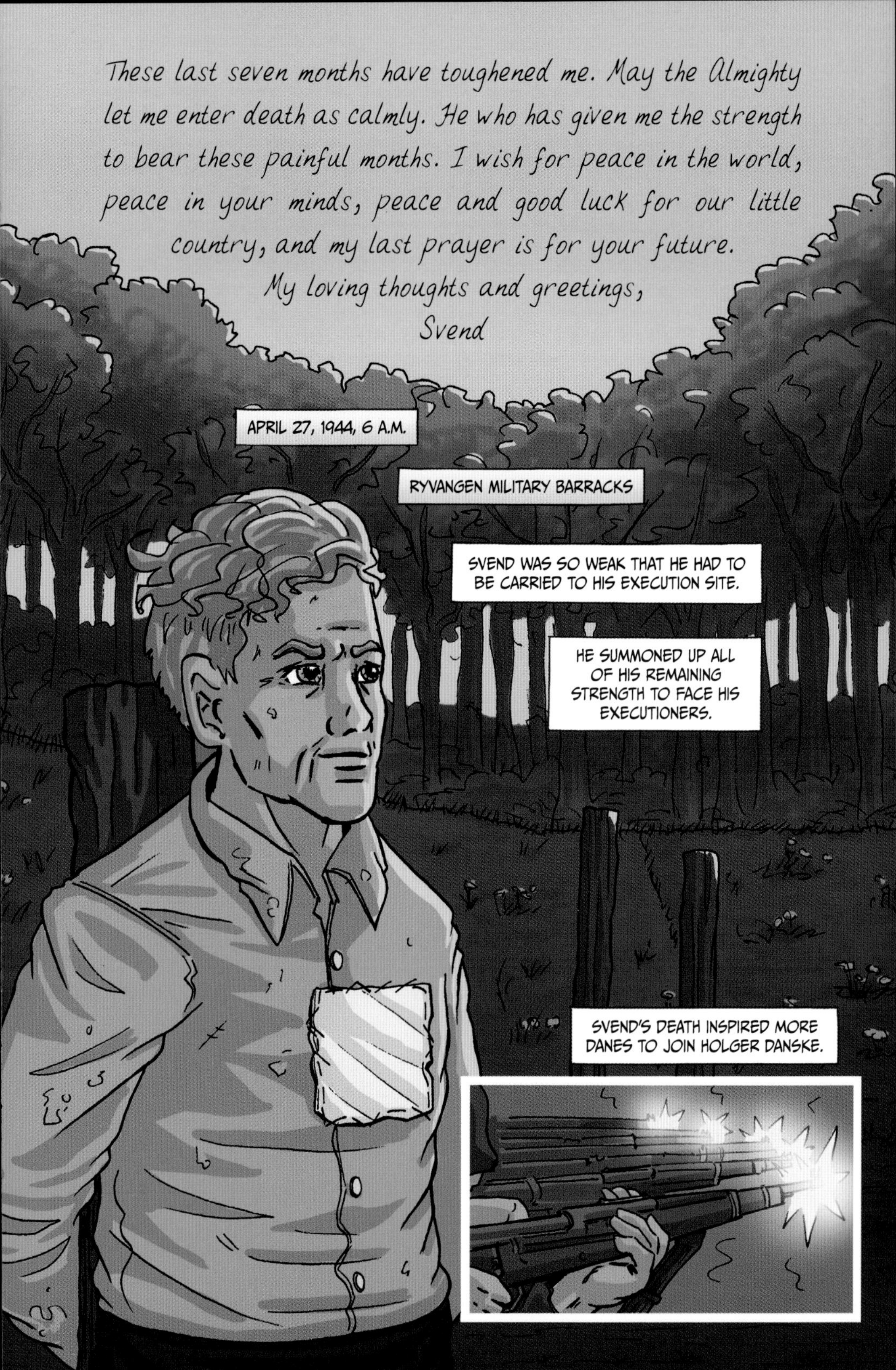
These last seven months have toughened me. May the Almighty let me enter death as calmly. He who has given me the strength to bear these painful months. I wish for peace in the world, peace in your minds, peace and good luck for our little country, and my last prayer is for your future.
My loving thoughts and greetings,
Svend
APRIL 27, 1944, 6 A.M.
RYVANGEN MILITARY BARRACKS
SVEND WAS SO WEAK THAT HE HAD TO BE CARRIED TO HIS EXECUTION SITE.
HE SUMMONED UP ALL OF HIS REMAINING STRENGTH TO FACE HIS EXECUTIONERS.
SVEND'S DEATH INSPIRED MORE DANES TO JOIN HOLGER DANSKE.

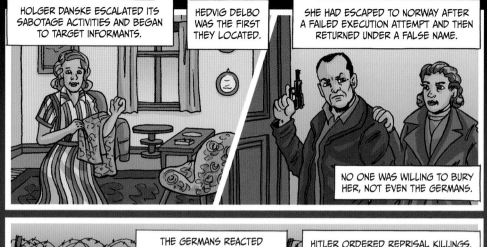

HOLGER DANSKE ESCALATED ITS SABOTAGE ACTIVITIES AND BEGAN TO TARGET INFORMANTS.

HEDVIG DELBO WAS THE FIRST THEY LOCATED.

SHE HAD ESCAPED TO NORWAY AFTER A FAILED EXECUTION ATTEMPT AND THEN RETURNED UNDER A FALSE NAME.

NO ONE WAS WILLING TO BURY HER, NOT EVEN THE GERMANS.

THE GERMANS REACTED HARSHLY TO THE VIOLENCE.

HITLER ORDERED REPRISAL KILLINGS. FIVE DANES WOULD BE EXECUTED FOR EVERY GERMAN SOLDIER KILLED.

THE GERMANS BLEW UP PART OF TIVOLI AS A PUNISHMENT.

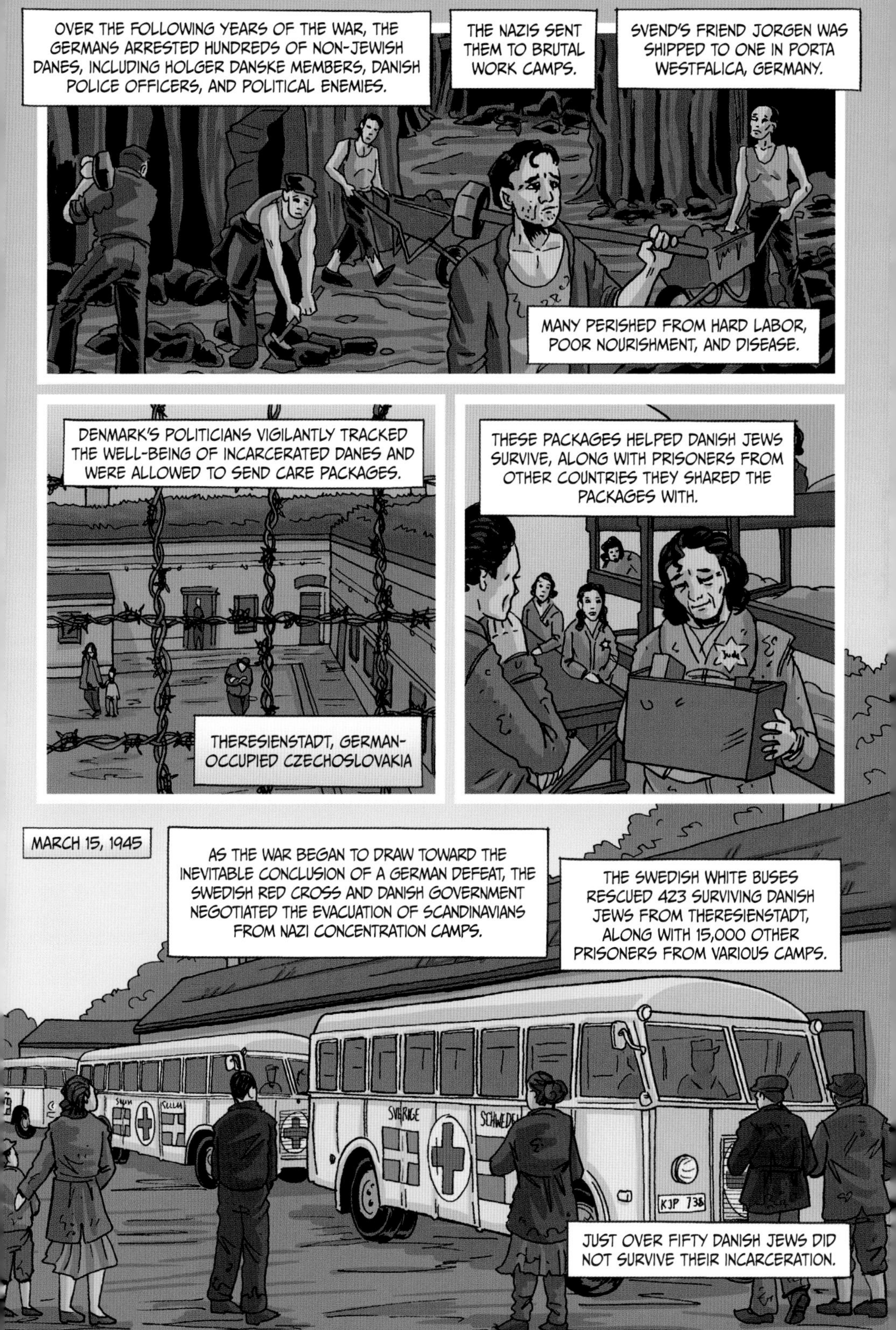
OVER THE FOLLOWING YEARS OF THE WAR, THE GERMANS ARRESTED HUNDREDS OF NON-JEWISH DANES, INCLUDING HOLGER DANSKE MEMBERS, DANISH POLICE OFFICERS, AND POLITICAL ENEMIES.
THE NAZIS SENT THEM TO BRUTAL WORK CAMPS.
SVEND'S FRIEND JORGEN WAS SHIPPED TO ONE IN PORTA WESTFALICA, GERMANY.
MANY PERISHED FROM HARD LABOR, POOR NOURISHMENT, AND DISEASE.
DENMARK'S POLITICIANS VIGILANTLY TRACKED THE WELL-BEING OF INCARCERATED DANES AND WERE ALLOWED TO SEND CARE PACKAGES.
THERESIENSTADT, GERMAN-OCCUPIED CZECHOSLOVAKIA
THESE PACKAGES HELPED DANISH JEWS SURVIVE, ALONG WITH PRISONERS FROM OTHER COUNTRIES THEY SHARED THE PACKAGES WITH.
MARCH 15, 1945
AS THE WAR BEGAN TO DRAW TOWARD THE INEVITABLE CONCLUSION OF A GERMAN DEFEAT, THE SWEDISH RED CROSS AND DANISH GOVERNMENT NEGOTIATED THE EVACUATION OF SCANDINAVIANS FROM NAZI CONCENTRATION CAMPS.
THE SWEDISH WHITE BUSES RESCUED 423 SURVIVING DANISH JEWS FROM THERESIENSTADT, ALONG WITH 15,000 OTHER PRISONERS FROM VARIOUS CAMPS.
SVERIGE
SCHWEDEN
KJP 738
JUST OVER FIFTY DANISH JEWS DID NOT SURVIVE THEIR INCARCERATION.

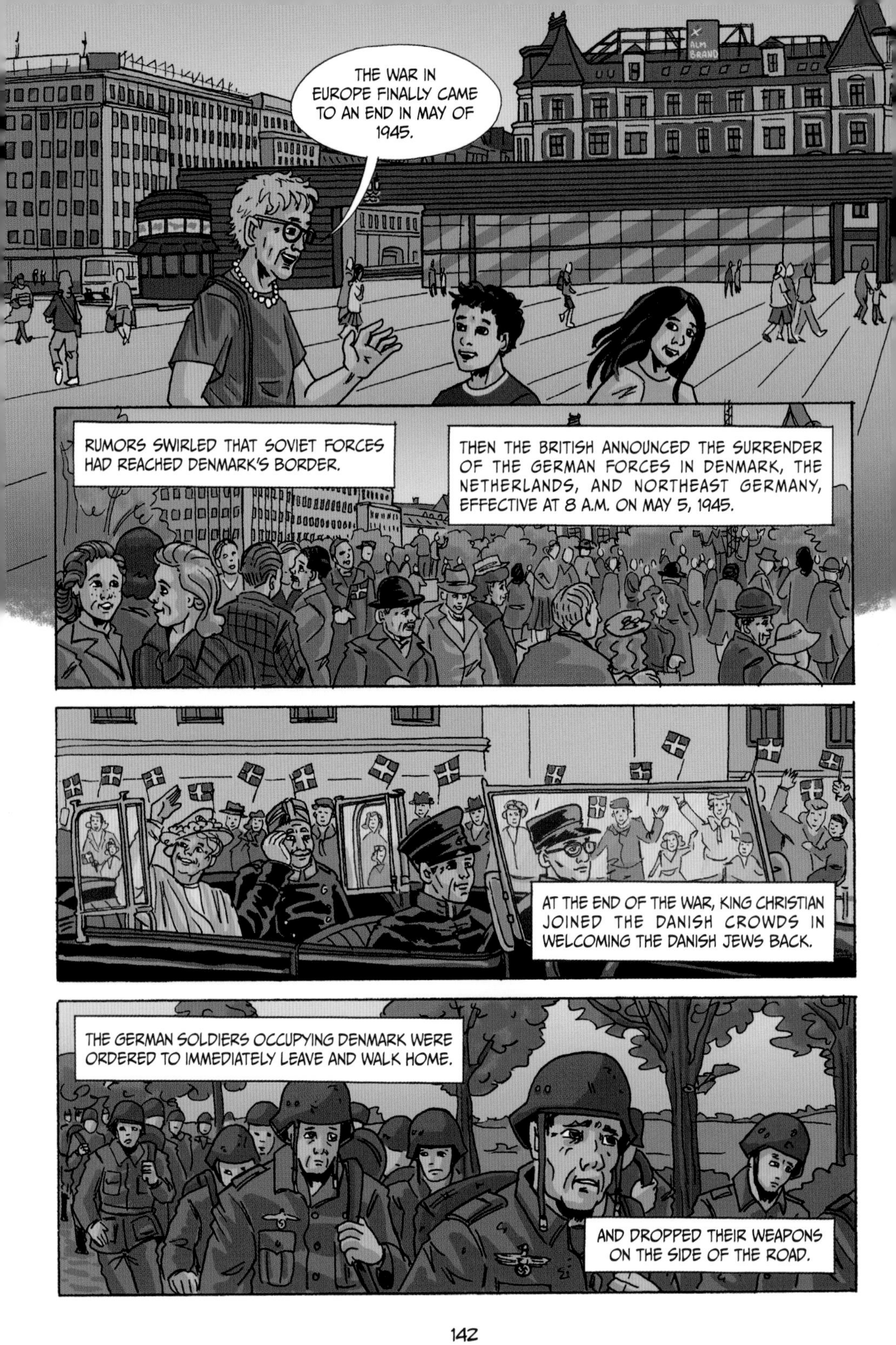
THE WAR IN EUROPE FINALLY CAME TO AN END IN MAY OF 1945.
ALM BRAND
RUMORS SWIRLED THAT SOVIET FORCES HAD REACHED DENMARK'S BORDER.
THEN THE BRITISH ANNOUNCED THE SURRENDER OF THE GERMAN FORCES IN DENMARK, THE NETHERLANDS, AND NORTHEAST GERMANY, EFFECTIVE AT 8 A.M. ON MAY 5, 1945.
AT THE END OF THE WAR, KING CHRISTIAN JOINED THE DANISH CROWDS IN WELCOMING THE DANISH JEWS BACK.
THE GERMAN SOLDIERS OCCUPYING DENMARK WERE ORDERED TO IMMEDIATELY LEAVE AND WALK HOME.
AND DROPPED THEIR WEAPONS ON THE SIDE OF THE ROAD.

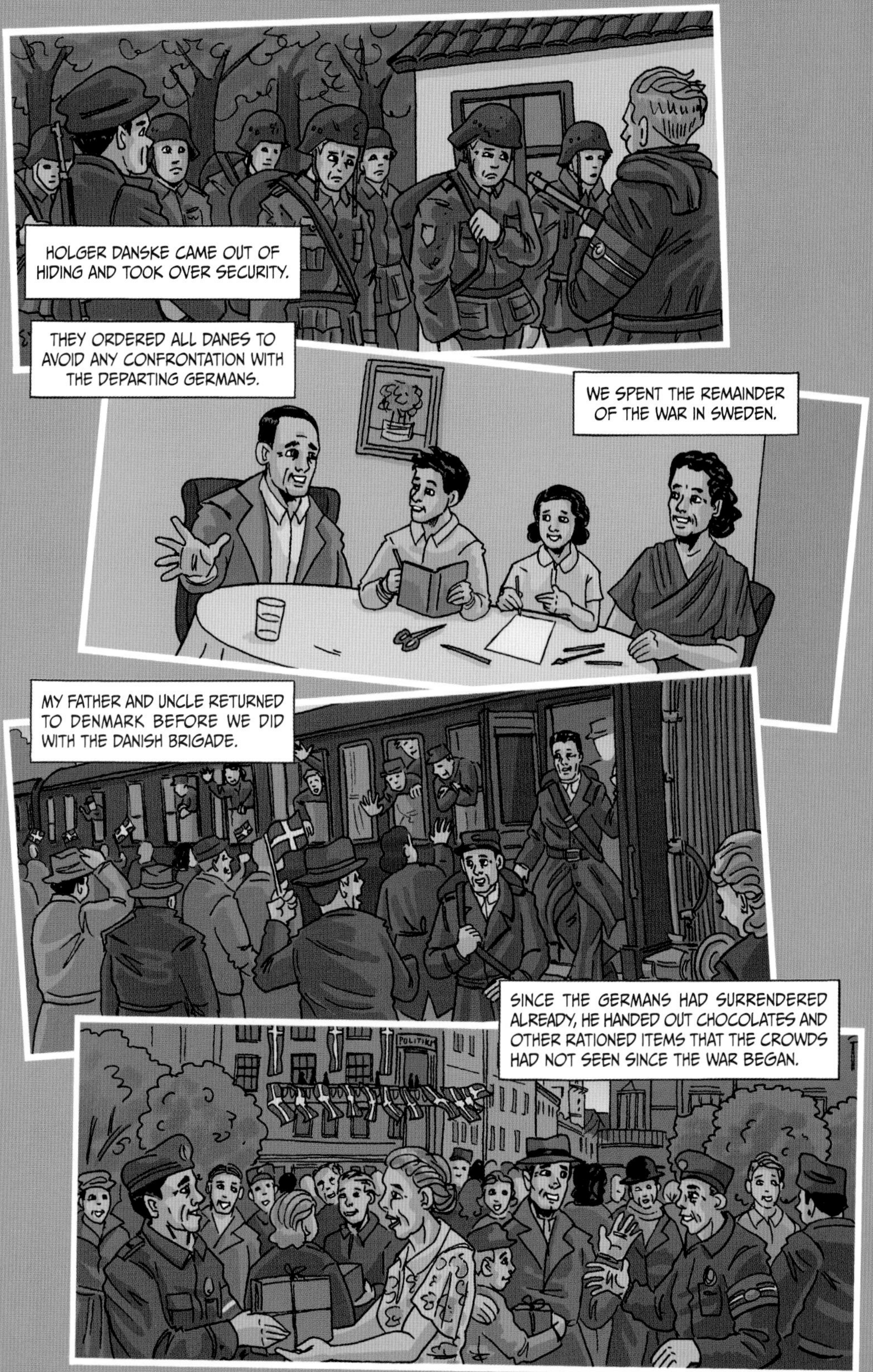
HOLGER DANSKE CAME OUT OF HIDING AND TOOK OVER SECURITY.
THEY ORDERED ALL DANES TO AVOID ANY CONFRONTATION WITH THE DEPARTING GERMANS.
WE SPENT THE REMAINDER OF THE WAR IN SWEDEN.
MY FATHER AND UNCLE RETURNED TO DENMARK BEFORE WE DID WITH THE DANISH BRIGADE.
SINCE THE GERMANS HAD SURRENDERED ALREADY, HE HANDED OUT CHOCOLATES AND OTHER RATIONED ITEMS THAT THE CROWDS HAD NOT SEEN SINCE THE WAR BEGAN.
POLITIK

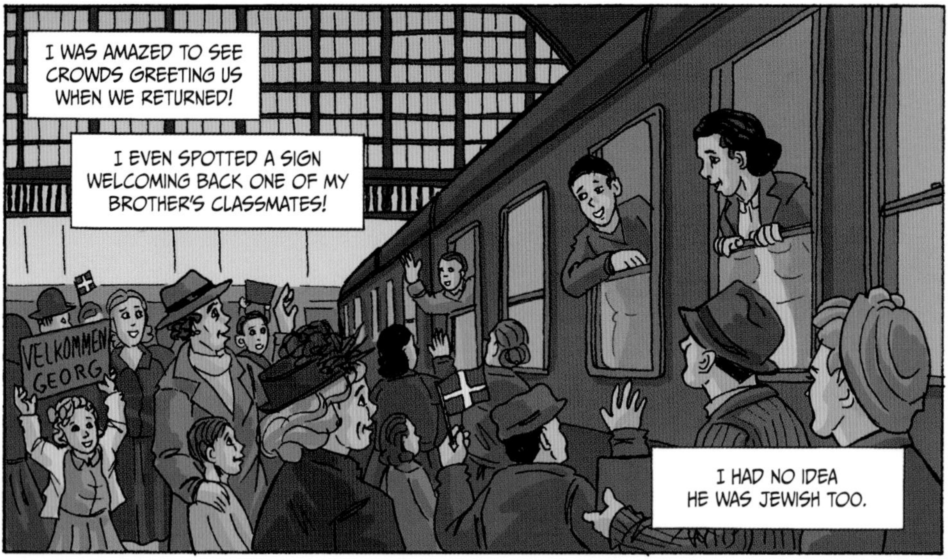
I WAS AMAZED TO SEE CROWDS GREETING US WHEN WE RETURNED!
I EVEN SPOTTED A SIGN WELCOMING BACK ONE OF MY BROTHER'S CLASSMATES!
VELKOMMEN GEORG
I HAD NO IDEA HE WAS JEWISH TOO.

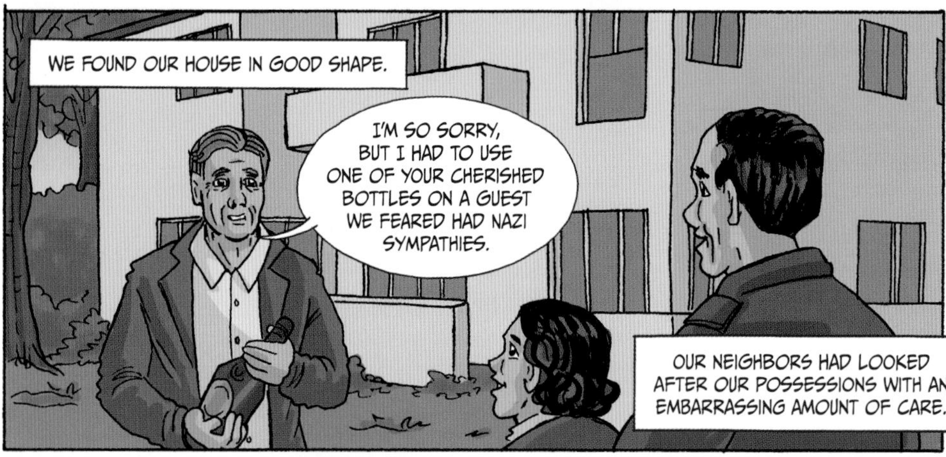
WE FOUND OUR HOUSE IN GOOD SHAPE.
I'M SO SORRY, BUT I HAD TO USE ONE OF YOUR CHERISHED BOTTLES ON A GUEST WE FEARED HAD NAZI SYMPATHIES.
OUR NEIGHBORS HAD LOOKED AFTER OUR POSSESSIONS WITH AN EMBARRASSING AMOUNT OF CARE.

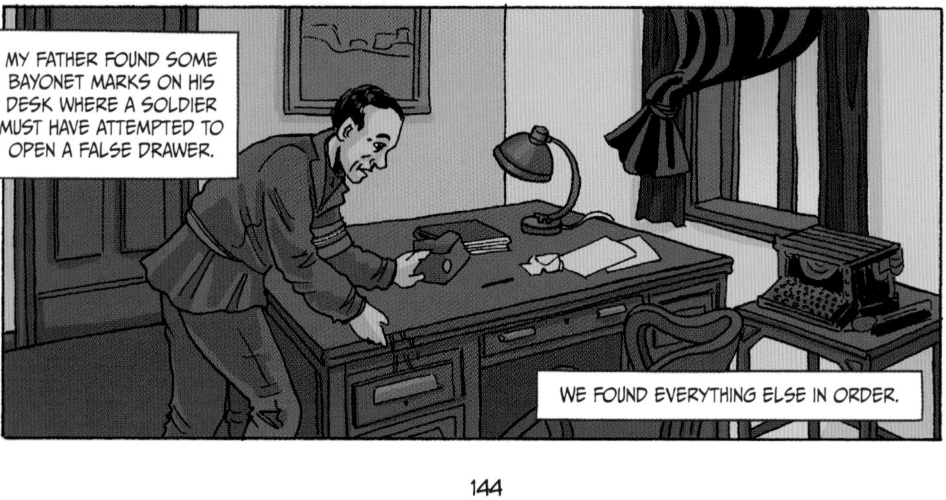
MY FATHER FOUND SOME BAYONET MARKS ON HIS DESK WHERE A SOLDIER MUST HAVE ATTEMPTED TO OPEN A FALSE DRAWER.
WE FOUND EVERYTHING ELSE IN ORDER.

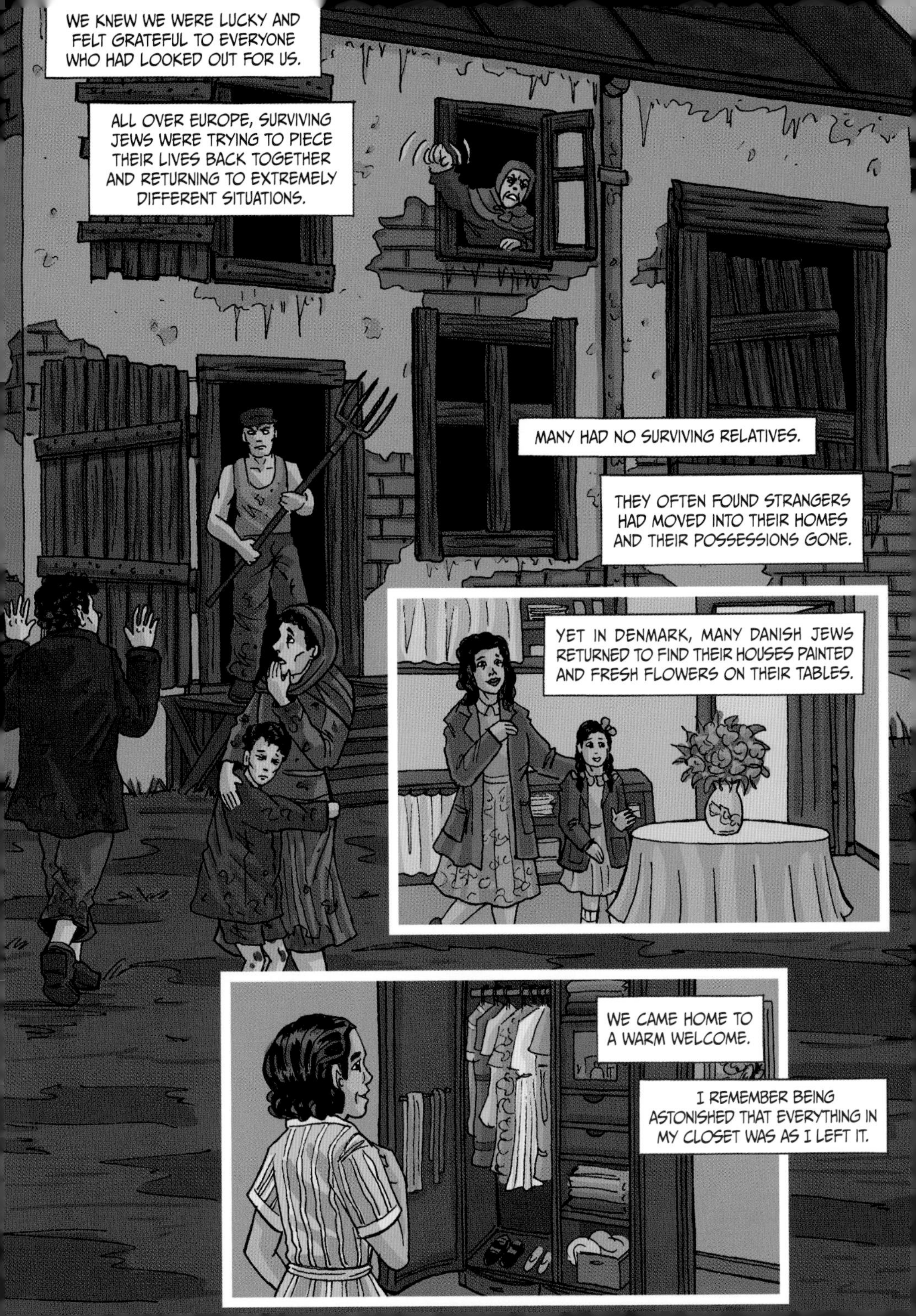
WE KNEW WE WERE LUCKY AND FELT GRATEFUL TO EVERYONE WHO HAD LOOKED OUT FOR US.
ALL OVER EUROPE, SURVIVING JEWS WERE TRYING TO PIECE THEIR LIVES BACK TOGETHER AND RETURNING TO EXTREMELY DIFFERENT SITUATIONS.
MANY HAD NO SURVIVING RELATIVES.
THEY OFTEN FOUND STRANGERS HAD MOVED INTO THEIR HOMES AND THEIR POSSESSIONS GONE.
YET IN DENMARK, MANY DANISH JEWS RETURNED TO FIND THEIR HOUSES PAINTED AND FRESH FLOWERS ON THEIR TABLES.
WE CAME HOME TO A WARM WELCOME.
I REMEMBER BEING ASTONISHED THAT EVERYTHING IN MY CLOSET WAS AS I LEFT IT.

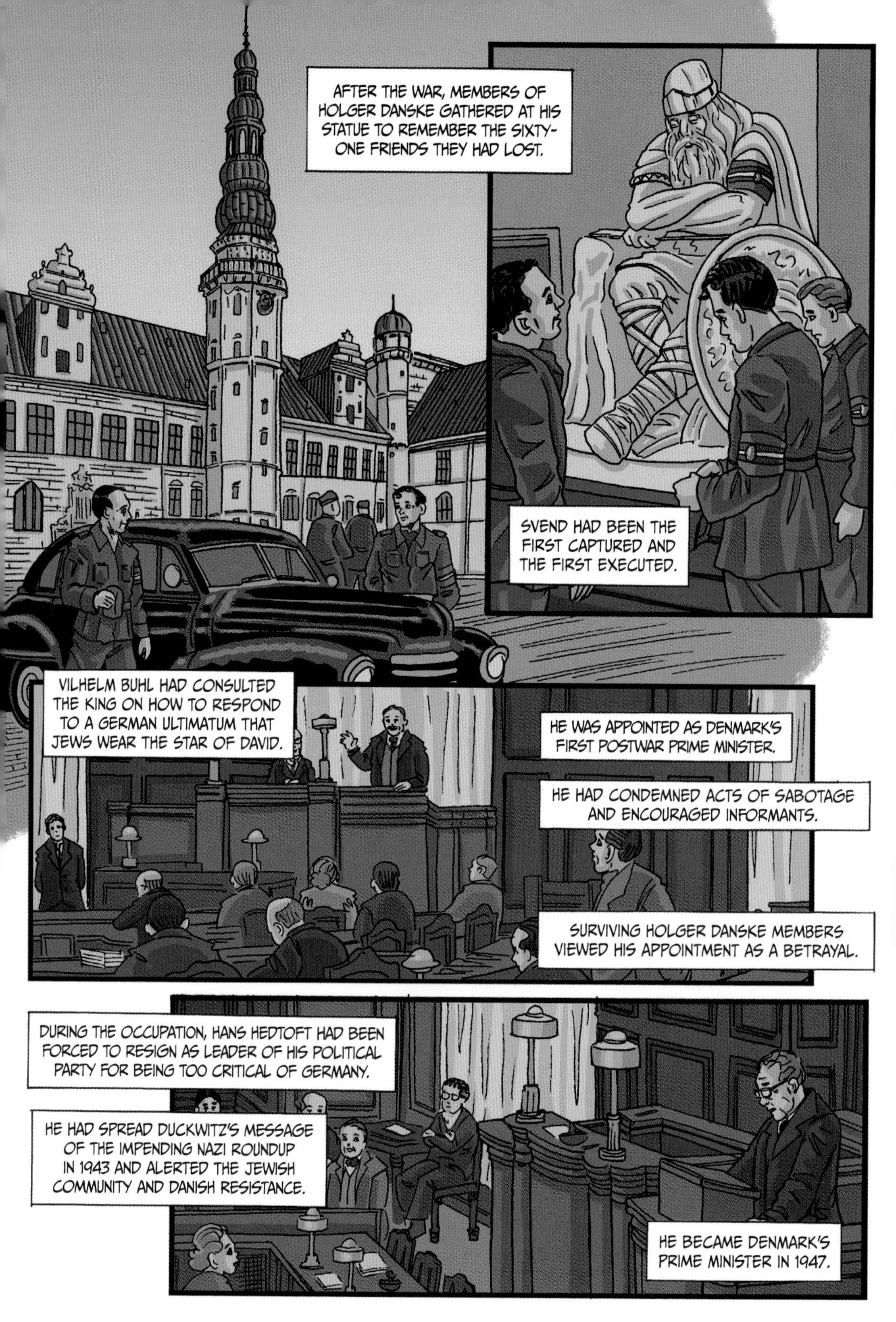
AFTER THE WAR, MEMBERS OF HOLGER DANSKE GATHERED AT HIS STATUE TO REMEMBER THE SIXTY-ONE FRIENDS THEY HAD LOST.
SVEND HAD BEEN THE FIRST CAPTURED AND THE FIRST EXECUTED.
VILHELM BUHL HAD CONSULTED THE KING ON HOW TO RESPOND TO A GERMAN ULTIMATUM THAT JEWS WEAR THE STAR OF DAVID.
HE WAS APPOINTED AS DENMARK'S FIRST POSTWAR PRIME MINISTER.
HE HAD CONDEMNED ACTS OF SABOTAGE AND ENCOURAGED INFORMANTS.
SURVIVING HOLGER DANSKE MEMBERS VIEWED HIS APPOINTMENT AS A BETRAYAL.
DURING THE OCCUPATION, HANS HEDTOFT HAD BEEN FORCED TO RESIGN AS LEADER OF HIS POLITICAL PARTY FOR BEING TOO CRITICAL OF GERMANY.
HE HAD SPREAD DUCKWITZ'S MESSAGE OF THE IMPENDING NAZI ROUNDUP IN 1943 AND ALERTED THE JEWISH COMMUNITY AND DANISH RESISTANCE.
HE BECAME DENMARK'S PRIME MINISTER IN 1947.

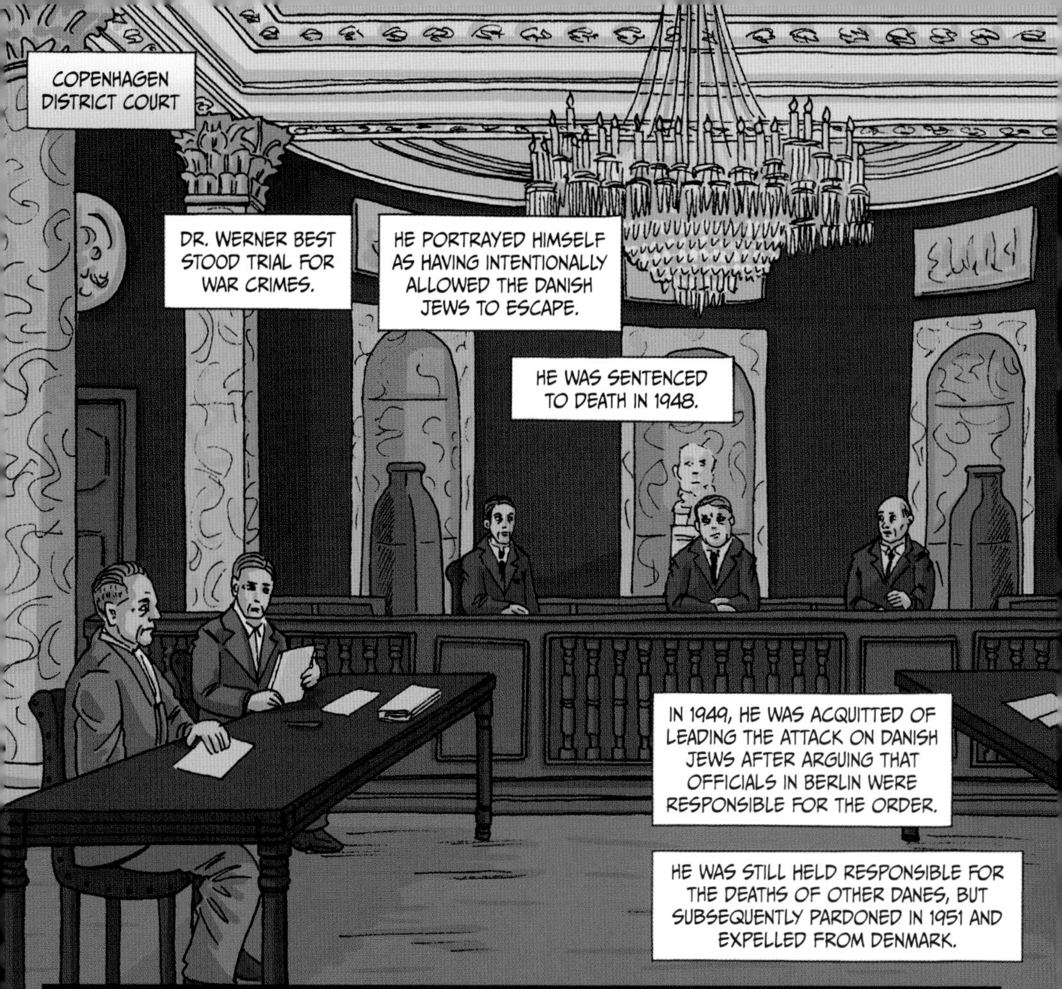
COPENHAGEN DISTRICT COURT
DR. WERNER BEST STOOD TRIAL FOR WAR CRIMES.
HE PORTRAYED HIMSELF AS HAVING INTENTIONALLY ALLOWED THE DANISH JEWS TO ESCAPE.
HE WAS SENTENCED TO DEATH IN 1948.
IN 1949, HE WAS ACQUITTED OF LEADING THE ATTACK ON DANISH JEWS AFTER ARGUING THAT OFFICIALS IN BERLIN WERE RESPONSIBLE FOR THE ORDER.
HE WAS STILL HELD RESPONSIBLE FOR THE DEATHS OF OTHER DANES, BUT SUBSEQUENTLY PARDONED IN 1951 AND EXPELLED FROM DENMARK.

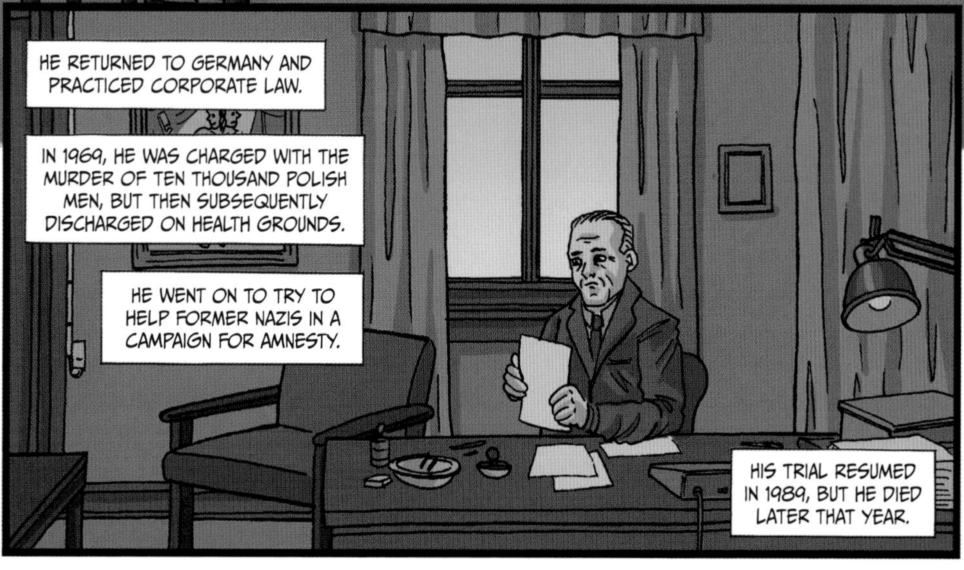
HE RETURNED TO GERMANY AND PRACTICED CORPORATE LAW.
IN 1969, HE WAS CHARGED WITH THE MURDER OF TEN THOUSAND POLISH MEN, BUT THEN SUBSEQUENTLY DISCHARGED ON HEALTH GROUNDS.
HE WENT ON TO TRY TO HELP FORMER NAZIS IN A CAMPAIGN FOR AMNESTY.
HIS TRIAL RESUMED IN 1989, BUT HE DIED LATER THAT YEAR.

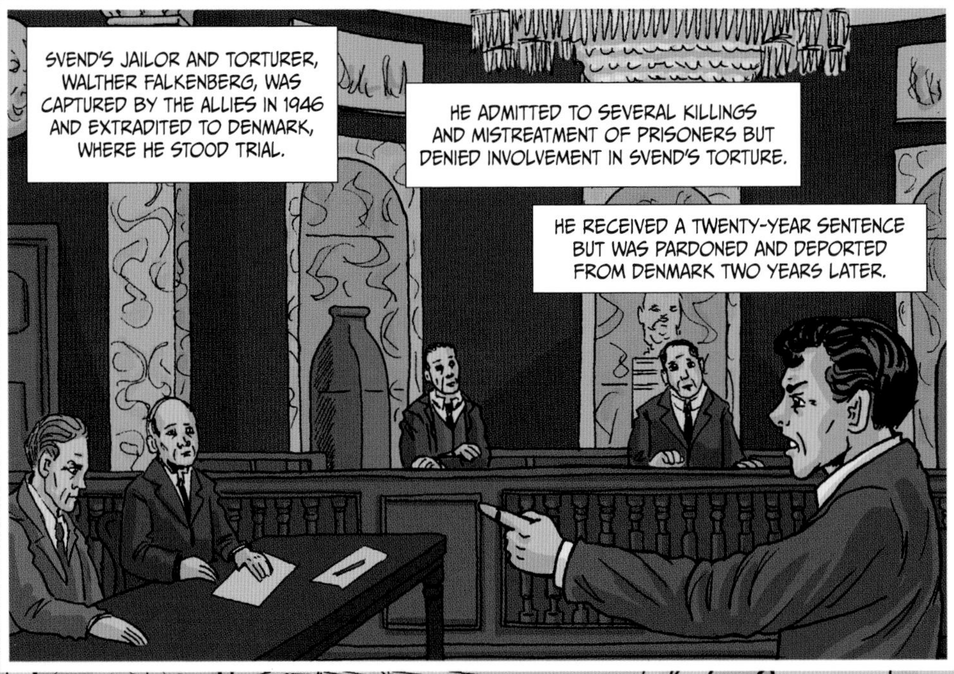
SVEND'S JAILOR AND TORTURER, WALTHER FALKENBERG, WAS CAPTURED BY THE ALLIES IN 1946 AND EXTRADITED TO DENMARK, WHERE HE STOOD TRIAL.
HE ADMITTED TO SEVERAL KILLINGS AND MISTREATMENT OF PRISONERS BUT DENIED INVOLVEMENT IN SVEND'S TORTURE.
HE RECEIVED A TWENTY-YEAR SENTENCE BUT WAS PARDONED AND DEPORTED FROM DENMARK TWO YEARS LATER.

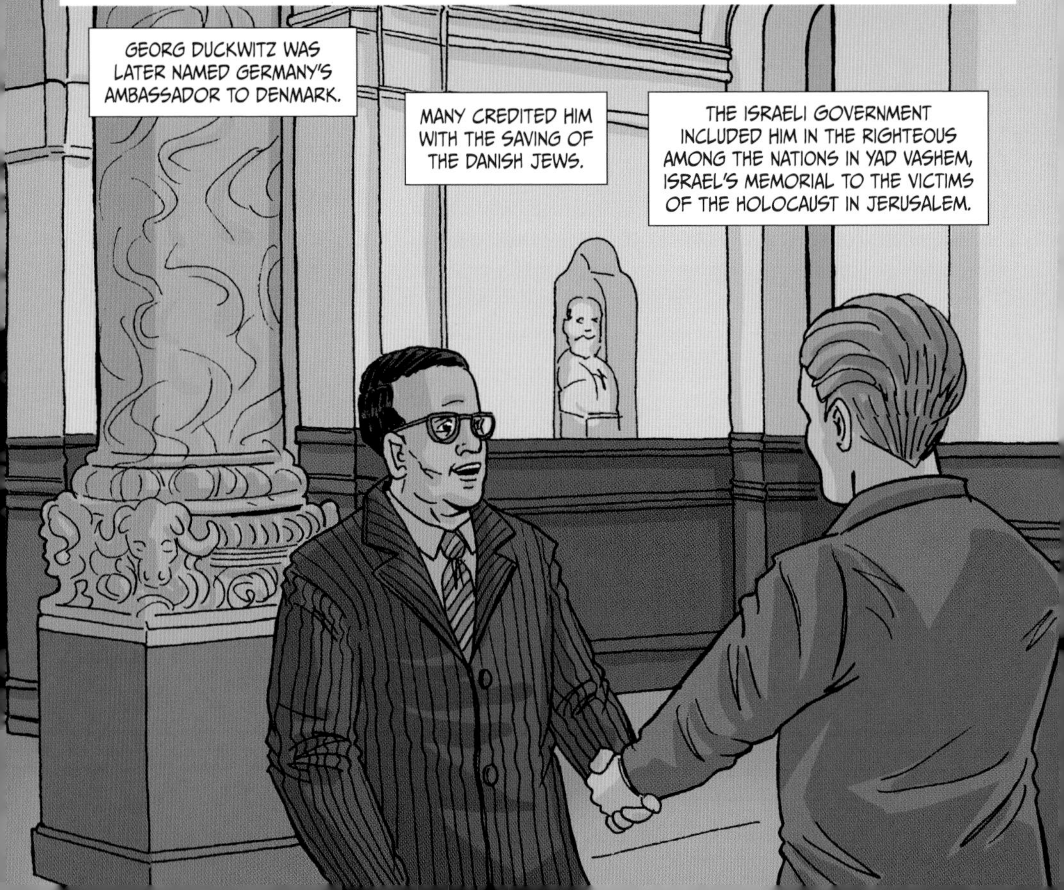
GEORG DUCKWITZ WAS LATER NAMED GERMANY'S AMBASSADOR TO DENMARK.
MANY CREDITED HIM WITH THE SAVING OF THE DANISH JEWS.
THE ISRAELI GOVERNMENT INCLUDED HIM IN THE RIGHTEOUS AMONG THE NATIONS IN YAD VASHEM, ISRAEL'S MEMORIAL TO THE VICTIMS OF THE HOLOCAUST IN JERUSALEM.

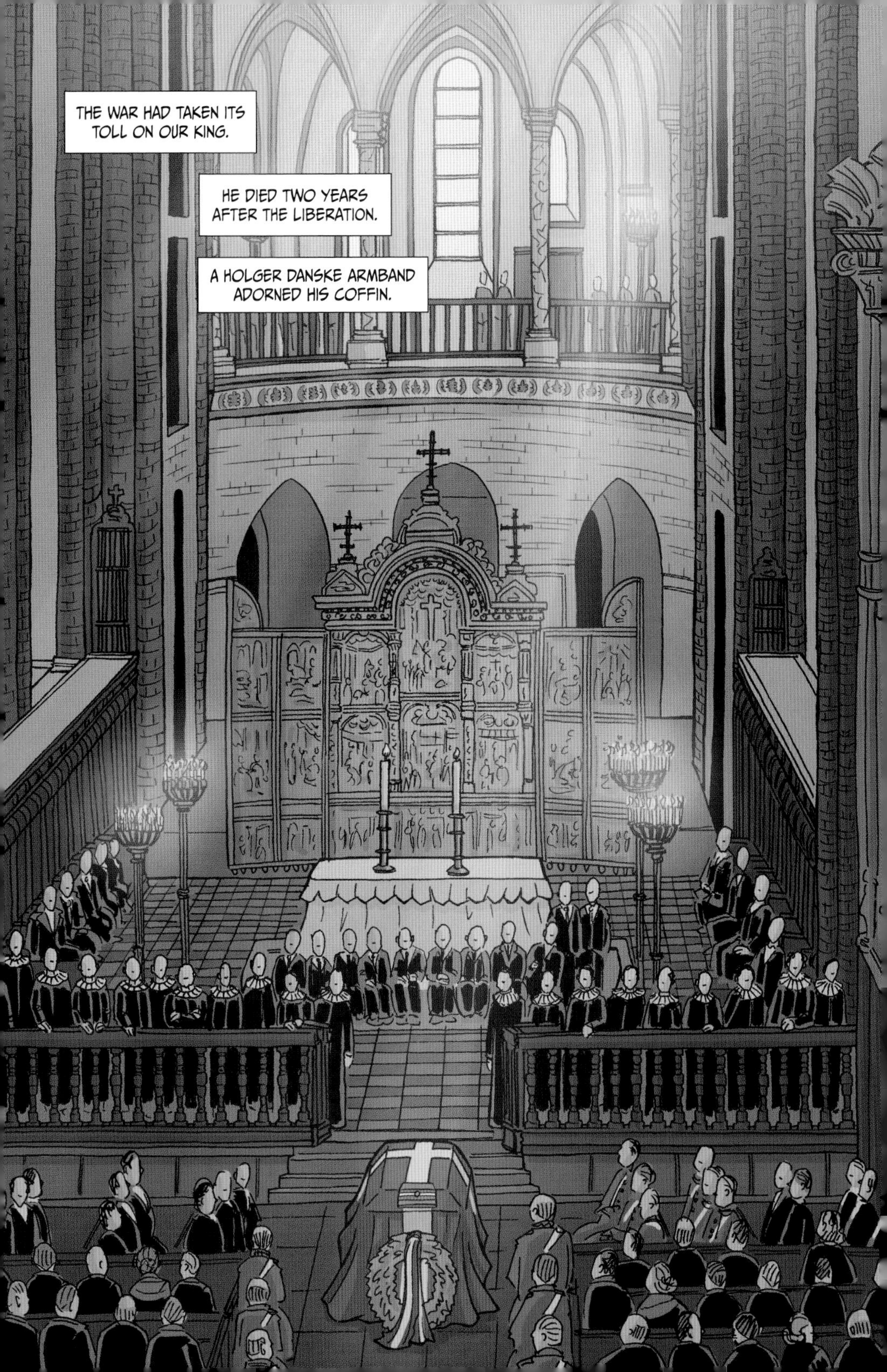
THE WAR HAD TAKEN ITS TOLL ON OUR KING.
HE DIED TWO YEARS AFTER THE LIBERATION.
A HOLGER DANSKE ARMBAND ADORNED HIS COFFIN.

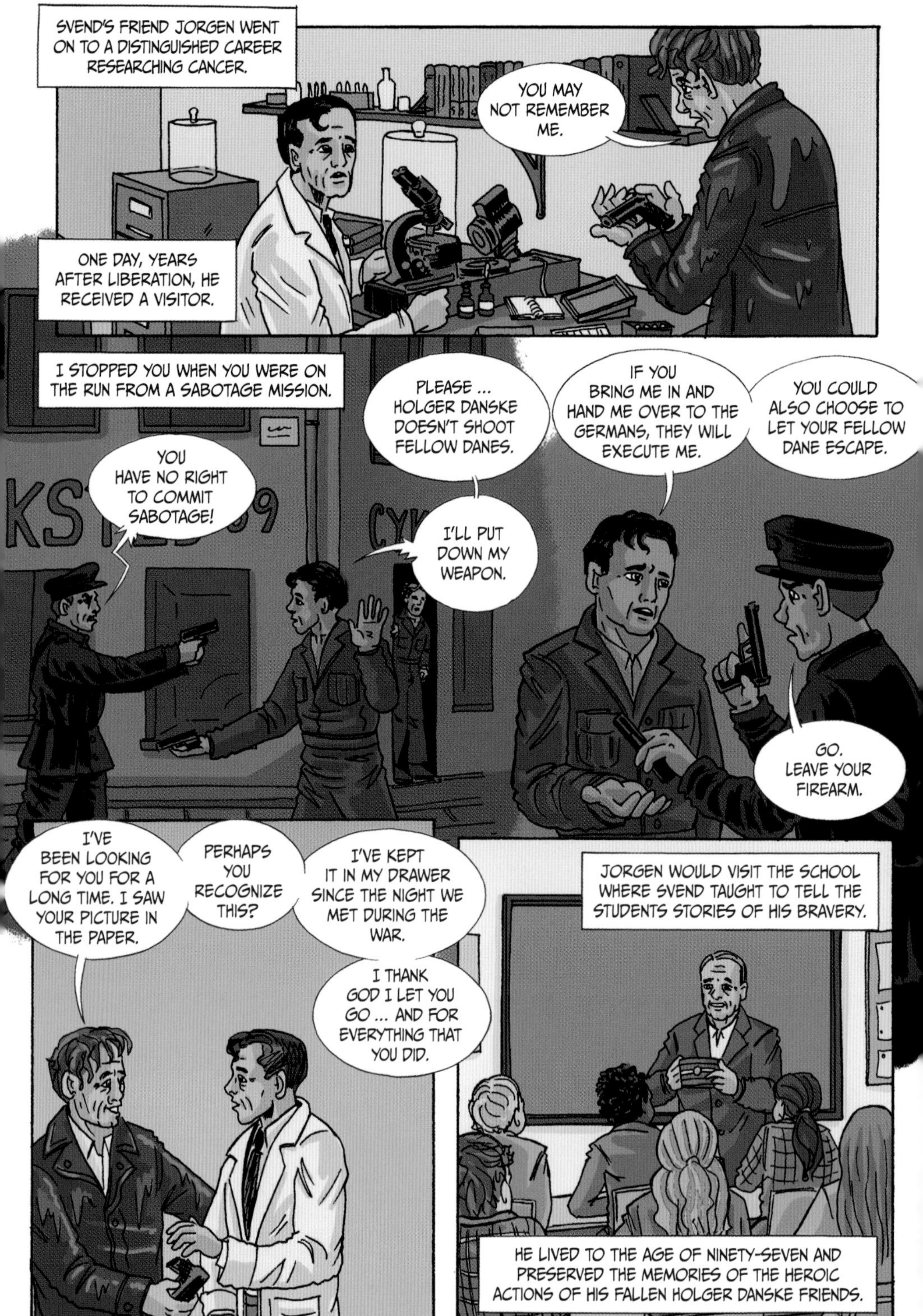
SVEND'S FRIEND JORGEN WENT ON TO A DISTINGUISHED CAREER RESEARCHING CANCER.
ONE DAY, YEARS AFTER LIBERATION, HE RECEIVED A VISITOR.
YOU MAY NOT REMEMBER ME.
I STOPPED YOU WHEN YOU WERE ON THE RUN FROM A SABOTAGE MISSION.
YOU HAVE NO RIGHT TO COMMIT SABOTAGE!
PLEASE ... HOLGER DANSKE DOESN'T SHOOT FELLOW DANES.
I'LL PUT DOWN MY WEAPON.
IF YOU BRING ME IN AND HAND ME OVER TO THE GERMANS, THEY WILL EXECUTE ME.
YOU COULD ALSO CHOOSE TO LET YOUR FELLOW DANE ESCAPE.
GO. LEAVE YOUR FIREARM.
I'VE BEEN LOOKING FOR YOU FOR A LONG TIME. I SAW YOUR PICTURE IN THE PAPER.
PERHAPS YOU RECOGNIZE THIS?
I'VE KEPT IT IN MY DRAWER SINCE THE NIGHT WE MET DURING THE WAR.
I THANK GOD I LET YOU GO ... AND FOR EVERYTHING THAT YOU DID.
JORGEN WOULD VISIT THE SCHOOL WHERE SVEND TAUGHT TO TELL THE STUDENTS STORIES OF HIS BRAVERY.
HE LIVED TO THE AGE OF NINETY-SEVEN AND PRESERVED THE MEMORIES OF THE HEROIC ACTIONS OF HIS FALLEN HOLGER DANSKE FRIENDS.

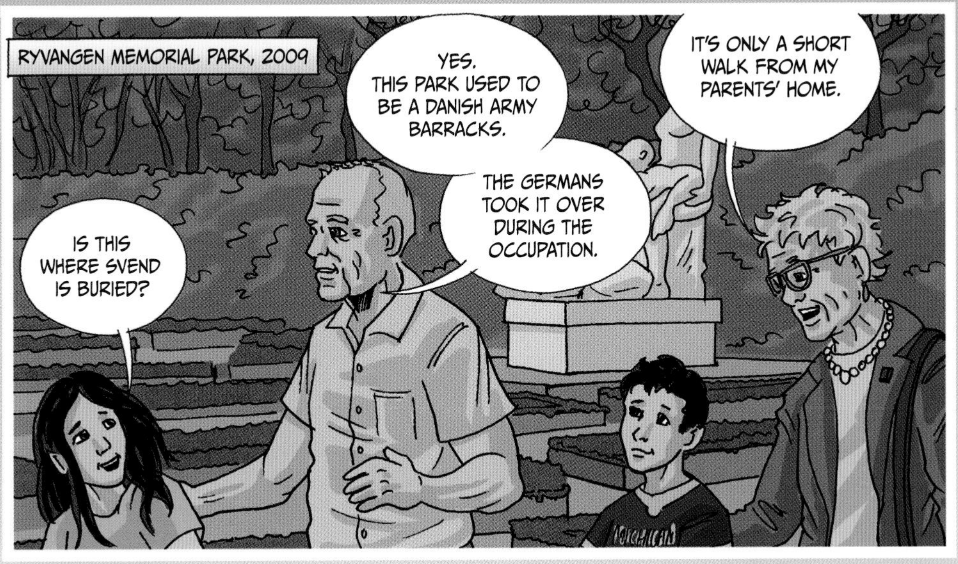
RYVANGEN MEMORIAL PARK, 2009
IS THIS WHERE SVEND IS BURIED?
YES. THIS PARK USED TO BE A DANISH ARMY BARRACKS.
THE GERMANS TOOK IT OVER DURING THE OCCUPATION.
IT'S ONLY A SHORT WALK FROM MY PARENTS' HOME.
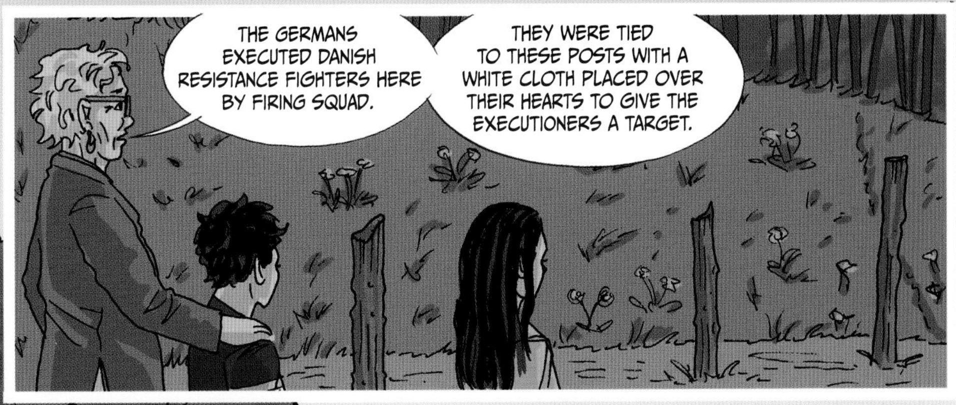
THE GERMANS EXECUTED DANISH RESISTANCE FIGHTERS HERE BY FIRING SQUAD.
THEY WERE TIED TO THESE POSTS WITH A WHITE CLOTH PLACED OVER THEIR HEARTS TO GIVE THE EXECUTIONERS A TARGET.
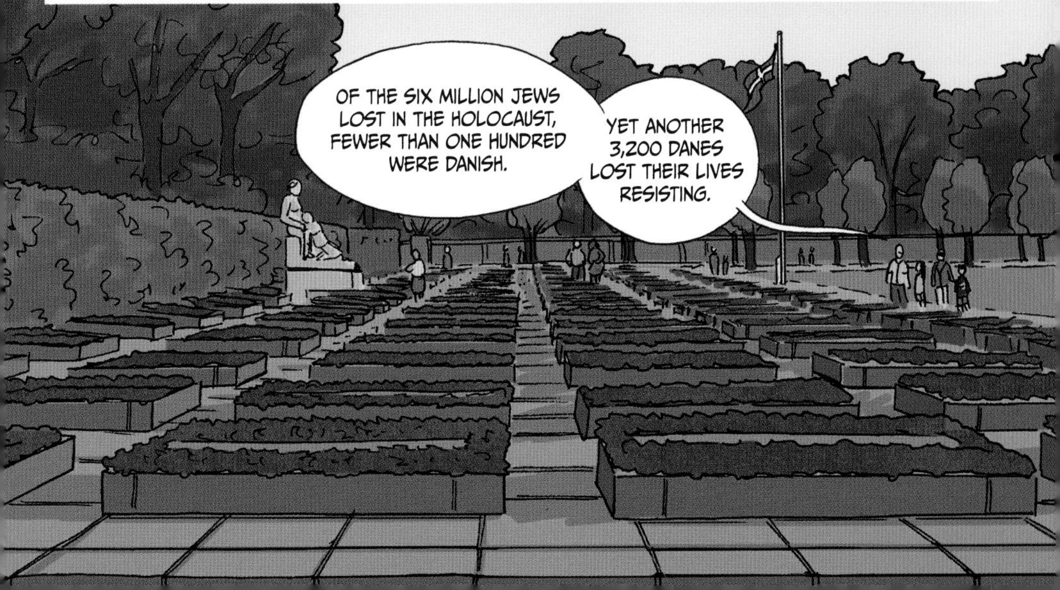
OF THE SIX MILLION JEWS LOST IN THE HOLOCAUST, FEWER THAN ONE HUNDRED WERE DANISH.
YET ANOTHER 3,200 DANES LOST THEIR LIVES RESISTING.

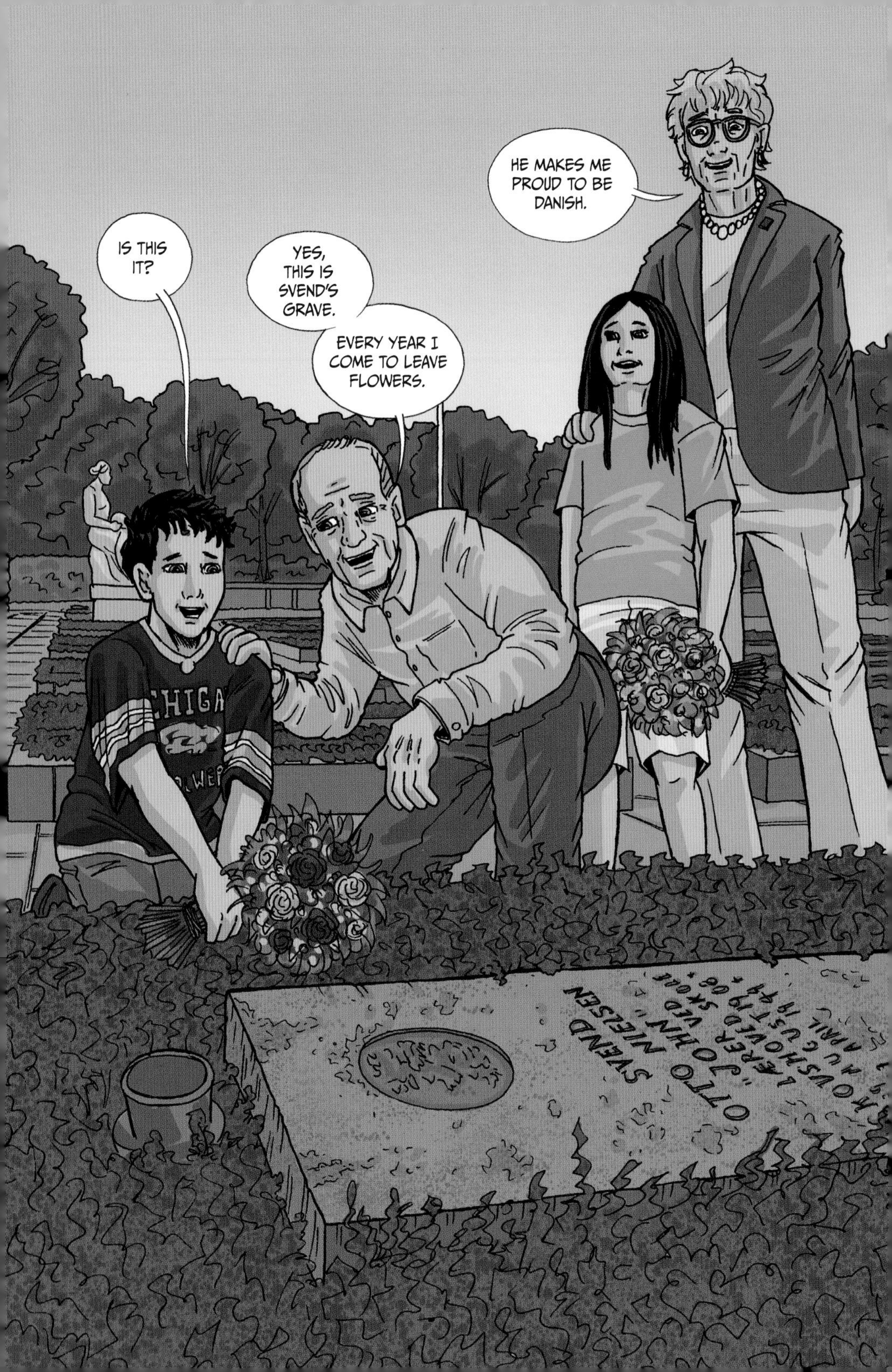
IS THIS IT?
YES, THIS IS SVEND'S GRAVE.
EVERY YEAR I COME TO LEAVE FLOWERS.
HE MAKES ME PROUD TO BE DANISH.

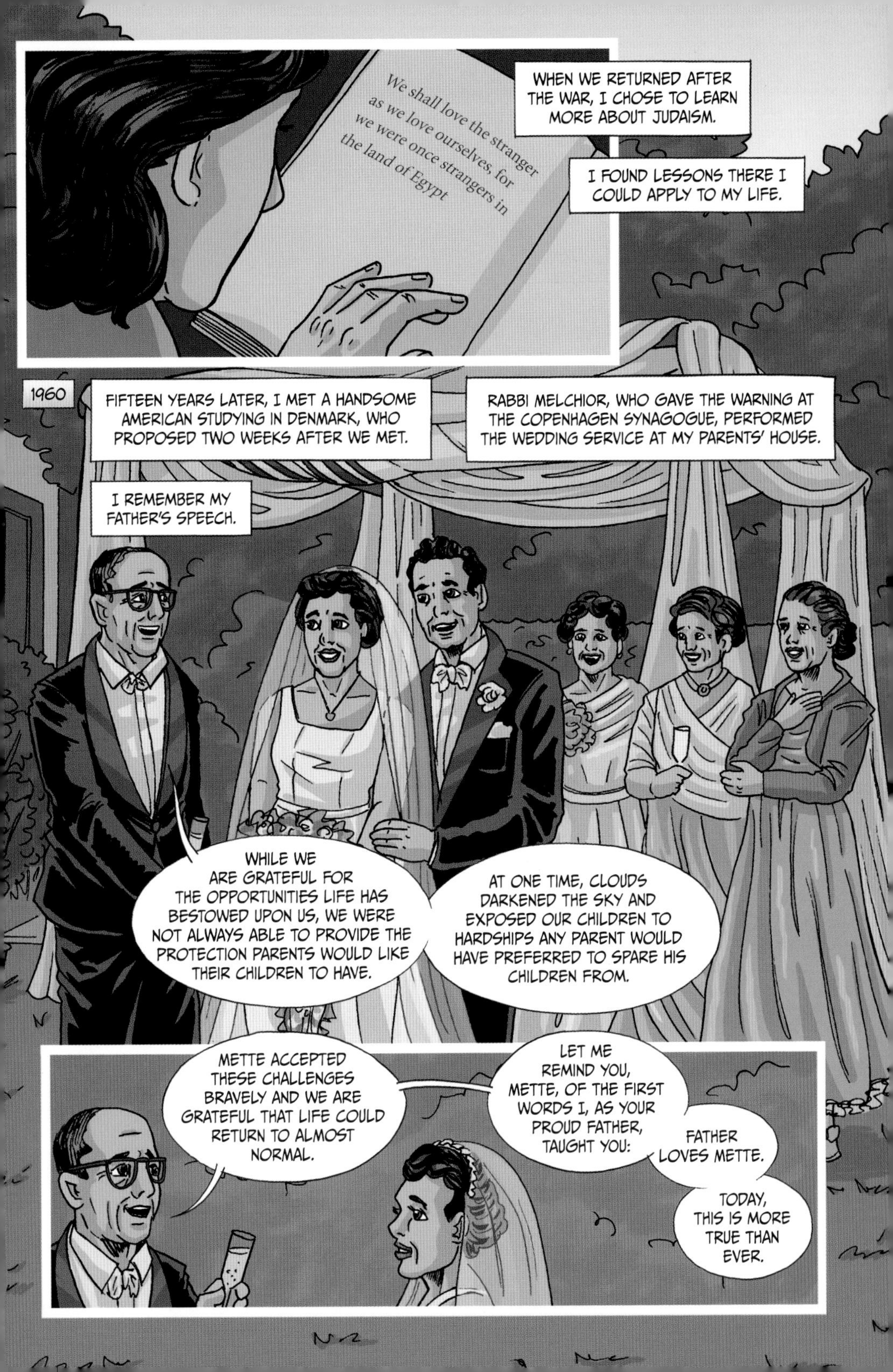
We shall love the stranger as we love ourselves, for we were once strangers in the land of Egypt
WHEN WE RETURNED AFTER THE WAR, I CHOSE TO LEARN MORE ABOUT JUDAISM.
I FOUND LESSONS THERE I COULD APPLY TO MY LIFE.
1960
FIFTEEN YEARS LATER, I MET A HANDSOME AMERICAN STUDYING IN DENMARK, WHO PROPOSED TWO WEEKS AFTER WE MET.
RABBI MELCHIOR, WHO GAVE THE WARNING AT THE COPENHAGEN SYNAGOGUE, PERFORMED THE WEDDING SERVICE AT MY PARENTS' HOUSE.
I REMEMBER MY FATHER'S SPEECH.
WHILE WE ARE GRATEFUL FOR THE OPPORTUNITIES LIFE HAS BESTOWED UPON US, WE WERE NOT ALWAYS ABLE TO PROVIDE THE PROTECTION PARENTS WOULD LIKE THEIR CHILDREN TO HAVE.
AT ONE TIME, CLOUDS DARKENED THE SKY AND EXPOSED OUR CHILDREN TO HARDSHIPS ANY PARENT WOULD HAVE PREFERRED TO SPARE HIS CHILDREN FROM.
METTE ACCEPTED THESE CHALLENGES BRAVELY AND WE ARE GRATEFUL THAT LIFE COULD RETURN TO ALMOST NORMAL.
LET ME REMIND YOU, METTE, OF THE FIRST WORDS I, AS YOUR PROUD FATHER, TAUGHT YOU:
FATHER LOVES METTE.
TODAY, THIS IS MORE TRUE THAN EVER.

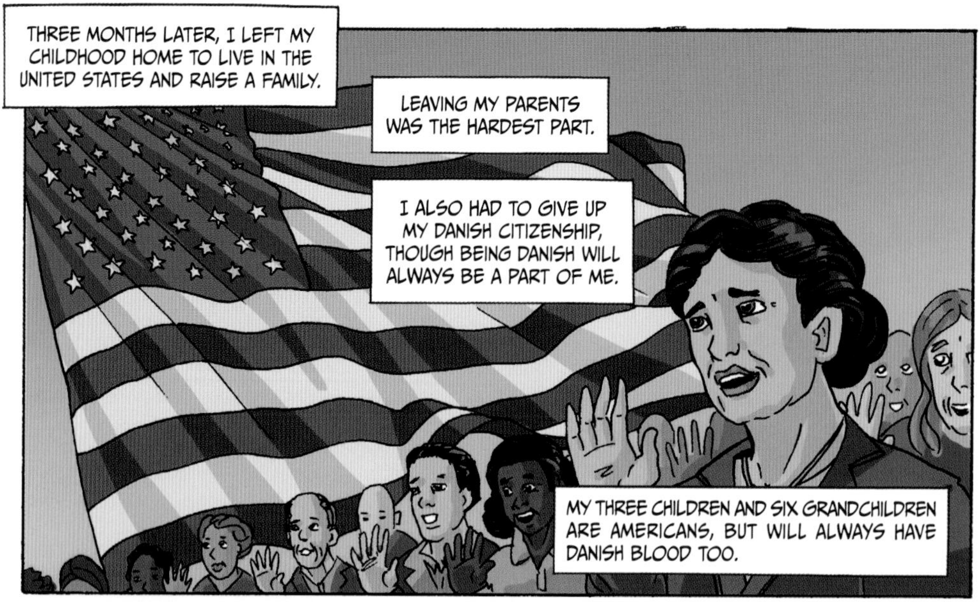
THREE MONTHS LATER, I LEFT MY CHILDHOOD HOME TO LIVE IN THE UNITED STATES AND RAISE A FAMILY.
LEAVING MY PARENTS WAS THE HARDEST PART.
I ALSO HAD TO GIVE UP MY DANISH CITIZENSHIP, THOUGH BEING DANISH WILL ALWAYS BE A PART OF ME.
MY THREE CHILDREN AND SIX GRANDCHILDREN ARE AMERICANS, BUT WILL ALWAYS HAVE DANISH BLOOD TOO.

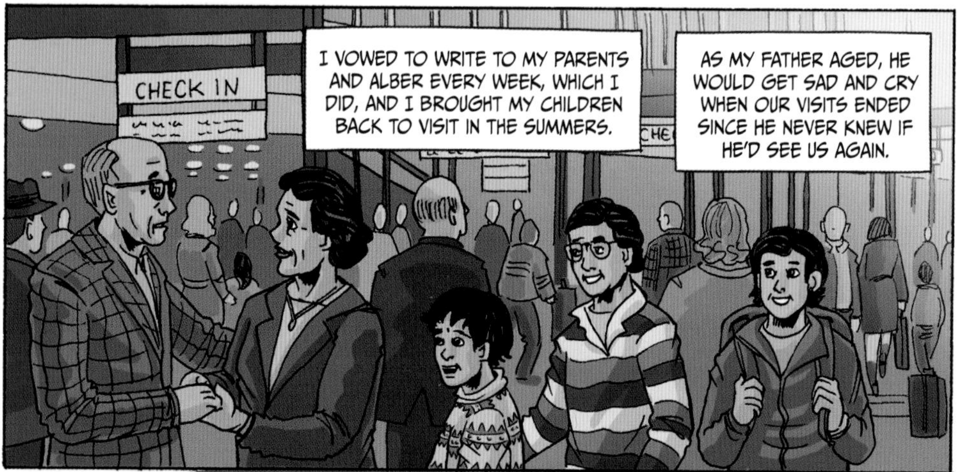
CHECK IN
I VOWED TO WRITE TO MY PARENTS AND ALBER EVERY WEEK, WHICH I DID, AND I BROUGHT MY CHILDREN BACK TO VISIT IN THE SUMMERS.
AS MY FATHER AGED, HE WOULD GET SAD AND CRY WHEN OUR VISITS ENDED SINCE HE NEVER KNEW IF HE'D SEE US AGAIN.

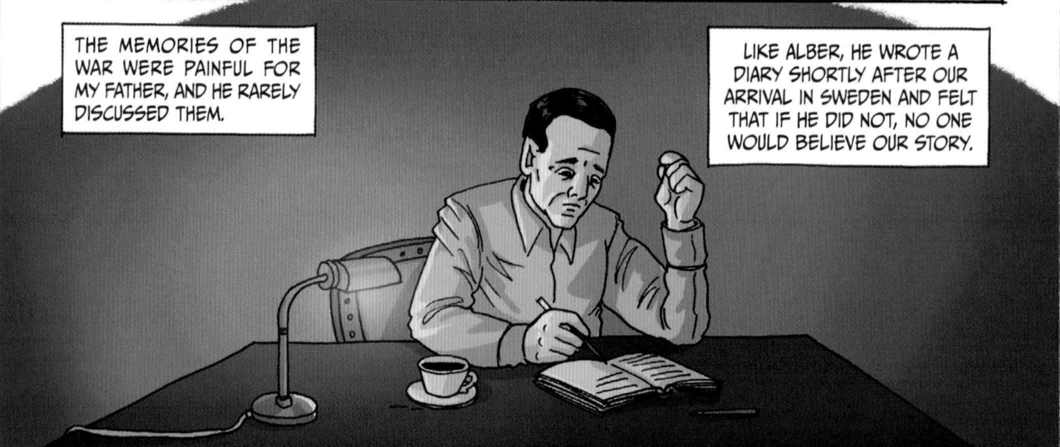
THE MEMORIES OF THE WAR WERE PAINFUL FOR MY FATHER, AND HE RARELY DISCUSSED THEM.
LIKE ALBER, HE WROTE A DIARY SHORTLY AFTER OUR ARRIVAL IN SWEDEN AND FELT THAT IF HE DID NOT, NO ONE WOULD BELIEVE OUR STORY.

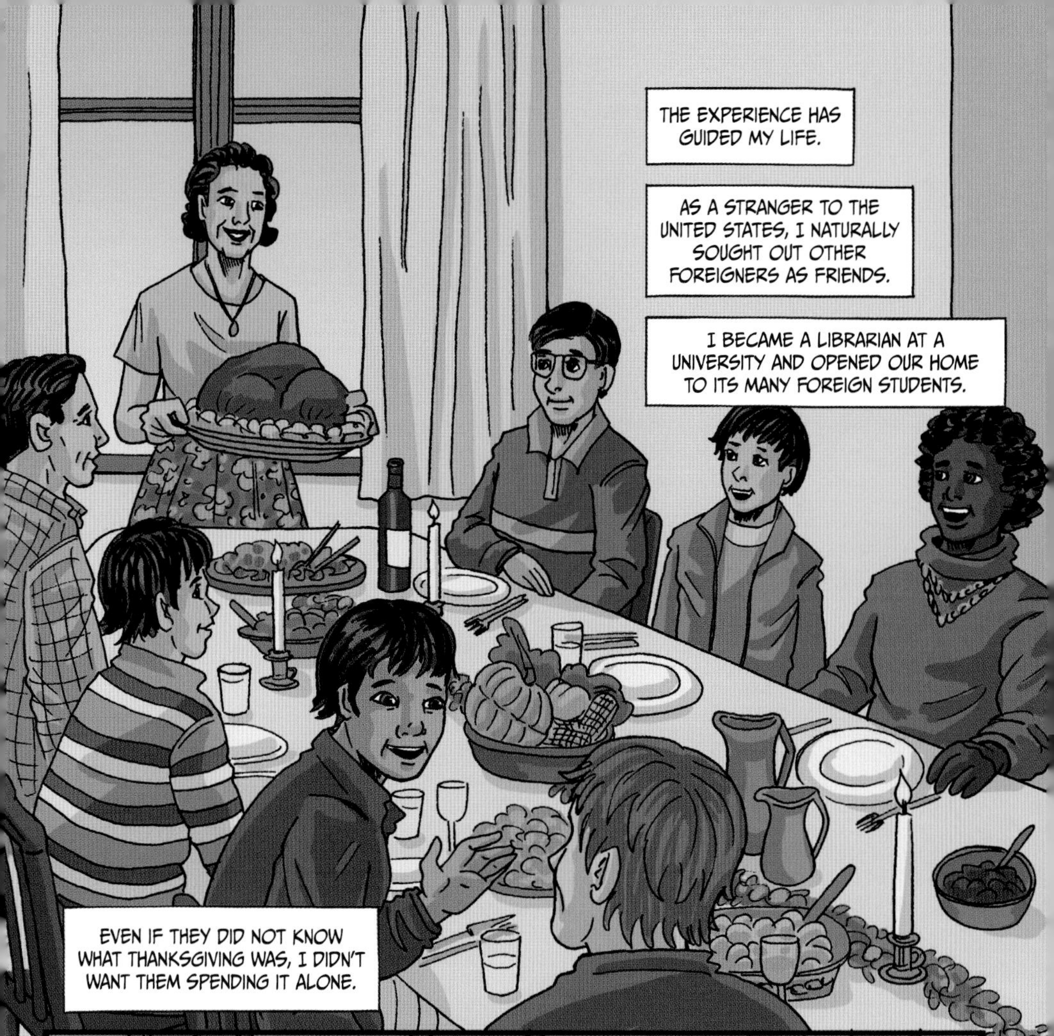
THE EXPERIENCE HAS GUIDED MY LIFE.
AS A STRANGER TO THE UNITED STATES, I NATURALLY SOUGHT OUT OTHER FOREIGNERS AS FRIENDS.
I BECAME A LIBRARIAN AT A UNIVERSITY AND OPENED OUR HOME TO ITS MANY FOREIGN STUDENTS.
EVEN IF THEY DID NOT KNOW WHAT THANKSGIVING WAS, I DIDN'T WANT THEM SPENDING IT ALONE.

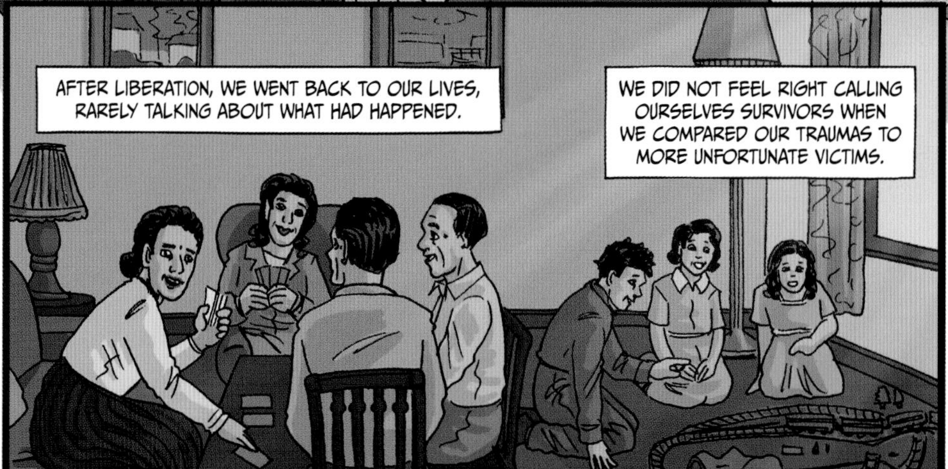
AFTER LIBERATION, WE WENT BACK TO OUR LIVES, RARELY TALKING ABOUT WHAT HAD HAPPENED.
WE DID NOT FEEL RIGHT CALLING OURSELVES SURVIVORS WHEN WE COMPARED OUR TRAUMAS TO MORE UNFORTUNATE VICTIMS.

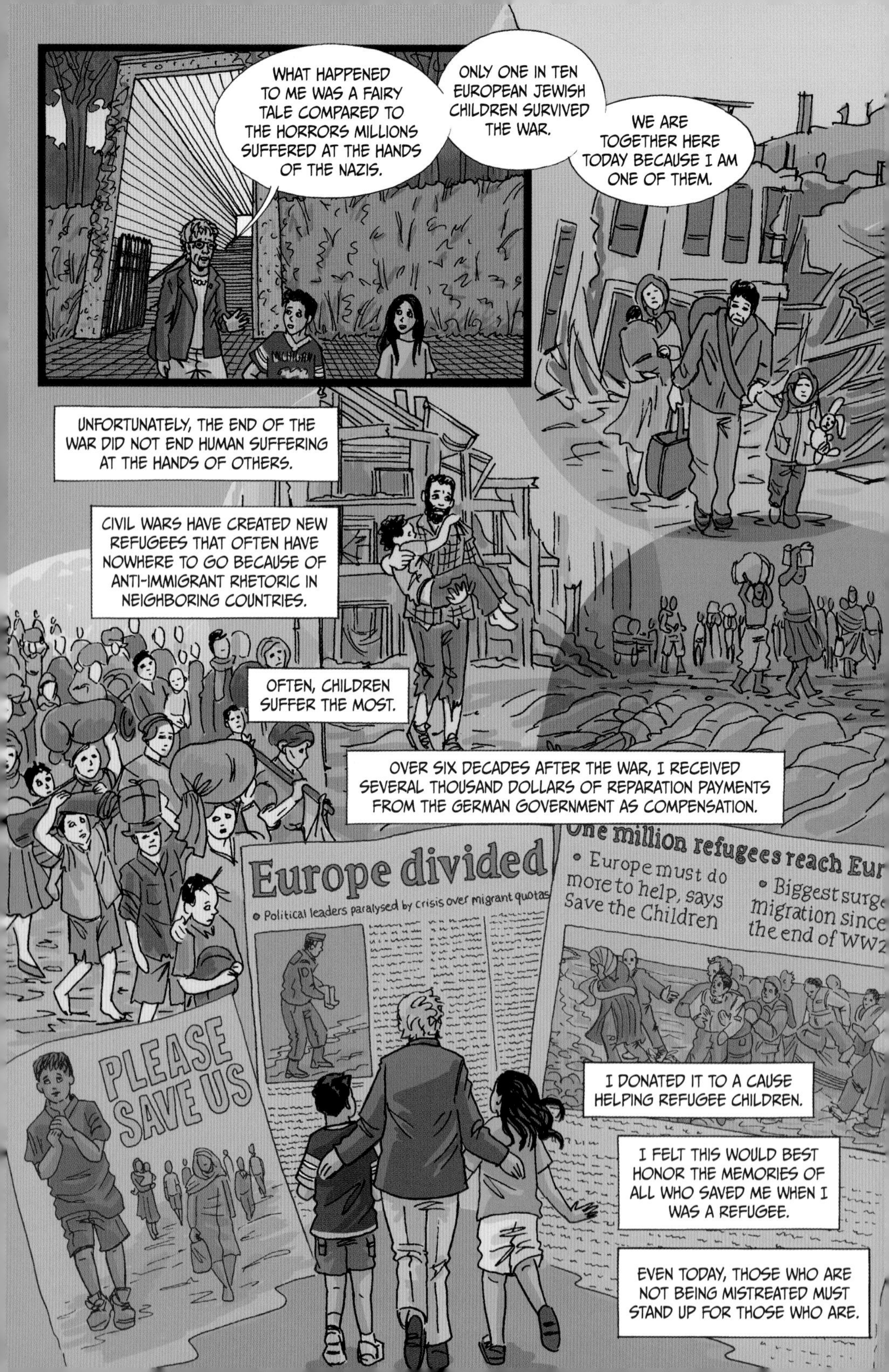
WHAT HAPPENED TO ME WAS A FAIRY TALE COMPARED TO THE HORRORS MILLIONS SUFFERED AT THE HANDS OF THE NAZIS.
ONLY ONE IN TEN EUROPEAN JEWISH CHILDREN SURVIVED THE WAR.
WE ARE TOGETHER HERE TODAY BECAUSE I AM ONE OF THEM.
UNFORTUNATELY, THE END OF THE WAR DID NOT END HUMAN SUFFERING AT THE HANDS OF OTHERS.
CIVIL WARS HAVE CREATED NEW REFUGEES THAT OFTEN HAVE NOWHERE TO GO BECAUSE OF ANTI-IMMIGRANT RHETORIC IN NEIGHBORING COUNTRIES.
OFTEN, CHILDREN SUFFER THE MOST.
OVER SIX DECADES AFTER THE WAR, I RECEIVED SEVERAL THOUSAND DOLLARS OF REPARATION PAYMENTS FROM THE GERMAN GOVERNMENT AS COMPENSATION.
Europe divided
Political leaders paralysed by crisis over migrant quotas
Europe must do more to help, says Save the Children
PLEASE SAVE US
I DONATED IT TO A CAUSE HELPING REFUGEE CHILDREN.
I FELT THIS WOULD BEST HONOR THE MEMORIES OF ALL WHO SAVED ME WHEN I WAS A REFUGEE.
EVEN TODAY, THOSE WHO ARE NOT BEING MISTREATED MUST STAND UP FOR THOSE WHO ARE.

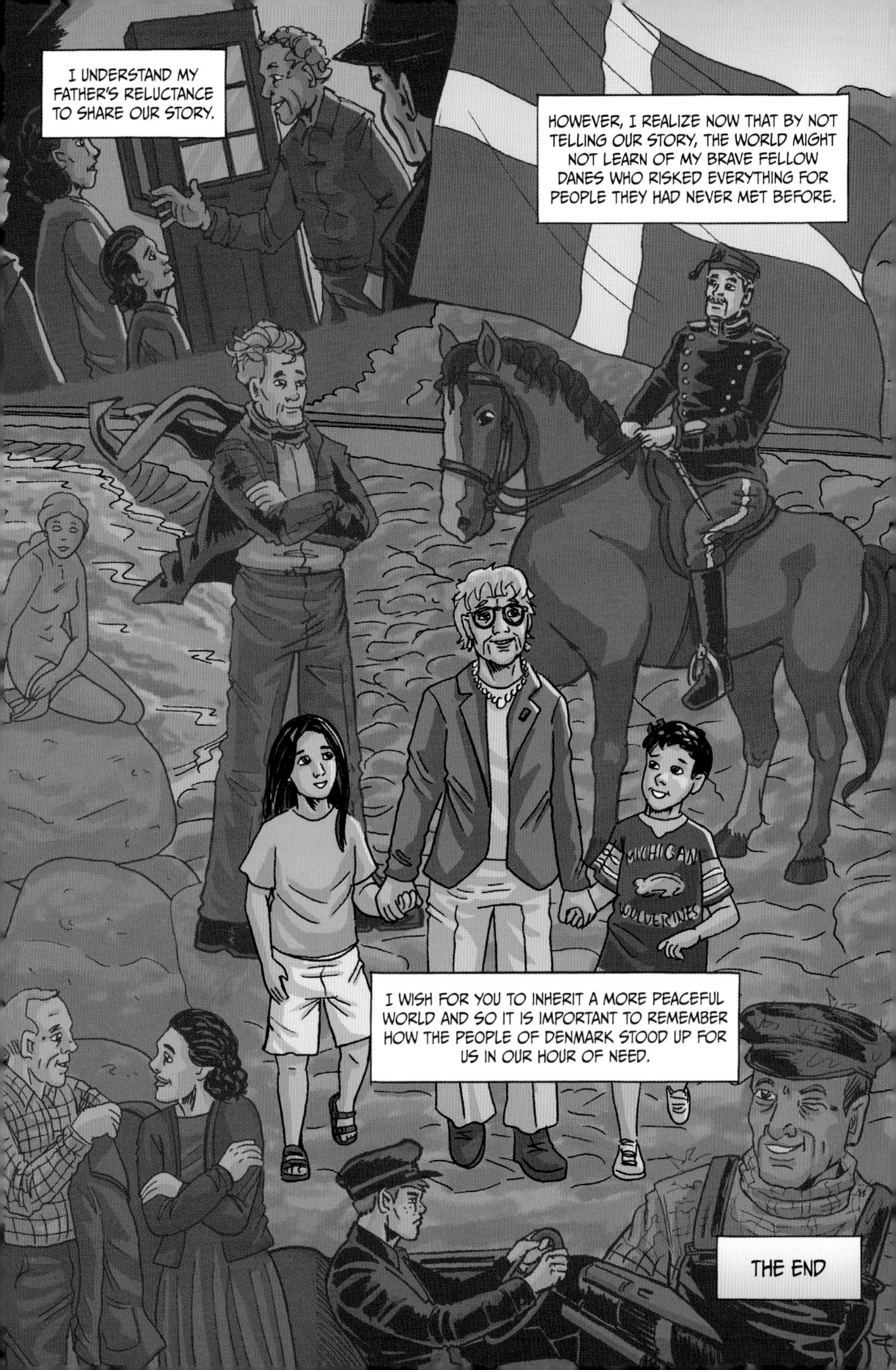
I UNDERSTAND MY FATHER'S RELUCTANCE TO SHARE OUR STORY.
HOWEVER, I REALIZE NOW THAT BY NOT TELLING OUR STORY, THE WORLD MIGHT NOT LEARN OF MY BRAVE FELLOW DANES WHO RISKED EVERYTHING FOR PEOPLE THEY HAD NEVER MET BEFORE.
MICHIGAN WOLVERINES
I WISH FOR YOU TO INHERIT A MORE PEACEFUL WORLD AND SO IT IS IMPORTANT TO REMEMBER HOW THE PEOPLE OF DENMARK STOOD UP FOR US IN OUR HOUR OF NEED.
THE END

From the Author

How would a young girl anticipating her ninth birthday react to suddenly learning she was Jewish, and because of that, she and her family were in grave danger? While I grew up safely and securely in Chicago, I had a curiosity about, but not a comprehension of, my mother, Mette's, escape from Denmark to Sweden on a fishing boat during World War II. She rarely spoke of her rescue from the Nazis, but it clearly had a profound impact on her life.

I knew she did not consider herself a survivor because she felt her experience paled in comparison to the horrors other Jews experienced throughout German-occupied Europe. The Danes welcomed her home after the War, and her prior life resumed. She felt a guilt about this contrast in treatment. Fortunately, I pushed her to sit for an interview with the USC Shoah Foundation, which Steven Spielberg created to record the memories of living witnesses. This encouragement led her to speak at a 50th anniversary commemoration of the rescue of the Danish Jews in 1993, hosted at Chicago's Anshe Emet Synagogue, and to numerous fourth grade classes that had just read Lois Lowry's *Number the Stars*, a fictional story about a young girl in German-occupied Denmark.

In 2016, my mother died too soon, but I am sure her innate Danish attitude would have considered her timing perfectly acceptable. Living to age eighty-one, she successfully raised three boys, became an integral part of her six grandchildren's lives, and never lost ties to her Danish family and friends over her fifty-six years living in the United States, faithfully writing to many of them every week. In the year after my mother's death, I finally followed through on my pledge to trace my family's escape route. I began to learn more about a man credited with helping my family secure safe passage, Svend Otto "John" Nielsen. I visited his gravesite with my children after learning that it was fewer than two miles from where I spent summers with my Danish grandparents. Then stars aligned, and on a research trip to Denmark for *Hour of Need* in 2022, I had the honor to meet the young daughter Svend left behind seventy-nine years prior.

Not many in the United States know that the people of Denmark proved themselves to be a bright spot during those dark days for humanity. *Hour of Need* reflects my family's Holocaust experience, which differed in many ways from other Danish Jews who survived or perished. Others had easier and harder passages to Sweden, different refugee experiences in Sweden, faced the brutal conditions of Theresienstadt or encountered hardships upon their return. While I would have preferred to capture as many other experiences as I could, I realized I would fail at truly telling any if I pursued this ambition. Out

of respect for those with different experiences from my family, I should qualify this by saying not all Danes rose to the occasion and some collaborated with the Nazis. Many, however, responded with a level of empathy and support not seen in other occupied countries. Where else do stories abound of Jews being welcomed home?

During my writing, I had the good fortune to meet hip-hop pioneer turned comic book creator, Darryl McDaniels (also known as DMC from Run DMC). He told me that comic books have the power to make a young person and an old person want to sit down and have a conversation with each other. One clear

lesson from bringing my mother's story to life is that the passage of almost eighty years has not healed all scars. I faced unexpected reluctance and resistance from close family members to talk about their experiences. I hope *Hour of Need* will heal some of these scars by providing a way for them to convey their experiences to their grandchildren.

I was inspired to adapt my mother's story to the graphic novel format after attending a talk by the late United States Congressman John Lewis and the co-author of his autobiography *March*, Andrew Aydin, in 2018. I hoped to achieve at least a fragment of Lewis and Aydin's success in making history relatable to younger generations. My journey to bring *Hour of Need* to life would have detoured into failure without Andrew Aydin "paying it forward" with advice; my wife, Lara's, support and patience; the belief in the mission of my project from the Illinois Holocaust Museum & Education Center's Susan Abrams, Kelley Szany, and Amanda Friedeman; my literary agent Dan Strutzel who believed in the mission of getting my mother's story told; my editor Charlie Ilgunas who could identify in *Hour of Need* the voice of his grandmother; art director Rob Wall for his patience with me; Christer Almqvist who, as a little Swedish boy, lowered apples down to my family and then almost eighty years later walked me through his childhood memories of the port of Ystad; John Hannover and the many others who played tour guide for me on my research trip to Denmark and Sweden; Arne Notkin for helping me navigate the Danish journalism and art scenes, Steen Metz for sharing his memories of capture in Odense and captivity in Theresienstadt; Jenny Friedes for giving me a masterclass on screenplay writing; the Danish Jewish Museum for reviewing the authenticity of my research; and the generous pro bono legal services from the talented attorneys at Much Shelist and Neal Gerber & Eisenberg.

Fate guided me into the talented hands of Tatiana Goldberg, whose connection to the project from her own family's experience at the hands of the Nazis only miles from where my grandparents lived made her pursue authenticity in her drawings well beyond what I could have imagined. *Hour of Need* benefited from the support of many affiliated with my alma mater, the Francis W. Parker School in Chicago, including one of its most popular teachers, David Fuder, a cast of students he recruited to focus group the script, and Principal Dan Frank.

I would also not be here if not for the moral courage of the Svends, the Jenses and the Jørgens my family encountered in their hour of need, and I hope their stories will serve as an inspiration to future generations. They did not know my family before they were in danger, but their passion for humanity and their willingness to stand up for those suffering from injustice is at the root of saving us all.

Author's End Notes

Hour of Need relied on the efforts of many who have tried to accurately record what happened in Denmark during and after the War, and I have included a bibliography of the primary sources that have supplemented the precious interviews I was able to conduct with family and friends who lived through those times.

While the events described in *Hour of Need* occurred, in some instances space and time have been rearranged for storytelling purposes. Some dialogue has been recreated or imagined from recorded history, and out of respect for non-historical figures, some names and characteristics have been altered. I added one notable experience to my family's journey that occurred to others making the same crossing that can be sourced to historical records. The confrontation with a German patrol boat comes from the recounting of the experience of other refugees detailed in *A Conspiracy of Decency*.

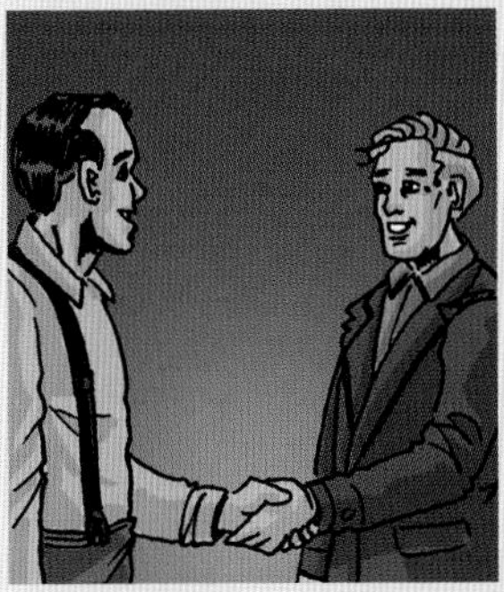

Svend Otto "John" Nielsen is a historical figure, and I have noted where I made him into a composite character of other brave leaders of the resistance. The details of Svend's activities come primarily from "The Giant Killers," an interview of Jørgen Kieler conducted by the Imperial War Museum, and Jørgen Kieler's writings in *Resistance Fighter*. I am not aware of how Jørgen, Svend, and Jens Lillelund came to know each other or join the resistance group Holger Danske II so my account of their initial interaction is imagined. Jens's confrontation with German soldiers on the day of occupation comes from an account in *The Bitter Years*.

Many of Svend's activities occurred in 1943, and while he was actively engaged in resistance activities prior to affiliating with Holger Danske II (a successor group to the original Holger Danske movement), Svend's involvement in Holger Danske's planning is fictionalized. My research indicates he acted independently of Holger Danske during the Jewish escape and joined the group at a later date. I also have not made a distinction between the original Holger Danske and Holger Danske II. While members of Holger Danske played a role in my

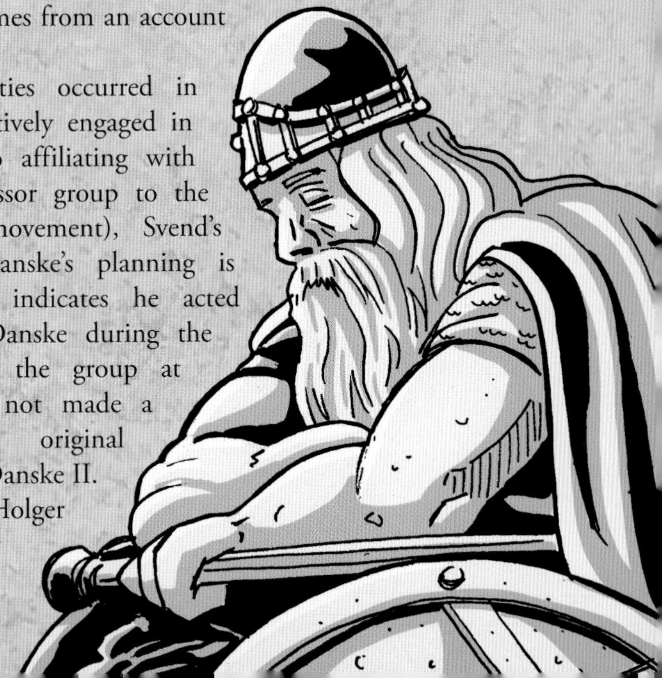

family's escape and the rescue of many others, it was one of several resistance groups involved, and many Jewish refugees found their way to Sweden through the spontaneous efforts of other Danes, including many medical professionals and clergy, not affiliated with a resistance group.

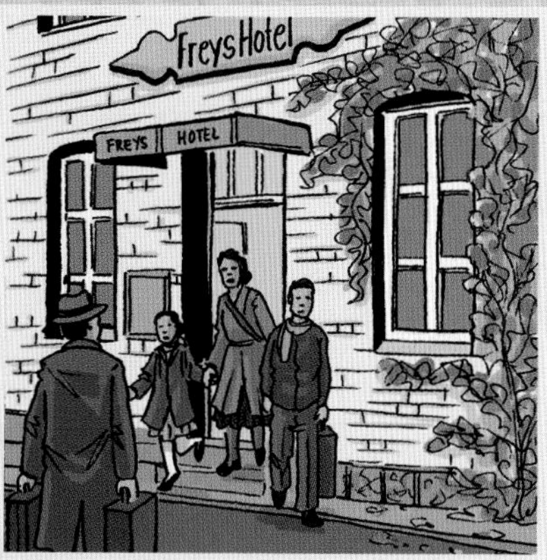
FreysHotel
FREYS HOTEL

Because of the large cast of characters involved in assisting the refugees at the Frey Hotel in Stubbekøbing (a hotel that no longer exists), I have created some composite characters and given Svend a premature introduction to my family. While he was reported to have actively arranged with local fishermen to secure passage for refugees, Svend was not the initial contact my family had with the Danish resistance. Instead, my family met August Jensen, who my grandfather likened to the swashbuckling action hero of that era, the Scarlet Pimpernel (a 1940s equivalent to Indiana Jones). Jensen's wife is the woman who generously agreed to take my mother's baby cousin on her bike to the coast.

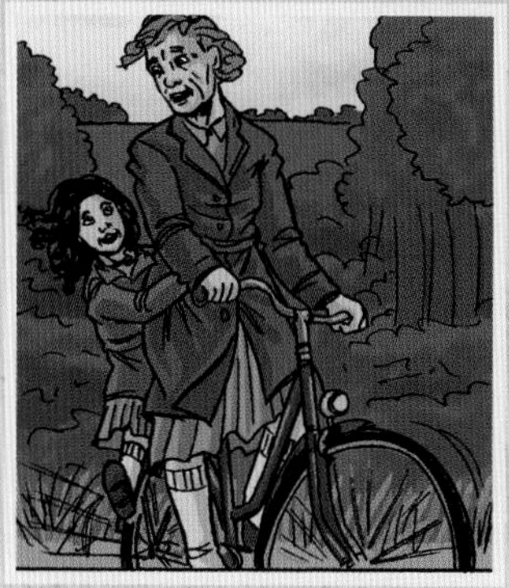

The myth that King Christian X and all Danes wore the Jewish star in solidarity survives to this day and is one of the few popularly known but inaccurate "facts" about the Holocaust in Denmark. This is in no small part due to Allied propaganda that took the king's stance and turned it into a myth. My mother provided me a firsthand account that she and her fellow Danish Jews were never pressed to wear the Jewish star, and many sources confirm this. The conversation between King Christian X and Finance Minister Buhl about wearing the star occurred in early September 1941, according to Knud Jespersen's exploration of King Christian X's personal diary, which he details in *Rytterkongen, et portræt af Christian 10. Countrymen* also provides the context that this conversation occurred while the Germans were successfully advancing into the Soviet Union and the United States maintained its official neutrality.

In neighboring Norway, however, which was invaded at the same time as Denmark, the Germans immediately imposed a mandate that the Norwegian Jews wear the Jewish star after encountering stiff resistance from the Norwegian armed forces. King Christian X and his brother, King Haakon VII of Norway, took different paths in how they confronted Germany when it simultaneously invaded both of their countries. Norwegians were more defiant, and many more Norwegians died as a consequence, including approximately half of Norway's Jewish population.

The Norwegians inflicted setbacks to the German war plans that influenced the War's final outcome. Whether one king's tactics were superior to the other's is fodder for a healthy debate.

Exploration of the Danish experience brings up several questions that may not be completely answerable. A theory persists that Werner Best aimed to get rid of the Danish Jews with as little effort and unrest as possible, and with an eye toward reputation washing at a time when the War was turning against Germany. This also may be self-serving revisionism. Were the Danish Jews "lucky"? Being persecuted is not luck and many suffered severe trauma, but their circumstances offered them a better fate than other European Jews.

Why was Denmark different? In *Nothing to Speak of*, author Sophie Lene Bak attributes this to primarily three reasons: the civil control maintained by the Danish government, the low level of antisemitism, and the relatively small size and high degree of assimilation of the Jewish population. As the first European nation to ban slavery, Denmark also had a history of protecting equality, including a constitutional protection that stayed intact for the period of time that the Nazis allowed the Danish government to continue self-governance. Denmark did have a restrictive pre-War policy that limited the migration of German Jews into Denmark, as Bo Lidegaard discusses in detail in *Countrymen*.

Were all Danes good and all Germans bad? That clearly was not the case. Some Danes welcomed the Nazis, and some Germans turned a blind eye. And lastly, do you need to have the courage and daring of a Svend Otto Nielsen to make a difference? This may be the easiest to address, as many Danes found their own ways to stand up for and help the oppressed.

The final words of *Hour of Need* are inspired by my mother's message to my children when discussing her experience: "hoping for a better world for my grandchildren."

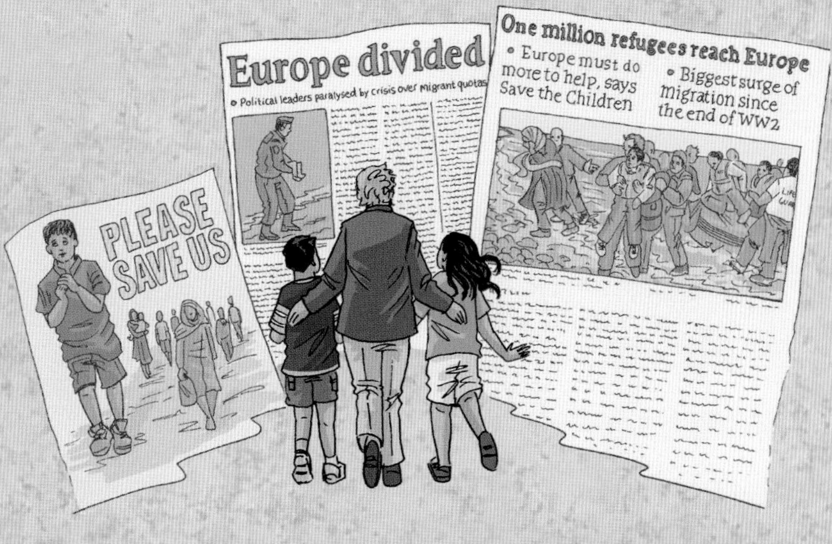
PLEASE SAVE US
Europe divided
• Political leaders paralysed by crisis over migrant quotas
One million refugees reach Europe
• Europe must do more to help, says Save the Children
• Biggest surge of migration since the end of WW2

Drawing from History

These comparisons between the art and historical reference photos show the accuracy and attention to detail of the creators in bringing this story to life.

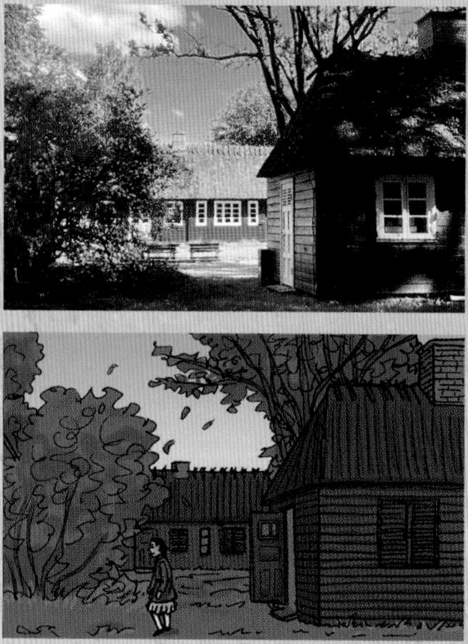

The camp Mette's family spent the night at in Falster, Denmark

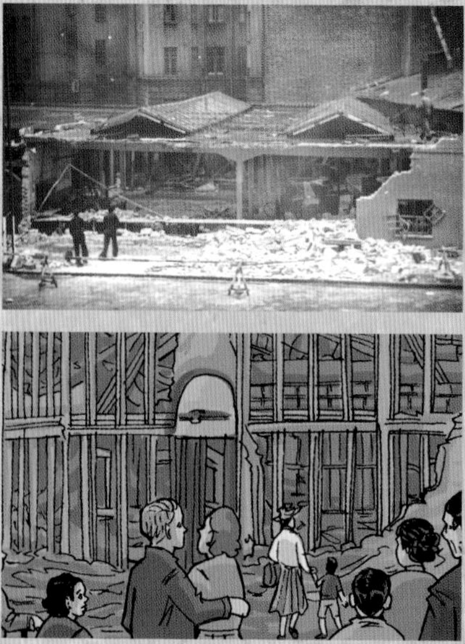

Holger Danske sabotage of Forum Copenhagen

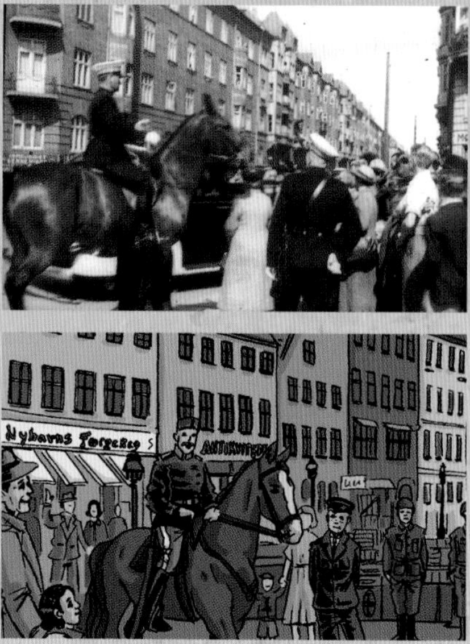

King Christian X atop his horse, Rolf

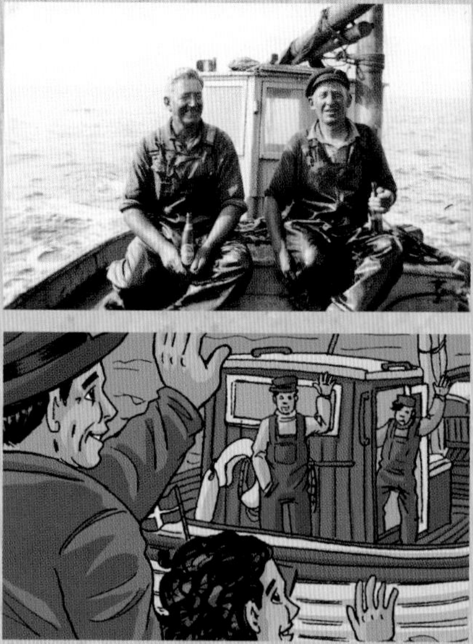

Danish fishermen on a boat similar to the one that transported Mette and her family

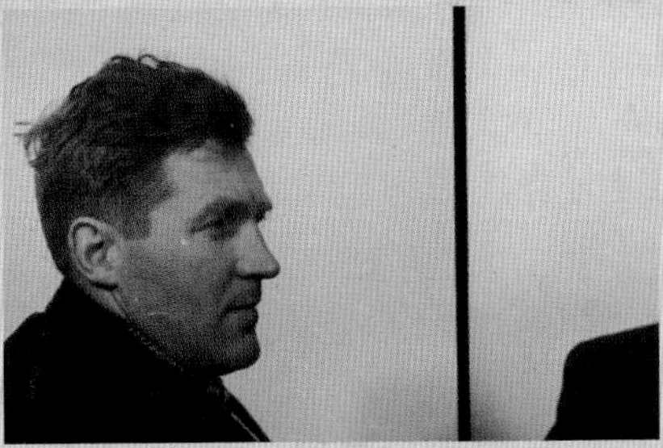

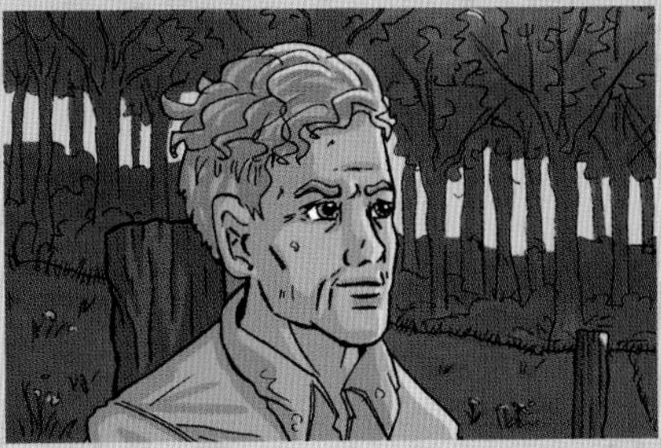

Svend Otto "John" Nielsen

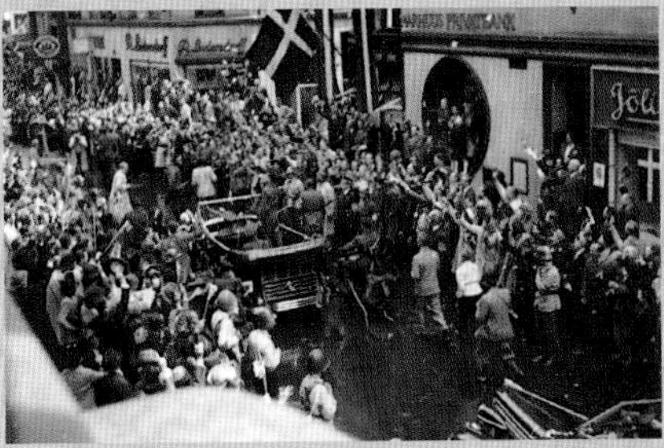

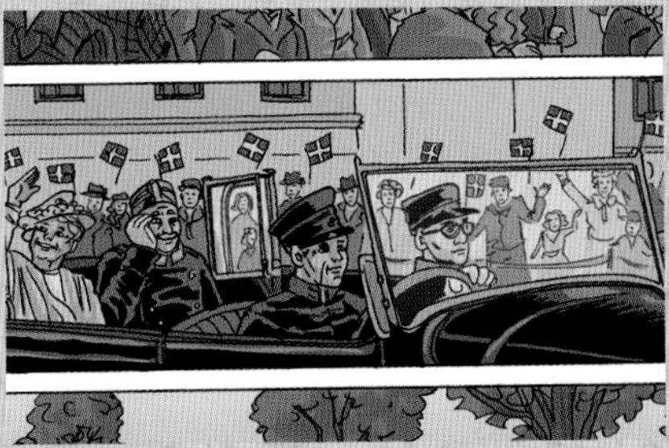

King Christian X celebrating
the end of the war

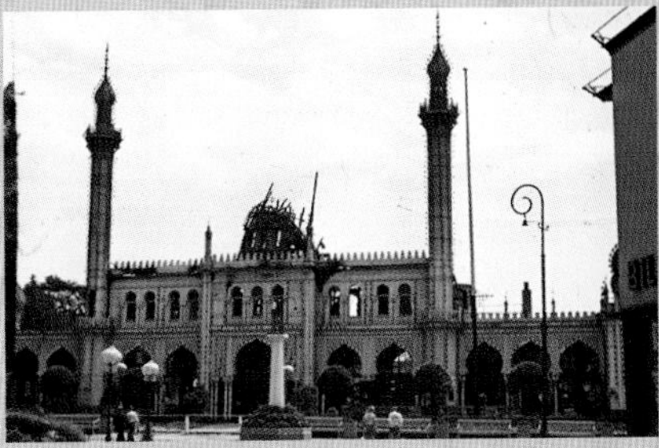

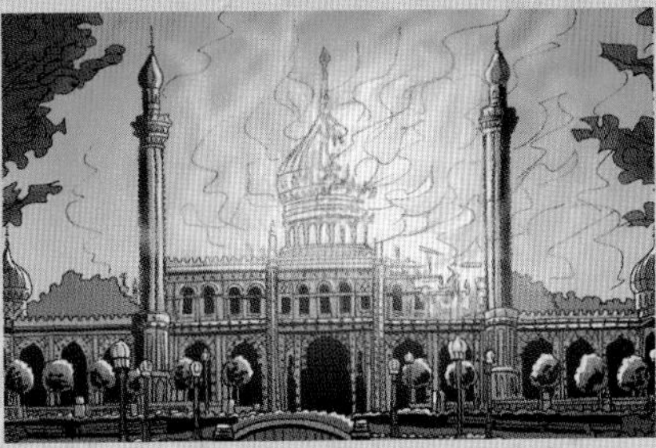

Tivoli Gardens fire bombed

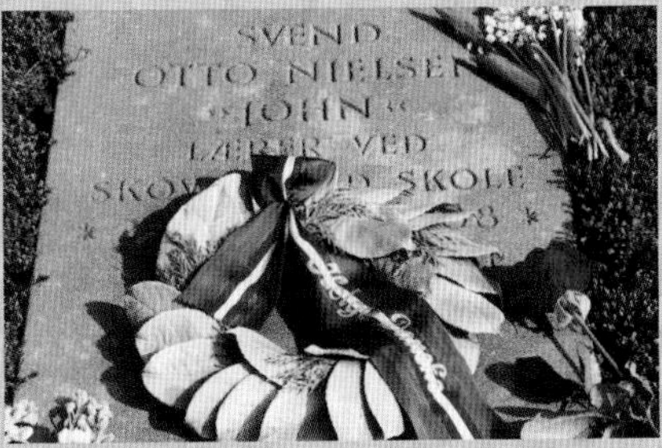
SVEND
OTTO NIELSE
JOHN
LÆRER VED

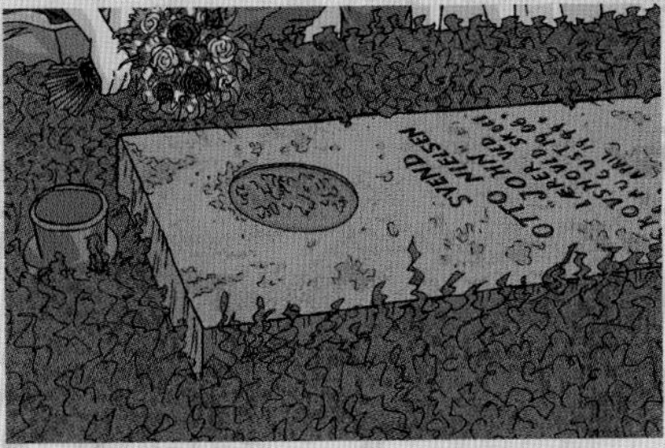

Svend's grave memorial

Photos courtesy of The Museum of Danish Resistance 1940-1945,
except for the Falster camp from the artist's personal research.

From the Artist

First of all, I'm grateful for the opportunity to work on a project with so much history, meaning, and passion behind it. I've written, drawn, and taught comics for years, and many of my own comics—while still important stories to myself and many readers—are most often pure fiction. But there are common characteristics between my own projects and *Hour of Need*. I do love working with female voices, characters with depth, and emotional stories, and *Hour of Need*, and the authenticity of Mette's story, has been a very special project for me.

My own family's brush with the Nazis can hardly be compared to the escape of Mette and her family or that of the many Danish Jews who went through so much persecution, hardship, and fear—some of whom did not survive. But my family's story did inspire a short comic for a Danish anthology of World War II anecdotes in 2015 and paved the way for my work on *Hour of Need*. The name of the comic is "My Beautiful Aunt." It tells the story of the night the Danish Jews were deported in October 1943 when my grandfather, a Jewish friend of his, and my then 3-year-old Aunt Gitte were picked up by German soldiers and put on a truck bound for the ship *Wartheland* and after that Theresienstadt. They didn't make it very far though. When my grandfather was still alive to tell the story, he claimed that

from My Beautiful Aunt

he and Gitte were let off the truck at a checkpoint by German officers who were convinced that they could not be Jewish because Gitte had the most beautiful blond hair and blue eyes. And well, they weren't Jewish. Because only our family name remains from a Jewish heritage my grandfather claimed ended two generations before him.

But even so, the thought of what could have been—and what did happen to Mette's family, who lived so close to my family—has inspired me to illustrate Mette's story with love, dedication, and as much visual historical accuracy as possible. I've been working diligently on getting everything right. I even made corrections to finished pages when, after I did a talk about my work at a Danish library, an elderly lady who remembered the war told me that there were blue lights in the streetlamps during the occupation. Of course, there's bound to be a mistake or two in there—not everything has been easy to research and not all historical accounts agree about every detail—but I've done my absolute best to bring the past to life and recreate everything from major historical events to the everyday details of life in Denmark during the occupation.

And I hope you've enjoyed reading this book as much as I loved illustrating it.

Historical Note from the Illinois Holocaust Museum

The Holocaust was an enormous and massive event, spanning more than a decade and nearly the entire European continent. The Nazi Party, which controlled Germany through its leader, Adolf Hitler, believed that people could be placed into categories, and those categories were ranked according to how much the Nazis believed each group contributed to society. People whom the Nazis believed to be "good Germans"—white people without disabilities who conformed to Nazi ideals and policies—were at the top of the scale. People of other ethnicities, religious minorities, and political opponents were placed in different places down the scale. In just a few years, the Nazis transformed Germany into a society where people had different rights and opportunities based on who they were, creating a culture where neighbors turned against neighbors and life was increasingly difficult for people considered to be less worthy.

As the German army invaded and occupied much of Europe in 1939 and 1940, the rules and restrictions of German society were quickly imposed on the local populations. According to the Nazis, people from Scandinavia, including Denmark, were "almost" as good as Germans, so Danish people faced fewer and less harsh restrictions than those imposed in other occupied countries. At first, Jewish Danes were not treated differently than Danes of other faiths.

Denmark was unusual in Europe for other reasons too. Prior to World War II, Jewish people in countries in Western Europe were largely assimilated—they practiced a different religion and celebrated different holidays and family milestones than their Christian neighbors, or they practiced no religion at all, but they lived, worked, and went to school as equal members of their communities. It usually was not obvious until you got to know someone who was Jewish and who was not. (In Eastern Europe, the situation was different—some Eastern European Jews were highly assimilated, while others lived in more traditional ways, living in communities that set them apart, wearing clothing and speaking a language, Yiddish, that made them immediately identifiable as Jewish.)

The Danish government, and perhaps most importantly, the Danish people themselves, made no distinction between citizens based on their religion or culture. Everyone had the same rights, and everyone was equally Danish. As a result, when Nazi authorities tried to impose restrictions on Danish Jews, they were met with opposition from both the Danish people and the remaining Danish government, including King Christian X himself. Some Danes participated in labor strikes to show their opposition to the occupation, and the Danish resistance, made up of ordinary citizens, was formed to carry out sabotage against the occupiers and to provide aid and shelter to those being targeted for harsher treatment, including Jews.

The relatively stable situation in Denmark changed on September 8, 1943, when SS General Werner Best, the administrator of the occupation in Denmark, suggested to Hitler that the German military be used to deport Danish Jews to concentration camps, as was being done to Jews in other occupied countries and in Germany itself. As preparations for the deportations began, Best began to doubt his decision and confided the plan to Georg Ferdinand Duckwitz, an official with the German Navy stationed in Denmark. Just before the final order for the deportations was given, Duckwitz and others warned non-Jewish Danes of the plan. Those Danes then successfully alerted the Danish Jewish community that roundups and deportation were to begin in a few days, on October 1, 1943—to coincide with the Jewish holiday of Rosh Hashanah.

Thanks to the warning, Danes—Jews and non-Jews alike—were able to organize and carry out one of the largest and most successful acts of resistance and rescue of the Holocaust, and indeed of all of World War II. Jewish Danes went into hiding; Danish police authorities refused to cooperate in the Germans' search by denying Germans the right to enter Jewish homes or simply not reporting the people they found in hiding. Many Danes, including the royal family, officials from numerous churches, and ordinary people, spoke out against the deportations. Members of the resistance and others helped Jewish families travel safely to the coast, where fisherman took them across the strait to Sweden, a country that remained neutral during World War II and welcomed the refugees.

Over approximately a month, hundreds of Danish fishermen repeatedly made this relatively short journey that was, nonetheless, filled with danger: German patrol boats scanned the route, stopping and searching the Danish vessels looking for Jews trying to escape. The journey was frequently taken at night; darkness provided additional safety from German eyes but made the waters more treacherous.

In all, approximately 7,200 Danish Jews and roughly 700 of their non-Jewish relatives were able to find safety in Sweden in this way. Not everyone was so lucky, however: nearly 500 Jews, including both Danes and people from other countries who had come to Denmark seeking safety, were captured by the Nazis and deported to Theresienstadt, a ghetto and concentration camp near Prague in occupied Czechoslovakia. These were primarily people who lived in cities and villages far from Copenhagen, the Danish capital, who did not receive word of the coming roundups or who were unable to make their way to the coast to be evacuated.

The Danish government and Danish Red Cross demanded information about their location and living conditions, which likely persuaded the Germans to allow these prisoners certain privileges and slightly better treatment at Theresienstadt: they were able to receive letters and care packages, and none were deported to concentration camps or killing centers in occupied Eastern Europe. Still, dozens of Danish Jews died from the harsh conditions in the camp.

In all, 120 Danish Jews died in the Holocaust, most either in Theresienstadt or during the evacuation to Sweden. Although tragic, this number represents one of the highest survival rates of any country in German-occupied Europe. Since 1963, Yad Vashem, the Holocaust Remembrance Authority and Museum in Israel, has recognized non-Jews who risked their lives to help Jews to survive the Holocaust by granting them the title Righteous Among the Nations. Of 27,921 individuals who have been recognized as Righteous (as of January 1, 2021), 22 of the Righteous are from Denmark. Given what you've learned about the Danish Resistance, you might be surprised that number is so small—and you'd be right: because the members of the Danish Resistance viewed their rescue efforts as a collective act, they requested that members not be recognized individually. Instead, a tree was planted to commemorate the Danish resistance on the Mount of Remembrance at Yad Vashem, and Illinois Holocaust Museum honors the people of Denmark collectively on its Ferro Fountain of the Righteous.

Amanda Friedeman
Associate Director of Education
Illinois Holocaust Museum & Education Center

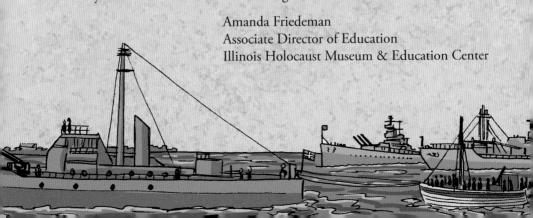

Sources

Børresen, Bo. "Christian den 10. var indlagt på Peter Bangs Vej." *Ugeavisen*, August 25, 2020.

Bertelsen, Aage. *October 43*. Museum Press, 1955.

"Danish Resistance fighter Jørgen Kieler dead at 97." *The Copenhagen Post* online, February 20, 2017.

Flender, Harold. *Rescue in Denmark*. US Holocaust, 1991.

Goldberg, Leo. *The Rescue of the Danish Jews: Moral Courage Under Stress*. NYU Press, 1987.

Glickman Lauder, Judy. *Beyond The Shadows: The Holocaust and the Danish Exception*. Aperture Foundation, 2018.

Hoose, Phillip. *The Boys Who Challenged Hitler: Knud Peterson and the Churchill Club*. Farrar Straus Giroux, 2015.

Hurowitz, Richard. "Op-Ed: How the Danes, and a German turncoat, pulled off a World War II miracle." *Los Angeles Times* online, September 30, 2018.

Jespersen, Knud J.V. *Rytterkongen: Et potraet af Christian 10*. Gyldendal Bookstorre, 2007.

Kieler, Jorgen. "Oral history interview with Jørgen von Führen Kieler." Imperial War Museum, February 1995.

---*Resistance Fighter*. Gefen Publishing House, 2007.

Lampe, David, and Birger Riis-Jørgensen. *Hitler's Savage Canary: a History of the Danish Resistance in World War II*. Frontline Books, 2014.

Lene Bak, Sofie. *Nothing to speak of: Wartime Experiences of the Danish Jews 1943-1945*. Translated by Virginia Raynolds Laursen. Museum Tusculanum Press, 2013.

Levine, Ellen. *Darkness over Denmark: The Danish Resistance and the Rescue of the Jews*. Scholastic Inc., 2001.

Lidegaard, Bo. *Countrymen: How Denmark's Jews Escaped the Nazis*. Atlantic Books, 2015.

Loeffler, Martha. *Boats in the Night: Knud Dyby's Involvement in the Rescue of the Danish Jews and the Danish Resistance*. Lur Publications, 2000.

Lutzer, Erwin W. *Hitler's Cross: How the Cross Was Used to Promote the Nazi Agenda*. Moody Publishers, 1995, 2016.

Mentze, Ernst. *5 Years: The Occupation of Denmark in Pictures*. A.-B. Allhems Förlag, 1946.

Petrow, Richard. *The Bitter Years: The Invasion and Occupation of Denmark and Norway*. Morrow Quill Paperbacks, 1979.

Shayne, Mette. Rescue of the Danish Jews (By Mette Shayne). 140 Cong. Rec. S16808 (daily ed. July 23, 1993). (https://www.congress.gov/103/crecb/1993/07/23/GPO-CRECB-1993-pt12-2.pdf)

Shayne, Ralph. "Privately owned journals," in the author's possession.

Thomas, John Oram. *The Giant-Killers: The Story of the Danish Resistance Movement, 1940-1945*. Taplinger, 1976.

Tveskov, Peter H. *Conquered, Not Defeated: Growing up in Denmark During the German Occupation of World War II*. Hellgate Press, 2003.

Veisz, Howard S. *Henny and Her Boat: Righteousness and Resistance in Nazi Occupied Denmark*. CreateSpace Independent Publishing Platform, 2017.

Werner, Emmy E. *A Conspiracy of Decency: The Rescue of the Danish Jews During World War II*. Westview Press, 2002.

Yahil, Leni. *The Rescue of Danish Jewry: Test of Democracy*. Jewish Publication Society of America, 1969.

More information on *Hour of Need* reference sources and Denmark during World War II can be found at www.ilholocaustmuseum.org